FATHER

AND

SON

Modern Fiction from Korea
published by Homa & Sekey Books

Father and Son: A Novel by Han Sung-won

Reflections on a Mask: Two Novellas by Ch'oe In-hun

Unspoken Voices: Selected Short Stories by Korean
Women Writers by Park Kyong-ni et al

The General's Beard: Two Novellas by Lee Oyoung

Farmers: A Novel by Lee Mu-young

FATHER AND SON

A NOVEL

Han Sung-won

Translated from the Korean by

Yu Young-nan
Julie Pickering

Homa & Sekey Books

Dumont, New Jersey

First American Edition

Copyright © by Han Sung-won
English Translation Copyright © 2002 by Yu Young-nan &
Julie Pickering

The publication of this book was supported by a grant from
Korea Literature Translation Institute.

ISBN: 1-931907-04-8
Library of Congress Control Number: 2002103285

Publishers Cataloging-in-Publication Data

Father and Son by Han, Sung-won, 1939--
Translated from the Korean by Yu Young-nan & Julie Pickering
1. Korean fiction--20th century--Translation into English
2. English fiction--Translations from the Korean
I. Title. PL992.62 895.734-dc21

Published by Homa & Sekey Books
138 Veterans Plaza
P. O. Box 103
Dumont, NJ 07628

Tel: (201)384-6692
Fax: (201)384-6055
Email: info@homabooks.com
Website: www.homabooks.com

Editor-in-chief: Shawn X. Ye
Executive Editor: Judy Campbell

Printed in the United States of America
1 3 5 7 9 10 8 6 4 2

Contents

Translators' Note

Han Sung-won was born in a rural village near the southern coast of Korea in 1939. He graduated from the Creative Writing Department of Sorabol Art College and, in 1968, made his literary debut with a short story entitled "Wooden Boat," winning the Newcomer's award in the *Taehan ilbo* daily.

Over the next decade and a half, Han married and supported his young family by writing fiction and teaching in high schools in the Chôlla region. In the mid 1970s, he added novellas to his repertoire and, in 1979, published his first full-length novel, *Tsunami (Haeil)*. Since then, he has published more than two dozen novels and a steady stream of short story collections and essays.

In January 1980, just before the Kwangju Rebellion and the vicious government crackdown that rocked his native South Chôlla Province, Han moved his family to Seoul. During this repressive period, Han began to question the role of the writer and literature in Korean society. He traveled the country, studying shamanism and traditional culture, and in his work explored more deeply the intersection of traditional culture, the natural environment, and industrialization.

Shamanism and images of the sea, born in his childhood, run throughout Han's work. Indeed, Han's writings are unique for his profound understanding and rich portrayal of shamanism, a traditional belief that is often thought of as mere superstition in modern society. Han is also known for his vivid characterizations of life along the Chôlla coast. He is a master of the local Chôlla dialect, using it to infuse his characters with life.

The hardships of Han's characters mirror the conflict and contradictions that have marked Korean history in the 20th century. Han examines the lives of individuals and families straddling the divide between tradition and modernity, between political freedom and capitulation, and between rural and urban life. These individuals, and their families, struggle to survive, physically and spiritually, as their nation marches, sometimes blindly, toward industrialization and urbanization.

Han is a prolific writer and the recipient of numerous literary awards, including the 1980 Literature Prize of the Korean Writers Association, the 1982 Literature Prize of the Republic of Korea, the 1983 Literature Prize for Korean Writers, the 1987 Modern Literature Award, and the 1988 Yi Sang Literary Award.

Han Sung-won's 1989 novel, *Father and Son*, focuses on the age-old struggle between the generations within the context of modern industrialization and the battle for democratic freedoms in Korea. In this novel, Chu-ch'ôl, a successful poet-publisher, is tormented by his son's antigovernment activities and lack of filial respect, by the cynical questioning of a cousin-turned-government agent, and, not least, by his own guilty conscience. Through Chu-ch'ôl and his extended family, Han explores the role of the intellectual in modern Korean society and the changing face of the Korean family as tradition gives way to economic growth and social upheaval.

The novel opens as Chu-ch'ôl and his wife leave Seoul to attend the funeral of Chu-ch'ôl's ne'er-do-well brother in their native village in South Chôlla Province. Though sympathetic about the brother's death, their main motivation for the trip is to find their eldest son, Yun-gil, who is on the run after participating in antigovernment demonstrations.

As they board the train leaving Seoul, Chu-ch'ôl catches sight of his cousin, Chu-ôn, whom he suspects is a spy for the government. As the story unfolds, we learn that Chu-ôn has been hanging around Chu-ch'ôl's house in Seoul, determined to uncover the whereabouts of Yun-gil.

For Chu-ch'ôl, the journey home stirs a mixture of guilt, lingering resentment, and fear. His son is a stranger to him, his own life's work is a bundle of platitudes, and his family's history and land are obligations: chains that bind, rather than matters of pride and love.

The narrative guides the reader deep into the history of Chu-ch'ôl's family, recalling their relative wealth before the end of the Japanese colonial period, the struggles that his father and grandfather endured during the post-liberation and Korean War periods, and then the crises of conscience that Chu-ch'ôl and his family experience under the authoritarian regime of the 1970s and 1980s.

The story shifts from the past to the present and back— illuminating the interaction between traditional values and spiritual forces, including shamanism and Buddhism, and modern values of prosperity and individualism. Similarly, the story shifts back and forth from Seoul and the small coastal village and surrounding mountains where Chu-ch'ôl grew up, juxtaposing the dreams and interests of the individual and those of the larger family.

Also central to the story, as the title reveals, is the relationship between fathers and sons: between Chu-ch'ôl's grandfather and father, between Chu-ch'ôl and his father, and between Chu-ch'ôl and his son Yun-gil. Time and history flow through these relationships, but no more easily than time and history flowed through Korean life in the 20th century. In the end, the son transcends the father, and at the same time, inherits from him the oppressive ties of history.

Yu Young-nan, Seoul
Julie Pickering, Seattle
March, 2002

Father and Son

1

The bus galloped across the wintry plain. There were only five people on board: the driver and the bus girl, Chu-ch'ôl, his wife and Chu-ôn.

"So what happened to Yun-gil?" Chu-ôn asked with an air of contrived concern. Chu-ch'ôl stared out of the window, pretending not to hear. The frost-covered pane distorted the world outside; the mountains, the clouds, the fields, the trees along the side of the road, the rivers, the villages–they were all refracted in dizzying patterns. Grizzled patches of snow lingered on the mountain slopes. The clouds were a murky gray, heavy with snow. Piles of straw dotted the fields, and a bleak morning fog hung over the dark brown earth, which lay plowed and fallow for the winter. The trees lining the road twisted occasionally, their gaunt branches stretching into the empty sky. Like an invading army spewing cannon fire, the bitter cold had reduced the land to a desolate ruin. The mountains and rivers were dying the way all living, breathing things die in the microbes or poisonous gas released by an attacking army.

Hye-suk sat huddled to Chu-ch'ôl's right, feigning sleep, her face buried deep in her muffler. Chu-ôn sat to his left, across the aisle. For some time, Chu-ch'ôl had sensed Chu-ôn's eyes groping the back of his skull, across his ear and left cheek like a cockroach's feelers. A shiver ran through his body. *He obviously didn't come for Chu-man's funeral. He's after Yun-gil.* Rage surged inside him. His stomach and chest burned. Was it the anger or the beer? His stomach felt hollow, as if he were getting hungry, and all of his energy seemed to be seeping away. He had eaten a bowl of *haejangguk* before boarding the bus, but it hadn't calmed his stomach. If only he had something to drink.

"I'm going to have to give that boy a good talking-to. He's in big trouble if he gets much further out of line."

Chu-ôn seemed to have been waiting for the chance to say this. Earlier in the ride he had taken out a cigarette; he was still pinching it by the filter, rolling it back and forth between his thumb and forefinger. His eyes rested for a moment on the tip of the twisting cigarette, then darted to Chu-ch'ôl's face again. Chu-ch'ôl could feel his gaze. He's toying with me, he thought. How am I going to get rid of this ungrateful bastard? He clenched his teeth, bearing down on his rage as he turned Chu-ôn's words over in his mind. *If he gets much further out of line....* Was Yun-gil out of line? But how had it started?

2

"Water flows as dynamic energy, and any force that obstructs it is reactionary energy. So what about you, Father? Where does your writing fit in?"

It was nearly sunset on a Sunday afternoon, in the autumn of Yun-gil's freshman year in university. Chu-ch'ôl had practically dragged his son from his room, where he had been ensconced for the day, and taken him to the mineral springs on the hill behind their house. They sat down to rest in a patch of eulalia grass. New stamen were just beginning to sprout, round and hard like scabs forming over a scratch.

Chu-ch'ôl pointed out the trees and plants to his son—the alders and cherries, the juniper, birch and beech trees, the poplars and oaks, the bush clover, azalea and rhododendrons. He explained the unique character of each species. He told the story of the mountain reeds, the eulalia, the scouring rush, the asters and the wild chrysanthemums. Man gives names to all things in this world, he explained, and using their proper names helps us understand them and initiate a spiritual exchange.

FATHER AND SON

Chu-ch'ôl wanted to instill a sense of artistic sensitivity in his son, a history major. It wasn't so much that he wanted Yun-gil to choose a career in literature. He simply wanted to cultivate in his son the eye of a scholar, in other words, the perception and wit needed to see directly into the heart of all phenomena.

Literature isn't the only field that requires artistic sensitivity. Politicians, businessmen, academics, merchants, bureaucrats, people in the judiciary, doctors, industrialists, laborers and farmers all needed it so far as Chu-ch'ôl was concerned. He had always believed that such sensitivity was beneficial not only to the individual, but to society and the state as well. If politicians ruled with artistic sensitivity, the country would be a more open and hopeful place to live in. Judges and prosecutors would better understand those living on the other side of the law, and criminals could expect sympathy and would no longer need to worry about unreasonable punishment. A patient treated by a doctor lacking in such sensitivity would clearly suffer, and laborers would be exploited at the hands of insensitive management. Chu-ch'ôl had always thought that Einstein's extraordinary discoveries, Churchill's grand politics and Kennedy's youthful vision were born of their artistic sensitivity.

Be that as it may, his son's question took him by surprise. Stunned, Chu-ch'ôl stared at the clouds floating between the tops of the eulalia grass. "Reactionary"—It was the term that stunned him. When he was a boy, the village children had taunted him for being the "reactionary's brat." A reactionary was someone who stood on the side of forces resistant to change, someone who raised obstacles to the dynamic driving force of the proletariat revolution—no simple middle-of-the-roader. It was only after reaching adulthood that he understood what it really meant.

Chu-ch'ôl's father had been a farmer who worked his own land in their home village of New Town. With two and a half acres of paddy and nearly five of dry field, he was the richest of the tideflat villagers; the rest worked less than a half acre of paddy and only an acre or two of dry field, or lacking that, depended on fishing or seaweed cultivation for their livelihood. As a result, the propertyless villagers who had joined the South Korean Workers' Party labeled Chu-ch'ôl's father "a hindrance to the creation of a new society where the wealthy's land is redistributed to the needy."

"Wait a minute. Where is your 'dynamic energy' supposed to be flowing anyway?" Chu-ch'ôl asked.

What was Yun-gil thinking? The wind shook the tops of the bush clover. The eulalia grass rustled metallically. The mountain shadows were beginning to settle, pale and purple, over the grassy spot where they were sitting. A desolate silence fell over the woods. The autumn wind made Chu-ch'ôl feel lonely. He was frustrated by the mood his son was creating.

"That's such an obvious question," Yun-gil replied. An awkward smile played on his lips as he stared down at the short stalks of cogon grass sprouting beneath his gray tennis shoes. Maybe he regrets asking me about my writing, Chu-ch'ôl thought. It's my fault if he does.

"I guess you're right," he said. "But do you know why I asked? Because your question reeks of Marxism. Apparently you've been reading a lot about Marx, Lenin and Stalin these days...but to tell the truth, I don't care much for them."

Chu-ch'ôl regretted his words immediately. Here he was, a father trying to talk to his son, and he came right out and said he didn't care for the very people his son respected.

"So if my father rejects someone, I have to reject them too?"

Yun-gil reacted just as Chu-ch'ôl had expected. His face hardened, and a gloomy look, dark as the mountain shadows, settled over his features. Why am I so tactless with this boy?

Chu-ch'ôl bit his tongue in frustration. Yun-gil was a quiet, thoughtful child. What little he did say ran deep and unseen, like an iceberg. He took after his mother in that respect. Chu-ch'ôl often got into trouble for his flippant remarks to Hye-suk.

"I'm not saying you have to reject who I reject. I'm just saying I don't care for their materialistic interpretation of history, the way they define human history as the history of class struggle. I'm for a free market economy. I think capitalism is better than communism in many ways. It makes life easier for people. It makes true human liberation possible."

Chu-ch'ôl babbled worthless theory. He simply wanted to clarify his own position and turn his son around, if, in fact, the boy was leaning toward Marx and Lenin.

Yun-gil glanced at his father, then stood up.

"Shall we go?" he said with an awkward smile. Eyes focused on the path, he started down the hill ahead of Chu-ch'ôl. His gait seemed heavy, laden with discontentment. His movements spelled loathing and rebellion.

"You'd better keep a close eye on your son once he's in college. Make sure he doesn't get involved with student activists."

Chu-ch'ôl recalled the advice of a professor friend. Suddenly he felt dizzy. His face flushed at what Yun-gil had said about his writing. Maybe his son had already joined the student movement. Chu-ch'ôl felt as if Yun-gil and his new friends could see right through him. He had tried to reflect the pain of Korea's alienated masses in his poetry, but each poem ended there; he never tried to touch the masses or offer any real solutions.

Chu-ch'ôl was forever the bewildered captive of a contradiction only he understood.

As a child growing up in New Town, Chu-ch'ôl was accustomed to his status as the rich man's son, but when he left the village to attend middle school in the city, he soon realized that he was really the son of a poor man. His classmates' clothes, their spending habits, lunches and books all proved it. Chu-ch'ôl rented a room and had to cook and clean for himself. His school uniform was made of muslin dyed and sewn by his mother, and his winter underwear was stuffed with thin cotton wadding and quilted at home. His lunch consisted of boiled rice and barley, with a spoonful of bean paste or spiced anchovies on the side. He had only his textbooks to study from, no reference books or dictionaries like the other students. Snacks were an unthinkable luxury. There were no special treats to take on school picnics, and he missed the senior class excursion because his parents didn't send the money. Such were his middle and high school years. He then went to Seoul for university, but there too he was forever running out of food. He felt inferior to classmates who didn't suffer like him and he detested people of great wealth. Still, when he returned to New Town, he was the rich man's son. There was no getting around it. None of the other villagers could afford to send their sons and daughters to school the way his father had. They were dirt poor.

From a logical point of view, Chu-ch'ôl's rich boy-poor boy contradiction was hardly a problem. It was simply a matter of changing the way he thought. The rich man's son was no more than a big fish in a small pond. Far better to admit he was the son of a poor farmer and fisherman and stand on the side of the impoverished masses wherever he went. As time passed, however, he came to think like a member of the bourgeois elite. He may have sung of the masses in his poetry, but he loathed the idea of them ruling the world for he knew that they would attack him as a pallid intellectual. He knew he would feel terribly wronged if they levied heavy taxes on the wealthy, in effect nationalizing all property.

FATHER AND SON

In addition to the house he was now living in, Chu-ch'ŏl owned a plot of orchard land valued at 100 million won. His wife had inherited it from her parents, and she and Chu-ch'ŏl were thinking of selling it one day to finance overseas studies for one of their children, something along those lines. But if the impoverished masses came to power, Chu-ch'ŏl might lose that precious possession. Even if it wasn't confiscated, he had the sneaking suspicion that he and his family would not enjoy their present comfort. Chu-ch'ŏl resented being included among the ranks of the "haves" because of his middle class fixation on security, but, while hardly becoming a poet, it was a natural enough response for an ordinary man.

Thanks to Chu-ch'ŏl's stubborn contradiction and the orchard land, the clash with Yun-gil was unavoidable. Their differences surfaced the morning after Chu-ch'ŏl bailed his son out of jail.

Yun-gil had been picked up for participating in a sit-in that had stretched on for several days. As it was his first offense and he wasn't deeply involved in any key organizations yet, Yun-gil was released into his parents' custody after they promised to take responsibility for him and provide proper guidance. It was well past midnight by the time Chu-ch'ŏl got Yun-gil into a cab and brought him home. Hye-suk was waiting by the front gate. Yun-gil hadn't slept or eaten properly during the sit-in, so his parents simply fed him and sent him to bed without showing any emotion. The next morning they woke him a bit after eight and gave him breakfast.

"Why don't we have a talk?" Chu-ch'ŏl suggested as he sat down across from the boy when he finished eating.

"I hope you will leave politics to the politicians and get on with your studies. Change has to come gradually. This idea that you can get rid of obstacles, everything you don't like, by physical force—all this stuff about revolution—it's just no good."

17

Chu-ch'ôl had stayed up all night composing a detailed speech, but he was rambling now. Even *he* found his argument feeble. It wasn't going to convince Yun-gil of anything.

"You kids are like saplings just beginning to grow. You have to cultivate yourself if you want to grow strong and tall. If you rush out and get involved in the labor movement or some anti-American democracy demonstration, you're just wasting time that you should be using to study. That's no good—not for you or the nation and the people. I'm not saying your sacrifices and dedication are meaningless. I just think they'd be a lot more meaningful if you waited until you've grown. I mean, throwing rocks and shouting slogans through a cloud of tear gas can be meaningful, but becoming a bookworm who studies in the library can be just as meaningful, even if the other students look down on you for it. Actually, it might take more courage to be a bookworm than to throw stones."

Yun-gil listened in silence, his eyes fixed on the floor in front of him. When Chu-ch'ôl finished, the boy shook his head slowly.

"I'm sorry, Father," he began in a low voice. "Your logic typifies the deceptive appeasement measures of today's so-called intellectuals. It simply echoes the fraudulent governing logic of our rulers."

Chu-ch'ôl was speechless. The morning sun bounced off the window frame and spread an amber light across the room like the ribs of a fan. Hye-suk was standing with her back to the door. When did she come in? he wondered. She hadn't slept or eaten for days. Her face was gaunt, her lips chapped. Shadows hung like dark purple bruises in the triangular hollows beneath her eyes.

"I can't believe he's our son!" she sighed bitterly as she turned her head to the ceiling.

"Who knows? Maybe the spirit of one of your enemies, or someone who hated Grandfather, has descended on me.

Parents give birth to their children physically, but they can't give birth to their spirits. Why do you even try to pretend to understand? Why do you try to get involved? It'll just break your hearts. Forget about me! You have given birth to me, but I don't belong to you. In the end, my body belongs to the wretched masses of this land."

Then the son began lecturing the father on political economy.

"You may call me a communist sympathizer, but I believe Marx was right in many cases. He was right about the conflict between the relations of production and forces of production and how it forms the root of the historical change that brings about human liberation. He was right about the connection between conflict, confrontation and class struggle. It's already been clearly proven. During the feudal period, the bourgeoisie was the dynamic class representing the forces of production, and the aristocracy was the reactionary class, right? In monopolistic capitalism, the proletariat is the dynamic class, and the bourgeoisie is the reactionary class. In the collision between a dynamic and a reactionary class, the dynamic class always wins. It's inevitable, all part of the great flow of history. The problem lies with the forces that resist the natural flow of history. In a class society, the state invariably strengthens its bureaucracy, courts, police force and military, and serves as a mouthpiece for the interests of the ruling class.

"In the clash between the forces of production and the relations of production, the ruling class uses a variety of measures to maintain the status quo. One method is to mobilize the state's legal force. Of course, that doesn't necessarily mean physical force. First, the state attempts to conceal class exploitation and suppress consciousness-raising within the dynamic class. When that fails, it is forced to mobilize its legal forces. That's why the struggle between the dynamic and reactionary classes is never restricted to the economic arena.

It always becomes a struggle for political power. Lately that's what our new rulers have been trying to do."

From time to time Yun-gil paused to moisten his lips. The light from the window glistened off them as he spoke. His pale, swollen face reminded Chu-ch'ôl of a patient with kidney disease. A sharp, metallic pain pierced his chest. He felt an excruciating regret, as if he had discovered parasites on the branches of a chestnut tree that he had carefully watered and fertilized.

"I've read those books," he replied, his features crumbling like fragments of a broken pot. "I know that theory in and out, how Lenin developed the concept of a dictatorship of the proletariat, how the proletarian masses are supposed to rule until the people's consciousness has been raised, and how the 'reactionary' bourgeoisie will be purged."

Chu-ch'ôl's heart fluttered nervously as he spoke. He paused to light a cigarette.

"I know it too," his son replied in an icy tone. His eyes were fixed on the floor still.

Chu-ch'ôl swallowed hard. "Well then, you must have read all about the communist countries that are even more rigid and hierarchical than the capitalist societies they despise.... And you must know that the Soviet Union and communist China are actually trying to introduce capitalist reforms..."

Hye-suk was still standing at the door. She looked back and forth between her husband and son. An even darker shadow had descended over her face now. She moistened her blistered lips, and interrupted in a pleading tone.

"Do you really think a few kids can change anything? Do you realize how many people have been crippled and died for dreams like yours? There've been hundreds like you since Korea was liberated from Japan, but they just come and go like the morning dew."

"You keep out of this," Chu-ch'ôl snapped. He turned back to Yun-gil.

"When I was your age, I was tempted by that sugary idealism too, but I gradually came to realize that it's all a lie. The communist countries have all launched ruthless purification campaigns in the name of their two-bit liberation, and they're all creating a new class society within their planned economies. I think a system that promotes the *gradual* creation of an ideal world, within the context of a free market economy, is better than a system that forces change. Classes exist under all forms of government, and left to themselves, they fall into a pyramid. I'm for a free market system that would lift the people at the lowest echelon to the middle to create an egg-shape. This can't be achieved through class struggle. It has to be achieved gradually, the way a tree grows, on the basis of the stability we have now."

Chu-ch'ôl flushed. I sound like some kind of government spokesman, he thought. But what could he do? Those were the ideas he'd been brought up on. His son grinned and spoke in sympathetic tone.

"You needn't say anymore. You must feel awful. I understand the contradiction you face. I know how it's been torturing you over the years."

Aghast at her son's impudence, Hye-suk looked at the ceiling and laughed.

It wasn't long before Yun-gil was forced into the army because of his involvement in demonstrations.

Winter's first snow fell the day he entered boot camp.

"Why does he have to go to boot camp in the middle of winter, of all times? It's not fair. I knew this would happen...from the moment he started acting up." Hye-suk was devastated. "Don't they see that they're just a bunch of idealistic kids?

Why can't they give them a little leeway and try to guide them in the right direction? Why are they giving them such a hard time? I can't believe this! How can they do this? How can they drag someone off and force him into the army in the middle of winter?" Spittle gathered at the corners of her mouth.

Chu-ch'ôl tried to comfort her when she returned, teary-eyed, from seeing her son off at the front gate of the army base.

"It's all for the best. By the time he's discharged and returns to school, all his buddies will have graduated. He won't have a reason to demonstrate any more. It's better this way. They've actually saved him from getting into worse trouble, from going to jail or getting expelled. I know it's cold and it'll be hard going but.... He'll just have to suffer through it. After all, it's all of his own doing. It's part of growing up. Don't let it get you too upset."

Yun-gil never wrote home. All they got was a mimeographed note from the commander of an infantry company on the front line: *Private Pak Yun-gil is presently serving under my command and performing his sacred obligation to the defense of his nation. He is in good health. There is no need for concern. Thank you.*

After a year in the army, Yun-gil came home on leave. The following year he returned once more. A few months later he was discharged.

Each leave lasted twenty days. He spent the entire time holed up in his room. He seemed to be writing something, and judging from the paper he discarded, it wasn't poetry. It looked like he was writing a novel.

"I guess you were right," Hye-suk said with satisfaction. "Army life really has made him grow up."

But Hye-suk was wrong.

FATHER AND SON

Chu-ch'ôl was seized by a disturbing premonition from the moment his son came home on leave. Something wasn't quite right. He pretended not to notice, for fear his wife would start losing weight and get fever blisters again. Then one night before Yun-gil was scheduled to return to the base, he sneaked into the boy's room to talk.

"I have a feeling you're hiding something from me. You know, I've always been very sensitive. You seem to be having a hard time in the army. Why don't you tell me about it? I know someone high up at army headquarters. Maybe I could pull a few strings for you."

Yun-gil was seated with his back to his father. All Chu-ch'ôl could see was the back of his son's crew-cut head. Suddenly Yun-gil spun around and shot a murderous look at his father. The whites of his eyes shone with a bluish glint. His pupils reflected the light like the steely blade of a knife. He pressed his lips together for a moment, forming deep dimples at the corners of his mouth, then spoke in a low, pained tone.

"Just try it and I'm deserting."

Chu-ch'ôl didn't know what to say.

It wasn't until after Yun-gil was discharged that Chu-ch'ôl learned why his son had become so spiteful. He didn't hear the story from Yun-gil himself; his son's girlfriend told him.

Yun-gil had been assigned to a reserve infantry regiment on the front line as soon as he finished boot camp. That was when the *t'aekwondo* training had begun. After learning a few basic moves, Yun-gil was sent into matches against better-trained opponents. Agile and fierce as wild beasts, they beat him relentlessly, pounding him until he collapsed. It wasn't long before he became a vicious monster himself. He had to if he wanted to survive.

Yun-gil returned to school immediately after his discharge. Soon he didn't bother coming home at all. He'd had a heated argument with his father. Chu-ch'ôl had kept scolding and advising, advising and scolding, all with the best intentions, but father and son ended up arguing. Yun-gil refused to accept anything Chu-ch'ôl said. He snarled at his father, spitting and glaring like a crazed cat. Helpless to control his own resentment and anger, Chu-ch'ôl slapped his son several times across the face with all his might.

"Get out of here! You can drop dead for all I care!"

Yun-gil let out a snort. "Fine," he answered in a husky voice as he jumped to his feet. "I'm leaving this stinking reactionary dump!"

And he stalked from the room without a backward glance. Overcome by the sense of defeat and rage boiling inside his head, Chu-ch'ôl ripped off his undershirt, tore it to shreds and flung it to the floor. His skin was streaked with red as the rage coursed through his body.

"I don't understand you," Hye-suk cried. "You're acting just like him! Why, he's only a boy! He hasn't even had a chance to recover from the army yet. Why are you acting like this? Can't you control yourself? Just wait! Do you think he's going to come back? What am I going to do? I can't take this anymore!"

She's right, Chu-ch'ôl thought as regret surged over him, but then he snapped back in anger.

"Forget about him! Forget he exists! Remember? He's the one who said he belonged to the 'wretched masses'! Our ties to him are broken. We're not his parents anymore!"

Chu-ch'ôl went into the bathroom. As he washed his face and poured water over his head, he was seized by frustration and loneliness. The misery and self-hatred made him retch. He pressed his eyes shut and bit down hard on his tongue. Maybe his son was right. Maybe I'm just trash, all contradictions and conceit.... Nothing more than a chunk of rotting flesh. Suddenly he felt like killing himself.

It wasn't long before life returned to normal, though. After all, fathers and sons have their own lives to live, he thought. Who isn't swayed by life's contradictions? Everything begins in contradiction, conflict and confrontation. Life and death, creation and extinction, good and evil—the significance of all being lies in the pendulum motion between opposites. In the end, all things are one. Left is right and right is left. There is no left and there is no right. That was how Chu-ch'ŏl rationalized his actions. He tried to forget about his son and break free of those aggravating thoughts.

On the night of the fourth day after Yun-gil left home, Chu-ch'ŏl returned from work late to find Hye-suk upset by a visit she'd had during the day.

"She was just a wisp of a girl, no bigger than a sparrow." Hye-suk's face twisted as she spoke.

"She said Yun-gil sent her. I couldn't believe it when I saw her. What is wrong with him? He's gone too far! That girl...why, I couldn't stand the sight of her—her face, her hair, her clothes.... She couldn't be more than four and a half feet tall, and she's skinny as a rail. Her skin's rough and drawn, and she has so many freckles it looks like someone poured black sesame seeds on her face. She's got these frog eyes—and they're the only thing about her that sparkled! Her forehead and cheekbones stick out, her cheeks are hollow, and her lips are thin and tight.

"She's smart enough, I guess, but there's not a hint of femininity in her. She could have worn something a little prettier, but no...she was wearing a baggy old tee shirt on top of a worn-out pair of blue jeans and torn sneakers. Her hair's kind of brown, and cut...not exactly in a pageboy or short like a man's. It's not even permed.... It's just cut in patches, like a rat gnawed it. And her hands are rough, like she's been pulling grass or digging around in the dirt. Why, she looked like some kind of factory worker! No, I take that back. I don't think you could find a factory worker dressed like her in this day and age.

"Anyway, I figured as long as she was here, I might as well ask her a few questions, so I sat her down and asked her about Yun-gil. You know, where he was, and does he have a place to stay, and is he getting enough to eat, and is he going to school.... Anyway, you would not believe that girl! She referred to him as 'Brother!' Without the slightest hesitation! I couldn't believe it! She said he'd been staying in her room and they might get married someday. I asked what she did for a living, and she said, 'Me? I dropped out of school. I'm with the labor movement now.' She kind of laughed and then nonchalantly added, 'Brother and I think alike. In a former life, we must have shared the same body, like an earthworm. Everything fits just perfect.'"

Hye-suk paused to see if he understood.

"So what are you saying?" he demanded brusquely, avoiding her embarrassed gaze. "Are you saying we should run over there and get him?"

"I know, but I can't accept a girl like that for my daughter-in-law. The very thought of it makes me want to die."

"Just forget about it. Our ties to that boy were severed long ago. What he does is his problem, not ours," Chu-ch'ôl said. But in his heart he had already begun working on a speech to persuade Yun-gil to come back home. He decided not to tell his wife about his plan. No point in raising her expectations.

Chu-ch'ôl lay awake at night, turning his scheme over and over in his mind. Think of the dreams I had for that boy! I've got to make him understand this contradiction of mine. He's got to realize that it's part of me. Yes, that's what I'll do. I'll go to him, and we'll open up and say what's on our minds. We'll find some kind of middle ground.

Chu-ch'ôl stole the girl's address from his wife's note pad, then went to her house late one night a few days later.

As he gazed out of the taxi window, he saw the moon slipping by, suspended between the roofs. Round as a ripe pumpkin or an advertising balloon floating high in the sky, it reminded him of his son's face. When Yun-gil was a baby, Chu-ch'ôl used to take him to his hometown to see his mother. The old woman would bounce her grandson in the air and exclaim, "He looks just like a bright shiny moon!"

The moon made the dizzying labyrinths of the city seem much larger. It awakened him to the existence of a distant, infinite vastness on the other side of space. There was more to the world than what was found here on earth.

It was late autumn. An unseasonable rain had fallen during the day, and as evening progressed, the wind had grown cold. The clouds had scattered, and finally, the moon peeked out. The asphalt was still wet; ginkgo leaves littered the ground like yellow butterfly corpses. The fluorescent light of the street lamps streamed down in icy threads. Chu-ch'ôl felt a flash of warmth at the thought of seeing the child he had abandoned. When Yun-gil had the flu as a little boy, Chu-ch'ôl would lay his hand on his forehead, hot as a brazier stone, and say, "You'll just have to wait it out. Your body's trying to grow more quickly. That's why it hurts so much."

Chu-ch'ôl believed that. Spring rains brought warm breezes, late autumn showers prompted winter's arrival. Children lost weight when they were ill, but once recovered, they gained quickly, growing by leaps and bounds. When old people caught a cold or the flu, they got more gray hairs and wrinkles. His son was suffering from an illness called youth now. The ordeal would provide him with an opportunity to mature.

Yun-gil agreed to see his father, but he was clearly annoyed by the visit. He refused to meet him somewhere quiet and cozy, like his girlfriend's room or a restaurant; instead he insisted they meet in a wine stall on the corner of a major thoroughfare, exposed to the damp, cold wind.

"The food at these stalls is outrageously overpriced, but I make a point of drinking here. These people can't afford to rent even the shabbiest little bar, so they're stuck on the streets. I figure I'm doing a good deed, giving them my business like this."

Yun-gil chuckled expansively as he perched himself on the long wooden bench. The proprietor of the stall, a squat man in his early forties, welcomed them with a good–natured smile. As Chu-ch'ŏl sat down beside his son, he thought how naive and arrogant Yun-gil sounded. The boy speaks with the self–righteousness and superiority of someone who thinks he's one of the chosen, he thought. After all, Yun-gil had always been an honors student. He had gone to only the best schools, and people were always raving about how intelligent he was. But did he have to flaunt that sanctimonious attitude in front of his father? The little jerk is trying to get back at me for slapping him!

They ordered chicken gizzards, roasted eel and mussel broth to eat with their *soju*. Back in Chu-ch'ŏl's time, young men turned to the side when they took a drink before their elders. Yun-gil was insolent by comparison, gulping down the liquor as he sat straight and proud in front of his father. Chu-ch'ŏl hadn't had a chance to teach his son drinking etiquette. It was too late now. He refilled Yun-gil's empty glass, almost as if he were a friend or acquaintance from school, and as he did, he recalled how he had cared for his son when he was delirious with fever as a child. "There's nothing to be afraid of," he said, squeezing the boy's hand and smiling. "Everyone has to be sick sometime. It's part of growing up."

A gust of wind whisked under the sides of the tent covering the wine stall. Chu-ch'ôl felt the chill run through his body. A dark cloud of steam and smoke rose from the eel the proprietor was roasting for the customers next to them. He turned the eel over with a pair of thongs. The man's face was deeply wrinkled. The flame in the kerosene lantern hanging over the table writhed in the wind. Milky white steam rose over the kettle of mussel broth. The people next to them smoked as they talked. Their conversation, peppered with swearing, suggested they were boiler workers. The thin man in a brown jacket with the dark stubble and unwashed hair spoke in the Chôlla dialect. His companion, a lanky fellow with a Ch'ungch'ông accent who, while similar in age, seemed insecure, chimed his agreement to everything the Chôlla man said.

"Let's go home," Chu-ch'ôl said. "I'm your father. I can't leave you here like this, and you can't turn your back on your parents forever, just because we disappointed you once. I know it sounds funny, but neither of us have had any practice at this father and son business. I guess the understanding and love shared by a father and son grow out of situations like this."

Chu-ch'ôl rambled on, almost as if he were talking about someone else. His son took a noisy slurp of mussel broth before he spoke.

"I'm sincere when I say this, Father. I always thought you were the greatest dad in the world. You were the one who gave me the courage to leave home in the first place.... Don't get me wrong. I'm not trying to mock you. It's just that.... Life is a form of suffering, a kind of penance, I guess. And no one can pay penance when they're cooped up like a hothouse flower. That's why I can't go back with you. How can I save the suffering without sharing their pain?"

As Chu-ch'ôl listened, he sensed a profound distance separating them, as if his son, who was right beside him, were sitting on the opposite side of a vast river. He felt as if his voice would never reach his son's ears, no matter how he shouted, as if the words would simply scatter, meaningless, into the air. It wasn't only his relationship with Yun-gil. All his relationships seemed empty: his marriage, his relationship with his daughter, a sophomore in university, his relationships with the president of the publishing company where he worked, with the other editors and staff.

"I understand. It's up to you. But I have a couple of requests to make. First, about that girl you've been seeing.... Just think of her as a friend. Don't plan on marrying her. A woman has to look gracious, you know, pretty and good-natured. A marriage affects more than the bride and groom. You have to think of the children!"

Chu-ch'ôl figured he might as well achieve at least half of what he had set out to do that evening, but Yun-gil shook his head.

"Father, let me make this perfectly clear. I'm the one who's going to live with the woman I choose to marry, and the children she bears are going to be my children."

"Listen here, young man! She's more than your wife! She's going to be my daughter-in-law, and the children she bears are going to be my grandchildren!"

That was what Chu-ch'ôl wanted to say, but he couldn't.

"All right, I understand," he said. "Let's say you're right. There's one more thing. I don't want you to get involved in any extremist activities. Violence is unforgivable, no matter what. I despise the radical left and communist sympathizers. I hate radicalism. Whether it's Marxist class struggle or liberation theory or Leninist revolution or the dictatorship of the proletariat—I'm against it all!"

FATHER AND SON

Yun-gil glared at his father. His eyes narrowed to knife points. A venomous blue light streamed from them, piercing his father like tiny needles. Chu-ch'ôl shuddered. Yun-gil shook his head again and chuckled as if it were all too absurd.

"So now my father's trying to make me out as the communist!" he snorted. "You've got me all wrong, Father. I merely sympathize with their ideas. I'm just advocating the overthrow of reactionary bureaucrats who oppose the great flow of history. We've got to get rid of the foreign powers who treat our bureaucrats like personal servants."

"You know that's the communists' logic, don't you? And all those terms you're using—they're almost all pro–communist!"

Yun-gil's eyes narrowed once more, streaming blue venom.

"Why shouldn't the people advocating democracy borrow a few of the communists' good points?" He said in a patient tone laced with sarcasm. "The communists often use terms like democracy and freedom, just like we do. Creating a better life for the poor, for those without, working on behalf of the laborers and farmers—do the communists have a corner on those ideas? Class clearly exists in our society. So why is everyone so suspicious of any discussion of it? Why is it pro–communist to talk about class?

"Korean Christians have borrowed plenty of terms from Buddhism, things like devotion and emptiness. The Korean Bible is full of quotes taken from Buddhist texts. 'Come unto me, all you that labor and are heavy laden, and I will give you rest.' That concept comes straight from Buddhism—the idea of freeing captive animals and birds. And all that business about 'Blessed are the poor in spirit for theirs is the kingdom of heaven...' That's taken from references to the pure–hearted in Buddhist texts. But that doesn't mean Christians are Buddhists. No one thinks they're heretics. And yet, this so–called free country of ours is riddled with preposterous taboos.

We're all so afraid of being called communist sympathizers for using 'tainted' expressions like 'comrade,' or the 'propertyless masses,' or 'class origins,' or 'self–criticism,' that we end up using substitutes that are completely meaningless."

"But Yun-gil, people like us, who are good but powerless, have to conform to reality. Remember that old saying: The virtuous man flows with the times."

"What? How can you say we're powerless?" Yun-gil snapped. The veins in his neck bulged. "We simply don't use the power we have. And why is that? Because of a few ridiculous preconceptions—the belief that we're all middle class, that our lives are fine the way they are, that nothing will change no matter who runs the government, the Korean people's fixation with security.... These ideas have robbed us of our passion!"

Chu-ch'ôl didn't know what to say. As he gazed vacantly into his son's face, he thought of a swamp. Yun-gil refilled his father's glass, then his own. "Perhaps you've had too much to drink, Father," Yun-gil said as he emptied his glass.

"It's a swamp," Chu-ch'ôl sighed. "A muddy, boggy, frightening swamp that every decent human being in this country has to fall into at least once in his life. Just make sure you don't end up drowning. You have to get out as soon as you can...but you'll have to do it on your own."

Yun-gil was drunk too. "Oh, Father," he slurred. "You and your generation are just a bunch of romantics. You think my generation cares about nothing but ideological struggle, but you're wrong. We're fighting to transform this immoral society into a principled unified nation."

Yun-gil smiled awkwardly, then reached into his pocket and pulled out a piece of newspaper folded into a small, thick square like the pasteboard cards children play with.

"I may be a history major but I finally plucked up the courage to write something. It's called 'The Riddle Story.' Why don't you read it when you get home?" He placed the square on the table in front of his father.

"Do you know what a riddle story is?" Yun-gil asked. "It's a new literary genre I invented: a combination vignette-riddle. I was going to call it 'The Riddle Vignette,' but I changed the title to 'The Riddle Story.' I figured we should respect our mother tongue and use a pure Korean word."

On the way home, Chu-ch'ôl asked the taxi driver to turn on the overhead light, and, eyes bleary with drink, he began to read his son's story.

* * * * * * *

The rats destroyed the family's peace. No one could sleep; everyone was a nervous wreck.

The house sat in the middle of a field. When winter came, the rats flocked inside. At night, they thundered about, waking the family with their fighting and squeaking. From the day the rats moved in, the family couldn't sleep.

The children were frightened by the rats banging and squeaking in the ceiling; they didn't want to sleep in their own room.

"What? You can't sleep because of a few rats? Don't be silly!" the parents shouted as they herded their children back to bed. The children went to sleep, but during the night they returned, one by one, to their parents' room.

The family bought mouse traps by the dozen and set them where the rats frequented. They baited the traps with pieces of beef gristle and squid dipped in sesame oil. They caught a few at first, but after one rat was captured in a trap, the others would not go near it. They seemed to smell the death of their comrades.

Next they tried rat poison. They mixed it with the rats' favorite foods—rice, sweet potatoes, dried anchovies, cookies, and the like—then placed it near the rats' hideouts and scattered it in the crawl spaces above the ceilings in every room. They were going to wipe out the whole pesky lot in a single stroke.

Their first attempt was a great success. The morning after they laid the poison, the parents found rats staggering around the wash basin and drain, bellies distended from the water they had drunk through the night. Several had simply stretched out and died. They collected the carcasses, counting more than a dozen all together. After burying the rats, the family slept soundly for the first time in a long time.

"We should have done this from the very beginning," the father sighed.

"Let's use poison again if they come back," the mother added.

The rats returned on the third day and began making a racket all over again. The father and mother smirked knowingly and, the following evening, set about mixing the poison again.

Things didn't turn out as they expected, however. The rats did not eat the poison. It was as if they knew that it would kill them. The parents stared in disbelief at the untouched heaps of poison. The children trembled with fear.

How could they get rid of the rats now? There were so many. The rats flocked in, fifteen or sixteen at a time, squeaking and snapping, loafing about, chasing one another back and forth.

So the family got two cats. They borrowed a large female from a relative who ran a shop and bought the second, a medium–sized male, at the market.

They figured the rats wouldn't dare come in when they heard a cat. "The cats'll catch 'em. We should have thought of this long ago," they thought. They were, however, sadly mistaken.

The father sent the male cat into the crawl space above the ceiling. The mother tied the female on a string in the granary where the rats often played.

The male cat fell from the crawl space and died with its eyes rolled back in its head. It had eaten the rat poison. The rats didn't go anywhere near the granary. They simply squeaked and scampered in the ceiling or along the eaves and roof as before. At some point, the rats learned to ignore the remaining cat's meows. In fact, the cat deserved to be ignored.

The father and mother bought another cat to replace the one that had died, but it wasn't particularly effective. They couldn't send it into the crawl space with all that poison. They simply hoped it would chase the rats away. But it didn't work. Finally, the father and the mother gave up on cats and began looking for a surefire method to get rid of the rodents.

By that time, the rats had come down from the attic and were chewing holes in the rice bags, leaving urine and droppings on the family's bedding, invading the closets, and gnawing holes in their clothes. The family spent their days maligning modern cats and cursing the rats.

Then one day a well–dressed stranger with a large suitcase appeared at their door. He said he had, until recently, been a high government official and possessed an amazing solution to their problem.

"I'm thinking of taking out an international patent," he said, "so don't tell anyone about this. It's a rat extermination system based on fratricidal logic."

His amazing solution worked like this.

"First, you need a large jar, then you make a balance by suspending a lever across the mouth of the jar, and you fasten chunks of tasty beef at each end of the lever.

"Once the balance is fastened to the mouth of the jar, a rat climbs up to get the meat. He circles the top of the jar a few times, then screws up his courage and crawls out onto the balance to take a bite. The balance tips, and the rat falls into the jar.

"Now, people say there isn't a man alive who won't pick up a knife and commit robbery after three days without food. As time passes, the rat's eyes begin to burn with a frightening glow. And then another rat goes after the meat and falls into the jar, just like the first one. After a day or two, the two hungry rats start trying to eat each other. The one who finally manages to eat his opponent is the victor.

"It isn't long before another rat is lured by the smell of the meat and falls into the jar like the two before him. The rat that has already eaten one opponent devours the newcomer. And so it goes. The rat begins to eat his comrades, first one, then two, then three, then four...then ten, twenty, and so forth, until he realizes just how tasty his fellow rats can be. Soon he's mastered the art of killing on the first try.

"Leave the jar for a year and the rat will consume nearly one hundred of his comrades. That's when you turn the jar on its side and release him. He'll eat nothing but rats after that.

"And if you give him a shot of liquor or hallucinogens, it's even more effective."

"That makes great sense!" the father exclaimed when the traveler finished. The mother and children clapped their hands and jumped up and down. The father and mother bought a jar so enormous the two of them could barely carry it. Then they constructed a balance just as the stranger had instructed. They placed two pieces of mouth–watering beef on each end of the balance and fit it over the mouth of the jar. So began their treacherous vigil waiting for the no–good rats to turn into vicious cannibals. This time they patiently endured the rodents' squeaky commotion in the ceiling and yard.

But readers, do you think the family's dream came true? The answer is located at the bottom of the editorial on page 2.

* * * * * * *

Chu-ch'ŏl turned the newspaper over and looked for the editorial. At the bottom was the answer to the riddle.

Fratricide is based on human logic, not the logic of rats.

Chu-ch'ŏl got out of the taxi and trudged up the steep path toward his house, hands buried deep in his pockets. He smiled bitterly when he realized how miserable he must look: the stern patriarch deprived of his authority. The cold wind raced up behind him and sent the dead leaves scurrying along the path drenched blue by the street lamp. Just like the rats scrambling to devour their brethren, Chu-ch'ŏl thought. The logic of fratricide...the logic of rats...

3

"Have you read that ridiculous riddle story? The one Yun-gil wrote, I mean," Chu-ôn asked, as he finally stuck the cigarette in his mouth and flicked his lighter. Chu-ch'ŏl stared out of the window, pretending he hadn't heard. He was lost in a dull confusion. Was his son really out of line? Or were the people who thought he was out of line the ones with a problem? Outside the window a wind, relentless as an army ready for battle, whipped the plain; the gaunt branches of the trees thrashed in the wind. Chu-ch'ŏl folded his arms across his chest and tucked his chin inside the collar of his sweater. The wind rushed through a crack in the window, a knife of cold. Grizzled flakes of snow mixed with the wind. Through the flakes, a village appeared, nestled at the foot of a low hill, as if wrapped in a winter muffler. At the entrance to the village stood an old spirit tree. Its leaves were gone now. It seemed to be waiting for something, eyes closed and quiet. Chu-ch'ŏl shut his eyes. His head filled with cherry blossoms floating on the chill breeze of early spring. White butterflies fluttered as they mated above a yellow field of rapeseed flowers. Clouds drifted over the mountains, the fields were shrouded in a misty haze, and sky larks soared above.

Chu-ch'ŏl's toes ached. He had suffered a severe case of frostbite in the army. Eyes closed still, he wiggled his toes. The cockroach rose before him. It transformed into an enormous black phantom, overwhelming his senses. The ride from Seoul seemed like a long journey through a nightmarish tunnel.

Night Train

1

They had received a telegram: Chu-man, Chu-ch'ôl's younger brother, was dead. His death gave them the excuse they needed. Chu-ch'ôl and Hye-suk felt terrible: it was a shame to have to use poor Chu-man, but they did. Free from prying eyes at last, they rushed to catch the night train.

For an instant, Chu-ch'ôl was caught in a fantasy: he was departing on a journey to another world where he could cast off his troubles and feel completely unencumbered.

As he took his seat, he made his usual bet. Whenever he traveled, be it far or near, on the bus to or from work, anywhere, Chu-ch'ôl always made a bet: Would he meet someone he knew or not? It was a way of hypnotizing himself, of cheating time. If he ran into a familiar face, it meant something bad would happen, and if he didn't meet anyone, he could look forward to good fortune. The bets filled him with expectations, much like setting out the pieces for a game of *go*. Perhaps it was because of these expectations that he did not concern himself with the rules of fair play. Whenever possible, he avoided looking at people in the face. And when he did look at them, he tried to avoid their eyes. He was afraid that if he looked into their eyes too long they might turn into someone he had once known. On public transportation he always adjusted his gaze so it fell on the chest of the person facing him. Often he dropped his eyes and stared at the floor or turned to look out of the window. As a result, or perhaps because he really was lucky, Chu-ch'ôl never ran into anyone he knew. Nor did he ever have any bad luck.

He decided to bet on this trip as well. The bet would be effective from Seoul Station until they deboarded in Kwangju.

He knew his game was nothing more than useless superstition, but still, he played it and soon was completely absorbed. The suspense chopped the time, which could be so painfully boring, into small pieces, and in the end, he was able to forget himself completely. It was a brilliant notion—a self-imposed cure, a means of hypnotizing himself. His bets allowed him to immerse himself in solitude, thereby escaping it.

At one time he thought of telling Hye-suk about this brilliant idea, but he didn't. His wife had long since developed her own secret formula. Every morning she got up at five and went to the spring behind their house. When she got home, she poured water from the spring into a white porcelain bowl and placed it on the rice box in the kitchen. Then she knelt down in front of the bowl, pressing her forehead to the floor in a deep bow. Sometimes she used another secret technique: she pretended to sleep. It was a false sleep. When something bothered her, she swallowed the torment in silence, as if in a dream. Chu-ch'ŏl realized that his wife's false sleep was her way of escaping, and he didn't try to interfere.

The idea of passing time with clever tricks first came to him as a student. He had learned nine–card solitaire from the woman who ran the boarding house where he lived. The game was played with a deck of flower cards from which eight cards— the rain and paulownia tree suits—had been removed. He bet on whether he could get the cards to come out even at the end. It was extremely difficult and tedious. He was lucky if he could do it once in ten games. Waging one's luck on coming out even was a pitiful business, so Chu-ch'ŏl applied a much simpler and more ingenious standard to his game. He bet that the cards would get stuck in the middle. It was impossible to come out even in nine–card solitaire unless you cut the cards just right. And as a result, he always enjoyed the good fortune of getting stuck in the middle.

It wasn't long before he was chastising himself for his petty games of solitaire, and having listened to his own advice, he gave up betting on cards.

He then developed a system of betting on books. It was after he started working at the publishing company and had had some success as a poet. One could say he had given up vulgar forms of gambling, such as solitaire with flower cards, for a somewhat more sophisticated pastime. But when he stopped to think about it, this new distraction was equally ludicrous. Whenever he started reading a book, any book, he bet on how far he would get before encountering a spelling error or a missing word. An error signaled great fortune in the near future; a flawless book meant he was in for bad luck. Of course, there isn't a book in the world without some kind of error, so Chu-ch'ôl could always expect countless good fortunes when reading. He sneered at the publisher's ineptitude each time he spotted his prey, but at the same time, he thanked them for the good fortune they offered. He realized how silly his bets were. He laughed at the thought of himself betting on such foolishness, and yet he never gave it up. He couldn't, and the older he got, the more thick-skinned he became. He knew he was being foolish, but he didn't do anything about it. It was that hypocrisy that caused him the most pain.

He had brought along one of his firm's new releases in hopes of encountering that secret good fortune. He was responsible for new releases so he had to look over the books anyway. Betting on books made him feel comfortable and safe, as if he alone had a secret weapon, an exclusive prescription from a wonder–working doctor, a magic talisman. If he ran into a familiar face in his first wager, he could always recover his losses by opening the book and betting on where he would find the first error.

The train rocked as it gathered speed out of Seoul Station. Hye-suk was sitting by the window. Suddenly she grabbed Chu-ch'ôl's wrist. Her fingers sliced into his arm, as if she were twisting a cord around it. Chu-ch'ôl jerked to his senses and turned to her.

"Look! It's Chu-ôn," she whispered urgently, indicating the entrance to the coach with a toss of her chin. She hunched down, pressing her forehead against Chu-ch'ôl's shoulder, and pretended to sleep.

Chu-ôn stepped through the door. His hair was shaggy, covering his ears, his face long like a horse's, and his complexion was dark. He studied each passenger's face as he headed down the aisle, one hand plunged in his raincoat pocket. How did he find us? Chu-ch'ôl wondered. His first bet had fallen flat and useless. Chu-ch'ôl felt his chest constricting. He turned to look out of the window. It had been bitterly cold for several days—hovering around minus fifteen degrees. Snow had fallen three days earlier, and white patches lingered in the shadows of the mountains and on the roofs of the villages they passed. The frozen earth was blanketed in darkness. The wind, cold and penetrating as a metal spike, barreled through the darkness like a tank armed with machine guns.

The windows cut off the darkness and cold. They reflected another world, like a scene from a black and white movie, a negative that had been enlarged. Everything was swept up in what seemed a delicate ink painting, all coarse and pockmarked details removed. The wrinkles, scars and freckles on the faces in the window were gone. The distinction between beauty and ugliness was unclear. Everyone in the window exuded an air of dark stillness.

It was sweltering inside the train. Hot steam ran through the pipes beneath the seats by the windows. The passengers had taken off their suitcoats and sweaters, overcoats and mufflers. Some sat in shirtsleeves, chatting quietly, while others gathered in groups of four or five to play flower cards. Still others slept, a sweater or overcoat covering their chest and shoulders. Their reflections shone in the window, as clear as a movie screen. Chu-ch'ŏl found his own image in the black and white scene. Hye-suk looked like she was really sleeping, her face tucked behind his shoulder. He stared at her sleeping reflection as he waited for Chu-ôn to reach them.

"Aha! There you are! I nearly went crazy looking for you, Cousin! I called your house and the kids said you'd left a half hour earlier, so I jumped in a taxi and got to the station one minute before the train left. I'm sitting in the next car."

Chu-ôn stood next to Chu-ch'ŏl's seat chattering in a manner unseemly for such a large man. He bowed to the attractive young woman wearing a maroon beret who sat across the aisle from Chu-ch'ŏl, showed her his ticket and asked if they might switch seats. She glanced at the ticket and stood up.

"Once I heard Cousin Chu–man died, I couldn't stay in Seoul. It's too bad. He was so young! You know how he doted on me when I was little!"

Chu-ôn sat down in the seat vacated by the young woman.

"She must have had a hard day," Chu-ôn remarked, glancing across at Hye-suk.

He called over the vendor and bought two bottles of beer, some dried cuttlefish, peanuts and almond crackers. He also bought a bottle of juice and a cola, for Hye-suk, he said, when she woke up.

"Actually, I came to comfort you and try to help you in your time of grief. You shouldn't carry the burden on your own. There's nothing like a good drink when you're faced with something like this. Have a couple of beers and go to sleep, or just sit back and pass the time. That's the best way to cope. Here you go! Have a beer!"

Chu-ôn handed Chu-ch'ôl a cup and filled it with beer. Hye-suk shifted to lean against the window, still feigning sleep. She was wearing a silk scarf around the neck of her loose–fitting gray cotton blouse. Tiny wrinkles, fine as strands of hair, creased her lightly powdered face. A blue shadow clouded the hollows beneath her eyes. She was like an insect that plays dead when in danger. Perhaps she's simply lapsed into a state of false sleep, Chu-ch'ôl thought. She was always closing her eyes like that at home. She would take a sedative and lie with her eyes shut, but she never fell into a deep sleep. She seemed to think all her thoughts, dream all her dreams, and hear everything that went on around her.

It all started shortly after Yun-gil left home. He made one last telephone call in early winter. They could barely hear him. Either the phone was tapped or it was a bad connection. Something whirred in the background, a combination of grass bugs whining and a ringing in the ears.

"This may be my last call," he said, "but don't worry. I'm fine." He paused, and then, "Good-bye." He never identified himself.

Yun-gil sounded slightly out of breath. Chu-ch'ôl gasped, temples pounding, at the sound of his son's voice. "All right," he said, but there was a click on the other end of the line before he finished the word. He must be going to hide down in the countryside, Chu-ch'ôl thought. When he mentioned this to Hye-suk, she seemed even more concerned.

"You know, it would be so much safer in the city where there's lots of people. We never should have told him about that place."

Hye-suk bit her cracked lips nervously. Chu-ch'ôl couldn't help thinking she was right. He had suggested that Yun-gil hide in the old fishing village, but now he wasn't sure. It was in the backwoods where few people lived, at the end of a deep ravine.

If his pursuers burst in on him suddenly, he would have nowhere to run but the mountains.

"Maybe we should call and have them tell him to hide somewhere else. Isn't there something we can do? Come on! We have to do something!"

Hye-suk badgered her husband night and day. He didn't know what to do. He thought about calling Chu–man or one of his uncles down in the village, but he was afraid the phones were tapped. And if someone ran down there with a message for Yun-gil, they were sure to be tailed. He thought of sending a letter, but they would probably intercept it. His hands were tied, he was helpless, and then came the answer to his prayers: a message from his uncle in Tideflat Village. Chu-man was dead.

Cruel though it was, the news of Chu–man's death was glad tidings to Chu-ch'ôl and Hye-suk. They had been choking with frustration since that last call from Yun-gil. No one could be sure when Chu-man would die, but his neighbors knew he would go in the near future. Everyone secretly expected him to die soon. It was obvious from his symptoms—the way his face grew darker and darker—and his behavior—the way he guzzled *soju* and ran around like a crazy man. Chu-ch'ôl and Hye-suk should have felt sorry for Chu-man, but as they rushed to board the night train, they were thankful for this excuse to visit their hometown without worrying about what others might think.

And then Chu-ôn showed up, like a cockroach, quick–witted and agile, crafty and sly. There was no way of catching him.

2

Hye-suk sometimes shook her husband awake in the middle of the night. When she first woke him that way, Chu-ch'ôl jumped from bed, thinking there was a burglar in the house. He searched the room for something to use as a weapon—on top of the wardrobe, under the desk, on the dressing–table, the television. Then he heard his wife whisper, "There are two cockroaches as big as my finger in the kitchen," and the adrenalin drained from him. Unable to control his anger, Chu-ch'ôl glared murderously into her face.

"Oh, I'm sorry, darling! I didn't mean to startle you! Please don't be mad. Come to the kitchen. They just came out from nowhere. They're as big as rats and so quick, and their feelers are so disgusting, I...." He could hardly be angry when his wife apologized so diffidently. Still, he grumbled as he followed her to the kitchen.

"I can't believe this. Imagine waking your husband in the middle of the night because you can't catch a couple of lousy cockroaches!"

Hye-suk poked him in the ribs. "Quiet," she whispered. "They were digging in the garbage can by the sink, but they ran away when they heard me coming." She pressed a fly swatter into his hand.

"I heard a rustling in the garbage can. Don't bother looking anywhere else. Go straight to the garbage can and whack them when they come out," Hye-suk said. They stood by the curtain that hung at the entrance to the kitchen. She flicked on the light and pushed him forward, as if to say hurry up and get it over with. He went straight for the sink. A faint rustle came from the garbage can; it sounded like arthropods crawling or rats gnawing grain. He bent over the garbage can, fly swatter poised. I'll knock the crap out of them. He had plenty of reasons to punish the insects. A knot of ill feeling squeezed his chest. How dare they sneak into my kitchen in the middle of the night! I'm going to kill the little bastards! The thin sound of his wife's breathing seemed to refract the light of the incandescent bulb overhead.

FATHER AND SON

Chu-ch'ôl grabbed the edge of the garbage can with his left hand and gave it a cautious shake. The egg and cockle shells, onion skins, empty milk packets and discarded cabbage leaves trembled slightly. Every nerve in his body was stretched taut as a guitar string. He shook the garbage can again, holding his breath as he waited for the roaches to crawl over the edge of the can. As he had hoped, a puff of black wind shot from between a cabbage leave and an onion skin. Chu-ch'ôl swung the fly swatter down as the cockroach came over the rim. Whoosh! He had missed. In the blink of an eye, the cockroach slipped through the crack between the sink and stove.

"Damn it!" Chu-ch'ôl snarled. There are bound to be more, Hye-suk cried. Determined to succeed this time, Chu-ch'ôl turned only to see another mouse-sized cockroach sketch a dark line in the direction of the previous escapee. Chu-ch'ôl didn't even get a chance to raise his fly swatter. He shook the can again. There weren't any more.

Chu-ch'ôl was desperate to relieve his rage. He poked the fly swatter into the crack. It was pitch black, a cockroach paradise. They were probably laughing at him, flashing their iridescent blue eyes and twitching their feelers.

"How am I supposed to catch these things?"

"They're awfully fast, aren't they?" Hye-suk was careful not to find fault with his technique, as if she feared her husband's temper.

"Can't expect much when you wake someone up in the middle of the night! Next time you see a cockroach, grab the fly swatter and get him yourself. There's nothing to it! Just whack him! Why do you have to wake up someone who's just drifted to sleep?"

Despite his wife's efforts to console him, Chu-ch'ôl muttered angrily as he returned to bed. The next morning before leaving for work he went to the drugstore and bought a can of their best insecticide.

"Go to work!" Hye-suk snapped. "I'll spray after I've finished the dishes and covered the food."

Chu-ch'ôl insisted on doing it himself. Accustomed to her husband's impatience, Hye-suk wrapped the breakfast leftovers in plastic and put them in the refrigerator. Chu-ch'ôl doused the roaches' hideouts with insecticide—the dank space behind the refrigerator, the back of the stove, the space behind the rice box and cabinets, the cracks in the linoleum. When he returned home from work that evening, he found the carcasses. There was still something chillingly evil about them—the black shells, the stiffened feelers, the light brown wings faintly visible inside the wing case, the half–crumpled legs. The care with which Hye-suk had left them on the kitchen floor reflected the depth of her animosity for the insects, and as he cleared them away, Chu-ch'ôl realized that she wanted him to share the thrill of exterminating the black hordes. He thought of the insecticide he had used to douse their dark, dank haunts, then tried to forget the unpleasant memory. That night Hye-suk looked relieved as she went to bed.

But four nights later, Chu-ch'ôl woke to Hye-suk's shaking again. He rushed into the kitchen, fly swatter in hand, but he missed them, just like the first night. Three cockroaches, as large as his thumb, scurried like a pack of mice into the crack between the sink and stove. The next morning Chu-ch'ôl used the remaining insecticide, and not long after, they discovered the carcasses scattered around the kitchen once more.

The commotion reoccurred once or twice a week from that night forward, and the next morning Chu-ch'ôl would spray again. After repeating the process more than twenty times, Chu-ch'ôl and Hye-suk were exhausted. Yun-gil's problems arose around that time, actually, and they could savor their

disgust for the black hordes no longer. "We'll have to seal off
the house this weekend and spray an extra dose," they decided
as they watched the cockroaches race through the kitchen and
bathroom. In the days that followed they knew the cockroaches
were dancing around their kitchen in the middle of the night,
but they waited.

"You just make sure the food's covered until we get rid of
them," Chu-ch'ôl warned. Every morning as he poured water
from the kettle, a repulsive taste filled his mouth. The black
hordes might have touched the rim of the cup with their legs
and mouths during the night, he thought, but he swallowed
anyway. Sometime later they stretched the interval between
extermination sessions to two weeks, then a month.

Chu-ch'ôl sensed a strangely ominous connection between
the cockroaches, his son Yun-gil, and his second cousin Chu-
ôn. Yun-gil left home around the time the black hordes began
their rampage, and that was when Chu-ôn began wearing down
their gate with his visits.

"Can't you just leave us alone? You're driving me crazy!"
Chu-ch'ôl practically spat at Chu-ôn in naked irritation.

Even Hye-suk was openly hostile. "Uncle Chu-ôn, please
come back later when I've calmed down a bit. Why are you
doing this? For some reason I get goosebumps whenever you're
around."

"Oh, what's wrong with you two? It's only natural that I
should come see you. After all, here I am in Seoul, where
they'll steal the shirt off your back if you're not careful, and
you two are the only people I know. You may dislike me, but
I've nowhere else to go. You can turn me around and push me
out of the door, but I'll keep coming back."

And so Chu-ôn kept disturbing them, bringing a bottle of
liquor, a pound or two of beef or a cake every time he visited.
Perhaps he didn't have anywhere else to go, but that didn't

make him any less diabolic; he was like the cockroaches. Chu-ch'ôl and Hye-suk shuddered each time they saw him. Chu-ôn refused to tell them where he worked or lived. He wouldn't even give them his telephone number. He was just like the cockroaches. It was impossible to tell where they lived or laid their eggs either. He showed up under the cover of darkness, just like the black hordes sneaking through the drainpipe or swooping in on the dark night fog. He telephoned in the middle of the night asking how they were. The connection was always distant and fuzzy, as if he were calling from a bottomless underworld.

If Hye-suk greeted Chu-ch'ôl with a displeased look when he returned home from work, it meant Chu-ôn had visited in his absence. He showed up during the day and hung around in Yun-gil's room, reading, sleeping, riffling through Yun-gil's desk drawers, sifting through his notebooks and books, digging through his hiking equipment and bags, strumming his guitar.

3

The train chugged through the muddy darkness. It blasted its whistle and seemed to shudder down the tracks. Through the dark reflections of the windows, reddish lights blinked as they slipped past in the distance. The air was hot and humid inside the coach. Perspiration clung to Chu-ch'ôl's forehead, backbone, crotch and buttocks. It was hard to believe that the cruel winter cold was clawing like a fierce beast outside. The beer had made him dizzy; he felt as if he were dreaming.

Chu-ch'ôl often dreamed of abandoning everything someday. It was as if shadows were whispering around him, like evil cockroaches. He put out two or three books each month but they just seemed to pile up in the storeroom, never selling a single copy. He was sure to be driven from his job. All the typographical errors he had discovered seemed to return, dancing across the pages like evil monsters. *Open the door! Where's your son? Open that closet! Where's the attic? Who sleeps in this room? Tell the truth! Where did you send your son? Are you going to talk or not? Get up and put your clothes on! Get moving!* He felt as if a gang of men with crewcuts and beige parkas or leather gloves and corduroy jackets would come crashing in at any time of the day or night.

He and Yun-gil were always arguing. His son's daring and his own timidity were constantly at odds. Yun-gil's radicalism defied him; it loathed his father's conservatism. Who knows? Perhaps Yun-gil's contempt for his father's cowardice and conservatism had driven him to become a radical.

"Don't even go near a demonstration. There's no point. You have to think of yourself, of what's good for you. Get killed and you're the one who loses out. I know you can contribute to the betterment of the people and humanity by getting involved, but you can make a much more profound contribution in other ways. Something much greater is waiting for you when you've matured and finished your studies. In a way, I'm like a tree. I don't want my fruit to fall before it ripens. I want to see it grow to its full potential."

Perhaps he was acting out of selfishness, as is the habit of the well-to-do. Yun-gil assailed his father's advice as worthless bourgeois egotism.

"I may have been born of your flesh but I'm not your personal property. I belong to the masses. If our country or national history needs me, unripe as I am, I have to serve and fall as I may. Who knows? Maybe our country, and this age we're living in, wants more of the unripe to fall. Just pretend that I was never born. You may be faced with great pain because of me, but you have to resign yourself to it. That's your fate for giving birth to me and raising me."

Chu-ch'ôl soon felt a cold breeze blowing from Yun-gil's younger sister and brother as well. He's right. I never should have expected anything. The feeling of betrayal grows in direct proportion to my expectations. Don't try to connect everything. Don't try to stick things together. Just live your own life. Cut off and separate. Forget about eternity. Concentrate on the moment. I have my life, and the kids have theirs. Sons and daughters may stray from the framework that their parents have drawn out for them, but that doesn't mean the parents have failed. Forget your expectations. Expectations connect things. You can't cut off and separate when you live on expectations. The more expectations you have, the greater the feeling of betrayal. That's the bone–wrenching truth. Why should I torment myself with such bitter betrayal?

But his heart wouldn't accept it. He knew no other way of life. Living together as a group was the only way he knew. He hadn't learned how to cut himself off and live separately. That was why he always felt saddened by a certain betrayal.

It is said that he who walks well leaves no footprint. Words chosen carefully are faultless. An accurate reckoning requires no counting sticks. A door shut carefully will remain closed without a lock. A well–wrapped package will stay wrapped without twine.... But I am none of those things. I leave footprints, I am at fault. I struggle to imprison others in my locks and strings, but I can't even do that right....

The loss and frustration were inescapable. He was engulfed in self–doubt. Somewhere deep inside, he felt his hatred for Yun-gil, his condemnation, pooling like a poisonous juice. He couldn't help thinking he was responsible for getting his son into this mess. After Yun-gil left home, Chu-ch'ôl kept imagining his son covered in blood, staggering along some dark mountain path, blood dripping from a wound made by a knife or gunshot. The image of the boy floating face down in a pond, like a discarded cigarette butt, lingered in his mind, still and dark as a film negative. Where can he be? Is he getting enough to eat? He needed only to hear the boy's mother worrying and the image rose in his mind. He couldn't bear the thought. What do all these images mean? Perhaps they proved that he really did wish his son dead. Each time he had these thoughts, he tried to visualize another Yun-gil, a happy healthy young man with a broad smile on his face.

But it didn't work. Who is the real me? he wondered. Is he a wolf, a demon, while the nice guy, the generous angel, the bodhisattva that everyone's always talking about is nothing but a phony? Who knows? Chu-man may have died from my curses. *Why don't you just drop dead, die, die, die....* How many times had I thought of that? Every time he heard that Chu-man had gone on another drunken rampage, that he had grabbed a knife or sickle or ax or whatever he could get his hands on, every time he heard that Mother had cut her hand or strained her back trying to stop him, Chu-ch'ŏl prayed to himself over and over: *Die, just hurry up and die.*

"I can understand why Cousin Chu-man drank so much. Your mother was living with him so you gave him money for land and seaweed nets and you helped him start up the processing plant, but it all bothered him. Everyone was always bawling him out for drinking too much. They didn't understand how he felt."

Chu-ôn bought four more bottles of beer from the vendor. His speech was slightly slurred now. Chu-ch'ŏl didn't want to discuss Chu-man's death. There were more urgent matters on his mind.

"He had an inferiority complex," Chu-ôn continued. "And he was frustrated. He was probably smothering in loneliness too. He knew you were worried about all the things you'd paid for.... You were afraid he might sell them lock, stock and barrel.

Who knows? He may have thought you paid for that stuff because your mother was living with him, not because you cared about him."

"Cut it out, will you? I'm sick and tired of hearing about him." Chu-ch'ôl glared at his cousin. Chu-ôn nodded deeply and apologized for upsetting him. When Chu-ch'ôl saw that subservient smile, he felt like killing Chu-ôn. He imagined getting him drunk, dragging him out of the coach and shoving off the train. And if that failed, at least he could take him out in the dark where no one was watching and kick the crap out of him. Then he chided himself for the thought and lifted his cup to his lips.

I have to figure out what this jerk does for a living, he thought. He had to know what to be on the look-out for. First he considered Chu-ôn's hair. It was long, hardly the hairstyle for a man working within a strictly regulated system. Next he studied his clothes. Chu-ôn was wearing navy blue slacks with a wool shirt. His corduroy blazer and raincoat were hanging on a hook next to the window. The outfit collaborated the conclusion Chu-ch'ôl had already made: Chu-ôn didn't belong to a group run according to strict rules. And he wore the same low-top dress shoes as everyone else.

But you can hardly identify someone by the clothes they wear, Chu-ch'ôl thought. A person involved in criminal investigation or surveillance would dress like an ordinary citizen to protect his cover. Yes, Chu-ch'ôl thought, I'll look through the pockets of his jacket next time he goes to the restroom. Maybe he carries an I.D. card. Chu-ch'ôl waited for Chu-ôn to excuse himself.

"How much does it cost to publish a book of poetry these days? You know, I've been writing poetry for some time. You influenced me. When I was in high school, I was a member of the literary club and our advisor was always raving about you.

He said that Pak Chu-ch'ôl was a greater honor to his alma mater than any government official or business man. When I told him I was your cousin, he took a special interest in me. All my friends envied me. That's when I got the idea of becoming a poet like you."

Chu-ôn offered cup after cup of beer. Chu-ch'ôl felt uncomfortable talking about his poems. Over the years he had played the poet, writing and publishing his work, but he was never truly able to live for poetry. He could hardly claim to have dedicated himself to his art. It was a source of embarrassment to him, a sign he lacked confidence in his work. That lack of confidence meant his poems were false, which, in turn, meant he was living a double life, the life of a hypocrite. It was a painful thought. The words he used in his poems betrayed him day and night. No, he secretly betrayed those words himself. His poetry cried for a pure life, for sensitivity, for the ability to feel pain and shame at a breath of wind passing through the leaves, for unity with the common people, for a bodhisattva's generosity, for poverty, for deliverance, for rebirth. But Chu-ch'ôl lived a filthy, trifling existence, the life of a swarm of flies. He knew no shame. He was selfish, he lived for himself, and he was constantly struggling with that burden. At some point he had started living a divided existence: Pak Chu-ch'ôl, the poet, Pak Chu-ch'ôl, the editor at a certain publishing company, Pak Chu-ch'ôl, the husband and father. He was told he wrote beautiful, fresh, powerful verse, but at the same time he was forever maneuvering to make sure the books he made for the president of his company sold well. He tried to select controversial books and used every means possible, ethical and unethical, to make them sell. It was all a matter of staging. He mobilized the services of popular literary critics, he made sure the newspaper reporters covering literature and publishing were writing articles...and soon the readers were eating out of his hand. The publishing company where he worked had become a factory that produced best-sellers, popular writers and controversial poets. He and the president were constantly proclaiming their commitment to the advancement of contemporary culture. The goal of a publisher was to sell books, wasn't it? To attract the attention of readers who didn't know what they wanted to read, they were like fishermen who used lights to attract fish at night. But in the end, most of the books they produced (with a few exceptions, of course) differed little from the literary achievements of other companies.

"Stop talking about poetry and tell me who you really are! What do you do? Who are you working for? How can you afford to hang around doing nothing? What job would let you spend all your time at our house?"

Chu-ch'ôl was feeling the effects of the beer now. Chu-ôn stared intently into his face for a moment, then turned his eyes to the ceiling and guffawed. The sleeping passengers jerked awake and glared at him for a moment, then returned to sleep, smacking their lips.

"All right," chuckled Chu-ôn, ignoring the other passengers. "I'll tell you everything. I may not look like much but I'm one of Seoul's top jewel appraisers. Every two or three days I make the rounds of the jewelry shops. I don't have to worry about money." He laughed again. "I'll bet you're wondering how I developed an eye for jewels. Well, anything's possible. You know what they say—Every man has his trade. If you don't believe me, I'll take you on a tour of the jewelry shops. Now have some more beer!"

Chu-ch'ôl peered into Chu-ôn's face as he filled his cup. He wanted to believe him, but somehow he felt Chu-ôn was toying with him. His face was cloaked in a veil of lies. Just wait, you little jerk. I'm going to rip off that veil. I've made it through the last fifty years on little more than my senses. And those senses tell me something's wrong here.

"So you still don't believe me, eh? Too bad my heart isn't a sock—then I could turn it inside out and show you. Heh, heh.... Will you excuse me for a minute? I have to go to the john."

Chu-ôn bowed deeply as he rose from his seat. As soon as his cousin had teetered down the aisle and out of the door, Chu-ch'ôl jumped to his feet and began rummaging through the pockets of Chu-ôn's jacket and overcoat. The middle-aged man in the seat next to Chu-ôn opened his eyes in narrow slits and stared up at Chu-ch'ôl. He wasn't asleep after all. Chu-ch'ôl's face burned and a shiver ran down his spine, but he simply apologized and returned to his search. It ended in disappointment, however. There was no wallet. He must have put it in another pocket when he took off his jacket. Chu-ôn's thoroughness drove Chu-ch'ôl even deeper into that dark dizzying pool of suspicion. Of course! It had to be a lie. When would that bastard have had the time to become a jewel appraiser?

4

"Nephew? Is that you? It's me, Uncle Kae-dong."

One Sunday in early spring six years earlier, Chu-ch'ôl received a call from Chu-ôn's father. His childhood name was Kaettong, "Dogshit." The old man had devoted his life to raising and educating the motherless Chu-ôn.

"What? Uncle, where are you?"

Chu-ch'ôl had been lying on the warm floor looking through some manuscripts. He bolted upright at the voice on the other end of the line. Kae-dong's face rose before him. One of his eyes was milky-gray, like the screen of a television that wasn't turned on. His face was tanned dark-red. Kae-dong was built like an ox. Chu-ch'ôl owed the old man. Chu-ch'ôl had started school at the age of five, and each day, rain or snow, Kae-dong, a family servant at that time, carried him to school and met him at the front gate to carry him home. When Chu-ch'ôl went to middle school and high school on the mainland, Kae-dong carried his book bags and bundles of rice and pickle jars to the terminal in Hoejin. As they parted, Kae-dong would squeeze his hand and give him a broad smile, revealing two rows of yellowed teeth. Chu-ch'ôl's heart always ached at the sight of him heading home with his empty A-frame carrier after unloading his belongings in front of the terminal at the end of the pier.

"I'm here in Seoul."

"Then come right over. Just get in a taxi and tell the driver to take you to the entrance of the April 19th Monument in Ui-dong. I'll be waiting with the fare."

Kae-dong arrived by taxi, as instructed, but when Chu-ch'ôl ran to open the door, the fare had already been paid. He handed Kae-dong a five-thousand won note, but the older man waved it away, the light reflecting off the amber lenses of his glasses. Chu-ch'ôl stared at him in disbelief for a moment. Kae-dong was completely changed. His hair had grayed, and thick lines had formed on his grizzled face. That was only natural, of course. What surprised him was how neat and clean Kae-dong's clothes were. He was wearing a jade green dress shirt, a brown tie with red stripes and a navy blue suit, along with a sparkling pair of wire-rim glasses.

After escorting him into the house, Chu-ch'ôl was again amazed to learn that Kae-dong's son was the cause of this transformation.

"Chu-ôn? I heard he graduated from high school several years back. So he's found a good job?"

Kae-dong laughed, exposing the yellowed buck teeth, and shook his head.

"Job? What job? Why, he's just started university."

Chu-ch'ôl thought back to the Chu-ôn he had seen as a child. He must be at least thirty, he thought. After finishing his military service, he must have worked to make some money before going to university.

"Where does he go to school? I'm surprised he hasn't come to see me, if he's going to school in Seoul..."

Frankly, Chu-ch'ôl disliked it when people stopped by, but Chu-ôn was Kae-dong's only son. He didn't say it out of affection for Chu-ôn. He felt an obligation to Kae-dong.

"He goes to K University. He's already in his second year. Must be mighty busy, though, 'cause I told him to come see you first thing last year and the poor boy still hasn't found the time."

"At any rate, he's done a fine job. K University is a good school. Just think of it, Uncle. You're finally enjoying the fruits of all the hard work you put into raising him. How old is he now?"

"Twenty-nine. It's 'bout time I found a nice girl for him but..."

"Don't worry! He's sure to find one on his own."

"You think so? When'll he find the time to graduate and meet a girl.... I have never paid his tuition or sent him any pocket money. I didn't even help him find a room. I'm just grateful that he's able to go to school under his own steam."

Behind the amber lenses of his glasses, Kae-dong's eyes misted over. There must be something I can do for his boy, Chu-ch'ôl thought. After all, Chu-ôn is Kae-dong's only child. We could ask him to come share Yun-gil's room. Then he wouldn't have to live in a boarding house or find a room and cook for himself. I'll have to discuss it with my wife, he thought.

"It sounds like he's a good student. How much is he getting in scholarships?"

Kae-dong shook his head.

"I haven't the slightest idea. I hear he gets some kind of monthly salary."

"A salary?"

Hye-suk brought in a tray of drinks and food. Chu-ch'ôl offered Kae-dong a glass. He remembered hearing something about honor students being paid to study. He looked at Kae-dong once more. How did Chu-ôn get to be such a good student? he wondered. When Kae-dong was a servant at their house, he made flutes from stalks of bamboo and played them whenever he had the chance. He was a good flute player and he memorized the Thousand-Character text by ear. Once he started working at Chu-ch'ôl's house, he quit night school, but he knew his numbers. He could add, subtract, multiply and divide. Kae-dong was the product of the union between the stepson of Chu-ch'ôl's great grand-uncle and a widowed beggar-woman who lived in a hut at the entrance to the village. The stepson had left home as a youth, only to return years later, empty-handed and gray. Chu-ch'ôl's grandfather had set him up with the beggar-woman. Kae-dong was a big strong man, but he had a bad eye. He worked in the family saltworks, and later ran errands for the local arm of the South Korean Workers' Party. As a result, he was dragged off to police headquarters, beaten senseless and tortured. Chu-ch'ôl's father got him released. After he recovered, he went back to work at the saltworks and met a wandering crazy woman. Chu-ôn was born of their encounter. When Chu-ôn was still a baby, the woman set fire to their house and died. Kae-dong's life revolved around his son after that. It was amazing, though, to think that Chu-ôn was so smart when his mother was crazy. Did Chu-ôn get his brains from his father or his crazy mother?

As Chu-ch'ôl sat gaping in amazement, Kae-dong stroked the suit he was wearing.

"Last night he took me out and bought me this suit. These glasses, too."

So the gutter spawns mighty dragons after all, thought Chu-ch'ôl. If Chu-ôn was such a good student, he was sure to cut a fine figure no matter what field he went into.

"What department is he in?" Chu-ch'ôl asked. Would Chu-ôn head into politics, the law, business or the cultural field? Kae-dong shook his head.

"I'm not sure. Ain't told me a thing. He don't answer my questions. But when I tell people he gets a salary for going to school, they say he must be in the law department. Shoo-in for a post as prosecutor or judge, they say. But I don't know. I don't have a hint. When I told him I was coming to see you, he gave me enough money for the ticket home and some pocket money and put me in the taxi. He said he had someone to see."

"Didn't you stay with him last night?"

"Yep, but we slept at an inn. Ain't been to his room. He said something about living in a dormitory with twenty other students."

Maybe he lives in one of those lodging houses for students preparing for the bar exam. Chu-ch'ôl envied Kae-dong his bright son and feared Chu-ôn. The people in their village had always pointed to Pak Chu-ch'ôl as the greatest success to ever come from their neighborhood, but it looked that Chu-ôn would be taking his place in the future.

"Wait a minute.... Your father told me you were in the law department at K University.... " Chu-ch'ôl glared at Chu-ôn when he returned from the restroom.

Chu-ôn looked up. "When did he say that?"

"A year before he died. He came to our house. In the spring of your second year at university, I think."

Chu-ôn squinted, then burst out laughing.

"Ehhh, what did he know? Who cares where you go to school or what you study? I just went to school because I was bored. It's a sad story. Let's drop the whole thing."

Aha! Chu-ch'ôl thought. He wasn't going to school after all. He looked down and clenched his teeth. The bastard duped his poor father and me. I may be a distant cousin, but he can't afford to ignore me.... What's he after? Never take in a stranger for he's not likely to repay the favor. That's what the proverb said, and here was Chu-ôn, biting the hand of his benefactor, as if he were trying to prove that old saw true.

Long ago, when Chu-ch'ôl was staying at his parents' home after being discharged from the army, he had seen young Chu-ôn playing hide-and-seek and kite-hawk in the yard with the children of the other farmhands. Chu-ôn was always the dirtiest and most ragged of the bunch. The crotch of his pants was torn, and dirty patches of skin peeked through the holes in his ragged shirt. His hair was like a crow's nest, teeming with nits and lice as big as barley grains.

"Oh, will you look at that poor lil' thing?" Chu-ch'ôl's mother clucked. "Just look at him!" She had been preparing a snack for the workers, but paused to grab Chu-ôn by the hand and drag him off to the well where she filled a tub, stripped off his rags and bathed him. She dug some of Chu-man's old clothes from the closet and dressed Chu-ôn. The little boy was like a crow that had shed its black feathers to become a magpie. That night when Kae-dong returned, happily drunk, from the fields, he swept Chu-ôn into his arms and laughed out loud.

5

"You bastard! Do you have some kind of grudge against me? How come you're so obsessed with catching Yun-gil? The boy is practically your nephew!"

Chu-ch'ôl tossed down another cup of beer and glared across the aisle at Chu-ôn. Chu-ôn looked up. His eyes were bloodshot. "What's that supposed to mean?" he asked.

"Don't play dumb with me! I know what you are. You're like some kind of a hunting dog." Chu-ch'ôl scowled. Chu-ôn's cheek flinched for an instant. Then a mocking smile spread across his face. He straightened up, relaxed his contorted features and laughed heartily. Chu-ch'ôl saw the insidious wickedness of the cockroaches' feelers in his face. Chu-ôn finally managed to control his laughter and filled Chu-ch'ôl's empty cup.

"Oh, Cousin! Why can't you trust me? I told you: I make my living appraising jewels."

Chu-ôn chuckled as he stole a glance across the aisle. Chu-ch'ôl tossed his beer in his face. Chu-ôn didn't seem the least bit surprised. It was almost as if he had expected it. He sat stiff as a stone statue for a moment, then slowly took his handkerchief from his pocket and mopped his face.

"Wow! One cold splash in the face and I'm sober," he laughed. Chu-ch'ôl felt a shiver run through his body. That composure, that self-assurance, that cunning—Did they teach them that? Well, let's see how composed and cunning he really is! Chu-ch'ôl jumped to his feet and grabbed Chu-ôn by the wrist.

"Darling, what are you doing? Oh no, you're drunk! Uncle Chu-ôn, I'm sorry. Try to control yourself."

Hye-suk stood up and grabbed Chu-ch'ôl by the shoulders. The passengers in the surrounding seats leapt to their feet to watch the squabbling drunks. Ignoring the stares, Chu-ch'ôl pushed Chu-ôn up the aisle. Chu-ôn hurried along, almost as if he had anticipated this happening. The other passengers craned their necks to see the two men stumble out the exit. Hye-suk forged her way through the stares and followed Chu-ch'ôl and

Chu-ôn out of the door. Three or four curious young men pushed their way ahead of her.

Chu-ch'ôl and Chu-ôn had disappeared into the restroom and locked the door before the others made it through the exit. Hye-suk pounded on the door, shouting for them to open it, but there was no response, only the sound of blows.

After pushing Chu-ôn into the restroom, Chu-ch'ôl grabbed him by the throat with one hand and slapped him across the cheeks with the other. He punched him in the shoulders, kicked him in the shins, and slammed his forehead against Chu-ôn's face.

"You lousy bastard! Tell the truth. Are you following me or are you really going to Chu-man's funeral?"

"Will you stop? Haven't you let off enough steam?"

Blood poured from Chu-ôn's nose. He grabbed Chu-ch'ôl's arms, twisted them behind his back, unlocked the door and escaped. Chu-ch'ôl chased after him.

"You miserable bastard!" he shouted. "You'd better get off at the next station! We can get through Chu-man's funeral without the likes of you! Don't ever show your face around me again, you stinking worm!"

His nose swathed in a handkerchief, Chu-ôn slipped into the next coach. Hye-suk shoved her snarling husband back toward their seats.

"What's wrong with you? Don't you realize what he could do?"

All of a sudden, Chu-ch'ôl was sober and felt the hot sting of the other passengers' stares. He returned to his seat and closed his eyes. It all seemed like a dream. He hated himself for drinking with Chu-ôn in the first place. On one hand, he felt he was right to beat up the bastard, but on the other hand, he was afraid his outburst might trigger some kind of retaliation against Yun-gil and himself.

He thought of the bet he had made as they boarded the train that night. He should have done something. He should have read a book. He should have wagered on those countless typing mistakes and misspelled words. That would have canceled out the bad fortune he had anticipated in his first bet. He never should have shared a drink with that sneaky bastard. Turning his regrets over and over in his mind, Chu-ch'ôl bit down on the tip of his tongue and fell asleep.

"We're here," Hye-suk said, shaking her husband by the shoulders. "Wake up! It's time to get off." The train had come to a stop. A flutter passed through the quiet air as the passengers bustled to collect their baggage. Their footsteps receded into the distance like an ebbing tide. Chu-ch'ôl closed his eyes again and pretended to sleep. He had learned that trick from Hye-suk. "Come on. We're the only ones left," she said angrily after a moment or two. The coach was completely empty. A cleaning woman, her hair wrapped in a white towel, was removing the seat covers. The bluish light of dawn etched dizzy ripples in the frost-covered window panes. The memories of life's frustrating routine, forgotten in the night, returned with the frigid wind blasting through the open door of the coach. Outside the cold was armed for battle. Chu-ch'ôl swallowed bitterly and was slipping on his jacket when Chu-ôn stepped through the door.

"So Cousin, have you sobered up?" Chu-ôn crinkled his nose in a smile. Thousands of tiny feelers seemed to squirm inside his grin. Rage rose in Chu-ch'ôl's throat like a wave of nausea but he gulped it down.

Holes

1

Thousands of holes pierced Chu-ch'ôl's body, like the holes in a bamboo flute. An icy wind blew through them. Chu-ch'ôl slumped in his seat and pulled his parka around him. A metallic whistling rose in his chest. It hurt.

The bus was rounding Ch'ôn'gwan Mountain. A broad expanse of newly reclaimed land unfolded before it. Another hilltop rose in the distance. It was Tôkdo, the island where New Town, Chu-ch'ôl's native village, was located. Chu-man had lived there but now he was dead. The sight of the island revived memories from the past, like the whistling of a bamboo flute.

Dark clouds filled the sky. A thin fog hung over the mountains and fields. Hye-suk was staring in the direction of Temple Hollow on the northern slope of Hanje Mountain. Chu-ôn was seated next to Chu-ch'ôl. He was looking in the same direction. Yun-gil was hiding there.

We have to get a message to Yun-gil. He's got to find another place to hide... Hye-suk thought.

I'd better get there before they have a chance to warn him.... Fearful Chu-ch'ôl and Hye-suk might realize what he was thinking, Chu-ôn tried to distract them. "Speaking of Cousin Chu-man, when I was a kid.... " He glanced at Chu-ch'ôl. "Every time he got drunk, he'd say his heart was punched full of holes."

Chu-ch'ôl closed his eyes. A woman's face rose before him. Her skin was puffy for lack of sleep. Her breasts were bound in a cotton corset to keep them from protruding from her blouse. She slumped slightly, as if ashamed of her bulging breasts. The woman was Chu-shim, Chu-ch'ôl's younger sister. She had died twelve years ago. Chu-man was devastated on the day of her funeral. The image of his grieving brother was still clear in Chu-ch'ŏl's mind. That day Chu-ch'ŏl finally understood the holes that pierced his brother's heart.

As he headed for Chu-man's funeral, the same flute-like holes pierced his own.

2

Chu-man was as stubborn as a brick wall and unpredictable. He was like a machine whose screws had come loose, like a sweater that was slowly unraveling, stitch by stitch. He was disconnected, at loose ends. It was as if the stitches that were supposed to hold him together had come undone.

From Mother's reports on her infrequent visits to Seoul, it was clear that Chu-man was living by fits and starts. For example, every year after he set a date to transplant the rice seedlings, he was a nervous wreck. He felt compelled to run from house to house, asking the neighborhood women to help with the transplanting and the men to carry seedlings from the beds to the paddies. There was no telling how many people he actually asked, but come transplanting day, thirty or more people showed up at his paddies. The problem was Chu-man had less than an acre of paddy to transplant. Once they set to work, there was barely enough room to move.

The same thing happened when they harvested the rice, when they scooped out the latrine and when they took compost to the fields. When it was time to set posts for the seaweed harvest, he always managed to scrape together the money for the materials, but when it came time to move the frames from patch to patch, to change the ropes or to bind the posts, he wasn't interested. They never had a decent harvest. And then Chu-man would start drinking and cursing.

"Lousy world! Life's too short for all this grunting and groaning," he sputtered, only to drop off to sleep and stay in bed until noon the next day.

Chu-ch'ôl had left his mother in Chu-man's care. A few years back, when Chu-man got married, Chu-ch'ôl could tell his mother was behind his brother's offer to "take care of her."

"I'll live with you. I can take care of the kids and help with the seaweed harvest. It'll be good for you. And your older brother's sure to buy you more land if you support me."

In reality, Chu-man wasn't supporting Mother; *she* was supporting him. She didn't have a moment's ease when she was away from him. On the rare occasion she came to Seoul, she invariably rushed back to New Town at the crack of dawn the following day.

MOTHER DEAD. RETURN HOME FOR FUNERAL ASAP.

It was a cold day in early winter when Chu-ch'ôl received the telegram and returned home. The first snow had just fallen at the summit of Ch'ôn'gwan Mountain. Dark gray clouds hung in the sky; the wind was sharp. The weather glowered like an old woman who had skipped breakfast to spite her daughter-in-law. Snowflakes were falling, fat and white as peonies.

Chu-ch'ôl took the money that his co-workers had offered in condolence, borrowed some more, and bought a bolt of thick white cotton for wrapping the corpse and two rolls of hemp cloth for mourning clothes. When he stepped from the bus in Hoejin, he wasn't prepared for the reception that he received from Yong-man, a second cousin.

"I'll bet that telegram was a real shock, eh?" Yong-man asked with an embarrassed smile. Chu-ch'ôl thought of Chu-man and all his antics, but he couldn't believe that someone would say Mother had died when she hadn't.

"So how did she die?" he asked.

"To tell the truth, Auntie ain't the one who died."

"What?"

Chu-ch'ôl was stunned. His face must have twisted in anger because Yong-man looked like a frightened child as he explained.

"Chu-shim died, but Chu-man figured you wouldn't come if he said that, so..."

Chu-man may have been right. Chu-ch'ôl never came down for Father's memorial rite in early spring. He could hardly blame Chu-man for sending the telegram.

Chu-shim was only twenty-nine. She had been living at home with Chu-man and Mother since leaving her husband's family five years earlier. Chu-shim and Mother had visited Seoul a month before. For treatment, of course, though her condition hadn't been particularly serious.

Over the years, Mother had kept Chu-ch'ôl up-to-date on his sister's illness. He had taken her to a major university hospital for a check-up already. This time they went to a well-regarded psychiatrist.

"She's suffering from paranoia and psychogenic angina. There's no need to worry, though. It will take some time, but she should get better."

After offering this diagnosis, the doctor paused, lips pursed in thought as he fingered the pen lying on Chu-shim's chart.

"By chance, has anyone close to the patient displayed similar symptoms? A maternal aunt or an aunt on her father's side? A grandmother or her mother perhaps...?"

Chu-ch'ôl said he didn't know of anyone. There weren't any crazy people in the family as far as he knew. He sometimes wondered if Chu-man didn't share some of his sister's symptoms, but he could hardly say that. Chu-man had never complained of a problem.

The doctor nodded and prescribed a tranquilizer and some vitamins. It wasn't a congenital heart condition. All she needed was peace and quiet. Chu-ch'ôl could almost see Chu-shim— seated in the doctor's office, dressed in a jade green sweater and light green pants—but now she was dead. It was hard to believe.

"How did it happen?"

"I ain't sure myself," Yong-man answered as he piled the bolts of cloth into his A-frame carrier.

Apparently it wasn't something that could be explained in a few words. Chu-ch'ôl didn't press his cousin.

Chu-ch'ôl's family home, where Chu-man had been living, was burned to the ground by communist party members during the Korean War and hastily rebuilt after the South Korean army retook the area.

The house looked like it had a gaping hole in the middle. From the front, the main building, a four-chamber structure consisting of two rooms, a central wooden porch and a kitchen, was obscured by a shabby outbuilding, which stood across a small courtyard. The main gate was at the center of this outbuilding. On one side of the gate were the outhouse and a storeroom; on the other the cowshed and an extra room. Both doors had fallen off the gate. The kitchen doors in the courtyard were gone too. The walls of the kitchen were black with soot. The kitchen's back door was missing too, but that wasn't apparent right away because the earth in the backyard, which rose behind the house, was a dusky brown, as dark as the kitchen.

From the front gate, the kitchen looked like a dark lifeless cave. Not the kind of cave that had a stream running through it, not the kind where hibernating pythons turned into dragons and flew away, not the mossy home of a mysterious spirit; rather it looked like a ghastly stone tunnel where, during the war, people were roped together like dried fish on a string and burned to death. It was dark and dead, without a single blade of grass, without a single drop of water.

On that winter afternoon several years back, when dark clouds hung low and heavy over the tin roof, Chu-ch'ôl felt as if an enormous hole, as large as that gaping kitchen, were being drilled through his heart. The courtyard and back yard were filthy. The ground oozed with pig urine. The chickens pecked at the compost piled next to the gate. The earth in the front and back yards was rough and unraked with rocks poking up here and there. The wooden porch at the front of the house was covered with dirt. The latticed paper windows were full of holes. That night, Chu-ch'ôl scolded his younger brother.

"Look! Isn't it about time you fixed the doors on the front gate? You've got two perfectly fine doors. How come you don't hang them? Same with the kitchen. All you have to do is fix the hinges, but you just leave them there.... Why, you can see right into the house from outside! It looks like it's been abandoned!"

"I kinda like it. Nice and open." Chu-man stole a glance at his brother and smiled foolishly. "I've been so busy, just haven't gotten around to puttin' the doors on," he added with a wrinkle of his nose.

"And how come you leave the yard full of pig piss?" Chu-ch'ôl demanded. "You've got to keep the pigpen scooped out and the backyard clean. It's a fire hazard, and it looks awful! Clean this place up so it looks like *people* live here! And what about those chickens? Are you just going to leave them to dig around in the compost?"

It was Mother's turn next. "He finds time to drink and run around, but he never has time to shovel the manure. I can't leave the house for a minute."

Chu-man frowned slightly, puffing out his cheeks in irritation. His bulbous nose twitched like an old alarm clock ready to go off.

"Geez, Mama!" he cried. "How can you say something like that? Life's too short..."

"Look how he talks," Mother grumbled to Chu-ch'ôl. "And he's supposed to be running this household! Why, if it weren't for me, this house would fall apart. Nothing would get done. If I didn't fix the cow's slop, the poor animal would starve. And that's not all!"

Chu-man refused to give in, though.

"Brother, listen to her! She makes it sound like she does all the work around here! No wonder the neighbors all think I'm some kind of half-wit." He turned to his mother. "All right, Mama. I'll leave and you can live as you please."

Mother looked up at Chu-man. Her mouth dropped open in disbelief. How could he say such a thing when she was working her fingers to the bone for him and his family?

"Brother, take Mama back to Seoul with you. Please. You don't have to worry about me. I'll make a life for my woman and kids. I don't care if I have to beg or borrow to do it! Just take Mama with you! I can't get along with her anymore. Damn this lousy world! Life's too short to make such a fuss night and day. I just can't take it! You take Mama and I'll go off and make a life for myself. I can't stand living in this lousy house! It's driving me crazy! You're angry 'cause I don't hang them doors, but you know what? I feel like I'll suffocate if I put them up! You don't understand how I feel, Brother. No one does!" Chu-man's voice broke and his eyes filled with tears.

As they climbed toward the pass leading to the village, Yong-man explained what had happened to Chu-shim.

"I just can't figure Chu-man out," he began.

The narrow path through the pine woods was steep and slippery with gravel. As the local people said, you had to "huff and puff" to make it over that pass, but Chu-ch'ôl had crossed it often enough as a child. He knew he had to pace himself.

"I just can't understand him. If it weren't for Auntie, he wouldn't be able to run that house. But one drink and he's complaining about how she refuses to live with you in Seoul, how she's always making life miserable for him. Who knows? Maybe none of this would have happened if it weren't for that fight the other night."

There had been a celebration in Hilltop Village three days earlier. Chu-man had spent the entire day drinking, and when he returned home around sunset, Mother scolded him.

"Everyone's already moved their seaweed nets. They've got their drying frames up and are ready to harvest, but you haven't done a thing! Please, I beg you! Pull yourself together. You should have had one drink and gone back to work. How can you be so stupid—drinking all day like that?"

Her anxious tone must have bothered him, or something may have happened at the party earlier. Chu-man reacted in anger.

"Stupid? If I'm so stupid, how come you insist on living with me? Go live with your smart son!"

Chu-shim was resting in the main room, and Mother was afraid Chu-man might upset her. "Oh, shush and go to your room. I can't stand the sight of you."

"A person can't even enjoy a drink around here, huh? It's too much, just too much," Chu-man grumbled as he climbed onto the porch separating the rooms. "Can't stand the sight of me? So why don't you go live with that smart son of yours?

Then I can live as I please. Damn this lousy world! Work like a dog but your hard-earned money always ends up in someone else's hands.... Well, I ain't gonna let myself be used no more. Just take everything and get out of here!" he shouted as he sat down on the edge of the porch.

The fool's mad because I spent some money on herbal medicine for Chu-shim, Mother thought.

"You ungrateful brat! Quit that whining! Where do you think the paddy land we're living off came from? Someone had to buy it for you." She steered the conversation in Chu-ch'ôl's direction, hoping to protect Chu-shim's feelings. Chu-man refused to give in, though.

"Brother didn't buy me that land out of the goodness of his heart. He owed it to me. He's the one who sold off his parents' paddy and made me work like a slave to pay for his education. He owed me!"

Chu-man was right, but Mother couldn't stand by in silence.

"Since when did your brother sell all the paddy land? Your father sold off more than half an acre when he was sick. Your brother sold much less than that. He's a good person. That's why he bought you six nice fields, so why don't you shut up?" she said, shoving him toward his room.

"I don't want your paddies or fields. I don't want nothing! Go live with that smart son of yours. I won't starve. Take Chu-shim and get out of here!" he hollered. He seemed to want his sister to hear.

Mother beat him on the back with her fists as she pushed him into his room.

"Just shut your mouth and you'll be fine. How come you have to spout off about everything? Don't you realize you owe him?"

She convinced him to lie down, half scolding, half cajoling, then returned to the main room. Chu-shim was lying on her stomach. Sometimes it helped her heart stop fluttering.

"Don't mind him. He's worse than a dog when he gets drunk." Mother was afraid that Chu-shim might have misunderstood what had been said.

Chu-shim sighed. "Why should I mind?" she asked in a broken voice.

"There's nothing to worry about. I still run this house. Don't pay attention to what anyone says. Just listen to me 'cause I'm going to make you better." Mother knew how her daughter felt. After all, she looked into Chu-shim's heart a dozen times a day.

"Your brother's all right. He just causes trouble when he's been drinking. Why, only yesterday he brought home five shad and told me to fix them for you. He said raw fish is good for sick folks. You know how much he cares for you. It's just when he gets to drinking. He's a fine person at heart."

But Chu-shim left the house that night.

Mother checked the outhouse first. Then, on a troubling hunch, she rushed to the shed and fumbled around the shelf where they kept leftover pesticide. It was gone. Mother woke Chu-man and dashed to Uncle's house. The two families spent the night combing the hills, fields and beach.

They found Chu-shim the next morning, as the sun rose over Sorok Island and the Noktong Peninsula across the bay. The sunrise was as red as the blood she had vomited on the dry grass. She was lying in front of Father's grave in Persimmon Hollow.

"It broke my heart to see Auntie crying like that. Bad enough she kept beating her chest, but then she'd cry out, 'Oh you miserable witch, you just tried to save yourself!' I don't know who she was talking about, but it near broke my heart. She hasn't eaten a thing. Don't look like she'll last long."

You just tried to save yourself! Just tried to save yourself! The words echoed through Chu-ch'ôl's heart.

He looked up at the cloud-filled sky. The cold had come early this winter. It had started with a rain that felt more like the late spring monsoons, then changed to snow. And just as the snow began to melt, a new storm brought more, which melted again, only to be covered with still more. The clouds peeking through the pine branches promised another storm.

A cock pheasant strolling through the bushes by the side of the path caught sight of the two men and took flight, its purple-feathered mate flapping behind him. The image of Mother pounding her chest rose with the pheasants over the woods toward the facing hillside.

You just tried to save yourself! Just tried to save yourself! Chu-ch'ôl understood what she meant.

The hill behind the house was terraced. The terraces were used for drying seaweed more often than farming, but the villagers planted peppers, zucchinis and sweet potatoes there in the off-season. The poles and straw used for the drying frames were piled like grass tombs along the edge of each terrace and at the bottom of the hill.

Long ago Chu-ch'ôl had spent many nights hiding among the poles and straw with his father. It was late summer the year he turned nine. The sun was hot during the day, but at night the air turned chill. Father hid in the pantry off the kitchen in the daylight hours. The pantry had been used as a granary since Grandmother and Grandfather had passed away. Its bamboo slat window was lined with a sheet of tin to keep rats out. The tiny room was as damp and dark as a cave. Father spent the day there, confined like a leper, and when the light faded, he took Chu-ch'ôl up the hill behind the house and hid under a stack of poles, sweating and shaking like an ailing ox. Chu-ch'ôl disliked the cavernous darkness of the pantry, but he hated the chilling darkness under the poles just as much. The darkness came from the pine grove, where the village's tutelary guardian stood among a cluster of stone baby graves. The darkness rode a stream down the hill, flowing past the upper village to creep around the terraced fields like the spindly legs of a goblin. Chu-ch'ôl couldn't see a thing: the straw thatch protecting the poles from the rain blocked his view. All he could do was listen—to a pinging sound that rang through the darkness, to the crickets, to the pained groans of his father rustling in the straw.

Chu-ch'ôl was afraid of his father then. The man was too silent. The boy couldn't understand why his father dragged him to the hill each night. All he could understand was his father's labored breathing, the heat of his hands, and the way they trembled as he bent to pull his son over the edge of the terrace.

Communist soldiers, clad in khaki uniforms and carrying rifles, came to the village. They gathered the villagers on the beach and gave a speech. It was summer when the cry of the cicadas in the trees by the beach reverberated through the entire village. That was the day Sam-ch'ôl's father and Sun-hûi's older brother started wearing red arm-bands and carrying swords as long as a man's arm, and that was the day Chu-ch'ôl's father stopped going out. He began hiding in the pantry after a trip to Hoejin with Sam-ch'ôl's father, Sun-hûi's brother and Uncle Kae-dong.

Ten days after the communist soldiers' visit to the village, Chu-ch'ôl returned home from the beach, where the children had been gathered to learn "Glorious be the Morning," to find three pairs of unfamiliar black rubber shoes under the porch off the main room. He could hear people talking in low tones inside. Mother was squatting in the kitchen with Chu-shim strapped to her back. She was listening to what was being said as she fed the fire. She rinsed a raw sweet potato and pressed it into his hand. Chu-man stood behind her, chewing as he sniffed up the thick yellow mucus that dripped from his nose. Chu-ch'ôl had just taken his first bite when the brusque voice of Sam-ch'ôl's father filtered through the door.

"Just do as we ask, all right?"

"Why should I hand myself in?" Father responded in a firm tone. "I haven't done anything wrong. Since when is being village chief or director of the Fishermen's Association under the Japanese a crime?"

"I know. I know. But you're part of the bourgeoisie. You've got to hand yourself in," Sun-hûi's brother retorted.

"Bourgeoisie? And what's that?" Father asked incredulously. There was silence for a moment.

"This is ridiculous," he continued. "Since when does a couple of acres make someone a capitalist landlord? When did I exploit the poor laborers or farmers? I was never involved in usury. I never had any sharecroppers. You need at least ten acres and sharecroppers to be a bourgeoisie, don't you? Just think! I only have a couple acres! When did I exploit anyone? You know, when I was village head and director of the Fishermen's Association I tried to help people. That's why I hired servants I didn't need and paid them more than the going rate. Think about it! It's all because our village is so poor. You know, I'd be a middling farmer in a larger village. No matter how you look at it, there's no reason I should hand myself in. I didn't touch a single penny of public funds when I was village head."

"Oh come on! Do you think people hand themselves in 'cause they're guilty? Look at the world today!" Sun-hûi's brother replied. He had been a farmhand in the upper village his whole life, but after the communists' arrival, he had come to New Town wearing that red arm-band.

"Just come with us tomorrow morning," Sam-ch'ôl's father ordered gruffly.

"You ain't committed no crime. Why, you saved a lot of skins during the right-wing's rule! You can hold your head high at a people's trial," Uncle Kae-dong added.

The following day Chu-ch'ôl's father, dressed in a white *hanbok* reserved for special occasions, crossed Hanje Mountain with Sam-ch'ôl's father and Uncle Kae-dong. Sam-ch'ôl's father was head of the People's Committee. The security police had given him the job because his oldest son had been killed during the Yôsu Rebellion in 1948.

"Don't worry. I'll stay with him," he whispered to Chu-ch'ôl's mother as they left.

"If there's a people's trial, I'll take his side," promised Uncle Kae-dong.

Father didn't return that night. Uncle Kae-dong came to the house late in the afternoon.

"He's going to sleep there tonight so you'd better send him some supper. The people's trial went real well," he said before leaving.

As the sun dipped over Hanje Mountain, Mother prepared the children's supper, then drew Chu-ch'ôl aside.

"I'm going to take Father his supper so you and Chu-man lock the gate and go to sleep."

Chu-ch'ôl's heart sank. He was afraid of the funeral bier ghost. His father stored the bier in the outhouse. He had gotten the bier years before when Chu-ch'ôl's grandfather died, and now he lent it out when there was a funeral in the village. The dusty old bier had carried Ho-ch'ôl's grandmother and Kil-ho's father too. Mother often complained that Father didn't burn it, but he simply snorted, "What's wrong with letting them use it to cart off those pitiful corpses?"

The local children said the funeral bier ghost came out at night. Kil-ho said he had heard it once on his way to market.

As Mother took Father's supper to town, little Chu-shim strapped on her back, a bloody sunset lit the mackerel sky, then stained their courtyard and roof red. It was almost as if Mother had been sucked into the fire.

Sunset passed and darkness descended. Chu-ch'ôl locked the front gate and took Chu-man into the main room.

"It's scary, isn't it?" Chu-ch'ôl whimpered. "Let's hurry up and go to sleep."

They lay down on the floor and pulled the blanket over their heads. Like most children with large eyes, Chu-man was easily frightened. He laid his head on his brother's chest and held his breath.

The following morning Chu-ch'ôl woke at dawn to find Mother sleeping beside him, Chu-shim in her arms. Father had not returned. When it grew light, Mother rose and began bustling around the kitchen. After feeding Chu-ch'ôl and Chu-man, she rushed off with a basket containing Father's breakfast. She returned at midday, her face as pale as a blank sheet of paper, and rushed to the saltflats. It wasn't long before she returned with Uncle Kae-dong, his face hardened like steel. Kae-dong wandered around the courtyard as he waited for Mother to cook Father's supper, stopping from time to time to roll a cigarette and sigh. Mother wrapped Father's supper and headed across the pass once again, this time with Uncle Kae-dong following in her footsteps.

That night Chu-ch'ôl woke to his father's groans. He was lying at the other end of the room, moaning in pain. The sound echoed strangely, bouncing from the ceiling to the floor to the outer walls. It echoed through Chu-ch'ôl's heart as well. Mother sat at her husband's pillow, preparing some herbal medicine to relieve the bleeding. The stench of the medicine filled the room. A kerosene lamp flickered in the corner. The shadow around its base looked like a deep black hole. Chu-ch'ôl sat up and looked at his father. His features were contorted in pain. He looked like he was having trouble breathing. An oppressive numbness occupied Chu-ch'ôl's heart like the dark shadow at the foot of the lamp. He straightened up, took a deep breath and crawled closer. His father took Chu-ch'ôl's hand. The corners of his eyes glistened in the lamp light. His breathing was uneven. Each time he drew a breath, his nostrils dilated, large and dark, as if they were drawing in the shadow from the lamp.

The following day Mother stuffed some pine needles in the mouth of an empty bottle, tied a stone to it, and lowered it on a long string into the outhouse hole. That was the day Chu-ch'ôl stopped going to the beach to learn the communists' songs. His father wouldn't let him go anymore. Chu-ch'ôl was bored, but he sat by his father's side blinking in wonderment as his father drank the yellow liquid that Mother had collected in the outhouse.

As he watched his father suffering, his face contorted and dark, Chu-ch'ôl imagined him dying. His father's eyes rolled back in his head, and they put him in a coffin and buried him. Mother wailed and pounded the ground. Then she pulled Chu-ch'ôl into her arms. He felt an electrifying thrill when he entered her sweet embrace.

He hated himself for these thoughts and turned from his father, biting his tongue. Chu-man and Chu-shim were sleeping beside him. He imagined them dead too. They had drowned in the well. The villagers wrapped their corpses in white cotton cloth, placed them in large jars and carried them to the mountain. Mother flung herself on their graves, wailing, then pulled Chu-ch'ôl to her and hugged him.

Chu-ch'ôl hated himself for thinking that. He bit down on his tongue again. He squeezed his eyes shut and turned over. This wasn't the first time he'd had such thoughts. They occurred to him at the strangest times, as he played with his pasteboard cards, as he sat in the outhouse. He secretly enjoyed the thoughts. He enjoyed them on the way to and from school, he enjoyed them as he took the ox to graze, as he cut grass for the newborn calves. He relished them, then bit down on his tongue in guilt and anger. Sometimes he beat the pigs oinking in the sty with a stick or thrashed the ox with the reins as he took it to the fields. And other times he squashed frogs in the rice paddies and stoned snakes he found crawling through the grass.

He felt that he was committing a sin against Father, Chu-man and Chu-shim. He prayed for his father's recovery in hopes of freeing himself from the guilt. "Oh gods in heaven, oh revered ancestors, please make our father well." He even prayed for Chu-man and Chu-shim. "Oh Heaven! Please heal the boil on Chu-man's head. And heal my sister's measles." He prayed out loud so he could hear the words. He prayed in the outhouse and as he cut grass for the calves. "What are you mumbling about?" his mother and friends would ask.

Ten days after returning home, Father had recovered enough to walk to the outhouse by himself. That very evening Sam-ch'ôl's grandfather came to their house. The old man had been like a brother to Chu-ch'ôl's grandfather. His bamboo pipe trembled as he climbed onto the porch and entered the main room where Father lay. Chu-ch'ôl had been playing pasteboard cards with Chu-man, although his little brother was hardly a worthy opponent. He left the game to follow the old man into the room. Father shooed him out, though. He sat on the front porch pretending to count his cards while he listened to what was being said inside. Sam-ch'ôl's grandfather whispered something but Chu-ch'ôl couldn't understand what he had said.

A moment later the old man spoke again. "Take my words to heart," he said as he stepped from the room, the long pipe protruding from his white beard.

That night Chu-ch'ôl's father took Chu-ch'ôl to hide in the stacks of bamboo poles for the first time. Years later Mother told him what happened that night.

After Chu-man fell asleep, she put Chu-shim on her back and climbed to the stand of bamboo behind their house. There was a pile of firewood lying on the ground. She hid there. She couldn't go any further because she was concerned about Chu-man, of course. She had the baby on her back and was afraid a burglar might break in while she was away.

The main gate and front yard were visible through the bamboo. She crouched on her knees watching. She had lost all track of time when the sky brightened to the east. Was the moon rising already? Dogs were barking on the beach in the lower village. Sam-ch'ôl's grandfather was right: they were purging the reactionaries that night. Her hair stood on end, and goose bumps covered her flesh. She heard a rustling at the corner of the house and the main gate squeaked. Then she heard someone jump over the wall. Through the bamboo she could see a dark shadow enter the dimly-lit yard.

That was when Chu-shim began to fuss. Mother shifted the baby to her lap and offered her breast, but the baby arched her back and whimpered as she took the nipple. A bug must have bitten her. The shadow in the yard approached the house. She heard the door of the main room open, then the door to the kitchen. Chu-shim kept arching her back and whimpering. The shadow looked inside the outhouse. Mother covered Chu-shim's mouth with her hand. The baby struggled for breath. Mother took the corner of the baby quilt and covered Chu-shim's face. The shadow went around the back of the house and circled the large condiment jars stored there. He hesitated by the back door to the kitchen, then returned to the front yard and climbed back over the wall.

The following morning when Father returned to the house and heard Mother's story, he sighed.

"Let's get out of here! Let's take a boat and get out of here!" she begged. Mother was terrified.

"And where would we go?" he asked. To another island, she replied. He just shook his head.

Father spent the next day hiding in the pantry, and as darkness began to seep down from the rocky pine grove to fill the shed and kitchen with black shadows, he took Chu-ch'ôl's hand and climbed through the bamboo grove to the stack of poles on the hill.

The house burned down that night. Local party leaders from Hilltop Village and New Town thought they could flush Father out by setting the house on fire.

Mother spent the rest of her life grieving over what happened that night. After having so much trouble quieting Chu-shim the night before, she put Chu-man and Chu-shim to bed in the main room and went to hide behind the pile of firewood alone. The moon rose around midnight. The sea rippled with silver waves, but the hills of New Town were submerged in darkness. Several black shadows climbed over the wall. Once in the yard, they scattered, banging doors as they searched the house. Mother's heart ached at the thought of the sleeping children. What if the black shadows stepped on them? She closed her eyes and rubbed her hands nervously. "Oh gods in heaven, please, please keep them safe," she whispered over and over.

The door-banging stopped and the black shadows scampered back and forth between the front and back yards. All of a sudden Mother heard a rumbling sound, like a battleship. Ah, the police are coming to save us, she thought. Then she smelled gasoline. A large black object seemed to be floating over the silver waves stretching across the strait to Sorok Island. But why the gasoline smell? Could the smell of the battleship's fuel reach all the way up the hill? Mother kept rubbing her hands and praying. Then, whoosh, the scene below was lit by a brilliant light. Flames engulfed the roof of the house. A man touched a torch to the eaves, then ran to the back of the house. The firewood in the kitchen was burning. The porch was burning. The ribs and paper on the bamboo door to the room where the children were sleeping were burning too. Then she heard their cries, shrill like cloth ripping. "Fire!" she shrieked, dashing down the hill. Her voice seemed caught in her throat.

"Oh no, my children! What should I do?" she screamed as she darted from the back yard to the front, oblivious to the danger. A black shadow popped over the wall. He whispered something to the men in the courtyard, then fled back over the wall. The other men followed him.

Mother broke through the burning door and went into the room. The crying children shrieked at the sight of their mother and retreated into the corner. She gathered them up and dragged them outside. Chu-man kicked and struggled, screaming, "Mama, Mamaaa!" Chu-shim jerked and gasped for breath as if she were having a convulsion, but Mother didn't have time to console them. She left them by the front gate and returned to the house, hoping to salvage some of their belongings. The fire had engulfed the wooden-floored room at the center of the house. Suddenly Father appeared and pulled her to the ground.

"Water, get some water!" he cried, then ran to the back yard. Only then did Mother realize that she had to put out the fire. She followed Father to the back of the house.

Chu-ch'ŏl awoke to the sound of a woman crying "Fire! Fire!" Somehow he knew it was Mother. He groped among the straw mats lining the pile of poles, but Father was gone. Looking down the hill, he saw the house on fire. He could almost see Father, Chu-man, Chu-shim and Mother in the flames. Suddenly a dark phantom appeared before him—a monster as large as the pile of poles that they had been hiding in. Its hair was tangled like a mass of dried weeds; its eyes, nostrils and mouth gaped open like a huge mortar. The monster leaped in the air, flailing its arms and shouting. The sound rang through the hollow mountain valley like an echo. Chu-ch'ŏl understood what it was saying. *Heave ho, heave ho! Die, die, die right now! Die, Papa. Die, Chu-man. Die, Chu-shim. Die, die, die...* Chu-ch'ŏl repeated the monster's call in his heart. His chest pounded, his blood seethed with a gloomy whine. He frightened himself as he shouted along with the monster.

"Papa!" Chu-ch'ŏl called as he bounded down the terraced fields. In his head he pictured his father, mother, brother and sister struggling inside the red ball of fire. Mother was the only one to escape. *Heave ho, heave ho! Burn, burn, burn! Die, die, every one of you!* was all he heard.

When he reached the bottom of the hill, the yard was bright as day. Someone was hauling buckets of water from the well and pouring them on the roof of the house. It was Father. Mother was wailing beside him. "The house is on fire, the house is on fire." Her sobs seemed to alternate with those of Chu-man and Chu-shim. It looked as if the two younger children were inside the fire. Chu-ch'ŏl jumped from the bamboo grove into the yard. He ran to the front of the house to find Chu-man and Chu-shim locked in each other's embrace. He picked up Chu-shim and lifted her onto his back. She attached herself to him like a leech, and Chu-man clung to his leg, inconsolable still.

"Mamaaaa!"

It didn't sound like crying. It was a deathly scream, a knife in the heart. Chu-ch'ŏl looked up at the burning roof and broke into tears.

FATHER AND SON

As a tongue of black smoke and fire lapped onto the outer porch, Chu-ch'ôl heard the roof creak, and flames shot into the sky. Suddenly the roof crumbled. The cracking sound and whoosh of the flames seemed to echo through his body. Chu-man and Chu-shim let loose a new chorus of wails and clung even more desperately to their older brother. It almost sounded like the cry of a chicken as its neck was wrung. His chest crackled like the fire, his body trembled as a wave of vertigo and nausea swept over him. He wanted to weep out loud, but the sound would not come. The monster's call kept ringing in his ears. *Heave ho, heave ho! Die! Die! All of you!*

"It's my fault," Mother once said. "I'm responsible for what happened to Chu-man and Chu-shim. Imagine how they felt when they woke up and saw that fire burning through the door! They've never been the same since." She must have been referring to herself when she cried, "You tried to save yourself!"

Chu-ch'ôl's back was dripping with perspiration by the time they reached the pass. "Let's stop and rest," he suggested. Yong-man leaned his carrier against a tree and plopped down wearily in the dry grass.

The pine grove at the top of the pass overlooked New Town. Several houses were roofed in slate. A narrow road snaked over the hill at the entrance to the village, slithered through the dark earth of the surrounding rice paddies and twisted its way out of town. Beyond the hill lay the sea. The water, flat and gray as the sky, was encircled by the faded ink-color shores of Sorok Island and the Noktong Peninsula.

Chu-ch'ôl gazed at his brother's house in the upper part of the village. The black coal-tar tin roof lay flat on its belly; a hill rose like a staircase behind it. Dark yellow bamboo frames formed another set of stairs, but there was no seaweed on them. It wasn't time for the seaweed harvest yet. Chu-man's house was the only house without bamboo frames.

Chu-ch'ôl recalled how Chu-shim used to remove the seaweed from the drying frames. She caught cold easily. One winter, he returned home to find her working at the frames, a white wool muffler wrapped around her head and neck.

They shouldn't have had her get married. She'd never had a decent night's sleep. She tossed and turned the night away, sighing in frustration.

"Mama, please send me to a Buddhist temple." She had pleaded with her mother on several occasions, but her mother tried to console her.

"Oh baby, what are you talking about? Don't you worry! Mama will make you better. You're not cut out for a nun's life."

Mother had tried every medicine known to cure chest spasms and insomnia. Not only did she buy the finest over-the-counter drugs, she also tried everything that the local herbal medicine shops had to offer. Chu-shim's illness didn't seem to improve, though. On overcast days, she beat her chest, complaining that she couldn't breathe. Sometimes she hid under her quilt to escape visions of great black things. She paced from room to room, from the house to the yard, and when it was really bad, she ran to the stream and spent the night walking the ridges between the rice paddies or the beach, only to return at dawn, clothes damp with the dew.

When Chu-ch'ôl returned home after completing military service, Mother told him about the medicine she had been buying. She said she had tried everything. She had taken her daughter to the finest acupuncturists who pierced the girl's soft flesh in every imaginable place. Now she didn't know where to turn.

Chu-ch'ôl took Chu-shim to a university hospital in Seoul. After registering at the front desk, she was given an X-ray and blood and urine tests. Then she was called to internal medicine. She told the doctor of her symptoms, about the pain in her chest, about the black things that came after her when she was trying to sleep, about her heart palpations.

"Your heart is perfectly normal," the doctor explained. "Don't worry, you're not suffering from heart disease. You just have a bad case of parasites. All we need to do is get rid of them. Get some rest and take this medicine," he said as he handed her a prescription. Chu-ch'ôl took the prescription to a pharmacist and learned that it contained a sedative and some vitamins. He bought her a month's supply of pills, then sent her home. He had to stay in Seoul to look for a job. Chu-shim had reached marriageable age, and her mother had received a matchmaking inquiry from a neighboring village. Determined not to miss the chance, Mother pushed Chu-shim to accept the proposal. Chu-shim, who seemed to have improved thanks to the medicine, acquiesced, saying she would take the leap since her mother was so anxious for her to marry.

Thrilled to have recovered the daughter she had lost so long ago, Mother made a list of dowry items for Chu-ch'ôl to get in Seoul. She spared no expense and provided her daughter things that only the richest country folk could afford—a sewing machine, a radio, a wardrobe, a vanity table, a kitchen cabinet.

Mother believed Chu-shim's symptoms would gradually disappear if she married and had regular relations with her husband. She had seen many girls whose mental problems cleared up with marriage.

Chu-shim was different, though. When she got pregnant and began to experience morning sickness, her symptoms reappeared, more seriously this time. Then one night she came running home. She had taken two or three sedatives but still couldn't sleep. To make matters worse, she had a miscarriage at three months. Soon she began to lose weight, and her heart palpitations worsened. She never returned to her husband's house.

The doors on the front gate still hadn't been hung. The kitchen gaped dark and sooty like a cave. Chu-man's wife, a stocky woman, and Yong-man's wife, who was slender, were working in the kitchen. Smoke from the firepit and steam rising from the large iron kettle crept through the kitchen door, over the eaves and onto the slate roof. Relatives had gathered in the front yard to make straw ropes for the funeral, and several pairs of rubber shoes were resting on the threshold of the side room where Chu-man and his wife slept. The family elders had gathered to discuss preparations for the funeral.

When Chu-ch'ôl stepped in the gate, the people in the yard stood and greeted him.

"Well, you sure got here quick."

"Took an express bus, eh?"

They were all distant uncles or cousins.

Chu-ch'ôl entered the main room to find Mother leaning against the wall at the far end of the room. She straightened up at the sight of her eldest son and began a new chorus of weeping.

"Chu-shim, oh my poor Chu-shim, your big brother's come!" she wailed, pounding her chest. "Oh you miserable witch, you just tried to save yourself!"

Chu-ch'ôl's heart ached. Uncle Tal-jin's wife, herself distraught, leaned over and tried to console his mother. "Don't cry. Let her have a peaceful journey."

Chu-man stumbled into the room. His breath reeked of drink. "What are you crying for, Mama? Chu-shim's lucky to be dead," he growled. He then took his brother by the hand and told him that the elders in the other room wanted to see him.

After receiving Chu-ch'ôl's bow of greeting, Uncle Tal-jin turned to the business at hand.

"We all feel sorry for her, but there's nothing we can do now. We were going to bury her today but your mother wanted to wait for you, even if it meant putting it off a day. But now that you're here, what's the point of waiting? Everything's ready. Why don't we get the funeral over with?"

The others agreed. Chu-ch'ôl glanced at his watch. It was almost four.

They carried Chu-shim's unadorned coffin up the hill behind the house and around two neighboring knolls. "Careful now!" someone cried, and the pallbearers answered, "Yes, up and over carefully."

"Careful now. Be gentle with her. Higher in front! Yes, up and over. Lower in the back! Yes, gently now..."

As the coffin crossed the ridge beyond the village, blossoms of snow began to fall, covering her bare coffin with white flowers.

Her grave was to be located in the pine grove below Father's tomb at Persimmon Hollow. The funeral took place quietly amidst the falling snow.

When the grave mound was finished, the entire hill was covered with a blanket of white. The needles on the pine trees were enveloped with a delectable layer of white, and the snow kept falling, rustling like a woman's skirt.

They returned to the house by the light of Yong-man's flashlight. Not long after the relatives had finished eating and left, something happened.

The snow in the courtyard made everything light. Inside Mother pounded the floor, lamenting the fate of her poor daughter buried in the snow. Yong-man and his wife sat in the corner by the door, their heads bowed. Uncle Tal-jin's wife sat next to Mother, blowing her nose from time to time and wiping her hand on the sole of her sock. Chu-man's wife sniffled as she sat next to Yong-man's wife, nursing her baby. Chu-man was nowhere to be seen. The others assumed he had passed out in the other room. Chu-ch'ŏl sat awkwardly; he didn't know how to console them.

An oil lamp, chimney dark with soot, hung from the ceiling, dimly illuminating the walls. The rest of the room was hidden in its shadow.

All of a sudden Chu-man burst in from the other room with a large bottle of *soju* in one hand and a bowl in the other. He had been finishing off the liquor that the pallbearers had left behind. The bottle was still one-quarter full. He staggered into the room and collapsed under the lamp.

"Mama, stop your crying! Chu-shim's lucky to be dead," he said as he poured some *soju* into the bowl. Chu-ch'ŏl didn't want to scold his brother or tell him to stop. Chu-man had quit elementary school in the fourth grade to help pay his older brother's university expenses. He had never had a chance to learn good manners.

Still, Chu-ch'ŏl couldn't help frowning. He hated the sight of his brother tottering around with a bottle. "There's nothing left to eat. Who is going to drink now?" he asked. Chu-man turned to Yong-man who sat uncomfortably in the corner.

"Want a shot?"

Yong-man declined and turned to the corner. Chu-man snorted and thrust the bowl in Chu-ch'ŏl's direction.

"Here, Brother, have a drink."

"No one wants a drink," Chu-ch'ŏl snarled.

"All right, all right. I'll drink it," Chu-man said, hanging his head as he picked up the bowl.

"Without any food to go with it?" Chu-ch'ŏl demanded, grabbing the bowl.

"Oh, that's all right. Don't worry," Chu-man retorted. "Damn this lousy world. Life's too short for all this." He jerked his brother's hand away and tossed the *soju* down his throat. Chu-ch'ôl picked up the bottle and gave it to Yong-man.

"What are you trying to do?" he asked Chu-man, then turned to Yong-man and told him to get rid of the bottle.

Yong-man put the bottle on the porch and returned.

"Don't you understand how I feel?" Chu-man asked, glaring at his brother. "I can't live without booze. I can't!"

"How come? Please, I beg of you. If not for your own sake, quit drinking for our poor old mother. Why can't you stop?" Chu-ch'ôl pleaded. Chu-man fixed his bloodshot stare on his brother, then dropped his head.

"Brother, listen to what I have to say and then do as I ask. Take Mama with you. I can't live with her anymore. You don't have to worry about me. I'll manage one way or another, me and the wife and kids."

Uncle Tal-jin's wife spoke in Mother's place.

"Chu-man, you shush up and do what your mama tells you. You can't do a thing without her. What about the kelp beds? What about the seaweed nets? What about the fields? You couldn't do anything without her!"

Chu-ch'ôl spoke next.

"You know when I see how you treat Mother, I feel like taking her back with me. I know she doesn't want that, though, so I'll just leave things as they are for now. Understand?"

Chu-man glared at his brother.

"Do I have to spell it out for you?" he cried, then turned to Mother. "Mama, please go with Brother. I just wanna sell off this land and try livin' on my own. Don't you understand?"

All eyes converged on Chu-man's face. *What are you talking about?* they seemed to ask.

"Chu-ch'ôl, don't pay any attention to him!" Mother whispered in a mosquito-thin voice, then dropped her head.

Chu-man tore open his overcoat to reveal a gray undershirt. He ripped the buttons open and exposed his pale chest.

"Look at this!" he moaned, thrusting out his chest. "Chu-shim was lucky to die." He was crying. The lamp sputtered noisily as it sucked up its oil. The sound seemed to come from the black shadow that billowed from the cave-like kitchen.

"I wish I could cut open my chest and show you how I feel!" Chu-man wailed. No one spoke. All of a sudden Chu-ch'ôl heard the voice again: *Die! Just die! Stab a hole in your chest and die!*

Suddenly Mother collapsed against the wall as if she were short of breath. "Oh you miserable witch! You just tried to save yourself!" she cried, beating her chest. Outside, the snow illuminated the night as it piled deeper and deeper, rustling like the starched white skirt of a woman in mourning.

A Festival for the Living

Chu-ôn picked up a broom made of millet stalks, the tiny husks still clinging to the stems like drops of dried blood. He moved slowly as he swept, but his gaze was trained on Chu-ch'ôl and Hye-suk. From time to time, the sleepy eyes lit up as if by a flash of lightning.

Chu-ôn was watching for a meaningful glance from one of the relatives gathered for the funeral, for a furtive poke in the ribs as someone passed, for a note changing hands, for the exchange of words in a dark corner. He was especially alert to Tal-gyun, Chu-ch'ôl's youngest uncle, who lived in a Buddhist temple on the slopes of Mt. Hanjae. He walked with a slight limp and was actually five years younger than Chu-ch'ôl. Tal-gyun was born of Chu-ch'ôl's great uncle's liaison with a woman who cooked at the temple. As a young man, he had wandered the country, from Kwangju to Seoul and Pusan, but returned home at the age of forty, with a pretty woman in tow. They now lived at the temple with his mother, who was almost ninety.

Chu-ôn gathered up the straw mats and feed sacks that were piled against the wall between the porch and the main room. He was clearing a spot for the coffin. Beneath the mats and sacks were a layer of leftover feed grain and dust, a few dried brown persimmon leaves and a dingy plastic bag.

When he saw the plastic bag, something crashed inside Chu-ch'ôl's heart. The blood rushed to the top of his head and he felt dizzy.

Chu-ôn leaned forward to sweep up the dust, then paused, picked up the bag and looked inside. Its contents were visible from the outside; it was several lengths of iron chain. Chu-ôn reached into the bag.

Of all people, why did *he* have to find that? Chu-ch'ôl muttered to himself. His heart pounded, almost as if he had been caught stealing, and his face began to burn.

Chu-ôn coiled the chain around his hand and pulled it from the bag. The chain was quite thick: a grade thinner than those used to control traffic in front of fine office buildings or factories policed by uniformed guards with gold-fringed hats, and a grade heavier than those used on German shepherds or guard dogs. Here and there the silver paint had worn off to reveal coffee-colored rust. Two pairs of cuffs were attached to the ends of the chain, and a gold padlock was fastened securely to each cuff.

Chu-ôn's face hardened as he studied the chain. Chu-ch'ôl grimaced, and a groan escaped his lips. He pulled out a pack of cigarettes, hoping to calm himself with a smoke. Chu-ch'ôl and his mother were responsible for the chain.

One day early last summer, his mother had called from the village post office. "I can't take it anymore. You've got to come down here. And bring something to tie him up with. We can't live like this any longer." Her voice was trembling.

"Do you mean you want me to bring chains?"

"You wouldn't believe how strong he gets when he's drunk. Why, two or three strong young men can't hold him down! We need chains, and no ordinary chains at that. I know it won't be a pretty sight, but what can we do? This is no time for pity. Just do as I say and bring something strong!"

The next day Chu-ch'ôl stopped at the hardware store on his way to the bus terminal. He had gone there many times—for a briquette stove, a coal bucket, a piece of stovepipe, a gas exhaust pipe, some wire, a few nails—and he depended on the store owner when it came to installing things. Neither he nor his wife knew the couple who ran the store by name, but they always exchanged nods when they met.

The owner wasn't in but the door was open. "Anybody here?" Chu-ch'ôl called as he stepped inside and looked around. He spotted a collection of chains hanging in the doorway like a bamboo curtain, chains of all descriptions, from thin ones perfect for tying a cat to thick ones that might be hung across a factory driveway. Next to the chains were row after row of dog and cat collars, ranging in size and color from dainty artificial leather collars fit for a small poodle to sturdy leather contraptions meant for large shepherds or hounds.

"Are you looking for a dog collar? How big is your dog?" The owner's wife asked as she emerged from the quilt shop next door. She began sorting through the collars and chains.

Chu-ch'ôl felt a cold wind rise in his chest. No, it's for a person. A person. I'm looking for a chain to tie up my crazy brother. The cold wind was a strange tangle of sorrow and guilt.

Do we have to chain him up? Isn't there some other way to stop him from drinking? No, Mother wouldn't have suggested this method if there had been any other way left. How many times had he fallen into a coma, forcing them to put him in the hospital? When he got out, he always promised to quit drinking, but it never lasted more than three months. He would start drinking on the sly, and it wasn't long before he was guzzling at all hours of the day.

The woman, with her white blouse and permed hair, gave off a distinct smell, but Chu-ch'ôl couldn't tell whether it was from soap, shampoo, water or simply her own unique odor.

"It must be a large dog," she said as she took down a chain of the second thickest grade. Chu-ch'ôl had been fingering it with the thought that it would be just right for locking a bike or pushcart.

He pretended not to hear what she had said. Chu-man is stronger than a German shepherd, he thought. A dog might pull on the chain or chew at it, but Chu-man would try to cut it with some kind of tool. We'll need something thicker.

"This strap should hold even the largest dog. Most people get leashes like this, not chains. It's made of rope covered with soft artificial leather. It doesn't hurt your hand when you take the dog out for a walk, and it looks nice too. Why don't you try it?" She took down a stout brown leather leash. It was as thick as a new-born baby's wrist.

Chu-ch'ôl shook his head. How are we going to tie him down? he wondered. An image from a television program rose in his mind: mental patients shackled in chains because they threw violent fits. Their hands were locked in cuffs. We might have to do that with Chu-man, he thought. They would have to put him in the main room, lest his children see. They would have to drive spikes into the door frame to hook the chains on and put shackles on his ankles. They would have to tie his hands too so he couldn't remove the shackles or use some kind of tool to pull out the spikes and break the chains.

Chu-ch'ôl bought two lengths of the chain that the woman had first offered: one for Chu-man's ankles, the other for his hands. He also got four large spikes, four leather dog collars, and four padlocks to fasten the chains to the spikes in the door frame. Better safe than sorry, he thought.

The woman put his purchases in a large plastic sack. It sagged as if it were about to burst. Chu-ch'ôl put the sack in his travel bag and hefted it onto his shoulder. The weight nearly pulled him over.

On the bus south, he kept imagining Chu-man, wrists bound and shackled, gnashing his teeth with a wild fury in his eyes. How did he end up like this? Chu-ch'ôl's heart was weighed by something much heavier than the chains in his bag. He was shackled himself.

Chu-ôn stared at the tangled chains, then glanced at the pencil-thick spikes in the door frame. One of the locks was still fastened to a spike. Chu-ôn's eyes flashed. Chu-p'yông, Chu-ch'ôl's youngest brother, was seated on the porch. He turned to look at Chu-ôn, then snatched the chains away.

"What's this?" he protested in a mixture of tears and anger. "What is this?"

Chu-ch'ôl wet his lips and stared silently at the corpse lying at the end of the room. He was seized by a bitter sense of disappointment, guilt and anxiety. Chu-man's body lay covered with a sheet. Alcoholism may not have been the sole cause of death, Chu-ch'ôl thought. Chu-ôn and Chu-p'yông probably thought he was responsible for his brother's passing.

"Get that stuff out of here. I can't stand the sight of it! Go bury it or throw in the reservoir. Just get it out of my sight!" Uncle Tal-jin snarled. His face was flushed from the *soju* that he had drunk earlier. His younger brother Tal-gyun grabbed the plastic bag from Chu-p'yông and went out to the yard. His limp was more conspicuous than usual.

Snowflakes, as soft and plump as cherry blossoms, were falling sporadically. The thick dark clouds overhead seemed part of the soot-blackened eaves.

Tal-gyun threw the chains into the corner of the shed adjacent the ox stall and returned to the house. Meanwhile, Chu-ôn, who had been staring intently at the spikes, suddenly turned to Chu-ch'ôl's mother, who was rummaging through the wardrobe like an old mother dog. He looked back and forth between the old woman and the spikes. His eyes shone with a bluish glint, like a hungry wolf that had discovered something good to eat.

The old woman pulled a bundle from the wardrobe. It was Chu-man's shroud. Her dark pupils were small as peas, her face the color of lead. A white towel was wrapped around her wiry gray hair. She spread the shroud on the floor, carefully unfolding the hemp pants and shirt and neatly arranging the waist and ankle ties, the overcoat, the long roll of silky hemp cloth, the ball of cotton, and a parcel of mulberry paper.

Her body seemed enveloped in a strange eeriness, as if she had been waiting for Chu-man to die, as if she had been preparing for it.

"Why couldn't you do as I asked? Why? It didn't have to come to this!" Chu-p'yông whimpered. His voice was tinged with frustration and anger as he stared at the snowflakes whispering down in the fields beyond the wall. No one acknowledged him.

"Oh Father who art in heaven! Oh Father!"

Chu-p'yông's face contorted as he clasped his hands together in prayer and murmured into the sky. The snowflakes kept falling, like flower petals on a spring breeze.

Chu-p'yông was the only Christian in the family. In a sense, by becoming a Christian, he had chosen to isolate himself from the household, which had long been dedicated to the Confucian tradition. Chu-ch'ôl and his mother had vehemently opposed Chu-p'yông's marriage into a devout Christian family, but he insisted on marrying the young woman, a deaconess in her church. In the end, Chu-ch'ôl gave them permission to marry. "You and your family can believe what you like, but don't you breathe a word of that Jesus talk to anyone else in this family," he had warned. In fact, he didn't grant his permission so much as surrender to his brother's wishes.

From a Christian's point of view, a seed had been planted in the Pak clan, until then ignorant of Jehovah, and the Savior's hand was set to work. However, from the Confucian Paks' point of view, Chu-p'yông's marriage signaled an invasion by the Christian god. Ever since Chu-p'yông joined forces with his future wife and embraced Christianity, he had pressured his older brother to accept and respect them as Christians. At first,

Chu-ch'ôl resisted. He was stubborn and conservative. "If you marry a Christian, I won't think of you as my brother anymore." Chu-p'yông, however, insisted that he wouldn't marry anyone else. Then their mother intervened. "Let him do as he pleases. What if we hold out and he does something really awful?" Chu-ch'ôl came up with the condition—that Chu-p'yông never breathe a word of Jesus to the rest of the family—but with absurd results. It was like asking a wolf with a lamb in its mouth not to hunger after more sheep—an empty and powerless appeal to the Buddha. Since his marriage, Chu-p'yông had been a messenger of the Good News to the Pak clan.

At first, he was mindful of Chu-ch'ôl, but gradually his evangelizing grew more blatant. Every time he came to the house in Hoejin, he sweet-talked their mother into going to church. He even succeeded in getting Chu-man and his wife to go. He visited all the relatives, preaching tirelessly.

It was only natural that Chu-p'yông should be saddened and bitter upon discovering the chains. He had called Chu-ch'ôl when he learned that Chu-man had started drinking again, this time after being hospitalized for liver failure.

"Brother, please send Chu-man to live with us. I'll take care of him and make him go to church. There's a good religious retreat center near here. We could send him there. Why don't you send Mother along with him?"

Chu-p'yông worked as a high school English teacher in Ch'unch'on. Chu-ch'ôl promised to discuss the matter with their mother, but he knew he could never send Chu-man there. Chu-p'yông left for school early in the morning and didn't return home until late at night. Chu-man could rush out to a bar at any time. Chu-p'yông's wife may have thought she could transform her brother-in-law by the power of her faith, but she was off visiting church members and preaching door-to-door as soon as Chu-p'yông left the house in the morning. Why, she even enlisted her husband's help with the baby's bath and diaper washing! How could she keep that drunkard in his room, convert him, and make him quit drinking? No doubt they planned on committing him to a religious retreat center recommended by a fellow believer. One of those places where they lock up mental patients and senile old people for several million won a head...

"It's obvious. They're going to send him to that retreat center. How can they possibly take care of him at home?" Hye-suk said. After tossing and turning all night, she had come to a conclusion. "We'd better let your mother decide. After all, he's her son. Just tell her what Chu-p'yông said. We don't want to get blamed for something later on."

It seemed to make sense, so Chu-ch'ôl called his mother and relayed his brother's suggestion. Mother was vehement.

"I've heard about those retreat centers. Why, they drive normal people crazy there! I don't care if he dies drinking, I'm not sending him to one of those places."

Chu-ch'ôl agreed and called his brother to relay their mother's decision. Chu-p'yông called several times after that, begging him to send Chu-man to Ch'unch'on. He swore that the retreat center wasn't what they thought, and he promised to turn Chu-man around on the strength of his belief alone.

"It's Mother's decision," Chu-ch'ôl replied. "What can I do? We just have to leave him at home and hope we can keep him from drinking. Besides, I don't trust those places any more than she does..."

Chu-ch'ôl made his opposition clear. Of course, he sometimes wondered if Chu-man might actually quit drinking if he went to one of those places. Maybe he would stay off the stuff if he got a little religion, but Chu-ch'ôl refused to believe it. He wanted to believe that even if they could get his brother to stop drinking without beatings or drugs, he wouldn't stay sober for more than a month after he was discharged. To tell the truth, he didn't want to lose another brother to the Christian god. If Chu-man gave up drink for religion, his mother would be the next to go. Then it would be Hye-suk's turn. Maybe he was simply afraid of losing his family to Christianity.

Chu-ch'ŏl bit his tongue and thought. If we'd committed Chu-man to a retreat center maybe he wouldn't be lying here dead. No. He might have died even sooner, depressed and helpless. Maybe it's all for the best. Maybe he was supposed to die.

"Brother, it's your blind conservatism and obstinacy that got our family into this mess," Chu-p'yŏng sobbed. The words pierced Chu-ch'ŏl's heart like knives, but he ignored them. Chu-man was dead. Further discussion was useless.

"You pushed him toward death by giving him the money for that factory. He wasn't cut out for that kind of thing. He didn't have the brains or the ambition. You knew that," Chu-p'yŏng said as he stared out from his place at the end of the porch.

That might be true, Chu-ch'ŏl thought. When he first gave Chu-man the five million won for the factory, he was uncertain.

It was a seaweed processing plant, a cooperative project. Seven partners invested five million each and managed it together. The problem was, to run the machines efficiently, the shareholders had to harvest between 50 and 100 mats of seaweed each. A small boat wouldn't do for that. They needed a three-ton engine-driven vessel at the very least. That would take another 3.5 million won to build. The seaweed factory had state-of-the-art technology. It was powered by an electric motor imported from Japan and burned oil to dry the seaweed. With a good harvest, the equipment would pay for itself and yield each partner five million won in profits the first year.

In late summer two years earlier, Chu-ch'ŏl's mother had rushed to Seoul to plead with him.

"Everyone has a share in a factory these days. Why'd anyone want to peel off those sheets of seaweed by hand? Why, you'd have to be crazy to do that. You know how cold it can get out there by the drying racks. Lately I'm ashamed to walk through the village! Why, even the dogs seem to have a share in a factory! Your brother's the only one who doesn't. Why don't you give him a little push? It would make him wake up and get to work. All you have to do is give him five million won. If he can't pay it back, I'll sell off the land and pay you myself. All he needs is a share in a factory. After that, it's as easy as pie. You boys shouldn't ignore him just because you're educated and he's not. Chu-man needs your help."

Chu-ch'ôl knew why Mother tried so hard to help Chu-man. It was because of her debt to him.

Whenever Chu-man or Chu-shim acted strangely, Mother pounded her chest and sighed, "Oh, you miserable witch, you just tried to save yourself!" After Chu-shim drank the pesticide and died ten years ago, Mother had repeated the same words.

She felt guilty. That's why she prompted Chu-ch'ôl to help Chu-man, to give him the money for the factory. She was tortured by her guilt. After Chu-man married and set up housekeeping, Mother often badgered her eldest son for money. Something had to be done about the paddies. The irrigation was no good, the land infertile. Could Chu-ch'ôl help them pay for improvements? It was hard to make ends meet on a half-acre of paddy. Could Chu-ch'ôl buy another half-acre? Just think of it as a favor to your old mother. Chu-man needed 300,000 won to set up his seaweed nets but where else could they go for money in the middle of the long, hot summer?

Chu-man must have known how his mother felt. He often complained how hard it was to live in the country, how he was sick and tired of it all. And then he would get drunk and start wandering through the village. Mother tried to placate him by getting Chu-ch'ôl to help. Chu-ch'ôl did what he could. He knew that Mother took care of Chu-man, not the other way around, but he bought Chu-man the paddy that Mother had asked for, always making sure that it was the best land available. He sent money whenever she asked and bought them clothes, socks and underwear for every season, as well as school supplies for Chu-man's children. They kept saying that they would pay him back at harvest time or after they brought the seaweed in, but soon the loans—a hundred thousand won here, two-hundred there—added up to more than five million won. One day as Hye-suk studied the family account book, she confronted Chu-ch'ôl.

"Look at this! Are you going to give all your money to your brother? He's a full-grown man!"

She often reminded him of the dangers of his actions. "It's not like paying off a gambler's debts. You know what they say—At least a gambler wins every once in a while. A drunk will eat you out of house and home."

"Stop giving him money!" she would cry. "For his sake if nothing else! You have to stop, cold turkey!"

Chu-ch'ôl ignored her, though. He too felt a certain debt to his brother. In fact, it made him feel small and timid, like his fear of water.

Chu-ch'ôl had always thought of water as a living thing. It had the power to paralyze people by creating a mysterious atmosphere, like the night fog that covers the mountains, fields and villages. Flowing water in a river or stream, standing water in a pond or well, deep blue water in a reservoir, ghostly green water at the foot of a waterfall—it lured passersby with its magical powers, then drowned them. At times, it employed the water demon who lived deep within its shadowy depths to lure young men or women from sleep and swallow them. On nights in late spring or summer it wept sorrowfully like a young widow or wailed like a pair of copulating animals.

Salt water was no different. It shrieked, it cried, it rumbled like a witch or evil spirit, to drown fishermen, to wreck ships, to sweep away women, young and old, who went out alone to collect clams or squid. Those waves and swells didn't occur naturally. They weren't caused by wind or currents. They were the product of the sea's dark will. The waves were like scales on the back of a monster. The sea was a living, breathing monster. The stones on the edge of the sea were alive too, as was the seaweed sprouting from them. They gave in to the sea's dark intent, trapped in an endless cycle of birth, growth, death and extinction. And the people living at the sea's edge yielded to those same dark waters, fishing, digging clams or collecting seaweed.

Chu-ch'ŏl was trapped within this consciousness. From early childhood, he had felt dizzy whenever he went near the sea. He was afraid to swim. The other children plunged into the water and dog-paddled from the age of five or six, but Chu-ch'ŏl didn't learn to swim until he graduated from high school. And even then, he couldn't bring himself to swim into the deep water. He swam a few feet out, only to return in haste, overwhelmed by a terrible fear that he might be swallowed or caught in some mysterious conspiracy of the sea. His body shrank whenever he went in the water, as if he were developing a cramp.

This fear of water continued to rule his life, even after he left the sea and moved to Seoul. For a man born and raised on an island, it was a source of great embarrassment and humiliation. It kept him from the sea; it made him ignorant of the sea. He couldn't help feeling that this ineptitude was tantamount to an ignorance of his roots and a major hurdle to his literary development. And so he devoted himself to the study of the sea. He tried to understand the lives of the fishermen and the people of the tideflats. He studied the marine animals and plants near his home village. He searched for poetic inspiration in the sea there and soon found that his soul resided in his home village, though his body was in Seoul.

In the end, he couldn't be sure if he had overcome his phobia or if he was forever trapped inside the dark, mysterious atmosphere created by the water.

Chu-ch'ôl was also afraid of the villagers' wagging tongues. They had the power to create a vast forest as terrifying and mysterious as anything that the oceans produced.

"He got a chance to study thanks to his poor widowed mother and his dim-witted brother and sister. It's time he woke up and started takin' care of them."

"Yep, he'll suffer the wrath of the gods if he doesn't take care of those poor things."

"You're right there. Why, they didn't even finish elementary school 'cause his schoolin' cost so much."

His mother relayed what the villagers said. She wanted him to feel an obligation to his family.

"Everyone in the village says Chu-shim wouldn't have died such a terrible death if we'd sent her to a temple for some learning or taught her to read. We never should have kept her at home like that."

After Chu-shim died, Mother sang the same tune whenever she saw Chu-ch'ôl. They couldn't let poor Chu-man take the same cruel road as his sister, could they?

Chu-ch'ôl sympathized with his mother, and in an effort to ease his guilt, which plagued him as much as his fear of water, he did as she asked. Chu-man bought into a seaweed factory and set up fifty seaweed nets as part of the bargain. He had a three-ton boat built and borrowed five million more to pay for it, playing on the guilt of his mother and eldest brother.

"Do you really think you can save a man with money alone?" Chu-p'yông cried. "He died because of that money. You're responsible. You were wrong. You're a selfish egotist who thinks of nothing but your own reputation and writing. You don't understand the true meaning of life. You used your poor brother and sister as tools in your writing. You sacrificed them for your poetry. You're a sham, a fake who doesn't realize that true salvation means salvation of the soul!"

"You little upstart! If you wanted to save your brother's soul, you should have come down here when he was alive!" shouted Uncle Tal-jin, his neck taut with anger. "What's the point of showing up after he's dead and blaming your older brother? Everyone knows Chu-ch'ôl did everything he could for poor Chu-man. Heaven and earth know it too."

Chu-ch'ôl nudged his uncle in the side. "Leave him be. He's just bitter and sad."

Chu-ôn was still standing in the middle of the porch, glancing back and forth from the kitchen to Tal-gyun, who was meandering around the yard. Chu-ch'ôl smoked in silence, ignoring his cousin. Uncle Tal-gyun hadn't acted the slightest bit suspicious.

"What's keeping you, Nephew? Hurry up and get in here!" It was Uncle Sông-ho, one of the relatives gathered in the room next to the kitchen. There, several family members and Yông-sam, the head of the village funeral cooperative, were seated around a small table of drinks and food. Eager to discuss the funeral procedures, they had been calling Chu-ch'ôl for some time. The relatives were unhappy because Chu-ch'ôl had dipped into his own pocket and sent two younger cousins to Kwansan for the coffin, a bier and the food needed for the funeral ceremony. Tal-gyun had already told Chu-ch'ôl and Uncle Tal-jin that the relatives planned to raise the money for the funeral themselves.

"Damn them," Uncle Tal-jin spat, his features drawn in a fierce scowl. "What's there to talk about? It's your decision. After all you're practically the head of the household. You already gave the money for a bier and food, so what more is there to do? Those cretins are making a fuss 'cause they ain't got nothing better to do now that they've drunk all that free booze! What a bunch of fools..."

"That Sông-ho butts into everything. I can't stand the way he's always stickin' his nose in other people's business," Tal-gyun snarled in agreement. He turned to Chu-p'yông at the end of the porch. "It's gettin' cold. Let's close the door. Are you comin' in?"

"Go ahead and close it," Chu-p'yông replied sullenly.

"Hey, Chu-p'yông, why don't you go ask your Uncle Sông-ho what that dead man has to show for himself?" Uncle Tal-jin called out sarcastically. "Hell, the poor fellow didn't have no property and his kids are still small. That's why we want a quiet funeral, with just his family and a few close neighbors. Why do we need to appoint a funeral director and invite the folks from the funeral cooperative? You tell them I said to have a quiet drink and get on home."

He paused for a moment, then muttered on. "Why, there are twenty-five people in that funeral cooperative. If we have a three-day wake, that'll take at least a 250-pound pig, ten boxes of booze and one hundred packs of cigarettes. Do those fools really want that kind of funeral for Chu-man? Why, he was practically a beggar! They'd better remember who died here. I know people like to sponge off a funeral, but those guys are going too far!"

Chu-ôn, who had followed Tal-gyun back into the main room, agreed. "Yeah, Sông-ho is old enough to know better," added Tal-gyun.

Chu-p'yông must have agreed too because he went to the other room to relay his uncle's message. As his footsteps faded, Uncle Tal-jin pulled a cigarette from his pocket and turned to Chu-ch'ôl.

"Your mother and Chu-man's wife already know what happened, but I better tell you, so you don't misunderstood." He paused, drawing silently on his cigarette.

They heard someone emerge from the kitchen and cross the yard to the faucet. Chu-ch'ôl caught a glimpse of black and yellow through the crack in the door. It must be Hye-suk, he thought. She was wearing black corduroy pants and a yellow sweater. Tal-gyun, who was sitting with his back to the door, sprang up, as if prompted by a sudden thought, and stepped outside.

"Just forget about that...you know, that chain thing," Uncle Tal-jin said, blinking repeatedly as if the smoke had gotten in his eyes. Chu-ôn, who had been staring at the pictures on the folding screen concealing Chu-man's body, stood up and went outside.

A noisy quarrel had erupted in the other room. Chu-ôn acted as if he were on his way to settle the argument, but Chu-ch'ôl thought otherwise. He knew Chu-ôn had gone out to see what Uncle Tal-gyun and Hye-suk were doing outside. That stinking rat! Chu-ôn clearly thought Yun-gil was hiding at Uncle Tal-gyun's house.

"You bought them, so we used them, but only once. He'd been drinking for ten days straight. He went crazy, beating up the kids, ripping the house apart. Then he took a kitchen knife and said he was going to kill the village head. Went after me too.... It got so bad we called Tal-gyun and Sông-ho over and tied him up with those chains. But it was only for two days. Couldn't stand to leave him like that. The poor fool cried his heart out. He promised he'd quit drinking and never do anything like that again, so we let him go. After that, we threatened him with the chains a few times, but we never tied him up. Thinking back now, I'm glad we didn't tie him up the other day when he started running around with that knife again. How would it have looked if he'd died in those chains?"

Mother sat in the corner, spreading out Chu-man's shroud, then folding it neatly, patting the bundle, and unfolding it again.

The voices in the other room grew louder. They could hear Chu-p'yông and Chu-ôn talking, and Tal-gyun's sarcastic remarks. Uncle Sông-ho's husky voice, pompous and scolding, rose above the others.

"What do you fools know? We don't need garbage like you. Go get Chu-ch'ôl!"

Uncle Tal-jin rose at Uncle Sông-ho's words. Apparently he felt only he could settle the matter. Chu-ch'ôl stood up. Uncle Tal-jin told him to stay, but he followed Tal-jin to the other room. Why were they making such a big deal about the funeral? Why did they think they had to take care of everything? As Chu-ch'ôl stepped out onto the porch, Tal-gyun rushed over from where he had been standing by the other door.

"Don't listen to Sông-ho," he whispered. "I don't know what they hope to gain by takin' over this sorry funeral, but you just tell 'em you wouldn't call in the funeral cooperative if it meant carryin' Chu-man to his grave on your back! If you hire all the members from the funeral cooperative, there's no way you'll get by on one pig!"

"Lousy bastards!" Chu-ôn grumbled. "Can't they work on the funeral without all this meat and booze? You know, the Family Rite Law was enacted so poor people like Chu-man could have a funeral without spending a fortune on it."

Chu-p'yông was standing on the threshold of the other room. "Uncle Sông-ho, how can you call me garbage?" he cried.

Chu-ch'ôl advised Tal-gyun, Chu-p'yông and Chu-ôn to keep their mouths shut as he followed Uncle Tal-jin into the room. Uncle Sông-ho, Yông-sam, the head of the village funeral cooperative, Chu-hwang and Chu-ch'an, two distant cousins, and Kil-sun, a friend of Chu-man's, were seated around a small table. They reeked of alcohol after several bottles of *soju* accompanied by kimchi and salted seaweed.

"Brother, you can't leave out the funeral cooperative," blurted Kil-sun. "We'll take care of everything."

"Hey! Keep your mouth shut, Kil-sun. We elders will handle this," Yông-sam snapped, then turned to Chu-ch'ôl. "First of all, you have to appoint a funeral director. You can't pay for everything out of your own pocket. How about making Sông-ho the director?"

From outside, Chu-ôn shouted, as if he had been waiting for this moment. "Stop all this nonsense! Poor old Chu-man doesn't need any funeral director or funeral cooperative. His relatives and a few close neighbors can bury him just fine. Quiet and simple, that's all he needs! They've already sent someone for the bier and coffin and the food for the ceremony. All we need now is some booze."

"Hey! You keep out of this," Yông-sam yelled toward the door, the vein in his forehead contorting like a worm. "We villagers'll take care of everything. What the hell would someone like you know anyway?"

"I was born and raised here too, you know."

"No, you're a Seoulite now. You aren't one of us," Kil-sun intervened. "Chu-man carried a lot of funeral biers in his time. Now it's his turn. He may not have had any money and he wasn't too smart, but that doesn't mean you can just sling him over your shoulder and bury him like some kind of beggar. He has a wife and children, so why shouldn't he ride a bier like everyone else? If you're going to have a funeral, you have to do it right. What would the other villagers think? Besides, I want to do what I can for my friend, and the people in the village want to do the neighborly thing. That's the way it's always been. Call us in and you can be sure we won't come empty-handed. We donate as much as we eat, you know."

It was Uncle Sông-ho's turn next. "He's right. The corpse doesn't belong to the Pak clan now. It belongs to the village. The clan can't bury him on our own." Despite his uncle's dignified tone, Chu-p'yông wasn't going to accept defeat.

"There's no need for more talk. We're *not* calling in the funeral cooperative and that's it. If the villagers won't carry the bier, I'll stick the coffin in an A-frame carrier and bury him myself."

"Yeah, you and I can take turns carrying him," Chu-ôn concurred.

"Right. You two smart-asses try carrying him up that hill! That'll be a sight to see," Chu-hwang straightened up and yelled in the direction of the door.

"You don't understand us. You're outsiders, plain and simple. Just sit back and watch!" Kil-sun sputtered.

Yông-sam placed Chu-ch'ôl's hand on his knee and gave it a firm slap. "Chu-ch'ôl, you decide. Are you going to appoint a funeral director or not? Are you going to use the funeral cooperative or not? If you really don't want us, I can make sure no one shows his face around here, but you know, that would be a sad and regretful thing for the deceased. You *have* to use us. If you don't, we'll pitch in anyway. We'll butcher a pig and have some booze brought over.... Of course, it'll all come out of our own pockets. And wouldn't that be a pretty sight? Anyway, the rest of you keep quiet and let Chu-ch'ôl decide. You just say the word, Chu-ch'ôl. What'll it be?"

Yông-sam's voice cracked as he spoke. Everyone waited in hushed silence.

Chu-ch'ôl bowed his head. All eyes were on his face. He could feel it burning. His heart was burning too. Yông-sam's words were full of truth. For these people, life wasn't something to be lived alone. It was something to be shared. The warmth of their feeling moved him deeply. Yes, Chu-man's funeral wasn't his personal responsibility; it belonged to everyone in the village.

"The same goes for the expenses," Uncle Sông-ho added. "I don't know how much you brothers were thinking of contributing, but this is what we planned on doing. We'll collect donations from the villagers and add it to what you boys put in. Then, when all the funeral expenses have been paid, we'll hand over what's left to the widow and her children. You just wait. I'll bet the villagers' donations add up to a lot more than what you brothers put in."

Uncle Tal-jin shook his head. "I don't care if the villagers end up giving three times as much as us. We're not the kind of people who'd want to profit from a funeral. We don't need a funeral director or anybody from the funeral cooperative. If you really felt sorry for Chu-man, you'd carry his bier for a lousy cup of *soju*."

"Why do you have to be so damned stubborn?"

"Stubborn?" Uncle Tal-jin countered. "Since when am I stubborn? I just can't stand the sight of you invading poor Chu-man's funeral like a swarm of flies! Stop smacking your lips over his misfortune!"

"Are you finished?" Uncle Sông-ho asked with an angry glare.

"You just watch your mouth, Tal-jin!" Yông-sam sputtered. "Do you really think we came here to sponge off you? This isn't a family matter. Chu-man was a member of the funeral cooperative. We have a right and an obligation to take part in his funeral!"

Uncle Tal-jin ignored him and turned to Uncle Sông-ho. "Yes, I'm finished."

Uncle Sông-ho gritted his teeth and glowered at Uncle Tal-jin, then turned away with a sigh, as if he realized he had to control his temper. Wetting his lips, he took out a cigarette and lit it with a blood-red disposable lighter.

Uncle Tal-jin grumbled on. "You keep gobbling up everything in sight and you're going to be punished, believe me."

Chu-ch'ôl sensed some unresolved feelings between the two men. It seemed to have originated long before Chu-man's death. Perhaps they had quarreled over who controlled the family's affairs, or maybe Uncle Tal-jin realized that Uncle Sông-ho, who usually handled these matters, had been less than scrupulous when it came to family finances. However, he couldn't let them bicker just so he could learn what had happened.

"That's enough. It's my turn now. This is my brother's house. I'll make the decisions, and I hope you'll cooperate," Chu-ch'ôl announced, looking earnestly from face to face. "I'll appoint a funeral director and engage the services of the funeral cooperative. Uncle Sông-ho, I'd like you to be director and finalize everything after discussing it with Uncle Tal-jin. The issue of the funeral cooperative, how they're to be fed, whether we're going to feed them beef or pork, how big an animal we'll need, what kind of liquor we'll buy and how much, how long the wake will be, where we bury him.... I'm leaving everything to Uncle Sông-ho. Of course, there will be things that you'll have to discuss with me, but I don't want to hear any more arguments. That would be an insult to Chu-man, to our mother, and to us, her unfilial sons."

Yông-sam gave Chu-ch'ôl's hand a friendly whack. "Good thinking," he said. "Good thinking. You know, when it comes to a wake, we country folk are like the blind man who kills his own hen for supper. Still, it'll be a good chance to wash the dust from our throats. All thanks to Chu-man, eh? You brothers just sit back and watch. We won't disappoint old Chu-man."

The people who had been sent for the coffin and food returned. As the body was readied for bathing and dressing, a pig's squeal pierced the air, drowning out the din from the kitchen and the visitors' laughing and talking.

Mother, who had been gazing absently at the corpse lying on the seven-star board in the middle of the room, suddenly slapped her hands on the floor and began to wail.

"Oh, my poor son. Now they slaughter a fat pig! After you're gone! If only I'd bought more meat and made you soothing broth when you were drinking...maybe you wouldn't have died so suddenly! Oh, you stupid fool, you stupid fool!"

She buried her face in the shroud, then lifted a corner of the sheet covering the corpse and stroked Chu-man's feet and legs. No one in the family had ever bathed or shrouded a corpse before, so Yông-sam, the head of the funeral cooperative, was called in. Reeking of *soju*, he asked for a hemp mourning hat, then blinking his blood-shot eyes, he crouched over the body.

"Chu-man, I'm going to give you your last bath and dress you in some fine new clothes. Then we'll send you off on a pleasant journey to the other world."

A basin of warm water and a bowl of pungent mugwort tea were brought on Yông-sam's instruction.

Mother crawled slowly to the head of the corpse and leaned forward on all fours, like some kind of animal. Chu-ch'ôl and Chu-ôn crouched across from Yông-sam. Chu-ôn stood at the corpse's feet, and Uncle Tal-jin and Tal-gyun stood behind Yông-sam. Chu-man's wife left her work in the kitchen and kneeled beside her mother-in-law.

Yông-sam removed the sheet. Chu-man was stretched out, hands neatly folded over his stomach and eyes firmly closed.

He was dressed in off-white long underwear. Everyone held their breath, except for Chu-p'yông who was sobbing, "Oh, Lord help us."

Suddenly Mother cried out. "What was I thinking? He wasn't going to live forever! How come I didn't dress him better? How come I didn't feed him better? I treated him like an ox, like a work horse! Why did I make him harvest the seaweed in that icy water? Why did I force him to work those poor fingers to the bone?"

All eyes lingered on Chu-man's face, then his throat, wrists and ankles. There were bruises on his face, scratches on one side of his forehead and along his cheekbones. Blood had dried dark-red along the scratches. But it was his wrists and ankles that captured their attention. They were swollen, like the limbs of an obese person, and were ringed with bruises. Some were red, tinged with pale pink and purple; others were dark blue and lavender. Everyone seemed to think Chu-man had died struggling against the cuffs and chains. Uncle Tal-jin rubbed his hands together, unable to conceal his embarrassment.

"Wh . . wh . . why are his wrists and ankles like that? His mother and wife know. Those...you know Chu-ch'ôl, the stuff you brought down from Seoul.... We only used them for two days, and that was three weeks ago. We never used them again. But look! The bruises have shown up after he's dead! I don't get it."

"Oh, Lord help us," Chu-p'yông exclaimed.

"Come on now! Chu-man's mother was with him until the end, so don't go pretending you know everything," Yông-sam muttered as he bathed the corpse's orifices with mugwort tea. "In ordinary times, no one gives a damn, but when something happens, everyone's a know-it-all. You all stop that second guessing. Chu-man went in his own time. You just pray that he has a comfortable journey. Om Namo Amitabhaya Buddhaya, Avalokitesvara Bodhisattva!"

"Don't worry, Chu-ch'ôl!" said Uncle Tal-jin. "Heaven and earth know what happened. So do your mother, your wife and kids. I swear he didn't die in those chains."

Mother snuffled her agreement and caressed the bruised wrists and ankles. As she leaned forward to brush her cheek against them, Chu-ch'ôl felt as if his heart would break. The bruises on Chu-man's body spread to his own heart. He had killed his brother with those chains.

One day in early spring two years ago, Mother had called.

"He's left it all—the factory, the seaweed business, the boat, the house, the paddies, the fields. He just up and left everything behind. He said he couldn't stand to live here any more. He told me to ask you to come down and sell it all to pay off his debts. He said he's going to find a job as a farmhand and send for his kids later. Doesn't make any sense to me. I know you're busy but you have to come down here right away!"

After Chu-man bought into the factory, the seaweed harvest failed two years in a row. Then a typhoon wiped out the seaweed mats as soon as they were set up the third year. They had to borrow more money to rebuild the frames. The typhoon grounded the boat too, despite Chu-man's efforts to save it. It took one million won to fix the hole in its side.

Chu-man idled away the autumn and winter drinking, and the following spring, he left home to find work as a farmhand. He turned his back on the sea where he had invested more than ten million won.

Chu-ch'ôl hurried down from Seoul. He squeezed the travel expenses from his office on the pretense of visiting bookstores in Pusan and Kwangju.

"There's nothing else to be done. You've got to sell the factory, the boat, all the equipment, the paddies and the fields to pay off the high-interest loans," Mother said. "The money you've sent from Seoul, the private loans from the village and the loans from the Fisheries Cooperative add up to twelve or thirteen million won. He just can't manage it. He asked you to come settle his debts 'cause he's scared. It's all my fault. I shouldn't have made him buy into that factory."

Chu-ch'ôl went straight to the factory and met the other shareholders, then visited his uncles. It was a bad year for seaweed cultivation, and no one was willing to buy Chu-man's share in the factory or boat, not even the land.

"The interest on his loans from the Fisheries and Agricultural Cooperatives was piling up." Uncle Tal-jin had explained. "And then all the people who'd loaned him money began asking for more interest. I guess he just got scared and ran. You've backed him this far. Why don't you settle his debts one more time and get him to come back and start over?"

Uncle Sông-ho agreed. If they sold everything, Chu-man would be left as rootless as a floating weed.

"What'll people say when they hear Chu-man's draggin' his wife and kids around workin' as a farmhand? Imagine what they'll think of you!" added Tal-gyun. "Sure, you could pay off his debts by selling all the paddy land, but no one'll buy it now. You'd never get what it's worth. I know you bought the land in the first place, but just pretend you're buyin' it all over again. You got to figure out a way to pay off his debts."

Chu-ch'ôl had ten million won in his savings account. He could take out seven million and ask Chu-p'yông to chip in the rest.

He went to Hoejin and caught a taxi to Songch'i Village at the foot of Ch'ôn'gwan Mountain, where they said Chu-man had gone. The taxi left the main highway after passing through the town of Kwansan and headed up a narrow mountain trail, weather-worn and pockmarked with rocks the size of a man's fist. The trail wound around the steep cliffs. After crawling up a twisted ravine, the taxi emerged in a small basin surrounded by mountains, as tall and majestic as those portrayed in traditional screen paintings. Most of the cultivated land was in dry fields; there were few rice paddies.

Songch'i Village sat at the foot of a steep slope, a cluster of thirty-some houses, all battered and crumbling. Most of the houses were thatched; less than a dozen were roofed in slate or tin.

On the outskirts of the village were several abandoned thatched houses. It looked like the villagers were leaving their homes and land for the big city. Much of the land lay fallow. In a field at the middle of the village, sprouts of barley stood dwarfed and brown for lack of attention.

Chu-ch'ŏl saw a man heaping soil around plants in a barley field on the side of a small hill, which rose like an island at the center of the basin. His heart tightened. From a distance, the man seemed no bigger than a kid goat, but Chu-ch'ŏl knew it was his brother. He didn't bother to go to any of the houses or wait to ask a passerby for information; he hurried straight toward the farmer in the field.

You stupid imbecile! How could you do this without a word to your older brother? Did you really think I'd let you work as a farmhand? Chu-ch'ŏl's heart burned. The tip of his nose stung at the thought.

The man's hair was a magpie's nest of tangles; his face bristled with black stubble. He wore a faded brown jacket and ragged pants splattered with white spots of mud from the tideflats. It was clearly Chu-man. A gust of wind caught the soil that he was shoveling and tossed it in Chu-ch'ŏl's direction. It did not reach his eyes but they stung just the same. He couldn't control the tears. When he reached the edge of the field, he kicked over a bag of fertilizer that was standing between the furrows. Startled, Chu-man paused from his work and froze, staring into his brother's face.

Head bowed, Chu-ch'ŏl walked up to Chu-man and grabbed him by the wrist. "But wh...what...," Chu-man stuttered, still carrying the shovel in his other hand as his brother pulled him along, snorting like a bull. Chu-ch'ŏl felt as if their arms were fused together, like a grafted tree, as if Chu-man's blood were rushing into him like the incoming tide only to ebb back into his brother's body once more. A wave of dizziness swept over him, but he didn't know how to control it.

They went to see Chu-man's employer, a graying man dressed in a white *hanbok*. Chu-ch'ŏl tried to apologize. "This fool owns an acre and a half of paddy land and nearly five acres of dry fields. He shouldn't be working someone else's land."

He snatched the shovel from his brother's hand and threw it into the man's yard, then marched from the village, with Chu-man huffing and puffing behind him.

After they had left Songch'i Village, Chu-ch'ŏl sat his brother down in a sunny patch of grass and plopped down across from him. He had to talk some sense into him. Chu-man stared at the ground. He seemed discouraged.

"If you're afraid of the sea, you don't have to cultivate seaweed. Just farm and raise animals. I'll go get the money in Seoul. I can clear your debts. All you have to do is take good care of Mother. I'll hold onto the paddy land and help your kids in the future. You just do as I say. Understand?"

Chu-man plucked the dry grass blade by blade.

"I'm sorry," he whimpered in a mosquito-thin voice, "I can't face you or your wife."

"You're such a fool! Is that why you drink yourself sick? Is that why you came here? Because you couldn't face us?" Chu-ch'ôl looked into Chu-man's leaden face. His eyes were gummy and lifeless. He reeked of alcohol. The words began to take shape in Chu-ch'ôl's heart. *Die! Die! If you can't live like a decent human being, better that you die now.* No, it wasn't just that. Chu-ch'ôl felt like killing him. He could strangle him, smash his head in with a rock, throw him in the reservoir, push him off a cliff.... But how would he live with himself afterward? *No, you bastard, don't make your brothers murderers! Kill yourself!*

After cleansing the corpse's orifices, Yông-sam stuffed them with cotton and carefully covered each one with a piece of snow-white mulberry paper. Chu-ch'ôl thought of their relatives and the villagers as he watched. They all must have hated Chu-man for the way he acted.

"I know it's wrong, but I can't tell you how many times I've thought of putting rat poison in his booze." Mother had confessed as much on several occasions. The others felt the same way, no doubt. Perhaps Chu-man had died from their curses.

Yông-sam wrapped the corpse in a long piece of white cloth, beginning at the head, then binding the neck, arms, torso, thighs and feet. Mother slapped the floor and muttered in the shrill whistling voice of a shaman. "You can go now. Don't worry about a thing. Your brothers will settle your debts. You don't need to pay them back. It all belongs to the family, no matter what they say."

As he listened to his mother, Chu-ch'ôl thought of the sense of obligation that must have tortured Chu-man. Perhaps this was his way of escaping it. Yes, all our lives Chu-man, Mother and I have been struggling to free ourselves from that feeling of indebtedness. We were always struggling to dump it on someone else in the family. And in the end, it was Chu-man, the least intelligent and most innocent, who was sacrificed.

Yông-sam was dressing Chu-man now. First pants, then shirt, vest, socks, ankle straps around the cuffs of the pants and overcoat. He's free now, Chu-ch'ôl thought. He doesn't have to take the burden with him. He can hand back the guilt that we have heaped on him. In that sense, Chu-man had gotten his revenge and Chu-ch'ôl had lost.

Yông-sam seemed to be reading Chu-ch'ôl's thoughts. "Remember this, Chu-man," he said as he picked up the straw rope used to bind the corpse. "Your brother Chu-ch'ôl bought you land, he backed you in that factory deal, and he came back and paid your debts when it all fell through. You may be going now, but you have to remember what your brother's done to help you."

He then wrapped the rope around the body, binding Chu-man's arms tightly to his sides. Chu-p'yông sat next to the corpse, eyes closed and hands clasped in prayer.

"Oh Lord, please embrace my poor brother's soul. Lead him to your world and lay his weary soul to rest."

After the corpse was placed in the coffin, the whispering and shuffling in the kitchen quickened.

"Man, I can't believe this!" Chu-ôn said as he burst in the room, shaking his head in disbelief. No one had noticed him leaving.

"They paid some guy for a 250-pound pig and it only weighed 220. You know, as a 'favor' to the pig's owner!"

"What? Who the hell'd do a thing like that?" asked Tal-gyun.

"Imagine! Trying to rip off a dead man!" Uncle Tal-jin sniped.

"Let them do as they please," Chu-ch'ôl said coolly.

After all, a funeral was for the living, not the dead, he thought as he stepped outside to urinate. The smell of pork broth assaulted him at the door. A group of men had gathered around the entrance to the kitchen off the side room. The women of the family were rushing around the main kitchen, steaming vegetables, cooking rice, soup and rice cakes. They reminded Chu-ch'ôl of plump flies swarming at the smell of food.

As he returned from the outhouse, Hye-suk approached him in the yard. She looked around anxiously, wiping her hands on her apron. He leaned forward to listen.

"Yun-gil's at Uncle Tal-gyun's house, but I think Chu-ôn has already figured that out. We'd better send someone to tell him to leave the island tonight."

"No, just let him be. If that bastard gets anywhere near our Yun-gil, I'll kill him," Chu-ch'ôl sputtered. He stalked across the yard to stand by the wall. He gazed out toward the sea, visible around the curving slope of the hill in front of the house. Had Chu-ôn come to arrest Yun-gil or was he there for the funeral? The sunset was fading. By the side kitchen, the neighborhood men were feasting on pig's intestines and *soju*, mindless of those around them. They laughed and talked as they plucked slices of intestines from the steaming broth and exchanged glasses of *soju*. Someone was reeling off a list of villagers who had died from drinking too much. The secret to a sound gut was eating along with your drink, the man explained. The villagers drank the pig's blood, extolling its benefits for the sickly, then sliced up the penis and testicles, claiming they were good for virility. Black clouds passed through the sky overhead, scattering a few snowflakes.

After eating and drinking their fill, the men moved the boiled meat to the shed and began working in the front yard in groups of two or three. They brought out straw mats to spread over the ground, then pitched an awning. They hauled firewood to the center of the yard and started a bonfire, wet some straw and set it by the fire, took the bell from the ox's neck.

From the loudspeaker at the top of the tree by the village meeting hall came a man's voice, somewhat slurred. One of the men from the drinking party must have gone to make the announcement.

"Attention, members of the funeral cooperative. Will all members please gather at Chu-man's house by eight o'clock this evening? In addition, we ask all village elders and friends of the deceased to attend the wake. Members of the funeral cooperative who fail to attend will be fined fifty-thousand won. If you are unable to attend, please send a substitute or pay a fine of ten-thousand won to the head of the funeral cooperative, five-thousand for missing the wake and five-thousand for not participating in the burial."

Darkness descended. The bonfire blazed under the awning that stretched high above the courtyard. Members of the funeral cooperative and people from the village sat around the fire. There must have been at least thirty of them. Someone had a drum. They were discussing ways of entertaining themselves through the night.

Chu-ch'ŏl stood at the wall, his back to the fire, as he gazed into the darkness settling over the mountain and fields. It's a festival, he thought. Chu-man was dead and they had come to confirm that they were still alive. They wanted to laugh and talk and enjoy themselves as they looked into each other's living faces. They paid lip-service to Chu-man, of course. "Poor fellow," they said. "Too bad he had to die." But they ate and drank, demanding more meat and vegetables and liquor, as if that were the way it should be.

The coffin was moved to one end of the porch, and the folding screen was placed in front of it. There they arranged the ritual food on a table. At the center of the table was a framed photograph of Chu-man. He had it enlarged and put in a frame himself. Perhaps he had anticipated his death. Yes, Chu-man had been preparing for this.

The ritual table was piled high with fruit, rice cakes, vegetables, colorful cookies, meat and fish. A pair of bowls, one of steamed rice, packed round and high like a fluffy white flower, the other of soup, was placed in front of the photograph. A candle burned at one corner of the table, and an incense burner sat on the ground in front of the table. The smoke from the incense sticks, tall and thin like tough green paddy weeds, permeated the air under the awning. Chu-man's eleven-year-old son, officially the chief mourner, sat on a straw mat between the incense burner and the bonfire. He was dressed in a mourner's coat and hat made of stiff yellow cotton and held a mourning staff in his hand. Chu-p'yông stood beside him, a mourner's hat on his head. Chu-man's nine-year-old son wore neither a mourner's coat or hat. He scampered back and forth between his brother and uncle, laughing and hitting his brother. Mother's wails drifted from the main room to mix with the clatter of the women working in the kitchen and the voices of the men gathered around the bonfire.

"It's all right, children. It'll be quiet now, like the calm after a storm. No one's going to beat you. There's no need to run off to someone else's house to sleep. No need to go to the tavern to get his booze anymore. You can finally lie down on this nice warm floor and sleep in peace. Oh my poor baby.... "

Uncle Tal-jin was trying to comfort her. "Chu-man can rest now. He doesn't have to fight those demons anymore. He's better off now. He's finally gone where he was supposed to go," he murmured in a slurred voice.

"It's time for me to go too," wailed Mother, pounding her fists on the floor. "This heartless mother was waiting for you to die! You were right. I didn't trust you. That's why I couldn't go to live with Chu-ch'ôl. But now that you're dead, I'll leave it all behind and follow you. Ohhhhh, my poor son."

Chu-ôn stepped from the room and ambled over to Chu-ch'ôl. After a few drinks, the visitors began to rise one by one. Yông-sam, the head keener, rang the ox bell.

"Hear ye, hear ye. The first bell has rung," he called, drawing the words out long and clear. People entered the gate in groups of two or three to join the others under the awning. The crowd circled the bonfire, following Yông-sam in the dirge.

"Sweet briar of Myôngsa, don't mourn your falling blossoms!" Yông-sam cried.

"Ooho, ooho, ooho, ooho, owayo," the funeral cooperative members replied to the beat of a drum. One by one the mourners began to imitate Yông-sam's dance-like gestures, gently waving their arms as they sang. The melodious sound lifted the threads of darkness that hung over the awning and disappeared into the night sky. Black clouds floated overhead. Between them winked blue and yellow stars. Chu-p'yông stood stock-still before the ritual table, his head bowed in prayer. Chu-man's elder son bent to the ground, the mourning staff in his hand. Chu-man's wife, dressed in mourning too, wailed. Uncle Sông-ho stood to the side, instructing them. In the storage shed, some of the younger relatives were setting a table for dinner. Pork was sliced, vegetables were heaped on plates, fruit cut. From the kitchen came pork soup, thick with tofu, sliced turnips and starch jelly. It was for the keeners who had worked so hard.

"Look at this!" Chu-ôn exclaimed as he approached Chu-ch'ôl by the wall. "It's just a party to them. They don't feel sad. They don't try to comfort the bereaved. They don't try to save on funeral expenses or pay for anything. They don't give a shit about anything except who eats the most and rips us off for the biggest share of the funeral expenses. I can't take this. It's too much!"

Chu-ch'ôl tried to ignore him, then shook his head.

"You're wrong. It may look vulgar to you. Like they don't have any manners.... Like all they care about is food, but maybe they're simply being honest. Maybe this is what it means to be human. When you think about it, a funeral is just a convenience, a festival for the living who want to be sure they're really alive."

He paused for a moment, then continued in a sarcastic tone.

"I'm more frightened by people who pretend to be upright and proper. They try to kill their targets from within, cutting off their oxygen so they suffocate, secretly informing on them..."

As he spoke, Chu-ch'ôl noticed something he wasn't meant to see. A shadow slipped around the corner of the shed. It was a woman with a large bundle under her arm. She dropped the bundle over the back wall with a loud thud, then sneaked through the crowd and pretended to head for the outhouse before slipping out of the front gate. At first, he didn't recognize her. Unsightly folds of fat covered her cheeks and neck. As he stared at her fleshy features in the reddish light of the gate, Chu-ch'ôl sifted through his memory, trying to remember who she was. Yes. He had met her in the street about a year before. She was Uncle Sông-ho's second wife. He had remarried after his first wife died. The woman picked up the bundle on the other side of the wall and stole noiselessly into the darkness.

"That bitch.... They can't do this," snarled Chu-ôn. He turned to go after her, but Chu-ch'ôl grabbed his arm.

"Just pretend you didn't notice."

The mourners stopped singing and circling. The young men from the kitchen lifted one edge of the awning and carried in the table of food. Large bottles of *soju* were lined up next to the table. The women squatted in the kitchen and began to eat from bowls of soup and meat brought in from the shed. Some called their children and began feeding them as they continued to chew, cheeks bulging, like hungry ghosts.

FATHER AND SON

Sông-ho was in charge of the food in the shed. "Can't mourn on an empty stomach," he said, raising his voice as he sent his nephew Chu-ho into the main room with a tray of food. "You go tell the Seoul uncles and cousins to eat hearty." It was strange: a silence fell over the household as soon as the food was served.

Chu-ch'ôl forced down a bowl of rice mixed with soup and drank several glasses of *soju*. His body felt heavy. He lay down in the corner of the room, and his mother covered him with a blanket. The dead have died, but the living have to eat, drink and sleep.

Through a thin veil of sleep, Chu-ch'ôl heard the second bell and the mourners' keening. He then heard the people eating again. Some time later, the third bell rang, then the keening and eating once more. The fourth and the fifth bells followed with the sound of hungry ghosts filling their bellies one last time.

He turned on his side. I wonder how much pork is left. Are they going to leave enough for the burial procession and grave digging tomorrow? Are we going to have to get more for the third memorial rite? How much will that cost us? What's the matter? Uncle Sông-ho will handle everything. After all, the villagers will pay for it. Chu-ch'ôl was drifting off to sleep once more when he heard fighting. He listened more carefully and realized someone was being beaten.

"You bastard! Who are you tryin' to fool? What do you have against me anyway? Why would you want to spy on my house at this ungodly hour? You wretched whelp of a crazy woman! You don't deserve the name Pak!"

Chu-ch'ôl stepped outside to find Tal-gyun yanking Chu-ôn around by the collar. No one intervened because Chu-ôn was letting himself be tugged around without a word in protest. He laughed nervously as he flopped from side to side. Tal-gyun grumbled on, unable to suppress his rage. The mourners were getting up to leave now that they had eaten their fill; they made way for the two men. Above the gate, the sky was growing lighter, though the snow kept falling.

"Chu-ch'ôl! Look at this son of a bitch! He's been actin' funny ever since he got here so I've been keepin' an eye on him, and you know what? I caught him sneakin' off to my place. He was gonna search the temple, and the day hasn't even broke yet!" Tal-gyun tightened his grip on Chu-ôn's collar and growled, "You bastard! Why would you want to go to my house? Figured Yun-gil was hidin' there, huh?" Tal-gyun growled as he shoved Chu-ôn into the main room. Hye-suk ran from the opposite room and pushed Tal-gyun back outside.

"Uncle, Chu-ôn isn't that kind of person. You don't understand. I know him. Please don't make a scene."

Chu-ôn laughed nervously as he wiped the blood from his lips with the back of his hand.

"Do you want me to tell you where I was going, Uncle? I was on my way to my father's grave. I didn't want anyone to know. You've got it all wrong! What would I want with Yun-gil? You don't understand. It's not fair. I'm telling you: I came down here for Chu-man's funeral. Nothing more. I'm not after Yun-gil."

Swiping at the blood once more, Chu-ôn sat down against the wall where Chu-man's corpse had lain the night before. Hye-suk grasped his hand and shook it.

"Don't worry. I believe you."

"Son of a bitch. No tellin' where his parents came from. He ain't no Pak as far as I'm concerned. I'd like to kick the shit out of him. That bastard would have turned my house upside down, and if he didn't find Yun-gil, he would have come after me with his questions. 'How come you hid him? You helped him escape! Where did he go?' I know he would!" Tal-gyun shouted over his shoulder as he strode toward the bonfire. He was drunk and angry. Chu-ch'ôl grabbed him and dragged him toward the other room.

"Can't you keep quiet? Think of poor Chu-man and my mother. She hasn't taken a sip of water, much less any food. This is no time to worry about Yun-gil!"

"What? How can we not worry about Yun-gil?" Tal-gyun bellowed, the veins on his neck and forehead bulging. "To tell the truth, people like me and Chu-man, and scum like Chu-ôn, and all the dimwits in this village could drop off the face of the earth and it wouldn't make a lick of difference, but bright young kids like Yun-gil have to be free to do and say what's right. You know what I mean? He's already gone so it doesn't matter now. He went to hide somewhere else, but I learned a lot from him while he was with us. He's a smart boy. Let me tell you: Our family has produced a remarkable man. You just wait. He's goin' be a lot smarter than you, Chu-ch'ôl. A lot more successful too. And that's the way it should be. Your son is gonna be an even greater man than you."

Tal-gyun's words refreshed Chu-ch'ôl, as if he had drunk a cup of peppermint tea, but fear soon spread over him like a dark cloud. Yun-gil wasn't trying to build on his father's accomplishments. He was trying to sweep his father away completely. His was an act of betrayal, a rebellion.

As morning broke, the snow began to fall more heavily. The world was white, as if covered in a quilt of cotton. Lovely white flowers clung to the gaunt trees.

"Ooooh, ooooh. How can you bury my baby in this snow?" Mother sobbed. "Wait until it's melted. Let him sleep here one more night."

Uncle Sông-ho ordered the pallbearers to carry the coffin from the house. They circled the yard three times, then headed out of the gate, toward the beach where the bier was waiting.

The bier was pure white. Not a spot of black showed under the blanket of fresh snow and the white paper flowers that were used to decorate it. The snow continued to fall until the pallbearers had completed the road rite and turned to leave the beach.

The bier headed up the snow-covered hill. The pallbearers stumbled on branches and crevices hidden by the snow, but they kept climbing. Sông-ho had paid a man from Changsan eight-thousand won to lead the dirge. He sang in a clear, high-pitched voice, and the drunken pallbearers echoed his tune in their own merry voices.

The grave was to be dug at the end of a ridge overlooking the sea and the village. The procession rested three times before it arrived at the grave site. Each time they paused, the pallbearers feasted on thick slices of pork and more *soju*.

Chu-ch'ôl and his wife trailed the procession at a distance. Chu-p'yông followed closely on the bier's tail, clasping the hands of Chu-man's two sons.

Chu-p'yông hadn't bowed at the ritual table or at Chu-man's coffin. He had simply kneeled and lowered his head in prayer.

"Come on. It doesn't look right," Chu-ch'ôl had said impatiently. "Just bow. Is it going to taint your religion to get down on your knees and bow to your dead brother? Just make up your mind and do it! Do you have to insult him? Chu-man could be superior to your god for all you know. Get down and bow. Do it, eh?"

Chu-p'yông refused. "It's my choice. Just leave me alone. My prayers are more likely to get him to heaven than your bows. I've learned a lot from this experience. I've been too passive in my belief I bent under pressure from you and let Chu-man die. From now on, I'm going to take an active role and save my nephews from their suffering. I'm going to guide them to the church."

"He's completely nuts," Chu-ch'ôl felt like muttering, as he watched Chu-p'yông following the bier, their nephews' hands in his. "I wonder how he got to be such a fanatic?" Chu-ch'ôl glanced at Hye-suk and decided it was better not to express this opinion out loud. Perhaps he and Chu-p'yông weren't so different after all. Chu-p'yông was just trying to repay his debt to Chu-man.

After a rest and another drink, the pallbearers hoisted the bier to their shoulders once more. Chu-ôn walked to the right of the bier, Tal-gyun to the left. What the hell does Chu-ôn do? Is he a detective? Has he come to get Yun-gil, or is he really here for Chu-man's funeral? Where was he going when Tal-gyun caught him?

"I'm not sure if I should tell you this, but Yun-gil came to the house last night," Hye-suk ventured, looking to the procession ahead of them. "He said he's staying at Uncle Tal-gyun's in Temple Hollow. Uncle Tal-gyun dug a cave in the hill behind the house. He says no one will ever find it. He hides there when he feels something in the air, but usually he stays in a nice warm room. He told me not to worry."

Chu-ch'ôl couldn't believe what she was saying.

"I'm so grateful to Uncle Tal-gyun's wife," she continued. "They barely have enough to eat themselves, but she fries him an egg everyday and washes his clothes.... And Uncle Tal-gyun's been especially kind to him. Once a week he goes out and traps a rabbit or butchers a chicken to feed Yun-gil."

Chu-ch'ôl was helpless against the confusion that burned in his heart. It soon turned into an awkward feeling of obligation, constricting him and making him feel guilty. How am I supposed to pay him back? Suddenly Tal-gyun looked so lovable, so noble as he limped along of them. At the same time, Chu-ch'ôl felt the arrogance pounding in his temples. I'll slip him a couple hundred-thousand won when I leave for Seoul, he thought. Chu-ch'ôl didn't want to feel indebted to anyone. But would two hundred-thousand repay Uncle Tal-gyun for his kindness? The image of his uncle attacking Chu-ôn rose before him.

As the coffin was lowered into the ground that day, Chu-ch'ôl thought of that immeasurable gratitude. "Don't worry," he murmured. "I'll take care of your kids. I'll put them through high school, college too if they want. Don't worry. I'll make sure they have a good life."

He also made another promise, too profound for Chu-man to understand.

"I'm going to write poems that transcend the sufferings of wounded people like you. I'm going to write poems that will prevent more people from being hurt, that will stop the ideological war and bring unification, that will pull the Korean people together by confirming their common bond."

He bit his tongue. Could a poem do that?

Chu-p'yông had once accused him of using his siblings as fodder for his writing. Chu-ch'ôl regretted that he hadn't told Chu-p'yông that he was using his brothers as targets for his evangelism.

Chu-ch'ôl smiled bitterly. He realized that he simply wanted to rid himself of the sense of obligation he felt toward his dead brother. He wasn't alone in that. They all felt the same debt— Chu-p'yông, Chu-ôn, the other relatives, the people from the funeral cooperative, the villagers.

"There's no better gift to the dead than laying one more piece of sod, one more shovel of dirt. We want him to stay warm on his journey."

"Chu-man and I always took turns helping each other with the fertilizer and pesticide."

"Yep, Chu-man had a heart of gold."

"There ain't a man in the village that didn't get a free drink off Chu-man at one time or another. Why, when he sat down for a drink at the corner store, he'd invite the crows to join him!"

"He never rode that new boat of his, but we sure made good use of it. 'First come, first served,' remember?"

"Yeah! Everyone who used Chu-man's boat, bring over another piece of sod!"

The young villagers bantered back and forth as they stumbled through the snow carrying sod. They were happy to do the job.

The winter sun fell quickly. They worked hard but the earth was frozen and the snow slowed their progress. Dusk had settled by the time they finished, and with it came more snowflakes, as white and fluffy as cotton balls.

They hurried down the mountain and gathered at Chu-man's house once more. At Uncle Sông-ho's direction, the younger relatives and the women who had been waiting at the house laid another table of food. It looked as if they were all going to stay there, enjoying themselves, confirming their existence, as long as there was pork, soup and *soju* to be had.

"That snow's covering my baby like a blanket," Chu-ch'ôl's mother cried, pounding her chest. "He must be frozen stiff out there!"

Chu-ch'ôl and Chu-p'yông sat in front of her. They didn't know what to say. She pulled Chu-man's sons to her bosom. "Where'd you boys put your father? You can sleep sound from now on. No need to hide anymore."

Chu-ho entered with a tray of food. He called Chu-ch'ôl onto the porch.

"Something strange is going on. Chu-ôn sneaked out around sunset, and Uncle Tal-gyun went after him. Looks like they've gone to Temple Hollow. Folks are saying Chu-ôn has a pistol. Somebody saw it fall out of his jacket pocket when he was digging sod for the grave."

The grave diggers huddled over the food, their spoons and chopsticks flying. The room off the kitchen was filled with people too. A few drunken voices rose above the others.

"I'm not kidding. They'll never be able to pay Chu-man back."

"Right, right. Now shut up and eat."

"What do you mean? Chu-ch'ôl did everything he could for Chu-man."

"Still, it wasn't enough. He could weave sandals with his hair and it still wouldn't be enough."

Snow was accumulating on top of the awning now. The snowflakes sparkled gold and silver in the light of the lamp hanging from the eaves. Beyond the awning, the yard was ankle-deep in snow. Chu-ch'ôl stared at the yard and thought of Chu-ôn and Tal-gyun running through the dark snow-covered fields: Chu-ôn ahead, Tal-gyun chasing behind him. They joined in a tangle of fists, hitting, kicking, biting. Soon they were covered in blood. Chu-ôn pulled out a pistol and a shot echoed through the ravine..... . Was Chu-ôn a detective? Was he one of their snitches? Had he come for Yun-gil? Isn't there something I should do? I can't just sit around like some kind of idiot. Maybe I should go up to Temple Hollow. Chu-ch'ôl felt helpless. Impatience and despair spread through his body like wildfire. Uncle Sông-ho emerged from the shed and came to his side.

"What are you doing out here? You know, I can't be sure till tomorrow morning, but it looks like the meat won't last through the third memorial rite. We're going to have to buy a side of pork at market or butcher another pig."

As Uncle Sông-ho spoke, a heavy-set woman dashed back and forth between the shed and kitchen. In a tinny voice, she asked the women in the kitchen to prepare five more bowls of soup, then scurried toward the group seated outside under the awning. It must have been cold up there, she said. Eat hearty! She was Uncle Sông-ho's second wife. Chu-ch'ôl remembered her dropping the bundle over the back wall and disappearing into the darkness.

She rushed up, skirts flying. "Nephew," she pleaded in a regretful tone, "what more can you do for him? He's dead, but everyone knows how hard you tried to help him. Don't be so sad. Think of your health. Go in and have something to eat. You know what they say: You have to keep on living."

Suddenly Chu-ch'ôl remembered the spikes in the door frame. I've got to take those out, he thought as he turned away, but the woman stood in his path.

"I'd better tell you before you hear from someone else," she whispered. "You mustn't give any of Chu-man's things to Tal-jin. Not the factory, not the boat, not the land, not anything. Why, before Chu-man died, everyone was already talking about how Tal-jin was after Chu-man's property. He's already using Chu-man's seaweed harvesting equipment. If you must, let him manage the factory and the boat, but we'll take care of the paddy land. You won't regret it."

Chu-ch'ôl suppressed a wave of nausea and dashed inside.

"Uncle, did you see this?" he cried to Tal-jin, pointing to the spikes. "How can you just sit there? How can you eat and drink with these things around?"

Uncle Tal-jin lowered his spoon. Chu-ch'ôl turned to shriek at Chu-p'yông.

"What are you doing? Go get a hammer and pull these things out!"

Chu-p'yông remained seated by the table of food and closed his eyes. He was running to his god.

Uncle Tal-jin called Chu-ho and asked him to remove the spikes. The young man brought a long lever and pulled them out with little difficulty.

Chu-ch'ôl grabbed the spikes and ran from the room. He gathered the bundle of chains from the shed and dashed out of the front gate. The snowflakes felt cold on his face and neck. A monstrous thought rose inside his brain like an angry viper. It's all because of these spikes and chains. First they bound Chu-man and now they were trying to shackle Yun-gil.

Slipping, sliding, tumbling along, he crossed the snowy ridges and dark ravines. When he reached the small pond near the path leading to Temple Hollow, he threw the bundle of chains into the water and dashed onward, toward Uncle Tal-gyun's house at the temple. The snow blinded him. Chu-p'yông's words filled his brain with white, like the blossoms of snow.

"You used Chu-man and Chu-shim as fodder for your writing. You just sat by and watched as they unraveled, stitch by stitch, like a couple of old sweaters. And then you wrote about it."

The words echoed through the ravine like the scornful cackle of a ghost. They turned to cold snowy dust and poured down from the dark sky, piercing his spirit like sharp particles of steel.

An Abandoned Temple in Winter

1

The snow was ankle-deep and the narrow path leading to Temple Hollow was slippery. The darkness was diluted by the snow, but Chu-ch'ôl kept stumbling and falling, sometimes tumbling off the path. Anxious and afraid, he felt as if he had left the secular world to enter the spotless world of snow. Would he ever find a way back to the life he had lived before?

The sky was dark and somber. The snow was still falling. Chu-ch'ôl was covered from head to toe, like a snowman. Why did Chu-ôn have to go to Temple Hollow tonight of all nights? He must be a police snitch. Why else would he brave that treacherous path in the middle of a snow storm? He was going to get Yun-gil. But why would anyone arrest his own relative? His father used to work for our family. He spent his childhood in the shadow of our roof. Would he really sell off a relative so he could make something of himself? What a heartless scoundrel! He had no conscience at all. I'd like to beat the shit out of him.

Chu-ch'ôl slipped and fell forward. As he pulled himself up by the branch of a dwarfed pine, he tried to get his bearings, but he was lost. He had turned up the wrong valley. The snow had turned the path into another world. As a child he had taken that path so many times—grazing the ox, following his mother or grandmother to the temple; he had thought he could find it with his eyes closed. There were fox holes in the stony cliffs in Big Hollow on the way to Temple Hollow, and every summer Chu-ch'ôl went there to chase foxes or start fires at the mouths of their holes. He was more familiar with Big Hollow than Temple Hollow, but now he did not know where he was. He had lost all sense of direction and simply stood in the snow, blinking around him. Finally he set off toward the southwestern ridge after comparing the heights of the surrounding mountains.

As he descended the slope on the other side, Chu-ch'ôl slipped and tumbled into a snow-filled depression. He wasn't hurt, only a few scratches on his face and neck, but he was seized by the feeling that he was falling down, down from a towering cliff. He struggled furiously to escape the snow-filled hole. How embarrassing it all was! He despised his son. People always say the newborn pup has no fear of the tiger. That was Yun-gil, all right. Chu-ch'ôl owned a good-sized house and an orchard, albeit in his wife's name, so Yun-gil belonged to "the haves," whether he liked it or not. But now he was trying to sell off his parents in the name of his own ideology. He pointed to them and attacked the "rotten nature of the bourgeoisie." He was ready to dedicate himself to the propertyless masses, if only to cleanse himself of his parents' crimes.

Chu-ch'ôl finally reached the entrance to Temple Hollow. He saw a light. The village had electricity now. It was a street lamp at the center of the village below the temple. A wave of foreboding swept over him when he spotted it. Was he in the right village? Had he turned up the wrong valley? He looked around the snow-covered pine grove at the entrance of the village, searching for the spirit posts that once stood there. When he visited the temple as a child, he had always been greeted by a huge pair of stone spirit posts. Their noses were as big as a man's fist, their eyes like brass bells, their ears as long as cucumbers. One bore the inscription "Great General Under Heaven," the other "Female General Under the Earth." Where were they? Had he missed them in the snow? Had they been moved? Maybe this wasn't Temple Hollow at all.

He looked up at the ridges surrounding the village; their outlines were clear in the diluted darkness. To the east was Sunrise Peak, piercing the sky like a hawk's beak, to the west,

Moonrise Peak, its summit round as an octopus head. Temple Hollow, a small village of twenty households, stood on the slope of a ridge twisting to the southeast of the temple. The houses crouched under the weight of the snow, lights glowing in their windows. The temple never had been visible from the entrance of the village.

The spirit posts must have been moved, he thought as he headed for the center of the village. To get to the temple, he had to go straight through the village. The snow kept falling. The street lamp stood in front of the village hall, a few steps from the village spirit tree. The snowflakes fluttered gold and silver in the stream of light.

Chu-ch'ôl jerked to a halt as he stepped into the circle of light. There was a small field behind the village hall and spirit tree. Barbed wire stretched along the edge of the field, blocking the path to the temple. Silver balls of snow had formed on the barbs. The fence posts were jet black crosses. He couldn't tell if they had been painted black or scorched in a fire. Each fence post was a crucifix. They stood tall and proud, like telephone poles, their tops and northern edges outlined in cotton-white snow.

A few paces past the village hall was a small store. A dim light shone through its glass door. Three men were seated on stools next to the display window, drinking. They looked out as Chu-ch'ôl passed. Conscious of their stares, he brushed the snow from his head and body.

The path grew darker as it neared the temple. The street lamp and the light from the houses did not reach far. He walked on, groping through the diffused darkness. The sound of televisions and radios slipped from the houses. The path wound to the right, steering away from a large forest of bare black branches that stretched eerily into the sky. It was a grove of persimmon trees. A barbed wire fence protected it from intruders. Here too the fence posts were shaped like crosses. Three houses stood to the right of the path; beyond them lay a field. Barbed wire divided the path from the field here too. He followed the black crosses another 100 yards, to find a building towering before him. A single light burned above its iron gate. "Temple Hollow Church," a sign said. A cross rose above the belfry. Barbed wire wrapped around the southeastern edge of the churchyard.

Chu-ch'ôl headed in the direction of the temple. The persimmon grove, with its dark branches layered with snow, stood on the left, the church on the right. A brook, which flowed from the temple, lay between the church and the path.

A cement bridge led to the church across the brook, but Chu-ch'ôl did not take it. Instead, he continued up the steep path along the edge of the persimmon grove. Suddenly a tall pole loomed before him like a huge black phantom. He cried out and took several steps backward. It was another cross strung with barbed wire. Why had they put it up in the middle of the path? How were you supposed to get to the temple? He examined the barbed wire. Six rows were strung at 8-inch intervals. There was no way to get around it, and yet he couldn't climb over it or stretch a hole wide enough to slip through. He paused and looked around. The village was surrounded by barbed wire. There was no way to get to the temple.

"Lost in time." For some reason, the phrase popped into his head. When had he last come to the temple? He had left his hometown after the Korean War, more than thirty years ago. The temple had been burned down during the war. No one restored it, and the monks didn't think of returning. Since that time, the old Widow Chông had lived with her son Tal-gyun in the temple living quarters, the only building to escape the fire.

In the intervening years, Temple Hollow had been transformed into a Christian village. Not only had the villagers been converted, they had blocked the path leading to the abandoned temple with barbed wire. Chu-ch'ôl remembered how the villagers, young and old, used to clasp their hands together and bow when they encountered the monks in the village. Now they seemed to have rejected the Buddha completely. They must have removed the stone spirit posts because they believed they were remnants of primitive idolatry. Chu-ch'ôl recalled the pagodas in the temple courtyard. Were they safe? And what about the statue of the Maitreya Buddha on the hill behind the main hall? With no monks to look after them and the temple enclosed in barbed wire, they had probably been smashed to smithereens by now.

Still, this was too much. How did Uncle Tal-gyun and his family get in and out? Did they have any contact with the villagers? A wall seemed to separate them. Chu-ch'ôl turned back. He had to ask directions at the store in the village.

As he opened the glass door, the men turned to look at him. They had been waiting for him to come back. They looked up together, as if one of the men had cried out, "Here he comes!" and then, they averted their eyes, again as if by prior agreement.

Chu-ch'ôl sensed a barrier in their averted faces. All three men appeared to be somewhere between forty and fifty. It may have been thirty years, but if they were natives of the village, they should have recognized him. They would have gone to the same elementary school, the only one on the island. Perhaps they had started school late, after liberation from the Japanese rule. That would put them a few grades behind him. Still, Chu-ch'ôl had always been class president or weekly monitor. They had to remember him of all people.

"Please excuse me, gentlemen" he began, regretting immediately that he had used the Seoul dialect. They would resent him for that. All three men studiously ignored him.

"How'd I be gettin' to the temple?" he asked in the local vernacular. The men kept their eyes on the glasses in front of them, pretending not to hear. They were drinking *soju*. A few pieces of roasted squid and a half-empty package of shrimp-chips lay on the table.

"How'd the temple folk be gettin' there?" he asked once more. "The road's closed."

"How should we know? Go ask somebody else," one of them answered gruffly, without raising his head. He was a heavy-set man with stubbly sideburns.

Chu-ch'ôl felt as if he had been punched in the stomach. The men began chewing noisily, as if on the large man's cue. They gnawed eagerly on the squid legs, munched on the shrimp-chips noisily, and tossed their drinks down with exaggerated gusto. The other two men were smaller. One had a thin face, shriveled like a dried date seed; the other was even shorter with crowded features.

"Look at that snow!" commented the short man. "When's it gonna let up?"

"We're in for a fine barley harvest, that's for sure," the thin man replied.

"The rabbits'll starve to death, though," added the large man.

"Let's go rabbit huntin' tomorrow, eh?" asked the thin man.

"I hope it keeps snowin' tomorrow and the next day too, even if we don't go out huntin'," said the large man.

"Looks like they couldn't get here 'cause of the snow, eh?" asked the thin man.

"Assholes! Why they makin' a fuss now? The bell's been gone for months," the short man complained.

The conversation was solely for Chu-ch'ôl's benefit.

They've taken me for someone else, he realized. I'd better tell them who I am.

"Don't you fellows recognize me? I'm Chu-ch'ôl. I used to live in New Town across the way."

"We know," said the short man in a haughty tone, "but that don't make no difference. You could be your great-great grandfather and we'd still have nothin' to do with you. Once we make up our minds, there's nothin' you can do."

"I'll give you directions since your son's tried to help us. You can't get to the temple from here no more. You know where the spirit posts used to be? Head up the hill toward Sunrise Peak from there."

Chu-ch'ôl stepped closer. "How did this happen?" he asked in an irritated tone. "What's going on here?"

"It's a long story. Why, you could write a novel 'bout it..."

"Go ask Tal-gyun. You'll be up the whole night with that story."

"But you keep your nose outta our business, no matter what he says. It ain't got nothin' to do with you. No point in you gettin' on our bad side too."

Chu-ch'ôl wanted to sit down and hear the whole tangled story. He wanted them to realize that he hadn't come for that, but he didn't have the time. He had to find Chu-ôn. He was afraid of what might happen between Chu-ôn and Yun-gil. Chu-ôn and Tal-gyun might have ripped each other apart before Chu-ôn ever saw Yun-gil.

"Let's meet again in the morning. It's not what you think. I didn't come here because of that. Please don't get me wrong."

Chu-ch'ôl pushed open the door and stepped outside. He had forgotten the cold and tingling in his toes but now they returned. He was wearing regular leather shoes. He couldn't remember how many times they had slipped off, forcing him to dig through the snow with his foot.

He returned to the spot where the spirit posts used to stand, then climbed toward Sunrise Peak. There was no sign of anyone preceding him. Perhaps he had taken the wrong path again. He was soon tripping over rocks and tumbling into the drifts once more. His shoe slipped off, and he crashed to his knees. He fumbled for the shoe, then headed in what he thought was the direction of the temple. The living quarters sat in a small basin beyond the persimmon grove.

Sea Cloud Temple was small; its main hall was the size of the average country house. On a hill to its right stood the shrine to the Mountain Spirit, a small structure slightly larger than the look-out sheds found in melon fields. About 200 yards from the main hall was the living quarters, shaped like a long ship. There had only been three or four monks in the best of times, but Sea Cloud Temple was well-endowed. The land on which the village stood and nearly 200 acres of dry fields and paddies belonged to the temple. The persimmon grove also belonged to the temple, as did the mountains surrounding the village.

It was because of this property that the temple had been burned down and the monks had failed to return. Pak Ho-nam, Chu-ch'ôl's grandfather's older brother, had managed the temple's assets. He squeezed high rents from the villagers, with the full support of the head monk who belonged to the sect that permitted monks to marry. Not only was the income from the rent plentiful, but the persimmon crop and the rice contributed by believers were abundant. It wasn't long before Ho-nam set up the young Widow Chông in the living quarters to cook for the monks. She was his concubine, of course. He spent his days in the village on the other side of the mountain, but came to her each night. Gradually he lost interest in his household in the village and spent more time at the temple, squeezing the villagers even harder.

With liberation, the young men who had left for the city returned. Some had been tortured by the colonial police for arguing with Ho-nam about their rents. Others were returning from labor camps or forced conscription into the Japanese army.

When a tenant objected to the rent, Ho-nam marked his house with a pine bough in the dark of night, and the next morning the police arrested the man. He also informed on recalcitrant tenants, accusing them of refusing to worship the Japanese Shinto shrine or engaging in socialist activities.

Five days after Emperor Hirohito surrendered and word of the Japanese's withdrawal began to spread, the young men of Temple Hollow set fire to the main hall. They dragged the monks from the living quarters and beat them before driving them, and their families, away.

Pak Ho-nam and the Widow Chông managed to survive somehow. The living quarters had escaped the fire. The young men had surrounded it, hoping to capture Ho-nam, but he was as agile as a tiger, thanks to his many years peddling goods from market to market. He leapt over a club wielded by one of the young men, kicked him in the back, and fled into the mountains.

The Widow Chông survived the attack thanks to the twin sons she had born in her first marriage. Ssang-do, the elder twin, had masterminded the temple fire. In the years between liberation and the Korean War, a Patricide Society was organized by the sons of Japanese collaborators and wealthy landowners. The people of Naedok Island all knew of it. Many of its members had been drafted into the Japanese army or labor gangs to save their fathers unnecessary embarrassment. Others had escaped to the big cities.

Most of these young men joined the Committee for the Preparation of Korean Independence right after liberation and later became members of the People's Committee and the South Korean Workers' Party. Every village on the island had its own cell that secretly carried on its patricidal duties throughout the Yôsu Rebellion and the Korean War.

Pak Ho-nam died by the sword of a rebel who had fled to the island following the Yôsu Rebellion in 1948. His death and the liquidation of reactionary elements around the time of the Inch'on Landing in 1950 were all related to the Patricide Society. The young islanders dreamed of a social revolution that would do away with the uneven distribution of wealth, but if they wanted to make a name for themselves in the resistance community, they had to expose and eliminate the irrationalities of their own households first. Otherwise, they would never find a place among the powerful.

Pak Ho-nam carried a shotgun with him wherever he went. To shoot pheasants, rabbits and doves on his way back and forth from the temple, he said. He always dressed in riding jodhpurs, a Western-style jacket, and a hunting cap. His eyes were usually bloodshot. He stood six feet tall, was immaculately shaven except for a magnificent moustache, and always glowed with health.

Chu-ch'ôl could hear his great-uncle's shotgun when he was walking home from school or was out grazing the ox. Ho-nam often strode through the village with a magpie, pheasant or rabbit dangling from his ammunition belt. Sometimes he went hunting on Ch'ôn'gwan Mountain with the local magistrate or police chief. People said that Nakamura, the Japanese man who ran the village brewery, frequently accompanied them.

Pak Ho-nam slept with his shotgun by his pillow. In part, he did it to protect himself from attacks from outside, but he was also afraid of his stepsons, Ssang-do and Ssang-gyun. He sensed a murderous glint in the elder boy's eyes. In fact, Ssang-do had never called him Father. Ho-nam often dreamed that his two stepsons were strangling him.

FATHER AND SON

Ultimately he died at Ssang-do's hand. Thanks to his stepfather, Ssang-do had escaped the draft, but he had secretly organized the local Patricide Society along with several other young men who shared his beliefs. Pak Tal-ho, Chu-ch'ôl's father, had also died because of the Society. Everyone who had been appointed local magistrate, head of the Fishery Cooperative or county clerk on the strength of Pak Ho-nam's influence was purged when the communists took over during the Yôsu Rebellion and the Korean War. Chu-ch'ôl's father had followed in the footsteps of his father and grandfather to become head of the Fisheries Cooperative and later had little trouble entering the local government as senior commercial clerk.

Perhaps his own son's radicalism was rooted in those events, Chu-ch'ôl thought as he slid into another snowy hole.

Chu-ch'ôl's father began buying up land when he was head of the Fisheries Cooperative and clerk at the sub-county office. On a small island where arable land was scarce, an acre or two of paddy and a half dozen acres of dry fields were impressive holdings. Ho-nam trusted his nephew Tal-ho. He called him the "heart" of the Pak clan and bragged about how Tal-ho would succeed him. Ho-nam was secretly planning to make his nephew local magistrate. He paid off the county magistrate and governor from the rents he had gathered for the temple.

"I'm too ignorant to be magistrate, so you've got to do it for me. I'll do everything I can to help you get the job. It's about time we had a great man in the family." Ho-nam called Tal-ho to his house to encourage him. He assumed that all power in the township would fall into his hands once his nephew was named local magistrate. "Small trees may not thrive under a mighty oak, but under a great man, little people grow like bamboo sprouts. If you become a great man, you can help your cousins."

It was only natural that the close relationship between Ho-nam and his nephew would alienate his stepsons and make them even more radical. Rumor had it the twins' father had drowned in the sluiceway at the local saltflats, a victim of Ho-nam's intrigue. The police said several suspects had been questioned but they had been set free. They all had airtight alibis, and the police had no evidence to speak of. The case of An Chong-su's death was never solved. Among the suspects were Pak Ho-nam and three men employed at his saltworks.

Pak Ho-nam and An Chong-su had been fighting over the rights to manage the property held by Sea Cloud Temple. As they grew older, the twins came to suspect that Pak was responsible for their father's death and despised him for it.

People said Ssang-do killed Pak Ho-nam.

Ch'u Ch'ang-dong, a young man from Temple Hollow, and Pae Il-do, from nearby Ox Mountain, had volunteered to serve in the 14th Regiment stationed at Yôsu. When they saw how easily the rebelling forces advanced through Kwangyang and Posong, they were thrilled and rushed home, confident that they could liberate their villages with the same ease.

After a night's journey they arrived at Temple Hollow and went straight to the twins. The four young men did not bother to contact the chairman of the local People's Committee. They killed Ho-nam as he slept, set the temple on fire, then attacked the local police box. The policemen were terrified and the police box fell with just two gunshots.

Pak Ho-nam died of stab wounds. While Ssang-gyun and Pae Il-do searched the living quarters and backyard, Ch'u Ch'ang-dong and Ssang-do crept inside without so much as a creak of the door. They had decided against a gun for fear the shot would spoil the rest of their plan. Ssang-do stabbed his stepfather through the heart with Chang-dong's military sword.

Miraculously, Chu-ch'ôl's father escaped with his life. He had a dream that night. His father appeared, dressed in a long white coat. The old man told him to run and hide. Already suspicious of the twins, Tal-ho leapt from his bed and ran to hide in the bamboo grove behind his house. After a few moments, just long enough to smoke a single cigarette, he heard a dog barking, and through the trees, he saw a pair of black shadows climbing over the wall. Flashlights pierced the darkness as they tramped through the house banging doors. Tal-ho could hear his wife and children screaming.

When the guerilla suppression forces retook the village, Tal-ho made a point of assisting the families of the twins and their two associates. He helped the young men who had participated in the rebellion get into the local Youth Association and tried to play down their actions. Tal-ho knew it wasn't over yet, and he wanted to earn the affections of as many people as he could while he was head of the Youth Association.

Pae Il-do and Ssang-gyun were working as farmhands in Yong-am. Tal-ho made them return to the village and surrender, and whenever Ch'u Ch'ang-dong's father or the twins' mother were taken to the police box, he coaxed the police chief into releasing them. Of course, they paid a good share of the bribes themselves by selling off land and livestock, but Tal-ho's contribution was significant.

Confident in the power of these good deeds, Tal-ho didn't bother fleeing when the communists came into power. Pae Il-do and Ssang-gyun began working at the Security Bureau and did their best to protect him, both covertly and overtly. During the early days of the communist rule, this worked, but in the end it wasn't enough.

Ssang-do and Ch'u Ch'ang-dong, who had been hiding in a nearby cave like beasts in hibernation, returned to the village. They weren't going to let Tal-ho get away.

Toward the end of the communist regime, he died of complications from a beating he received after a People's Tribunal.

"I'm proud to be the grandson of a Japanese sympathizer and reactionary element," Yun-gil had once told his father. "It gives me strength to carry on the fight."

Chu-ch'ŏl was especially horrified by his son's sympathy for the Patricide Society. "I'm sorry, Father, but it sounds like a good idea to me. I've been thinking about what role the Society would play today. Of course, we couldn't actually kill anyone. We have to overcome our fathers with a kind of spiritual, ideological, historical and philosophical patricide."

It was snowing still. The white snow thinned the darkness but Chu-ch'ŏl could not see through the thick, fluffy flakes. He flailed his arms like a pinwheel. The branches of bush clover, chestnut and oak trees scratched his face and neck.

After climbing some distance up Sunrise Peak, he glimpsed a light flickering through a pine grove ahead. It must be the temple, he thought. He should have been glad, but he felt weak. His life seemed as treacherous as the snowy path he was climbing. The fateful ups and downs of three generations—his father, himself, and his son—seemed so pitiful, so sad.

What was happening at the temple? His impatience made him slip all the more.

2

Chu-ch'ŏl paused at the end of the temple living quarters. It looked like an enormous ship. At the bow, on the northeast end, was a kitchen, followed by five rooms, all in a row. There were two lights, one in the room next to the kitchen and the other in the last room, in what would be the ship's stern. The lights faintly illuminated the courtyard, but the belfry at the far end of the courtyard was enveloped in darkness. The bell was gone. Chu-ch'ôl recalled what the men at the store had said.

"Looks like they couldn't get here 'cause of the snow, eh?"
"Assholes! Why they makin' a fuss now? The bell's been gone for months."

The living quarters were silent. Somewhere in the darkness a branch snapped under the weight of the snow. From one of the rooms came the sound of even breathing. It joined the rustle of the snow and brushed over him. Where were Uncle Tal-gyun and Chu-ôn? Were they here or had they managed to kill each other on the way up the hill? And where was Yun-gil?

Chu-ch'ôl cleared his throat, then lifted a snowy foot and thumped it on the stepping stone beneath the front porch. The second door creaked open.

"Who is it?" scratched the voice of an old woman. The pungent odor of feces and rotting flesh drifted from the room. She looked like a ghost in the dim light filtering from the next room. Her hair was as white as leeks, her face wrinkled, and her cheeks hollow. She leaned an ear toward him. Though nearly deaf, she wanted to hear what the stranger had to say.

It was the old Widow Chông, Pak Ho-nam's concubine and mother of Ssang-do and Ssang-gyun.

Recalling her beauty in middle age, Chu-ch'ôl stepped closer. "It's me, Chu-ch'ôl," he said. His voice echoed over the snow-covered courtyard.

"Who? Ssang-do?" she asked, turning her ear to him once more. Her voice whistled like wind from a pair of bellows.

The door to the room next to the kitchen burst open and Tal-gyun stepped onto the porch.

"How did you get through all this snow? Come on in. Are you all right?"

Tal-gyun sounded like he was trying, unsuccessfully, to hide his anger. As he showed Chu-ch'ôl into the room, the old woman's door creaked shut. Chu-ch'ôl looked up to see a younger woman standing with her back to the door, staring at him. It was Tal-gyun's wife. How had she managed to get the old woman back inside so quickly?

"It's cold. Quick, come on in," Tal-gyun urged. The two men used the respectful form of speech for the uncle was younger than the nephew. Chu-ch'ôl struggled to move his feet. His legs were shaking.

"You could have waited till daylight but I know.... This son of a bitch.... What's he tryin' to do anyway? I can't stand this. I'm gonna have it out with him tonight, whether it kills one of us or not," Tal-gyun growled as he watched Chu-ch'ôl clamber onto the porch.

Chu-ch'ôl took off his wet socks, rubbed his feet with a rag and stepped across the room to sit on the warmest part of the floor as Tal-gyun directed. Chu-ôn stood just inside the door, looking down at him. He seemed uneasy, as if he had done something wrong, yet his cheeks and lips puffed out in a dissatisfied expression. Chu-ch'ôl looked up and, in an indifferent tone, told him to sit.

"I'm glad you're here," Chu-ôn said, sitting down. "Now I can tell you how I really feel."

Chu-ch'ôl tucked his hands under his buttocks and looked around the room. A latticed window opened onto the backyard, and on the wall next to it hung a woman's skirt and sweater. A ragged child's corduroy jacket, a few pieces of underwear and some socks were scattered across the floor. Next to them lay a dark red blanket and a crumpled quilt with cotton batting poking through the seams. Two grimy pillows lay on top of the blanket. In the corner next to the door was a flat bush clover basket filled with boiled sweet potatoes. Brownish sweet potato skins and a few half-eaten pieces were scattered along the edge of the basket.

Chu-ch'ôl dropped his head. He remembered the taste of the boiled sweet potatoes he used to eat on winter nights as a child. Tal-gyun's wife and children must have been banished to the old woman's room when Chu-ôn and Tal-gyun arrived. Where was Yun-gil? Was he down at the stern of this unwieldy ship? Why wasn't he in here? Was Chu-ôn going to arrest him tomorrow? Would he really do it, just to fulfill his duty? And would Yun-gil follow him obediently to Seoul or would he run off? And what about Tal-gyun? Would he just sit by and watch? What am I supposed to do? Chu-ch'ôl thought. Aren't I supposed to punch Chu-ôn out and rave at his cruelty?

"Your clothes are all wet and we ain't got nothin' for you to wear! At least the room's warm...don't have no decent blankets." Tal-gyun bit his lip at his ineffectualness.

Chu-ôn sat with his head bowed and hands tucked between his thighs, waiting for a chance to speak. When Chu-ch'ôl took out a cigarette and brought it to his lips, Chu-ôn flicked open his lighter and extended it in Chu-ch'ôl's direction. Tal-gyun reached for a sooty tin can and placed it in front of Chu-ch'ôl. The door opened quietly and a woman's face appeared. She looked from face to face, without the slightest embarrassment or shyness. Her eyes lingered on Chu-ch'ôl, crinkling in a smile. The woman reminded him of the Hahoe bride's mask, with her half-moon eyes, long face, and guileless, yet wanton smile.

"Get to bed, woman! What are you hangin' round here for?" Tal-gyun thundered.

She smiled nervously, seemingly intimidated by her husband's tone. "Me? I figured our guests were hungry so I thought I'd make some supper and heat the room a bit." The sluggish drawl and pouting lips suited her shiny face and neck.

"We don't need any food. Shut the door and go to bed!" Tal-gyun clattered, his eyes seething with anger. The woman ignored him and stood at the door, glancing back and forth between Chu-ch'ŏl and Chu-ôn. Tal-gyun jumped to his feet to push her out and slam the door. Chu-ch'ŏl was embarrassed, but Tal-gyun smiled awkwardly. "Her problem's she likes people too much. She's always tryin' to help out, even when I haven't asked her to..."

The room was still except for the sound of Chu-ch'ŏl exhaling from his cigarette. Dishes rattled in the kitchen. A branch snapped nearby. The three men sat in silence. Then Chu-ôn spoke.

"Excuse me, but I'd like to have a smoke."

Chu-ch'ŏl pushed his cigarettes in Chu-ôn's direction, but Chu-ôn pulled a pack from his pocket. Tal-gyun lit up as well. A door opened and shut at the other end of the building. Then they heard a man's gravelly cough. A pair of rubber shoes shuffled toward their door.

As he drew on his cigarette, Chu-ch'ŏl had an eerie feeling: Who was that coughing? Something told him it wasn't Yun-gil. Was there another man here?

The door opened and Tal-gyun's wife poked her head in. A cold wind rushed through the door. Chu-ch'ŏl had grown accustomed to the warm room. Tal-gyun glared at his wife.

"I told you to get your ass into Mother's room and go to sleep. Why do you keep stickin' your nose in here?"

The woman ignored him and stepped inside. She crossed the room, placed an earthenware bowl in front of Chu-ch'ŏl, then sat down, her legs folded neatly to the side, and looked at him. "Our *tongch'imi* is famous," she beamed brightly. "We ain't got nothing but boiled sweet potatoes, so if you get hungry, have a sweet potato and drink some of this *tongch'imi* stock. It'll make the sweet potatoes go down better."

When she smiled, her thick lips pulled back to reveal pale green gums. She kept smiling and her eyes traveled slowly back and forth, the whites showing around her irises. It wasn't out of friendliness, Chu-ch'ŏl thought. Either she was a bit off in the head or she was a nymphomaniac who went after every strange man she met. The woman gazed shyly at him and swallowed several times. Her breathing was shallow.

"All right, you've brought the *tongch'imi*, now off to bed."

Tal-gyun gave his wife a poke and she left without protest. Then an old man's face appeared at the door. Chu-ch'ŏl felt goose bumps forming all over his body. Tal-gyun turned away as soon as he saw the old man and began puffing furiously on his cigarette. Chu-ch'ŏl and Chu-ôn stared at the stranger in mute bewilderment. He glanced from face to face, then tottered inside.

Chu-ch'ŏl gave Tal-gyun an inquiring look, but Tal-gyun was staring at the ceiling. Chu-ch'ŏl had no choice but to face the old man, who by then had collapsed with his back to the door.

"I'm afraid I don't know you, but please come over here and sit on the warm spot," Chu-ch'ŏl offered. The old man shook his head in irritation and looked across at him. Chu-ch'ŏl smelled death on the man. Suppressing a shudder, he studied the man's face. Who is he? A face leaped from the depths of his memory. Yes, it was Ssang-do, the chief of the commando unit during the communists' rule. The one who carried two swords. No, it was Ssang-gyun. Chu-ch'ŏl felt a stabbing pain that pierced his heart like slivers of ice.

"You're Uncle Ssang-gyun, aren't you?" he asked hesitantly. He did not know how to act. He hadn't seen the man for decades. His father had treated Ssang-gyun and his brother well but they had repaid him with death. Actually, Ssang-gyun had gone to the Security Bureau several times to see if he could help; Ssang-do was the one who had taken Father in. Later, he went to hide on Chiri Mountain, and ultimately fled to North Korea. No one knew what happened to him after that.

Chu-ch'ôl stood and bowed deeply to the old man. Ssang-gyun took Chu-ch'ôl's hands. His eyes filled with tears, his lips and cheeks trembled slightly. The old man looked like a corpse; his hair and eyebrows were half-white. His cheekbones stuck out, and his cheeks and eyes were hollow. His neck was no thicker than Chu-ch'ôl's wrist, and his skin was the color of dust. Chu-ch'ôl looked down at the old man's hands. They looked like gnarled rakes, as if they had been covered in artificial leather to hold the bones together.

"Imagine seeing you before I die! The spirits must be watching over me," Ssang-gyun labored to move his lips and tongue, forcing the words out in a metallic whisper. His vocal chords were swollen. He stretched his neck, as if trying to swallow. Gasping for air, he shook Chu-ch'ôl's hands. The passing years have filtered out much of the pain and sorrow that had sliced at his bones and melted his skin, Chu-ch'ôl thought. I mustn't curse these people.

"Chu-ôn, get down and bow. It's Uncle Ssang-gyun. You must have heard of him. He's the second son of this household." Chu-ch'ôl then turned to Ssang-gyun. "This is Uncle Kae-dong's son. You know, Uncle Kae-dong, the one who used to work at the family saltworks."

Ssang-gyun shifted to face Chu-ôn who rose awkwardly and made a deep bow. Ssang-gyun took his hands as he had Chu-ch'ôl's and gathered breath to speak.

"So Dog Shit's son's all grown up! That old Dog Shit.... Do you realize how he used to look up to me? He was always calling me his big brother."

Chu-ôn's face hardened at Ssang-gyun's use of his father's childhood name. Kindling snapped in the kitchen and an acrid smoke seeped through a crack in the door. Tal-gyun's wife was stoking the fire that heated the *ondol* floor.

"Your father's in paradise now, Chu-ch'ôl. He did a lot of fine things when he was alive. I owe him my life! I tried to get them to take his name off the reactionary list, but they had me outnumbered..."

Ssang-gyun's metallic rasp grated Chu-ch'ôl's nerves like the scratch of a needle. Tal-gyun snuffed his cigarette out in the tin can and turned to Ssang-gyun. "Just shut up and get out of here. We have somethin' we need to discuss among ourselves."

"And why should I leave?" Ssang-gyun said with a scowl. There was a mesmerizing light in his eyes. "I've got a few things to say myself. I know they came here 'cause of Yun-gil. He's my relative too, you know."

"Keep your nose out of it. Why don't you just try to live the rest of your life in peace and repent all the terrible things you've done? You should be spendin' your final days chantin' Om Namo Amitabhaya Buddhaya!" Tal-gyun snapped.

Ssang-gyun struggled for breath as he stared at Tal-gyun.

"How many people have you killed anyway?" Tal-gyun continued. "You lived by the mercy of this world and now it's time you bent in silence and humbled yourself. How many dogs have you beaten to death? That's a violation of the Buddhist law against killin', ain't it? If you want to escape the knife mountains and the burnin' hell, you'd better chant till you take your last breath! Now get the hell out of here!"

Ssang-gyun seemed mystified. His lips and cheeks quivered as he struggled to speak.

"Can you really avoid hell by chanting?"

"That's what Mother says, and she's goin' on one-hundred!"

Ssang-gyun closed his eyes and lowered his head. Suddenly the door burst open and a young face with shaggy hair and a sprinkle of black stubble appeared. All eyes flew to the door. It was Yun-gil. He was dressed in a dark brown corduroy jacket with a fur-trimmed hood and a pair of baggy black pants.

"So you've come," he remarked sullenly, without so much as a bow to his father, then sat cross-legged by the window overlooking the backyard. Avoiding their eyes, he stared at a point over the door where Ssang-gyun sat. After a few moments, he reached for the bowl of *tongch'imi* and took a sip, then picked up a sweet potato and began to eat.

"I told you to stay put. Why'd you have to come in here?" Tal-gyun asked gruffly.

Yun-gil swallowed. "Just wanted to make my own case," he answered curtly.

Chu-ôn straightened up and looked at Yun-gil. "Thanks. I came to see you. I've got to talk to you, even if it takes all night."

"Ha," snorted Tal-gyun. Frowning deeply, Chu-ôn took out another cigarette and lit it, this time without asking the older men's permission.

"Don't you even think of draggin' Yun-gil to Seoul in handcuffs!" Tal-gyun warned. Then he turned to Yun-gil. "He ain't no relative. He's a cop. He's got a pistol and he's goin' to take you in. I heard he gets one million won and a promotion if he does."

Ssang-gyun's eyes flew to Chu-ôn's face. Yun-gil snorted as he munched on the sweet potato. "What's wrong with getting arrested if it helps Uncle Chu-ôn get a promotion?"

Chu-ôn tossed his head back and laughed loudly. Chu-ch'ôl snuffed out his cigarette and straightened up. The back of his neck felt tight, his chest full, and his head heavy. He felt completely helpless. He simply wanted to lie down on the floor, to forget everything and sleep.

"You've got me all wrong!" Chu-ôn turned to Tal-gyun. "I'm telling you: I didn't come for Yun-gil. I came for Chu-man's funeral. I just wanted to talk to Yun-gil as long as I was here."

"All right. Let's say you're tellin' the truth. You've seen him, so now what are you gonna do? Are you gonna let him go or are you gonna tell your buddies to come get him?" Tal-gyun was insistent.

Chu-ôn was equally determined. "That's none of your business. I'll do as I like."

"Fine. Just remember this. You're in the middle of the mountains here. The law's a long way off and the fists are right here. You'd better watch out or you won't get out of here in one piece. Look at my leg! Do you know how it got this way?" Tal-gyun spat out the words and clamped his mouth shut in a stubborn scowl.

"Why are you getting so worked up? Give him a chance to say something!" Ssang-gyun rasped. He then turned to Chu-ôn. "You should try to pay back the kindness your father got when he came to the Pak clan. He found a job, thanks to them, and got married and was able to raise you to what you are today."

No one appreciated Ssang-gyun's comment. Chu-ôn glowered, stubborn as a mule, and Tal-gyun nudged Ssang-gyun in the shoulder, pushing him toward the door.

"Brother, why don't you keep your nose out of our business? You've got enough problems! Just take it easy and try not to make life difficult for Mother. She's already got one foot in the grave. What did she ever do to you? How come you're always bickerin' with her?"

Ssang-gyun did not answer. He simply struggled for breath. Chu-ôn snubbed out his half-smoked cigarette and turned to Ssang-gyun. "Kindness, what kindness did my father ever get from them? Don't you ever mention my father again! And quit calling him Dog Shit!" Chu-ôn grabbed the bowl of *tongch'imi* and took several gulps of the tangy stock. "To tell you the truth, I can't remember how many times I wanted to kill my father. Do you know why? I'll bet Uncle Ssang-gyun knows. My father was the most pathetic man to walk the face of this earth. He *was* a fucking piece of dog shit! You know why? Yun-gil's right here, but all these rich assholes who run around saying they're part of the people's movement when they've never had a single hungry day in their lives...they are no better than my dick as far as I'm concerned. And now that I've brought it up.... Yun-gil, we've got things to discuss tonight."

The sound of kindling snapping and fire crackling in the firehole continued. The acrid smell of smoke filled the room. Chu-ôn was seething; his face was flushed, his nostrils distended. Yun-gil munched on the sweet potatoes as he listened. From time to time he took a sip of the *tongch'imi* stock. Ssang-gyun must have decided it was going to be a long night for he had crawled next to Chu-ch'ôl and stretched out on the floor.

"Brother, go lie down in your own room!" shouted Tal-gyun. Ssang-gyun ignored him and closed his eyes. Tal-gyun poked the older man in the side and jerked on his arm, but Ssang-gyun was immovable. Tal-gyun hurled the immobile arm to the floor.

Chu-ch'ôl thought of a large ship as he listened to Chu-ôn. Buried in that blizzard, the temple's living quarters were like a ship, slowly moving out to sea. I must be patient, he thought, settling back on the sidelines.

"Damn it! I may be the runt of a dog-shit beggar but I've got literary talent. I could be a first-rate writer if I put my mind to it."

So began Chu-ôn's story.

3

Chu-ôn's memories of his father began with the moaning of the reeds in late autumn, with the waves roaring like a herd of wild beasts, with the milky fog that lapped over the village like a living, breathing thing. Father's hair was always as coarse and unkempt as the reeds in the mudflats along the shore. One of his eyes was cloudy, like the muddy sea peeking through a break in the fog. It was not uncommon for the men of the village to beat him like a dog headed for a mid-summer's stew, and for Kae-dong to writhe on the ground like a worm when they finished with him.

"Those fucking bastards," Chu-ôn cursed whenever he thought of them.

Chu-ôn didn't know his mother. He dimly remembered gazing at the reeds and mudflats and sandy beach as he sat in his father's fish basket or rode back and forth on his father's back, steeped in the sour scent of his sweat. He often felt dizzy as he bounced along on his father's back, watching the sea roll in like a herd of bulls.

Sometimes he woke to find himself riding through the reeds. The white blossoms giggled, nodding their heads in the sunlight. Bundled in a thickly padded coat, he gazed into the air. The blue sky and white clouds swayed overhead; the lapping of the waves against the stern of the boat and the faint whisper of the sea intoxicated him. The smell of the tideflats was always with him.

Later, when he began to understand words, his father told him the sad tale of a man who raised his son without a mother. Drunk and sobbing, Kae-dong told the same stories over and over again: how he chewed barley to make a milky solution to feed the baby, how he begged the village women to share their milk, how he carried his son everywhere in a fish basket, how the baby fell asleep sucking his father's tongue like a nipple. Chu-ôn felt like he remembered it all.

He also remembered all Kae-dong's own experiences for his drunken father had tearfully recounted each one, from earliest childhood.

Kae-dong grew up in the house of the Moon Cake Shaman in Changsan. His mother left him there and never returned. His father had been tortured to death by the Japanese security police. It was a cruel legacy for a small boy. Kae-dong's grandfather had died fighting in the Tonghak Rebellion of 1894. His grandmother had put out the boy's eye on purpose. She did not want him to go out and become a leader of men.

He was named Kae-dong, "Dog Shit." His family had given him a humble name to protect him from jealous spirits.

He grew up with Knothead, the crippled son of the Moon Cake Shaman. Kae-dong only had one good eye but he could play the flute and the hourglass drum, gong and round drum more deftly than Knothead. He could make paper ceremonial flowers all by himself, recite all the words to the shaman's rites, and he danced well too. He learned the Ten Thousand Characters from old Mr. No, Knothead's father, a shaman himself, and could recite them backward and forward. He also knew his figures without the help of counting sticks. He and Knothead studied side by side, but he was soon acting the role of the teacher. From the age of fifteen, he followed the shaman to larger rites and filled in when necessary. He understood immediately what needed to be done. He was a gong player when there was none. He was the flute player when no one else could, and he played the fiddle when needed, too. He drank himself silly and, between rites, sang to the beat of an hourglass drum. People looked down on male shamans, but he led an exciting life. And every time there was a big rite, he ran into Pyôl-sun, the daughter of the shaman from Wolp'yông, who would always throw him a shy yet meaningful glance. On his way home he looked forward to the next rite in hopes of meeting her again.

If Kae-dong had continued to work as a shaman, Pyôl-sun might have been Chu-ôn's mother, but one day a farmhand from Pak Yong-nam's house came for him. He followed the man back to New Town where he was forced to kneel on the front steps and listen to a lecture from Yong-nam.

"You stupid fool! You've got Pak blood in your veins. You can't go around playing the shaman with those crazy folks from Spirit Hollow! You quit this very minute and come work for us. If you keep playing around with that hocus-pocus, I'll poke out your good eye and break both of your legs!"

From that day forward, Kae-dong lived in a straw hut by the saltworks.

One winter morning he found the body of a young woman on the edge of the flats. Passing fishermen and salt merchants spat on the body as they headed toward the pier. Some clucked in disgust. "What a terrible sight!" one man said. "If you're not gonna bury her, at least cover her with a straw mat or something!" Kae-dong found a mat to cover the body. Her skirt and blouse were ripped open by the waves, her hair was snarled like a tangled skein of hemp. He could see her pubic hair and navel, the plump mounds of her breasts and the round nipples. The body was swollen. She looked like a fat woman. No one claimed the body, and after two days Pak Yong-nam came out and ordered Kae-dong to bury it on the sandy hill above the saltflats.

Kae-dong wrapped the corpse in the straw mat and carried it up the hill. He dug a hole in the sand, spread the mat inside, and laid the body on top of it. He tore what was left of her tattered clothes to cover her breasts, pubic hair, navel and face, then folded the mat over her. A vision of the corpse opening its eyes and rising from the grave passed before his eyes and he hurried to shovel sand over the grave. Kae-dong met several women after that. Perhaps it was because of her ghost.

Chong-wol was the first. She was the kitchen maid at Pak Yong-nam's house. It was her job to bring Kae-dong's meals to the saltworks twice a day. Every morning she would come, balancing a basket with his breakfast and lunch on her head, and in the evening she returned with supper and carried the empty dishes back. At first she did not like Kae-dong because of his eye, yet she was painfully shy with him. While he ate, she squatted in front of the hut, rolling the hem of her skirt as she gazed out at Black Island. People said the densely forested island was haunted. The Moon Cake Shaman went there to prepare for special rites. Whenever someone had a new boat built or the fishing boats were heading out to sea, the owners would commission a rite of the shaman. And twice a year, before the first and eight full moons, she went to the island to prepare for the village tutelary rites. Sometimes families hired her to conduct three-day services to the spirits in hopes of protecting family members or curing illnesses. Some rites lasted ten days. Kae-dong had been to the island several times with the Moon Cake Shaman.

"Wanna watch her perform a rite sometime? Unclean women ain't supposed to go, you know," Kae-dong often teased her as he handed her the empty food basket, and Chong-wol smiled bashfully and ran off, skirts flapping.

One day he heard that Chong-wol was being forced into the Japanese Comfort Women Corps. Man-su, who worked at the saltworks with Kae-dong, said she could get out of it if she had someone to marry her.

"I hear they're gonna ship 'em out by boat. All you have to do is go up to the officer and tell him you two are engaged.

What do you got to lose? Tell'em you already did it and she might be in a family way."

Early the next morning five girls, one from each of the nearby villages, were marched past the saltflats, accompanied by their respective village heads, and a policeman with a sword hanging from his belt. Kae-dong approached Pak Tal-ho, the head of his village.

"Chong-wol and me.... She...she might as well be my wife," he whimpered.

Tal-ho, the son of Pak Yong-nam, seemed confused for a moment, then shook his head. "That policeman's not going to believe you."

Kae-dong went to the policeman and repeated what he had said to Tal-ho. The policeman was Korean. His face flushed. Then he began to bellow. "You idiot! Throwing salt on this sacred mission! I ought to kill you!" He slapped Kae-dong across the face and beat him with the sheath of his sword. When Kae-dong dropped to his knees in pain, the man booted him in the head. When he collapsed on his side, he kicked him in the ribs. Kae-dong was still writhing in the sand as the policeman loaded the young women onto a boat and left.

Later he learned Tal-ho could have made the policeman leave Chong-wol behind, but he had his own reason for volunteering his kitchen maid for service in the Comfort Women Corps: his father had been sleeping with the girl for some time. Tal-ho was afraid word would get out so he had taken this opportunity to banish her from the village.

Man-su had seen Chong-wol being loaded onto the boat.

"She kept wiping her eyes and looking back at you lyin' there in the sand."

Times were hard. Young men were conscripted into the Japanese military and labor camps, and the colonial authorities demanded regular quotas of brass, sappy pine, grain and cotton seedlings. Kae-dong did not have to worry about being drafted. Shit, he thought, I wish I could go. He envied the young men going off to war, surrounded by well-wishers, dashing heroes in their blood-red headbands and sashes emblazoned with the words "Victory in Battle!" But what could he do with only one eye? He just carried load after load of grain and sappy pine and cotton seedlings to the dock at Hoeryong.

After liberation, Ssang-do came to Kae-dong's hut and asked him to do some errands. "When the good times come, I'll make sure you get the saltworks," he promised, grasping Kae-dong's hand. "But don't tell anybody I was here, no matter what. You and me—we got nothing. Our fathers left this world bitter men. One slip of the tongue and the good times'll never come."

It was Kae-dong's job to go from village to village, summoning Tok-ch'il, Tong-man, Song-gon and Pu-ch'il to secret meetings. Ssang-gyun and Pu-ch'il came to the saltworks to paint slogans on pasteboard signs. *Long Live Field Marshal Kim Il Sung! Punish Japanese Collaborators and Evil Landlords! Long Live the People's Republic! Down with American Imperialism!* Under the cover of darkness, Kae-dong pasted the signs around the village, on the Spirit Tree and the walls of the mill, on the gates facing the alleys. They buried the paintbrush, ink stone and leftover pasteboard under a pile of straw mats in the salt warehouse.

One night the mimeograph machine was stolen from Taeri Elementary School. Song-gon and P'an-gil, two young men from Taeri, were responsible. They brought it to the saltworks and disappeared like the wind. Kae-dong hid it between some old straw bags behind the warehouse. Three days later Ssang-gyun and Pu-ch'il made flyers, and the following night Kae-dong went through the village, throwing them over the walls of rich pro-Japanese villagers and pasting them on the Spirit Tree and mill walls. The flyers demanded that the landlords and pro-

Japanese profiteers wake up and return what they and the Japanese imperialists had stolen.

Then the Yôsu Rebellion broke out, Sea Cloud Temple burned down, Pak Ho-nam was murdered, the young men connected to the murder fled, and their underlings were arrested, to be beaten until their backsides were bloody. Fortunately no one revealed that the saltworks was their secret meeting place. The anti-guerilla forces streamed over the island like a swarm of wasps, but nothing happened to the saltworks, Man-su or Kae-dong.

One afternoon in late autumn Kae-dong ran into Pyôl-sun on his way back from delivering a load of salt to the dock in Hoeryong. To his great surprise, she was dressed in a ceremonial green blouse and red skirt. Her face was powdered, she had circles of rouge on her forehead and cheeks, and on top of her head was a bride's crown. She was getting married, and Knothead, the son of the Moon Cake Shaman, was to be her groom.

Shaman No, Knothead's father, was delighted to see Kae-dong and asked him to let them use the salt skiff to cross the harbor. It seemed the ferry was under repair and they needed someone to carry the bride's procession.

A northwesterly wind roared with the force of a raging fire. The villagers believed the wind god stirred the wind to sweep away the layer of yellow sand that settled over the mountains and sea at that time of year.

Since he had to return to the saltflats anyway, Kae-dong rowed the bride and her guests across. His heart pounded the whole way. If he had stayed at the shaman's house, Pyôl-sun might have been his bride, not Knothead's. He felt sad, depressed, and angry. He despised Pak Yong-nam for dragging him to that dilapidated hut by the saltworks.

Knothead and his mother were waiting at the ferry landing. A shaman's wedding rarely had many well-wishers. Only a handful of old women from Spirit Hollow accompanied the groom's party.

As Kae-dong touched the bow of the skiff to the broad black rock that marked the ferry landing, waves crashed against the stern and the skiff bobbed violently. The guests scrambled onto the rock, trembling with fear. Soon everyone was hollering for someone to bring the bride ashore, but no one volunteered.

"Hey, Bridegroom! Why don't you carry her over on your back?" someone quipped. Considering Knothead's crippled leg, it was clear they had only meant to tease him. Kae-dong stood on shore, clutching the bow rope, but the skiff kept banging against the rock. It would splinter apart if they waited for the bride to jump ashore herself. Pyôl-sun shivered in the stern, her face green with fright. Kae-dong jumped into the skiff like a bolt of lightning and swept the bride into his arms. As he leapt back to shore he caught a whiff of the camellia oil in her hair and the fresh powder that covered her face and neck. That scent would torture him for years to come.

"Kae-dong, leave the skiff here and help carry the bride's palanquin. We found someone to lend us a palanquin but there's no one to carry it," the bridegroom's father explained as Kae-dong set the bride down on the black rock.

Kae-dong was drunk on her fragrance. Unable to tell them he needed to get back to the saltflats, he said he would.

He threw the anchor into the waves and lifted the palanquin to his shoulder. A bachelor still, he was setting aside his business to carry the bridal palanquin of a shaman family everyone looked down on. That was how he met the beggar woman.

As he carried the palanquin up the hill a young woman, clutching a white bundle of clothes, followed him. She picked some wild chrysanthemums and asters along the edge of the road and stuck them in her hair and at the bodice to her dress. When Kae-dong, dripping in sweat, finally set the palanquin down in the shaman's yard, the beggar woman handed him a bunch of flowers. In the confusion of the moment, he accepted it and someone called out, "Come on you two! Why don't you get married today?"

"Yeah, why not?" laughed the others. "Looks like you were made for each other!" Kae-dong felt the blood rushing to his face. It was hot, as if someone had poured burning coals over him. He threw the flowers to the ground and returned to the ferry landing. The woman followed him at several paces. He drew in the stern line and pulled the skiff closer to the rock. Just as he was about to climb in, the woman hopped past him and settled into the seat at the bow. He ordered her out, but she only wrinkled her nose and shrugged. He had no choice but to row back to the saltworks with her.

When he reached the edge of the saltflats, he shooed the woman onto the dike, anchored the skiff and went into his hut. The woman followed him, still clutching the bundle of clothes in her arms. The scent of Pyôl-sun, now Knothead's wife, lingered in his nostrils. Her weight and warmth remained in his arms and chest, her pale features blooming in his mind like a magnolia.

"You miserable hag! Get out of here before I beat the shit out of you!" Kae-dong snarled, shoving the woman away. She did not want to leave, though, and when she turned to him, whimpering, he slapped her on the shoulder. He struck her in the head and shoved her out of the door. She sniveled noiselessly and turned reluctantly toward the village. That night she returned with a large bowl of rice she had gotten begging in the village. He sent her away once more and went to Pak Yong-nam's house for supper. Chong-wol had not returned after liberation. A widow, well over forty, had taken her place in the Pak kitchen, but she was not as spry as Chong-wol and never had the time to deliver his meals to the saltworks.

The next morning he woke to find the beggar woman lying beside him. He beat her once more and sent her on her way. She was clearly half crazy. She grinned foolishly and devoured her food as if she were starving. She followed him around like an obedient wife. When he beat her, she shrunk back in sadness, as if it hurt to be beaten by her husband. Who was this woman? She had to be someone's daughter-in-law, someone's daughter. How had she ended up like this?

After beating her and sending her off to the village, Kae-dong set to work, scooping water from the saltflats, and waited for Man-su to come with his breakfast. The woman returned with another bowl of rice from the village. She watched him carefully as she settled down to eat in a patch of sun by the corner of the hut. He debated whether to beat her again, but decided to ignore her.

"Come on, Kae-dong, why don't you just shack up with her and be done with it?" Man-su joked when he arrived. As Kae-dong wolfed down his bowl of barley, Man-su packed his pipe with dried radish leaves. "From what I hear, she's a real sad case. They say she's the daughter-in-law of that Nok-dong granny across the way, but the family got wiped out in the trouble. I know they were in cahoots with the Japs and everything, but I feel sorry for her. She was the only one to survive. Her husband and parents-in-law were all shot and burned."

Kae-dong looked at the woman. She wasn't bad-looking. She wouldn't have given him a second glance if she hadn't been crazy.

"I'm serious! Why don't you sleep with her tonight? You know, people say one night with a man can make a crazy woman snap back to normal."

Kae-dong fumed at the suggestion. Man-su looked down on him because he had only one eye and no family.

"You sleep with her! I'll stay in the village tonight. I'd rather slam my dick in the door than sleep with that crazy bitch!"

In the middle of the night, Kae-dong was dragged off to the police station and beaten. They took Man-su too. Song-gon had been implicated in the theft of the mimeograph machine, and in the process of torturing him, the police had learned of the involvement of the saltwork boys. Now the police wanted to know who had used the mimeograph machine. They were trying to uproot the secret circle like a vine of sweet potatoes. They tortured the boys with leg-screws, beat them with sticks, pinned them to the floor and poured water spiked with red pepper powder up their noses. Kae-dong and Man-su had to talk, but they only gave the names of men who had already fled.

The police then told them to name anyone who had ever visited the saltworks, for any reason. Illicit sales of salt were exposed, and everyone who had ever stopped for a smoke or a joke on their way fishing got a taste of the policemen's sticks. Kae-dong and Man-su were released after three days, thanks to the good graces of Pak Tal-ho, but they couldn't walk. Man-su's family and a servant from Tal-ho's house had to carry them home. When Kae-dong returned to his hut on the back of Tal-ho's servant, the beggar woman hugged him and wept.

Abandoned in his hut like an old mop, Kae-dong lay groaning when Pak Tal-ho arrived with some medicine for his oozing buttocks. He gave it to the whimpering woman, who squatted by the door, then explained how to make a medicinal brew of fresh seaweed and dog shit. A servant brought a basket of food from the house every day, and the woman set about gathering dog droppings. Five or six times a day she pressed a chipped bowl of the pungent liquid upon him, and each time he would rise on his knees like an animal and drink it. When he finished, she would giggle with delight. She sounded like a baby in swaddling clothes, gurgling at its mother when she clicked her tongue or nodded in fun. The woman helped him eat and go to the outhouse, she washed his face and hands and neck with a wet towel, and was always careful not to provoke his anger.

When the wounds healed and the pain began to recede, Kae-dong went back to work at the saltworks, scooping water from the flats, sweeping salt into piles, and carrying heavy bags. The night after his first day back at work, he slept with the woman. It was his first time and she clutched his shoulders and wept from start to finish.

The next day the woman went begging to the village and returned with enough rice for two people. She asked him to eat with her since the servant from Pak's house was late that day.

The rumor spread through the village.

The beggar woman went from house to house asking for food. "Can I please have another spoonful?" she pleaded. "I'm gonna share it with my husband. And how about a little more kimchi?"

"Who is your husband?" the village women asked. "Dog Shit," she replied with a shy smile.

Sometimes the village women were naughty. "What do you do with your husband at night?" they asked. "Which part does he like best?"

The beggar woman answered frankly. She even lifted her skirt to reveal her white belly and proclaim, "I've got a baby."

She really was pregnant. Kae-dong had to act the part of her husband. He started by preventing her from going to the village to beg. He shared the food from Pak's house or smuggled a bowl of rice after eating in the village. It didn't work as he planned, though. As her stomach grew, she wanted more: meat and eggplant, cucumbers, melons and persimmons. If she heard someone was making red bean porridge, she went to ask for a bowl. When a family was holding ancestral rituals, she begged for rice cakes, and if a household was hiring temporary farmhands, she asked for a bite of the sour watercress they served with the workers' lunch. She would have eaten even more, like a pig with its snout to the ground, if people had not teased her. "Your baby'll die if you eat that," they said, and she spat out whatever was in her mouth. She even tried to make herself vomit. The kids enjoyed watching her and often gave her a piece of rice cake or sweet potato, only to tell her they had put rat poison in it just as she was about to finish. She clenched her teeth and rolled her eyes and shook her fist as if she were going to beat the teasing brats to death. Then she stuck her finger down her throat and vomited.

In early spring, the year the Korean War broke out, the woman gave birth on a straw mat laid on the floor of the hut. She lost consciousness for a while, and when she awoke, she seemed quite normal. She clutched the bloody bundle of a baby in her skirts and wept with uncontrollable sorrow. When Kae-dong asked her to eat the seaweed soup he had made in a pot hanging over a fire at the opening to the hut, she startled awake and began grinning like a crazy person again.

She slipped back and forth between reason and madness after that. When she was feeling normal, she clutched the baby to her breast and cry. Then she shuddered and started to grin as if she had never been crying.

Man-su's wife brought an old baby blanket and rags to use as diapers, and Pak Tal-ho sent some baby clothes his wife had packed away. The beggar woman wandered through the village with the baby on her back. She flitted over the hills, across the fields, in and out of the alleys like a butterfly.

My baby, what a baby, kanggang sullaeyeee.

My baby, a diamond plucked from the sky, kanggang sullaeyeee.

My baby's a divine peach, kanggang sullaeyeee.
Like the sun, like the moon, kanggang sullaeyeee.
His eyes are bright stars, kanggang sullaeyeee.
His mouth is a red cherry, kanggang sullaeyeee.

The song never left her lips.
"Oh, what a pretty baby!"
"Kae-dong sure has a fine son!"
"His face is as bright as a full moon!"

The village women heaped their praises on the child whenever they ran into her on their way to the well or in the alleys around the village. And each time, she shifted the child from her back to look at him, as if to confirm what they said. She remembered the women who praised her child and later offered them the rice cakes, sweet potatoes and persimmons she collected on her rounds through the village. Sometimes she would even sneak some salt from the saltworks and give it to the women.

There was a long dry spell that year, and the saltworks were particularly busy. One day in early summer she laid the baby down in the hut, made a torch of an old straw mat, and began igniting fires in the corners of the hut. The storage building next door, where dried fish and anchovies were kept, was infested with mice, and their lice had invaded the hut. The baby was covered with red bites that were fast developing into oozing sores. He cried constantly. After getting the fretful child to sleep, she decided to get rid of the lice once and for all.

She was thrilled to think she could burn the villains that had been torturing her son. The walls of the hut were covered with clay, and the roof was made of straw thatch draped over a rafter and held down by a few thick ropes. The end of one of these ropes ignited. She didn't realize the fire was spreading to the roof and continued touching the torch to the walls and piles of straw bags.

"You horrible lice! Leave my baby alone!" she shouted. The hut filled with smoke. The baby cried fitfully. Red balls of fire leapt from the white smoke. The woman was surrounded by flames. She shrieked and fumbled around the floor. Finding the baby, she dashed out of the door.

"Oh, my poor baby! You almost got burnt! Who set our house on fire? They deserve to die!"

Clutching the baby she ran toward the sluice gate. Her skirt was on fire but she didn't know it. The flames gradually crept up her body. She screamed, never thinking to extinguish them. "Why's this fire followin' me?" she cried. "What am I gonna do with my baby! Oh my poor baby!"

She collapsed and rolled in a ball of fire, the bundle in her arms still. It was not her baby, though. It was the wooden pillow her husband used in the summertime.

Kae-dong was pedaling the water wheel, like a squirrel on a treadmill, the sweat dripping from every pore. He had moved more than half of the water from one flat to the next when he noticed a cloud of milky smoke rising from the hut. A red tongue of fire lapped through the smoke, and at the same time he heard the baby's terrified screams.

He leapt from the water wheel and ran toward the hut. That was when the woman emerged from the smoke. Her skirt was on fire.

"You stupid woman, jump in the water," he shouted.

She did not seem to hear him. She ran around in circles, as if she had been stung by a bee. She was holding something in her arms, but Kae-dong could tell it wasn't the baby. It was too small. She had reached the middle of the bank between the saltflats but he still heard the baby shrieking from the other direction. When he reached the hut, the roof was on fire and the baby's crying had stopped. The corner where the baby usually slept was empty except for the thick white smoke. He groped through the straw on the floor and found the grimy blanket. The baby was lying on it, but he wasn't breathing. Kae-dong wrapped the lifeless body in the blanket and rushed outside. As he stepped through the door, the roof crashed to the ground. The flames lapped even more fiercely now. Kae-dong ran for the bank, shaking the baby, slapping his cheeks and buttocks, sucking his nose.

He buried the woman on the sandy hill above the saltflats as he had done with the woman's corpse that had floated in on the tide. He lived alone after that, raising the son he had somehow managed to revive.

The communists came into power. The People's Army arrived in the village and everyone was ordered to assemble on the beach. Ssang-do and Ssang-gyun were there along with Pu-ch'il, Song-gon, Tong-man and Tok-ch'il. Pu-ch'il strapped a red arm band on Kae-dong who stood holding the baby. Kae-dong was confused. "The saltworks are yours now," Pu-ch'il explained. "The time has come for the propertyless masses to live with dignity. Ssang-do and Ssang-gyun are going to head up the security bureau and local people's committee. I'll tell them to assign the saltworks to you and Man-su."

That night, when he returned home, Kae-dong danced a jig with the baby in his arms. If he and Man-su split the salt harvest, he would be a rich man in no time. He could buy a house, give his son a good education, and live like a king. Knothead had been dead for a year by then. Now that the communists were in control, shamans were no longer untouchable so he could take Pyŏl-sun as his wife. The waves splashed against the bank in front of the saltworks. There wasn't a cloud in the sky. The stars blinked blue, yellow and red, like tiny eyes. No, like flowers or tiny bells. They seemed to laugh, shaking their petals and ringing in celebration of Kae-dong's overnight success.

It turned out to be nothing more than a dream, though. The People's Committee, Security Bureau and local party committee all took a share of the harvest, and when the right-wing police came back in power, Kae-dong was nearly shot for trying to take over the saltworks and diverting profits from the sale of the salt to the communists.

The police chief jailed the communist sympathizers in a warehouse. Rightists, who had been persecuted by the communists or who had somehow managed to avoid the earlier purge, sat in the jury's box and named the rebels one by one.

"What shall we do with this bastard Kim? As vice chairman of the People's Committee, he had Hwang Sang-su murdered for reactionary behavior."

Tribunal rules allowed the suspension of executions on the word of a single juror, but when the jurors remained silent, the police chief nodded to the door and the accused was taken to the killing field. Kae-dong was saved on the word of Pak Sang-ho from Sinsang. Pak said Kae-dong had testified on Pak Tal-ho's behalf when he was brought before the People's Tribunal and had been rebuked by an officer from the People's Security Bureau for his loyalty. Kae-dong was thus spared, but he could not work at the saltworks anymore. He built a shack at the entrance to the village and eked out a living fishing from the quay, trolling with an old wreck of a boat and helping with the farm work at Chu-ch'ôl's place.

That was the end of the saltworks. The real owner was Chu-hong, Pak Ho-nam's eldest grandson. He had been a captain in the Korean War and made quite a name for himself, but then he was wounded during the January 1951 retreat and discharged. He sold everything—the house, the land and the saltworks—and left for the city. The new owner of the saltworks rented the land out to tenant farmers.

Kae-dong lived in his shack and did odd jobs around the village. He emptied outhouses, embalmed corpses, dug graves, gathered old bones when a grave was moved, buried the bodies of wandering lepers that no one else would touch, killed dogs for summer stews, and slaughtered pigs and oxen, all with the baby on his back.

He was often the victim of terrible and undeserved beatings. When someone sneaked into a young widow's bedroom, her relatives swarmed over Kae-dong's shack and beat him to a pulp. From that day forward, he kept his eyes to the ground wherever he went. He feared what might happen if he looked at a woman carrying a water bucket or fish basket through the village.

He was nearly killed one summer three years later. Chu-ôn was six at the time. The seaweed harvest had failed three years in a row, and the villagers decided to stage an extra large Sea Spirit Ritual. The rite was held every year on the Harvest Moon, but this year was going to be special. They selected the widowed shaman Pyôl-sun to perform the rite. The villagers took her a large bag of rice and asked her to go to Black Island and offer a sacrifice to the Sea Spirit.

Kae-dong couldn't sleep the first night. This was a golden opportunity to make Pyôl-sun his own. But no, he thought, shaking his head as he rocked Chu-ôn in his arms. He couldn't violate a shaman while she was offering a sacrifice. Still his heart fluttered at the thought of her alone on the island. All he needed to do was row across. She was sure to accept him. The scent of Pyôl-sun on her wedding day stirred in his nostrils and his nerves seemed to tingle. That night he dreamed of a woman beckoning him into a nearby forest. She was wearing the winged robes and red skirt of a shaman. It was the beggar woman. No, it wasn't. He looked again: It was the corpse that had drifted into the saltflats. He took a closer look and it was Chong-wol. No, it was Pyôl-sun. He followed her. She walked across the water to Black Island. He tried to follow her and sank. Gasping for air, he woke.

The next night he rowed his old boat to Black Island but was caught by a band of villagers guarding the island. He hadn't realized that the ceremonial masters of the village rite were standing guard over the island, lest anyone interfere with the shaman's preparations. When the sacrifice to the Sea Spirit was over, a village assembly was called and Kae-dong was beaten. He told them he had gone to the island to check his nets, but it was no use. For the rest of his life he suffered from headaches and pains in the chest and ribs because of that beating.

Pyôl-sun decided to live on Black island after the rite was completed. She set up a tent on the southern shore. The Moon Cake Shaman, her mother-in-law, tried to coax her back, but Pyôl-sun refused. When she wasn't offering sacrifices to the Sea Spirit, she dug clams and gathered seaweed, which she cooked in a pot balanced between two stones. People said she had been possessed by the Dragon King while preparing for the rite to the Sea Spirit. The villagers sometimes took her a bag or two of rice in hopes of a good catch.

Kae-dong went out fishing with Chu-ôn every night, except in winter. He moored the boat between Naedok Island and Black Island. When Chu-ôn awoke in the middle of the night, his father would be smoking in the stern, lonely and quiet as a ghost. In the early morning, he woke to find the boat anchored at one end of the island and his father climbing back in, smelling of the island grass.

Kae-dong did not go near the island before the annual sacrifice to the Sea Spirit. At those times Chu-ôn jerked awake at the sound of an enormous fish and a sudden listing of the boat, only to find his father climbing over the gunwale, panting from the long swim. Kae-dong would collapse in the bottom of the boat and start bailing the water that had collected while he was gone. The shaman's candle flickered on Black Island. Kae-dong swam to meet her in order to avoid the prying eyes of the ceremonial masters guarding the front of the island.

Pyôl-sun died that winter. She had contracted bronchitis after spending so many nights in the cold damp woods, and she was weakened by her pregnancy.

When the villagers learned Kae-dong was responsible for the baby in her belly, they threatened to kill him for violating the sacred island and seducing Pyôl-sun. When the seaweed crop failed, they got drunk and beat him again. He never left the village, though. After the beating he had a few drinks and cried, little Chu-ôn clutched in his arms.

From time to time, Kae-dong would pause from his chores in the village and look down at Black Island. "Listen, Chu-ôn," he would say. "You've got to make somethin' of yourself. Then you buy a piece of land overlookin' Black Island and bury me there."

It was a modest wish, and yet his longing was palpable. Chu-ôn had heard the wish so many times his ears ached for his father repeated the words every time he had a drink.

4

"I came home for winter vacation my second year in middle school and Father was drunk. He grabbed hold of me and started crying again. As I sat there in his arms, I wished he were dead. For no reason. Well, I pitied him, that's all. From that night forward, whenever I ran into one of the people who had beaten him when I was little, I imagined myself killing them. That's why I became a government spy after high school. I wasn't going to get into a reputable university after studying at a high school in the boondocks. Besides, I had hardly studied. So I entered a second-rate community college and became a spy. I bought a backpack and books with the money they gave me. I got a fake student I.D., and started attending K. University. I was supposed to incite demonstrations. I'd get things started, then sneak out the back and point out the student leaders. I'd also report when and where the next demonstration was planned. I studied Marxism and Kim Il Sung's Juche thought, and made friends with the students. We'd start the demonstrations together. Then I'd report on them when the time was right. I was like a vine: I was going to grow up the string that controlled me. I wanted to become bigger and more powerful than the people I wanted so much to kill. That's how I became what I am today."

Chu-ôn chain-smoked as he talked. Ssang-gyun lay on the floor, eyes closed, quiet as a dead man. Chu-ch'ôl was listening, though he had to struggle to keep from collapsing from exhaustion. Tal-gyun leaned against the wall, his hand to his forehead. Yun-gil sat with his eyes to the corner, chewing on a sweet potato. From time to time the sound of snapping kindling drifted in from the kitchen. It was still snowing. They could hear branches breaking under the weight of the snow. Chu-ôn exhaled a puff of smoke and continued.

"Actually, I'm grateful to my grandfather and father and that beggar woman and Pyôl-sun the shaman. They're the ones who made me what I am today. I'm grateful to the villagers who were so cruel to my father too. They gave me a taste for blood. They're the reason I'm a rightist."

Chu-ôn snickered and Yun-gil chuckled along with him as he munched a piece of radish from the *tongch'imi*. Tal-gyun glanced from Chu-ôn to Yun-gil. They seemed to have come to some kind of understanding.

"You could say I'm from the most basic class," Chu-ôn continued. "By birth, I should be leading the people's movement. But I wouldn't do it. I know the far left is all a sham. When I was in high school there was a gang. The sons of the local minister and police chief and the school principal all belonged. Whenever there was trouble, those boys were always in the middle of it. They were the ones who stabbed boys from other gangs, they were the ones who gang-raped girls out on dates in the park, they were the ones who put on masks and robbed their own houses. Now why was that? Because they had a complex about not belonging to the basic class. They were afraid that they would be isolated and ignored by the other boys if they didn't take the lead and cause trouble. Their fear made them act even more brutally. I came up here through all this snow because I wanted to talk to Yun-gil. Heart-to-heart. He's leaning dangerously close to left-wing adventurism and I want to talk to him. I want us to open up and be frank with each other."

"It looks like that complex applies to you, too, Uncle," Yun-gil said, taking a sip of the *tongch'imi* stock.

The room was too warm. The floor had gotten so hot they could barely sit on it. Chu-ôn mopped his forehead with his handkerchief, then looked down, reflecting on what Yun-gil had said. He reached for the *tongch'imi*. Ssang-gyun lay in silence.

"Hey, we're burnin' up in here," Tal-gyun yelled in the direction of the kitchen. "Stop feedin' that fire!"

The sound of the snapping kindling had stopped some time earlier. The door opened silently and Tal-gyun's wife appeared. The woman created a strange mood as she stood in the shadow of the paper door, beyond the warm pool of light streaming from the room. She was outlined by the bluish cast of the snow and looked strangely sly and seductive. She was smiling, a shy, innocent smile that had a way of mesmerizing men. Perhaps she cared for nothing but the sensual pleasures of men and women. Was Yun-gil safe with her?

"Why did you stoke the fire like that? Shut the door and get to bed! Right now!" Tal-gyun bellowed, rising to pull the door shut. His wife seemed accustomed to such treatment for she looked deliberately from face to face before closing the door silently. She won't sleep as long as she hears our voices, Chu-ch'ŏl thought. She'll toss and turn, her heart pounding over the smell and sound of the two strange men. She's like an animal, he thought. A wild beast living in a pristine forest, a red-blooded female animal.

"As far as I'm concerned," Yun-gil continued, "Uncle Chu-ŏn is no more than a hunting dog for the far right. No matter how well you perform on the job, they'll always distrust you for your roots. That's why you've taken the front line, manipulating people in the student movement and arresting them at all costs. You don't want to be accused of favoritism toward your family, so you've decided to go after me, to prove your loyalty. You said you wanted to be frank. How about being frank with yourself?"

"I didn't come here to catch you. You've got to believe that. I swear, I came for Chu-man's funeral," Chu-ŏn said in a plaintive, yet firm tone. "There's something I want to tell you. The democratic movement is good in the purest sense, but you have to avoid violence. Look what happened at the U.S. Information Service demonstration. You were there. Why throw Molotov cocktails at a cultural center? There's no excuse for an armed attack on innocent civilians. A man was killed and two more were injured. They were just using the library! You can try to glorify your anti-Americanism and anti-imperialism, but that was murder. This isn't Iran, or the Philippines, or Japan or France. We're a divided nation. Ideals are fine, but wait until Korea's unified. Ask your father. He'll agree with me, and I think Uncle Tal-gyun will too."

Chu-ôn did not bother to include Ssang-gyun. Yun-gil chewed more slowly now, as if he were getting full. His lips curled into a smirk. Chu-ch'ôl rolled a cigarette back and forth between his fingers.

"Well, I'm too ignorant for any of this," Tal-gyun said gruffly, staring at the door. "But after listenin' to Yun-gil, I can't help thinkin' he's right. If we're gonna unify this country and live together in a real democracy, we've got to get rid of the blue-eyed foreigners who back the dictatorship and treat us like slaves."

Chu-ôn snorted in reply. "You can blame whoever you like, but Korea isn't going to be unified. The U.S. and Japan are on this side, and the U.S.S.R and Red China are on the other. They'll never let us unify. What's in it for them? No, all we can do is try to prevent another war, increase our GNP and exports, and live a good life. Look! We've built all these factories and the whole world's in awe of our exports. What's the point of all this talk about anti-Americanism and anti-imperialism and unconditional unification? Do you want Vietnam-style unification, where they throw out everyone who's got enough to eat? If the United States turns its back on us, our factories will collapse. If they withdraw their troops and nuclear weapons, there'll be another Korean War and the whole country will go communist. A lot of people will die, and everyone else will have to start over from nothing. You can't just whine about nationalism; you've got to be realistic. As long as Korea's divided, we've got to accommodate the Americans. That's what I wanted to discuss with Yun-gil."

"Do you know what I feel when I hear you? Despair. That's the most serious problem facing our young people today. We have to rise up against that despair. Uncle Chu-ôn, how can you be so thoroughly corrupt? Why did they bring nuclear weapons to our country? It wasn't to protect us. They want to use our country as a bridgehead to take over the world.

"They're always saying North Korea has more weapons than South Korea. 'They have more soldiers. They're moving troops to the front line. They've bought dozens of MIGs from the Soviet Union.' The American newspapers make a big fuss. Then they sell their own expensive airplanes and rockets to our government. Soon American products will be flooding in without tariffs and Korea will turn into another American state. Our culture will deteriorate, and all that will be left is American culture. Don't tell us that there'll be another Korean War and Korea will go communist if the U.S. turns its back on us. Don't tell us that our GNP is higher than North Korea's. The North Koreans don't want a war. It's true! They don't live as well as us, but that's because of Kim Il Sung's self-reliance ideology. They eat less, they have fewer clothes, they don't enjoy themselves as much, but at least they haven't sold out to the major powers. Do you really think the North Koreans would prostitute themselves to the Chinese and Soviets? Do you think they do everything the Chinese and Soviets tell them to do? They don't. That's why their development has been a little slower than ours. They aren't slaves to China and Russia, politically, economically, or culturally. They can meet the South Koreans and discuss unification any time they want. They don't have to ask the Chinese or Soviets. South Korea's the problem. The South Koreans have to go to the U.S. for everything. Even the president needs their approval. That's why every young man with a conscience wants the Americans out. We want the Americans to take their nuclear weapons and get out of our country. We want Koreans to sit down with Koreans and discuss unification. Get rid of the masks and arms. And if we can't achieve this with words, we'll have to resort to violence."

Yun-gil paused to moisten his lips.

"Uncle Chu-ôn, why don't you take off that cloak of lies? Who are you playing the hunting dog for? Don't tarnish your grandfather's reputation. He gave his life for true human liberation. If he knew what you are doing now, I'm sure he'd turn over in his grave."

Chu-ôn lit a cigarette and grinned. You know what they say, the newborn pup has no fear of the tiger. Don't be a fool. Take my advice. Besides, I've got you in my noose already. You think you're pretty hot stuff but there's nothing you can do about the power that rules this land. Chu-ôn's face betrayed both confidence and arrogance.

"Listen up 'cause I'm going to be frank with you. Some time ago we had this discussion down at the office. I can't tell you who was there, but we were talking about people like you, people with corrupt thoughts. We were trying to figure out how many there really were. How many people can you really call anti-establishment? We estimated there are about ten thousand of them nationwide. Include their families and that makes about thirty-five thousand. Of course, there's no telling for sure.

"So we were wondering what we should do with these people. Should we clear off an island and stick them there? You know, intern them. But what law could we use? The Social Stability Law. Put simply, we'd be sweeping out the bad.

"Yun-gil, I'm just asking you not to waste your life. You're like an egg throwing itself against a rock. It doesn't bother the rock. The egg's the one that breaks. Ten thousand eggs can break but the Korean people will live on. You guys talk about getting rid of the Americans and the imperialists and all the conservatives and holding a constitutional assembly to establish a unified nation, but wake up! Don't you realize who's got the knife by the handle?"

Chu-ôn was getting excited. His words turned violent. He seemed to imply that he was only telling Yun-gil this because they were related. He puffed his chest out confidently for he believed that Chu-ch'ôl and Tal-gyun shared his feelings.

"I've listened to you two long enough. Now it's my turn," Chu-ch'ôl said. "Let's say a beggar boy came into a tearoom but the waitress sent him packing. What if he grew up to be a prosecutor? He might demand a heavy sentence for any defendant who happened to work in a tearoom. What if he became a general? He might be cruel and punish his subordinates unnecessarily. What if he became the president of a big company? He might misuse his wealth. He might put out a contract on someone or try to buy political power. Just think what the world would be like if we were all bent on revenge. Revenge is the most dangerous thing in the world. And Chu-ôn, you seem to be filled with it. Your life is governed by your determination to revenge your grandfather and father. You would have attached yourself to the ruling hierarchy even if it were socialist or communist. Let's be frank, Chu-ôn."

Chu-ôn looked up and burst out laughing. Tal-gyun nodded. "You're right," he said.

Ssang-gyun's breathing grew raspier. His eyelids, sunken and blue, quivered. He was listening to everything that was being said. Yun-gil was looking at the window, his back to his father. He knew where Chu-ch'ôl was headed. Now that he had finished with right-wing Chu-ôn, he would push Yun-gil to the far left and launch his attack. His father was conservative, rightist, nihilistic, opportunistic and revisionist. He pretended to be pure but he never acted on his conscience. Men pure in thought and passive in conscience stood by and watched the right-wing fascists take power. His father had taken the middle-of-the-road approach, fluttering back and forth between the right and the left like a bat. Yun-gil knew why. His father had seen so many deaths in the turbulent course of history. Yun-gil believed that a handful of rightists were able to run the country because the middle-of-the-roaders had been rendered powerless by nihilism and defeatism.

Chu-ch'ôl cleared his throat and continued.

"I can't blame you for doing your job. After all, you're supposed to be arresting the so-called anti-establishment element. I just wish you'd act out of goodness instead of revenge. Why do you have to play handmaiden to people like that? Can't you find another way to make a living? Can't you change your direction? I feel sorry for you. You need to wake up too. What do you mean: intern ten thousand people on an island? Are you nuts?"

Chu-ch'ôl's voice trailed off in despair. It was impossible to enlighten simpletons like Chu-ôn to the merciful love of the Buddha or Jesus, he thought. The realization sent him tumbling into a dim sense of discouragement. Chu-ôn simply smiled into space, his features as blank and emotionless as an ox. Chu-ch'ôl struggled for the energy to continue.

"The world operates on the law of opposites. If there's a radical right, a radical left naturally develops to counteract it. The right came into power on the coattails of the Americans who came here after dropping their nuclear bombs on Japan. Once they'd consolidated their power, the right had to persecute their opponents with ever greater intensity in order to stay in power, and the resistance grew in proportion to the persecution. Finally, the far left decides all conservatives, starting with the far right, have to be wiped out. Good people on both sides suffer as a result. Frankly, I'm on the right. I believe that we need gradual improvement, not radical reform. Yun-gil always criticizes me for my 'cancerous' bourgeois thoughts but I can't help thinking the recent wave of democratization started with people like me, invisible people who advocate gradual improvement.

"Now we have to be careful about a reactionary backlash against democratization. If the surge for gradual improvement is a dynamic force moving our society, the radical theories of the far right and far left, and the call for unconditional anti-Americanism and anti-imperialism and unconditional unification are all reactionary forces. The problem is we have to decide what is gradual improvement. What is the best path to democracy? It's clearly not communism or socialism..."

Chu-ch'ôl faltered. He felt a wave of helplessness spread through his body. He couldn't tell if that was what made him hesitate or vice versa. He was speaking without conviction. He was afraid of what Yun-gil might say. "Why should you align yourself with the haves, Father? What do you have? A house? An orchard? A monthly salary of one million won from your job as an editor at that best-seller factory? Is that what makes you afraid to stand with the masses? That's peanuts compared to what that asshole's in-laws have amassed. Are you really afraid of losing it?" Chu-ch'ôl wiped the sweat from his face with his handkerchief.

"Enough of this fightin'! It all sounds good to me. When Yun-gil talks, he makes sense. When Chu-ôn talks, he makes sense, and now that I hear what Chu-ch'ôl has to say, he makes sense too.... That's why the world's such a mess: everyone thinks they're right. I just don't like fightin'. And since I came back here to live, that's all there's been. Fightin' and more fightin'. The people from Temple Hollow are tryin' to beat the life out of me." Tal-gyun complained as he lit another cigarette.

Chu-ch'ôl thought of the barbed wire and black crosses he had seen on his way to the temple, the men he had encountered at the store. Ssang-gyun burst out in a fit of coughing. Chu-ôn took a sip from the *tongch'imi* bowl. Yun-gil kept gazing at the window, his back to the room.

"People just want what other people have. That's what it all comes down to." The door opened silently as Tal-gyun spoke. His wife peered in, her mask-like face outlined in the bluish light of the snow. She was holding a tray of food. The rasping voice of the old woman called from behind her.

"You stupid whore! Why don't you get to sleep? One whiff of those men and you're back there like a bitch in heat! Get in here!"

"Who asked you to bring this? Why are you makin' such a fuss?" Tal-gyun snapped.

The woman ignored him, though, and studied each face in the room. The smell of make-up wafted through the door. No, it was the smell of her body. Tal-gyun limped to the door, grabbed the tray and slammed the door in her face. She had sliced some radishes and sweet potatoes. Beside them were a handful of wooden matches to pick them up with. Tal-gyun set the tray in the middle of the room and went on with his story.

5

Tal-gyun pined for home. He was exhausted. He made his living junk-collecting. He pushed a cart around town, clanking a huge pair of scissors to announce his arrival. He carried a large bag of popcorn to reimburse people for what they gave him. No one had ever taught him how to use the scissors, but he played them well, making them sing like a gong in one of the farmers' bands he had heard as a child. And when he clanked the scissors, he felt happy. His step grew lighter and his shoulders danced to the rhythm. Soon his cart was piled high with old newspapers, iron boiler pipes, door frames, broken tape recorders, cartons, empty bottles and plastic containers. He exchanged these for cash, which he used to buy a comforting drink of *soju*.

When he first left Temple Hollow, he had planned to return as soon as he had saved enough to purchase an acre of paddy land. But money wasn't easy to come by. With only the sky as his roof, he wandered the country until he was over forty, but he still didn't have enough money to buy a single patch of land. He didn't have a wife either. He might end up a nameless corpse in a public crematorium.

So what if I don't have any money? I can farm the fields by the temple, tend the persimmon trees, and in winter I can go down to Sinsang and hire myself out for the seaweed harvest. I shouldn't be so greedy. What's so great about being rich? I'll go back when I find a woman who's willing to live with a poor man. I'll go back to my poor old mother. She's been waiting so long.

No sooner had he made up his mind than he began to hear the iron bell at night. As a child, he had heard it every day, morning and evening, but at the time he left the village, the bell at Sea Cloud Temple had been silent.

There was no one to ring the bell now. The monks had not rebuilt the temple. They had not returned to live in the temple. I'll go back and ring the bell myself, he thought.

I'll go as soon as I find a woman. But who'd want to live in that poor village? As he pushed his cart through the streets, he looked into the faces of the women passing by but none of them seemed right.

Then one sweltering summer day he parked his cart in a shady corner of the junk yard and took a nap. He was bowing before the Buddha in the Main Hall when someone came up and took his wrist. The hand was as cold as ice. He looked up and saw a woman. Her face was painted gold. "I am the Bodhisattva of Compassion," she said with a smile. "Let's go to your village together. I will be your wife." Tal-gyun was afraid, overwhelmed, and jerked from his sleep. It had been a dream, but a woman was looking down at him. It was O Ch'un-ja, the woman who later became his wife. She was eating a piece of corn. She broke it in half and thrust one half at him. The smile never left her face; it reminded him of the Hahoe bride's mask. She was wearing a purple blouse and a white slip-on skirt. When he saw her smile, his throat tightened. That night he slept with her in a cheap inn nearby. Even now, he didn't know where she came from or what she had been doing before she met him. She wouldn't say. He had named her O Ch'un-ja, the spring child. He watched her carefully, but she seemed to care for nothing but eating, sleeping with her husband, and flirting with other men. Sometimes he wondered if Ch'un-ja was simply dreaming a long dream, and he would get scared. What if she woke up one day and left him to return to her old life? I'd end up a rooster crowing into the sky, just like the lonely woodcutter who lost his fairy wife, he thought. His mother used to say that the fairy was able to leave the woodcutter because she had only two children to carry. If there had been three, she wouldn't have been able to carry them into the sky. Tal-gyun wanted to have three children as soon as possible, but it didn't work out. They had two children in the first two years, but there were no more after that. A family planning worker came from the local health center and tried to persuade him to have a vasectomy or Ch'un-ja to have a tubal ligation. He felt like he was going crazy.

When he returned to the village the bell was still there. The problem was the villagers wouldn't let him ring it.

He couldn't believe how the world had changed. Before he left Temple Hollow, everyone revered the Buddha. They went to the Buddha for everything: for babies, for good harvests, and for cures to their ills. They even went to the Buddha when their oxen and pigs gave birth. The first rice of the harvest was offered to the Buddha, and the first persimmons, chestnuts, sesame seeds, melons and watermelons were placed on an altar before him.

But now the path to the temple was blocked with barbed wire. They used scorched wooden crosses as fence posts. They built a church with a spire that pierced the sky on the path between the village and the temple, and they took down the two stone spirit posts that used to stand by the entrance to the village. They chiseled off the Buddhas carved in relief on the rocks behind the village and spray-painted a red cross in their place. The Maitreya Bodhisattva on Sunrise Peak had been destroyed as had the Buddha by the signal tower, and the villagers knocked down the pagodas that once stood in the temple courtyard.

Then one day they broke Tal-gyun's leg for ringing the bell. Soon after, a gang of thieves broke into the living quarters one stormy night, tied Tal-gyun's family up, and stole off with the bell. They wore masks and wouldn't let anyone turn on the lights. They never spoke a word and disappeared like a puff of wind. Tal-gyun couldn't tell if they were from Temple Hollow or if they had been called in from a nearby village.

The next day Tal-gyun reported the robbery to the police. According to the police, the bell was a valuable cultural artifact. Investigators were sent from the local police station, the national police and the Office of Cultural Properties. The strange thing was that Sea Cloud Temple was not listed with the Office of Cultural Properties. Nor was the bell. The people from the Office of Cultural Properties, afraid they would be accused of carelessness, told the police that the bell had no cultural value, and the police hastened to close the case, declaring it the work of some second-hand dealers. Later, the owner of the bell appeared asking the police to reopen the investigation, but it never was resumed.

The bell was owned by the foundation that ran the Buddha's Light High School in town. The people of Temple Hollow hated that foundation.

When the monks failed to return after the temple burned down, the villagers suddenly felt rich. There was no one to collect the rents on the land or fruit trees. The Pak clan wanted nothing to do with temple finances after Ho-nam's death. The land belonged to the tenants now. Some people farmed an acre, others three acres or more. Some people cared for just one or two persimmon trees, others ten or twenty. When the persimmon harvest was good for several years in a row, people said they wouldn't exchange their trees for paddy land. There was no need for fertilizer or pesticides with persimmon trees, no transplanting or weeding or spreading compost. Tending a persimmon tree was easy as pie and required none of the fuss of farming. The people of Temple Hollow paid no rent for several years. They attributed their good fortune to the Buddhas and Maitreyas carved in the surrounding mountains. The Buddha in the temple's Main Hall was gone, but the villagers found their own Buddhas in the mountains and made regular offerings with great care and respect.

Tal-gyun's family, on the other hand, grew poorer with each passing day. They had eaten well when the monks were collecting rents and watching over temple affairs, and the villagers were making generous offerings of food to the Buddha. But now that Pak Ho-nam was dead and the temple abandoned, they had nothing. It was this poverty that had driven Tal-gyun to leave.

A year after he left, two men from the Buddha's Light High School Foundation came. They went around the village with a list of the temple's property, checking who worked which land

and demanding rents from that year's harvest. They even charged rent on the chestnut and persimmon trees. The former head monk had donated all temple property to the school foundation when the school was established. The villagers agreed to pay the rents at first but then they held a town meeting.

"It's not fair. How could they turn over the temple's assets to the school foundation without letting us know? After all, the temple was already abandoned. The rents we paid over the years more than cover the price of those fields. We can't just sit back and watch!" said Ko Ch'ang-sôk. He had been village head for three years after his discharge from the army as a sergeant.

"We've got to stick together. Let's tell them we won't pay, even if it means we can't work the land," said Pae Tong-jun. A chaplain's assistant while in the army, he had failed in an attempt at seaweed farming in Sinsang and had returned to the village to tend an acre and a half of paddy land and ten persimmon trees.

"Let's just say we won't work the land if they charge rent. Who'd come all the way up here to work this land?" added the current village head, Song Chae-dong. A heavy-set man, Song had graduated from agricultural high school and made a good income growing black mushrooms.

These three young men formed the nucleus of village resistance to the foundation's demands. Pae brought his friend, the Reverend Kim Mok-ho, to the village. They built a church in the field next to the path leading to the temple. The field belonged to the temple, of course. Pae told the villagers that every paddy and field, every persimmon and chestnut tree belonged to God. If they wanted to tend God's possessions they had to become God's children, and in order to become God's children, they had to renounce idol worship.

Once they had built the church and started destroying the stone spirit posts and the Buddhist statues in the mountains, the people of Temple Hollow hated Tal-gyun's family. The villagers abandoned the Buddha and turned to God for the sole purpose of taking over the temple land and trees.

With the bell gone, Tal-gyun lost his taste for life. He could still hear it, reverberating across the fields to echo off of Sunrise Peak before floating into the sky. He was determined to find it. He went to the village and asked around; he sneaked down to the village store at night and eavesdropped on the people drinking inside.

One day Tal-gyun noticed that the villagers were all carrying iron candlesticks as they left the church. He nearly shouted when he saw them. The next day he went to the police. What if the villagers took the temple bell to a foundry and melted it down into candlesticks? he said. The policemen just laughed.

Maybe they buried it, he thought. He dug in the mountains and fields and, thanks to the recent dry spell, even searched the nearby ponds and reservoirs.

Then, beginning two years ago, Tal-gyun was faced with a more serious problem. His wife started roaming around the village at night while he slept. At least, he first became aware of it two years ago. For all he knew she could have been doing it for years.

Ch'un-ja grew restless at the sound of men laughing or talking or singing in the mountains and fields. One night as she stole from the house, Tal-gyun pretended to be asleep, then followed her at a distance. She peered into the dark church and stood outside the store watching the men drink and talk. Then she went inside and smiled coquettishly at them, moistening her lips and batting her eyelids. When they offered her a drink, she accepted it gratefully. When they took her hand, she wriggled bashfully but never pushed them away.

One day Ko Ch'ang-sôk's wife came running into the temple courtyard. "I hear you're letting your wife run wild on purpose! People say you let her run around like a bitch in heat because you can't get it up!"

When Tal-gyun asked what she meant, the woman told him what everyone in the village knew. "They say if a man hasn't done it with Tal-gyun's wife, he must not have any balls."

Tal-gyun sent the woman on her way and confronted his wife. He grabbed her by the hair and threatened her with a knife, demanding to know who she had met and what they had done. She rubbed her hands together, begging him for mercy and promising never to do it again, but that very night he caught her sneaking out. He beat her again, and she rubbed her hands together and begged for forgiveness. He beat her every time he caught her, but there was no use scolding her. She simply begged for forgiveness, and in the next instant forgot everything. She didn't understand that what she had been doing was wrong. She didn't understand that it was immoral to have sex with other men. Once he realized that, he simply tried to keep her from going out. He didn't beat or scold her when she managed to escape his watchful eye.

Instead, he did everything he could to find the lost bell. He decided to join forces with the school foundation. They were happy for his cooperation and sent an official letter to the police, urging them to reopen the case. They even slipped some money to the detectives handling the investigation. The detectives delved into the origins of the candlesticks, but they couldn't find the bell. The very idea that someone stole the bell and melted it down into candlesticks was the stuff of fiction, and the investigation ran into a brick wall once more.

The school foundation had hoped for an easy solution to the problem of its recalcitrant tenants in the investigation of the stolen bell. Failing that, they took the matter to court. The school won hands-down, of course. Late last autumn the villagers were ordered to pay regular rents to the foundation.

The people of Temple Hollow didn't appeal the verdict, but they didn't pay the rents either. Fearful of what might happen, the school foundation refrained from sending a bailiff to settle the matter with force. Instead, they tried to reach an agreement with the villagers, offering a cut in rents and an extension of the due date. The tenants snorted in disgust and sent notification that they would not pay a single cent. As far as they were concerned, the rents they had paid over the years more than covered the price of the land. Furthermore, the land should be turned over to them free of charge. They even threatened the use of force if their demands were not met.

6

"I don't understand how they can be so stubborn," Tal-gyun sighed as he turned to Chu-ch'ŏl. Clenching his teeth in a grimace, he drew a deep breath. He looked like he would do anything to get back at the villagers.

"I'm not askin' for much. My dream's simple enough. I just want to live in a peaceful village where the sound of the temple bell fills the fields and mountains and sky. I wanted to make Temple Hollow into that kind of village where people offer fresh grain and fruit to the Buddha, where people share the rice-cakes they make for family ancestral rites with their neighbors, and where the clear sound of the chantin' and the wooden clapper never rests. But it ain't easy. I feel like I've run into a brick wall. I don't like fightin', not with anyone. But I had to fight for the bell. You just wait. I'm gonna find it. I'm gonna get rid of those thieves and make this a quiet, beautiful village. I'm gonna do it, if only for my own innocent little children."

Tal-gyun sighed and lit a cigarette.

"Huh?" Ssang-gyun snorted. "What's so simple about that dream?"

Tal-gyun looked down at him in loathing. Chu-ch'ôl and Chu-ôn turned to the old man too. Yun-gil was still facing the window.

"It's none of your business anyway. Why don't you go sleep in your own room?" Tal-gyun spat.

"Dreaming of a quiet, peaceful village is the most frightening thing in the world," Ssang-gyun murmured. "Your ambition is what's frightening. Hitler wanted to make Germany peaceful for his own people so he started a war and killed the Jews. And the Communists insist on class struggle to create their own ideal society."

"What?" asked Tal-gyun.

Chu-ch'ôl felt Tal-gyun was being swept up in a kind of religious war. There is nothing more sinister. When a believer becomes a fanatic, he ceases to think. He's trained to believe his god like a hunting dog, to attack people of other religions on command. Ssang-gyun may have been right: Tal-gyun's dream could get him into a religious war.

"You fool, you don't have a house, much less a temple. This house belongs to the temple and the Buddha's Light High School Foundation got deed to it without you ever knowing it. You stupid oaf, don't you realize they could come here tomorrow and throw you out on your ear?" Ssang-gyun paused to catch his breath.

"What a crock of nonsense!" Tal-gyun snorted in reply. "Why should they throw me out when I'm doin' exactly as they say? My mother's dedicated her life to this temple. She cooked for the monks. Why would they throw her son out?"

"That's why I called you a fool. Don't you realize why the villagers are standing up to the foundation? They want to break free from the slavery that they've lived under for so long! If they're successful, that paddy land you're working will be yours. You won't have to pay rent. It'll be yours outright."

"I know that! I just don't like the idea of takin' someone else's property. It's just like the communists. Why are they tryin' to take it by force, instead of earnin' money and buyin' it, fair and square? It's highway robbery, no two ways about it. It's unthinkable under the Korean system of private property." Tal-gyun's voice rose in irritation. "Look at this! We're fightin' right now! Fight, fight, I'm so sick of it! That's enough! I only told you about my problems with the people in Temple Hollow 'cause I was hopin' at least our family could live in peace."

"How can you be so stupid? Don't you understand? If you figure in all the rent the villagers have paid over the years, they have a right to the land!" Ssang-gyun wheezed.

"Since when? A tenant pays rent for ten or fifteen years and he has a right to the land? Whose law is that? North Korea's? The Soviet Union's? China's?"

"The temple's burned down and there ain't no monks, so what's wrong with it?"

Tal-gyun looked up and laughed in frustration. "Brother, you sound like those Jesus freaks in the village."

Tal-gyun paused for a moment, then seemed to remember something. "Ah, I get it. You're the one who convinced the villagers to have it out with the foundation."

"Huh? Like I got nothing better to do! What's wrong with you? Don't you realize why I came in here tonight? I'm as good as dead but I came in here 'cause I had something to say."

Ssang-gyun wanted to save Yun-gil. They had talked a lot during Yun-gil's stay at the temple. They both agreed that wealth had to be redistributed and the foreign powers had to be driven out before Korea could be unified. Their biggest difference lay in the question: What could be done now? He thought the situation was hopeless, but Yun-gil was optimistic. Yun-gil spoke of revolution.

"Somewhere I heard about the Patricide Society. You know, patricide began with Oedipus. It's rooted deep in the human subconscious. I think it could accelerate the passage of history, push it in the right direction. Killing one's father is an act of revolution. Compromising with one's father means compliance and stagnation. History begins when sons kill their fathers. It's the same principle as dialectic materialism: an eternal struggle between father and son. That's why our generation is in such agony today."

Ssang-gyun's life and the society in which he lived had been ruined by radical ideas like that.

Ssang-gyun had achieved nothing. Everything in his life had ended in failure. Like Yun-gil, he had dreamed of social reform based on the logic of the Patricide Society, but he realized it was nothing more than a fantasy. After hiding in the mountains for a while, he turned himself in and changed his way of thinking. He tried his hand at all kinds of jobs. He strapped a wire cage on the back of a bike and traveled around buying dogs, which he then sold to dog soup restaurants. It wasn't long before he tired of shouting, "Dogs, dogs, sell your dogs," and settled down on the outskirts of Kwangju to raise them himself. If his mother had known what he was doing, she would have died of shock for she had spent her life in a Buddhist temple. At any rate, he made lots of money and soon bought extra cages to raise more puppies. A neighbor who was in the same business helped him rupture the puppies' eardrums with a wire so they wouldn't bark. It was an expensive venture raising the dogs to maturity. He was forced to take out some high-interest loans, but he figured dog prices would soar in the summer and his earnings would pay off the loans.

However, the dog soup business was wiped out in a single day. The television news reported that dog meat had been found to contain bacteria which destroyed the human liver. The following day officials from the Ministry of Health and Social Affairs began inspecting dog soup restaurants. It was just like the time people stopped eating raw fish because it was said to contain vibrio bacteria. Everyone quit eating dog.

It all began when a foreign animal rights group threatened to boycott the Seoul Olympics if Koreans kept eating dog meat. Fearful of what might happen, government officials lied to the public, hiring an unprincipled scholar to testify to the presence of the bacteria.

No one confronted the Ministry, though. The bottom fell out of the dog market overnight, and suppliers and restauranteurs went bankrupt.

Ssang-gyun's wife died of a broken heart. His son, a relief driver, was hit by a truck and killed. Ssang-gyun had them cremated and drowned his sorrows in drink. Then one day his throat began to hurt. It was swollen. He could not swallow and his voice grew husky, as if he had been shouting. His tonsils swelled and then his lymph glands. There was a lump on his glands the size of a ping-pong ball. His body felt heavy. It was hard to move. Lumps developed in his armpits and groin. The local pharmacist told him it looked like larynx cancer and urged him to go to a hospital. My life's not worth the price of a hospital room, he thought. It was all a matter of karma. Weighed down by that tremendous fate, Ssang-gyun returned to his mother. She threw her arms around him and cried. "Where have you been all this time? Did you marry? Do you have any children?" She mistook him for Ssang-do who had escaped to North Korea. Mother lived to see Ssang-do again, and Ssang-gyun struggled to suppress his urge to kill her.

The previous morning Ssang-gyun had seen his mother devouring the pork Yun-gil had brought from Chu-man's funeral. He couldn't stand it any longer. She had always been such a devout Buddhist. She wouldn't even speak of meat. But her spirit had left her body already. There was nothing left, only the spirit of an animal or evil spirit. Ssang-gyun was returning from the outhouse when he saw her. A broken roof tile lay on the ground before him. He picked it up and hurled it at her. "Why don't you just drop dead?" he shouted.

When he opened his eyes, he was lying in his room. Yun-gil was looking down at him. He had collapsed after throwing the tile.

"Everyone has their own share of life. Why did you try to take your mother's away?"

He was lucky to meet Yun-gil now, as he waited to die. Yun-gil showed him something he hadn't seen before. As he listened to the young man, he felt as if his body were growing lighter and starting to float.

"Attachment can make you sick, but it can also make you well. If you want to escape the physical and spiritual pain that you see as your karma, perhaps you should shift your attachment to something larger, something beyond yourself."

Yun-gil felt an obligation to liberate Grandmother Chong and Uncle Tal-gyun from their lifetime of slavery. Ssang-gyun just closed his eyes and listened.

"I've been meeting with the people in Temple Hollow. I know you're sick, so just rest and wish me luck in my efforts."

Ssang-gyun took Yun-gil's advice and began to focus his mind on the confrontation between the villagers and the school foundation. He lay in the middle of the room, still as a corpse, but the more he thought, the more he felt as if he were leading the villagers in their struggle. He forgot his own pain.

When he heard that Chu-ôn had come to the temple he couldn't stay in his room. He had heard about Chu-ôn from Yun-gil. Yun-gil was waiting for Chu-ôn. He knew that Chu-ôn would show up on some pretext sooner or later.

Ssang-gyun opened his eyes and glowered at Chu-ôn. His eyeballs looked as if they were made of glass.

"Even the blackest magpie knows how to be grateful, and a snake never harms the man who saves him. You lay a hand on Yun-gil and the gods will punish you. Don't you realize your father owes them? A son has to pay his father's debts. That's the way it should be."

Ssang-gyun was holding Chu-ôn's hand. Chu-ôn nodded as he looked into the black pits of Ssang-gyun's eyes.

"He's studied a lot," Ssang-gyun explained, "but he's still young. You've got to protect him. Please. It's my final wish."

Chu-ôn nodded again. Tal-gyun snorted in disgust.

"You might as well pray to the wildcat not to eat the family chicken." He trusted no one.

The door opened quietly again. It was the woman. She was holding a small table. She had made ramen noodles. Tal-gyun snapped at her in anger but took the table and placed it in the middle of the room. The woman stood at the doorway studying the men one by one. Her grinning face resembled a phantom waiting to bewitch them.

Chu-ch'ôl avoided her gaze. Moistening his lips, he thought of Yun-gil. The boy caused trouble wherever he went. I'll have to get him out of here first thing in the morning. If the villagers kept refusing to pay the rents, the police would come to investigate and Yun-gil might be caught. They may have already started investigating the villagers. In the bluish light of the snow behind the woman he sensed a dark conspiracy. It seemed as if a wave of people were silently sweeping down on the temple's living quarters, a long boat in the darkness. Yun-gil was a carrot: the promise of a cash reward and a special promotion.

"Yeah, now I understand. People are always sayin' never trust the human animal, and they're right," Tal-gyun's features had hardened. They were full of the pain of betrayal as he scooped the noodles into the bowls stacked on the table. He had done so much for Yun-gil. He had slaughtered him a chicken at least once a week, he had dug him a shelter in the hill behind the temple, he had bought him new bedding. He did all he could for Yun-gil. Everyone knew the boy was brilliant. But now.... How could Yun-gil betray him like that? How could he conspire with the villagers he hated so much, the villagers who had caused him so much pain?

"I know you're young and inexperienced but how could you do somethin' like that? I can't believe it!" Tal-gyun cried, after he had finished serving the noodles. He looked into the air and sighed.

Chu-ch'ŏl felt Yun-gil was wrong too, although he knew the boy had acted out of some kind of conviction. Obviously Yun-gil would disagree. He had thoroughly rejected the concept of family loyalty. So why had he come down here and stayed so long? Why did he have to hurt this innocent man? Chu-ch'ŏl hated his son's cold-blooded selfishness. If he'd known Yun-gil was going to end up like this he wouldn't have educated him so much.

"Please don't be angry with me, Grandfather. I know you're upset but try to be patient. You won't regret it, I'm sure." Yun-gil turned to look Tal-gyun straight in the eyes. His face was filled with arrogance. He was so self-righteous. As long as he was convinced that he was doing something for the people, there would be no compromise, no yielding. He looked down and continued.

"Please try to understand. I'd never betray anyone. Sakyamuni Buddha never hated or betrayed anything in his long struggle to serve the masses, and it's the same with the people working for the people today. Sometimes it might look like we're betraying the reactionary forces, but that's just temporary. In the end, everyone will benefit."

"I know I'm ignorant but don't try to trick me with your fancy talk. I ain't gonna give in 'cause a bunch of talk. Anyway, I understand what you're sayin'. You have your ideas and I have mine. I ain't gonna let it get to me. Let's have it out, just you and me. Imagine an old grandpa and his smart-ass nephew fightin'—what a pretty sight that would be!" Tal-gyun chuckled bitterly.

Yun-gil is like a cancer cell, Chu-ôn thought. This peaceful village is covered with a black cloud because of him. The villagers are the ones who will be hurt by the fight Yun-gil is stirring. Chu-ôn was trying to convince himself that he needn't feel guilty about arresting Yun-gil. Better to get him now, for his own sake and to prevent his father from feeling any more pain. With cancer, early detection and removal of the cancerous cells were best for the patient.

7

In the depths of sleep, Song Chae-dong, the village head, heard tree branches snapping under the weight of the snow. With his sleeping wife in his arms, he thought of Pae Tong-jun. That night as he returned from the store, he began to suspect Pae and the minister, Kim Mok-ho. Maybe they had conspired to get rid of the bell. Who else would do it?

The people of Temple Hollow were puppets in their conspiracy, he thought. They had abandoned the Buddha and replaced him with God and Jesus. They had done it for the rents, no other reason. The people from the school foundation had shown up, completely out of the blue, and demanded the back rent. They had even levied rents on the persimmon and chestnut trees. And now Pae and Kim were using the villagers for their own purposes.

The younger people submitted to them easily but the older villagers said they couldn't give up the Buddha. The young people held meeting after meeting. They decided that each person had to take responsibility for his own parents. They told them that they had to serve Jesus if they wanted the land they had worked so hard over the years. It was only right. They had to believe in Jesus if they wanted a better life. Some of the older villagers accepted their sons' arguments immediately, but others refused. They said they would be punished if they abandoned the Buddha for a few measly pieces of land. Religious quarrels broke out in several families.

Despite the elders' objections, there was no turning back. The young men managed to overcome their parents and each claimed a plot of land. Some took up knives and threatened to kill the whole family when a parent was particularly obstinate. Others begged their parents to simply pretend to believe in Jesus, while still serving the Buddha in their hearts. That was what bothered Song Chae-dong. For nearly a year he had been fighting with his old mother. Finally he told her, "I can't live in this village if you're going to be so stubborn. I'm leaving. Have a good life with your Buddha," and packed his belongings. Only then did his mother give in. It was with such tactics that the young people convinced their parents to forsake the Buddha.

Thinking back, Song felt as if he had been pushed by some great force. He released his wife from his arms and turned on his back. Her body hadn't changed, but somehow it felt colder and harder that night. He thought of Tal-gyun's wife, her eyes half-closed in pleasure.

A few days earlier he had run into her in a field of dry reeds at sunset. He was climbing the main ridge to Sunrise Peak to check on the oak boughs he had cut for mushroom frames when he spotted her. She must have seen him first for she was already smiling that droopy-eyed smile of hers. As he drew nearer, he saw three oak boughs lying on the ground beside her. You miserable thief! He stopped and glowered down at her. Sensing his anger, she began rubbing her hands together, begging for mercy. Suddenly the sight of her long face, the droopy eyes, the long, thin grasshopper eyebrows, the full, pouting lips, the skin, white as the inside of a gourd, sparked a fire in him. He recalled what the men in the village had said: Just push her down and she'll put out right then and there. They said her flesh was warmer and softer than anything they'd ever felt before. The women called her the village pisshole. He had teased Ko Ch'ang-sôk and Pae Tong-jun for sleeping with her. "I'll lend you my dog next time she's in heat," he said. In the past he had always ignored the woman.

But when he saw her alone in that deserted field, his manhood was awakened. She smelled of dry grass, like a wild animal. She seemed part of a wild, virgin forest.

He squatted down and the woman's body went limp like a centipede that had been stung. As a child he had stolen sweet potatoes from other people's fields, frantically digging up the long vines, yanking the sweet potatoes out one by one, like so many wild rabbits. He ripped open her clothes with the same intensity, his heart racing as her hidden parts were revealed. He felt dizzy. She lay on her back, blinking lazily like a copulating sow. As he plunged into her, she cried out, like a doe caught in a snare.

He couldn't get the incident out of his mind. It was like the secret taste of tart berries picked on a desolate mountain in winter. It was as if he were a wild dove that had soared high in the sky and returned to the wintry forest. No, it was a dream. He sucked her tongue and lips. She was no ordinary woman. She was like the woman from the legend, the one who put the cintamani in the school boy's mouth. She had changed Temple Hollow into a fantasy world, an unfathomable bewitching swamp.

He didn't say anything about her to others. He wanted to find a way to meet her again, alone.

He turned in bed once more. Outside he heard someone walking in the snow. He held his breath. Was it Tal-gyun's wife? People said she gave meaningful looks to the men she had slept with. She even visited their houses. It must be true. His wife did not stir. I'd better go out and get rid of her before my wife wakes up, he thought. I'll take her to the shed and satisfy her. No, I'd better ignore her. Let my wife get rid of her if she wakes up.

The footsteps drew nearer. It was more than one person. He bolted upright. Suddenly he remembered the bell. He had heard the police were going to reopen the case. Then he remembered Pak Yun-gil. Chu-ch'ôl's genius son was staying at the temple. They must have reopened the investigation because of him.

The bell was only an excuse; the police were clearly more interested in getting the villagers to pay their rent. When the school foundation sent a man around offering a cut in the rents and an extension in the pay period, Song had suggested they go along with it, on the condition they write off the overdue rent. Almost everyone, except Ko Ch'ang-sôk and Pae Tong-jun, agreed, but then Yun-gil intervened. He encouraged the villagers to fight for the land. Thanks to Yun-gil, Ko and Pae were able to get the others to confront the head of the foundation with their demands.

"Song! Hey, Song Chae-dong!" a familiar voice called from the gate. It was Constable Chi from the local police box. As he stepped outside he saw two plainclothes officers standing beside the constable. One was as large as Song, the other stocky and of medium height. They smelled of sweat and liquor. They must have had a drink before venturing into the heavy snow.

"Sorry to wake you, but we need a guide," Constable Chi whispered. He did not introduce the other men by name but said, "These gentlemen came about the bell. They have conclusive evidence that Pak Tal-gyun conspired with some outsiders to sneak the bell out of the temple."

Baffled, Song stared at the constable. As far as he was concerned, Tal-gyun was honest and naive to the point of stupidity. How could he do such a thing and pretend he didn't know what had happened? Song couldn't believe it and was immediately suspicious of the constable.

"Take us to him," the large man rumbled.

As Song led them through the snow, Constable Chi drew closer and whispered, "A college student named Pak Yun-gil has been staying at his house for some time, hasn't he? He helped Tal-gyun smuggle the bell out. I heard he's hiding in a cave behind the temple. You know all about it, don't you?"

Song looked into the sky. It had stopped snowing. Would Yun-gil do something like that? The boy was always saying he had dedicated his mind and body to the masses. Why would he go sneaking behind their backs like that? Song shook his head. Something was wrong.

From the very beginning he hadn't approved of the way Yun-gil, an outsider, had tried to interfere in their affairs. He had shouted at him, telling him to mind his own business. City folks and poor country folks are different, he had said. He had even thought of asking the police to run a check on Yun-gil. He suspected the boy's motives. Still, he couldn't believe that Yun-gil and Tal-gyun would steal the bell, though he could hardly argue with the police about it.

Song knew it wouldn't be right to lead them straight to the temple. The boy was probably fast asleep. I have to stall them, Song thought. You have to protect the animals that take refuge in your house. As they left the village and climbed the main ridge to Sunrise Peak, Song deliberately stumbled and slipped.

"How come you blocked off a perfectly good road with barbed wire and make people take this long way around?" Constable Chi complained after taking an especially painful fall himself.

8

Ssang-gyun lay on the floor wheezing. Tal-gyun sat cross-legged, looking back and forth between Chu-ôn and Yun-gil. Chu-ôn was waiting. He was exhausted. For two months he had been plotting to meet Yun-gil face to face. He had used up his patience. Now all he had to do was make sure he didn't miss his chance. It was time to quietly reap his reward.

Where are those guys? he wondered. What's taking them so long? He sucked peevishly on his cigarette.

"What did you plan on doing with me once you got here?" Yun-gil sounded as if he were trying to start a quarrel.

Chu-ôn exhaled and turned to Yun-gil with a frown. What a pathetic pup, he thought. Right, just keep playing the fool.

"What do you mean? You got me all wrong. I didn't come to get you. I just wanted to make you realize that what you've done is wrong. You're not helping our society or our people."

"Thanks, but you've come a long way for nothing," Yun-gil replied in a disdainful tone.

"Come on! Let's talk this out. What do you think is going on in our society? What is reality for you? People can't live drunken on ideals."

"If you want my respect, quit acting so haughty. You're the one that said you're a member of the basic class so take off that mask and start living the truth. Devote yourself to the common people, the people of your own class. Life's too short! Why do you insist on living such a despicable existence?" Yun-gil demanded.

Chu-ôn tossed back his head and guffawed.

"I may be jumpin' the gun but I'd like to tell you somethin'," Tal-gyun intervened. "You boys can say what you like, but make sure it ends in talk. I don't want nothin' bad happenin' here. Understand?"

Chu-ôn and Yun-gil did not answer.

Chu-ch'ôl went outside to urinate. It's no use talking to Chu-ôn, he thought. That filthy piece of scum! Still, Chu-ch'ôl hoped that Chu-ôn could open Yun-gil's eyes. He knew Chu-ôn wouldn't be able to turn the boy around completely; he simply hoped that Chu-ôn could make the boy a little less radical.

His shoes were gone from the stepping stone beneath the porch. All that was left was a pair of men's white rubber shoes. He slipped them on and headed for the outhouse. As he passed the kitchen, he paused.

A dim electric light burned inside. Tal-gyun's wife was crouched by the firehole, doing something. She looked up and smiled. The coals burned red in the fireplace. Her face appeared flushed in the reddish glow of the light bulb. Is she roasting sweet potatoes? He was about to move on when he saw what she was doing.

Several pairs of shoes were lined up on the hearth. That's where his shoes had gone! She was drying them. They were all men's shoes. He felt something hot shot up his spine. It wasn't because she was sacrificing her sleep to dry the guests' shoes. It was because of the reddish light, the gaping black firehole, the glowing coals. Strangely, it made him think of a wild creature's womb. How often did you find a primitive woman drying the shoes of her male visitors, with an idiotic smile on her face? The temple was a mysterious swamp, he thought.

He hurried to the outhouse, but urinated outside, on the white snow. As he turned to return to the room, he sensed someone coming, and hid around the corner of the outhouse on reflex. Four dark figures were moving through the snow. One went around the back of the living quarters, another to the front courtyard. A large man approached the outhouse. He must have seen Chu-ch'ôl. Chu-ch'ôl felt the blood rushing to his head. They must be part of Chu-ôn's gang, he thought. Yun-gil would be arrested now. He had to do something. He had to get word to Yun-gil. Should he call out, "Run, Yun-gil!" or demand to know who they were. He stepped out of the shadows and approached the large black figure.

"You're from the police, aren't you? You've come for Pak Yun-gil. I'm his father. My relatives are trying to get him to surrender. Please don't make any hasty decisions. Yun-gil is almost ready to surrender," he lied.

However, before the black figure could answer, something happened.

"Pak Tal-gyun, I want to talk to you," Song Chae-dong called from the front courtyard.

"Ssang-do, run! They've come to get you!" came the Widow Chông's raspy voice.

The light went out in Tal-gyun's room. Then they heard the sound of the door being kicked open.

"Who is that?" hollered Tal-gyun. A shriek rang through the darkness. Then something tumbled and crashed to the ground. Chu-ch'ôl felt dizzy. Chu-ôn and the plainclothesmen must be beating Yun-gil and putting him in handcuffs. The large man next to him drew a pistol and dashed toward the living quarters.

As he stepped to the porch, a shadow sprang from the darkened room and darted across the courtyard. The man with the pistol called out, "Stop!" and fired two shots. The fleeing shadow headed toward Sunrise Peak. The church bell in the village rang through the darkness. It was time for early morning services.

Chu-ch'ôl let out a sigh of relief as he watched the shadow disappear into the snowy forest.

"Ssang-do! Hurry!" The Widow Chông's voice was drowned out by the bell.

Yun-gil was barefoot. The snow reached his calves as he trudged across the ridges and valleys. His toes and the soles of his feet stung. They felt as if they were being cut to pieces by the sharp stones and branches. I can't let them catch me. I've got to think of the others. They're depending on me. That's my duty. It's more important than my life. Anyone who was caught, even if he had no choice, had to submit to self-criticism. It was your duty not to be caught. And if you were, you must never give the names of your comrades, even if they threatened to kill you. If someone was exposed, everyone believed that it was the fault of the one who had been arrested. Sell out your friends to escape torture and you were sure to receive severe criticism when you got out of prison. If you wanted to avoid that criticism you had to do your best not to be caught.

Yun-gil felt like laughing out loud. Thanks to his uncles and the *t'aekwondo* skills he had so painfully earned in the military, he had managed to escape Chu-ôn's noose.

Ssang-gyun had grabbed Chu-ôn's ankle the minute he heard his mother's cries and the voices outside. Tal-gyun had turned off the light, and in the confusion, Yun-gil had kicked down the man climbing onto the porch and fled, fists flying, out of the courtyard.

He wanted to laugh but couldn't. He had nowhere to go. He limped through the snow like a wounded leopard, leaving a clear trail of footprints behind him. As he stumbled up the mountain he longed for the room Tal-gyun's wife had kept so warm. Where do I go? Where do I go now?

Chu-ch'ôl followed the footprints up the ridge, Yun-gil's sneakers in hand. His own shoes, so carefully dried by Tal-gyun's wife, were soaking after a few yards. He slipped and tumbled in the snow drifts. He rolled into the ravines more than once, and each time, he was overcome by a ponderous feeling of despair. He refused to surrender to it, grinding the despair between his teeth and scrambling after his son like a wild beast. Their footprints twisted dizzily through the snow. For Chu-ch'ôl, the footprints were evidence of the destiny they shared as father and son. He felt his son's warmth radiating from them. He wanted to cry out, he wanted to vomit blood. When the red glow of the morning sun ignited over the distant sea, Yun-gil's footprints were filled with bloody shadows.

An Unlit Window

1

On the hill above Temple Hollow the eulalia blossoms had dried and faded. They were almost white now, as if someone had painted them silver. A sensuous woman was standing in the tall grass, smiling shyly at Chu-ch'ôl. Twisting her shoulders bashfully, she moistened her lips. Chu-ch'ôl felt lust burning in his groins. He looked around. There was no one there, only eulalia grass. He took the woman in his arms. She collapsed to the ground. Her bare flesh sucked him in. It was ripe and deep, like a marsh adorned with the colorful flowers of a pleasure palace. As he swam through it, she writhed beneath him, then cried out like a doe caught in a trap. He groaned like a mountain animal and ejaculated. A wave of guilt swept over him. He shouldn't have done it. She was Tal-gyun's wife. His own aunt! She grinned like a Hahoe mask, her arms wrapped around his neck.

He opened his eyes. His crotch was cold and damp. A wet dream! How humiliating! He was almost fifty. It was only a dream, but why her of all people?

A white circle of light spread across the opaque window. The moon had risen. Its light stung his eyes, but a thick gloominess filled his head, like the eerie blue darkness that pours from the eyes of nocturnal animals, like the venom of a centipede in chicken porridge.

It may have only been a dream but he hated himself for what he had done. The guilt and embarrassment overwhelmed him, but at the same time, he could feel the return of the bluish darkness that had seared his consciousness before he fell asleep.

The darkness came from his son's room; it was alive and wriggling. It had settled behind the closed door and lurked inside, plotting as if it had a mind of its own. Sometimes it stepped out but it always returned. It was like an enormous monster that had escaped from a magic lamp in a puff of smoke. He disliked Yun-gil's room because of that darkness. He felt as if it held a grudge against him.

He had left Yun-gil's light on that night. To fill the room with light instead of darkness, but that made it even worse. The fluorescent bulb did not radiate light. It emitted particles of darkness that had transformed into light. He scolded himself for his silliness, left the light on and went to bed in his own room, his wife beside him, but the particles came after him, squirming inside his brain. He couldn't sleep. Blades of light bouncing off the surface of a pond that lies sunning itself like an animal in the bright midday sun, they wounded his consciousness. He tossed and turned, pressed his palms against his eyes, but he couldn't sleep. Finally he gave up and went into the living room. The light seeping through the crack under Yun-gil's door was cruel and villainous. The particles, now transformed to light, were bouncing up and down behind the closed door. Chu-ch'ôl felt as if they acted on Yun-gil's will. He screwed up his courage, opened the door and turned out the light.

Hye-suk lay flat on her back under the quilt. In the dim moonlight Chu-ch'ôl could discern the contours of her body. She was lying with her legs straight, hands folded halfway between the mounds of her breasts and navel. Even her head was perfectly straight. She looked like a monk meditating in the prone position. Her breathing was smooth and even.

After Yun-gil's arrest, Hye-suk refused to sleep under a quilt. How could a mother sleep under a thick quilt in a heated room when her son was lying on a drafty cement floor? When Chu-ch'ôl covered her, she kicked off the blanket and closed her eyes, arms folded tightly across her chest.

"He's got his life and we've got ours." Chu-ch'ôl tried to explain, but she wouldn't listen. He finally came up with a scheme: He declared he wouldn't use a quilt either and curled up like a shrimp on the cold floor. When she covered him, he kicked off the blanket again and again. She finally gave in and covered herself to prevent her husband from sleeping in the cold.

Hye-suk wasn't asleep. She had probably taken a tranquilizer. Perhaps her head was filled with the darkness of Yun-gil's room too. No, her spirit was with her son, in solitary confinement. She was being tortured in some secret room in the prison basement too, resenting her husband's ineffectiveness and indifference.

Why don't you talk to that friend of yours? You know Chang Ki-ho, the prosecutor. Would it dirty your immaculate name to meet him? Who cares about your reputation if you can help your son? What's more important: maintaining a father's reputation or rescuing a son from insanity or death by torture? It makes my flesh crawl to think I've lived with such a cold, heartless man for all these years! You're not human. You're just a miserable poet. A fake, a cold-blooded animal. You disgust me!

Her thoughts must have made her angry with him. She bristled like the eulalia grass. Without the slightest provocation, she lashed out at the people around her. Still, Chu-ch'ôl never told her what he had been trying to do for their son.

He carefully lifted himself from the bed. He had to go to the bathroom and clean his foul body. He was ashamed, afraid that Hye-suk might sense that he had had a wet dream, that he had violated his own aunt, even if it was in a dream.

He chuckled scornfully at his timidity and stared at the moon's rays whirling like a mandala on the window pane. The blue darkness inside his head intensified. Yun-gil had always been a luminous body inside his mind. The boy's light had continued to burn inside him even after he had gone into hiding. Chu-ch'ôl could feel him there, like the warm, comforting feeling after a good meal. Perhaps a son could betray his father and still remain a light in his father's mind. But since the day of Yun-gil's arrest, darkness had filled Chu-ch'ôl's consciousness. He had tried to escape it; he had struggled like an ox being led to the slaughterhouse. He was so ashamed of the way he was acting. How Yun-gil would despise him if he knew. Chu-ch'ôl clenched his teeth, determined to tell no one how he had struggled to escape.

But it wasn't that. He was acting out of a sense of paternal obligation. It was a lie: all that business about Yun-gil being a light in his father's consciousness. It was all an incredible contradiction. For some time the image of Yun-gil, lying covered with blood, had been running through his mind. Sometimes he pictured the boy wandering through the air, a million particles of darkness. I am evil, he thought. Do I wish my own son dead? But what would I gain from that? Chu-ch'ôl bit down on his tongue as if to punish himself.

A shadow was etched on the window pane. It was an old chestnut tree. The shadow was delicate, like ink painting; the refracted moonlight whirled between the shadows of the branches. He felt dizzy. Was it the light spinning, or was his health deteriorating? After Yun-gil was sent to jail, Chu-ch'ôl had tried to make love to Hye-suk but each time she shoved him away. How could he act so shamelessly when their son was in jail? He was still aroused by his wife, so his health must not be that bad. Then why was he feeling dizzy?

Maybe I had the wet dream because Hye-suk won't let me get close to her, he thought, stepping into the living room. The darkness wrapped itself around him. Yun-gil's door was closed. Chu-ch'ôl felt a cold wind blowing from it. As he reached for the bathroom door, the round face of Chang Ki-ho rose before him.

"Hey, what's the Superman calling a lowly fly like me for?" Chang asked when he answered Chu-ch'ôl's telephone call. There was a timbre of arrogance and mockery in his voice. Chang had once come up to Chu-ch'ôl at a reunion and said, "I used to be infatuated with Nietzsche too." They had been in the same eighth grade class. They had even sat next to each other for a semester, but now they only met at alumni functions, and Chu-ch'ôl secretly despised Chang for his reputation as a political prosecutor. Chu-ch'ôl didn't want to admit that he was classmates with a man who used the Anti-Communism Law to imprison dissidents, all at the beck and call of those in power. He had nothing to gain from their acquaintance. In fact, it threatened his career as a poet. Chu-ch'ôl was known for his bold, meticulous activist poetry. When the ruling party offered him an exorbitant sum to write the lyrics for their theme song, he refused. He had a reputation for distancing himself from people who cooperated with the government, and he was careful to maintain his untarnished image.

He had dirtied himself for his son. It would have been nice if things turned out as he expected. He met Chang Ki-ho because he was willing to risk everything for Yun-gil.

But the moment he saw Chang in that tearoom, he lost hope. He hated himself for even thinking of asking a favor of this short stocky man.

Chang puffed himself up as he sat down across from Chu-ch'ôl. He must have guessed that Chu-ch'ôl had a favor to ask. They drank a cup of green tea, then went to a Japanese restaurant. After a couple of drinks, Chang puffed himself up even more, tucking his chin in the folds of his fleshy neck and speaking in a deep resounding voice. Chu-ch'ôl tried to be patient. After all, Chang's profession had made him that way.

He waited for the right moment, then explained why he had asked to meet him.

"I know this might put you in a difficult position, but I have to ask you a favor. You see, my oldest boy's been getting into a lot of trouble lately. I didn't come to you before because I didn't want to put you on the spot, and frankly I have my pride, but things have gotten really bad and I have to do something. My wife is a wreck, and I haven't slept for days. After a lot of thought, I decided to talk to you. Don't take it too seriously. If you can help me, great. If you can't, I'll understand."

Chang stared down at the table, his lips firmly pursed.

"Hum, so he's gotten into some trouble." Chang frowned. Chu-ch'ôl was encouraged to see him taking the matter seriously.

"They've already taken him in. I've heard they're really tough once they've got them in custody. Beating them, not letting them sleep, torturing them.... I've heard electrical and water torture are just part of the routine. You have to help us."

"Uh, huh." Chang looked at Chu-ch'ôl, his eyes glinting behind his glasses.

Chu-ch'ôl looked away. Chang's eyes were sneering at him. You asshole, they seemed to say, all these years you've treated people who cooperated with the ruling party like crows or maggots feeding on dead bodies. Now you're finally getting what's coming to you. The unspoken words pierced Chu-ch'ôl's heart like needles.

"You know what it's like in there, don't you?" Chu-ch'ôl wanted to ask but he bit down on the words. It would have been like getting down on his knees and begging Chang to save his son.

Chang lifted his glass and emptied it in silence, then handed it across to Chu-ch'ôl and poured him some wine. He picked up a ginkgo nut from the plate of snacks in front of him and stared down at the table, chewing thoughtfully. Finally, he slipped his hands between his thighs, tucked his chin in his neck once more and spoke.

"Don't worry. Drink up. If I didn't help your son, who would I help?"

A strange feeling shot through Chu-ch'ôl's heart. His throat tightened. He felt he might weep with happiness. At the same time, an inexplicable emptiness and sorrow rushed over him. He was lying on the ground like a crumpled, rotting piece of paper. Chang Ki-ho and Yun-gil were stepping on him. He felt despised, rejected as if he were covered with excrement. His face cramped in a grimace and he bit down on his tongue.

Chang poured him another drink. He thought Chu-ch'ôl was struggling to control his joy. Chang lifted his own glass and offered a toast. "Drink up. What are classmates for anyway?" he declared expansively.

Chu-ch'ôl absorbed the alcohol well that night. He normally wasn't much of a drinker. He was punishing himself. He accepted every glass Chang offered him, as if his intestines were a great wine sack.

"You know, this is an opportunity to change your way of thinking," Chang said. "Everyone's always talking about the masses, but who are the masses? They're an apparition, a figment of your imagination. And that means your poems are completely empty. A handful of communists are playing you fellows like a violin. I can understand ignorant laborers or naive students falling for the communist line, but I can't figure out why respected intellectuals and people from the middle class would follow them so blindly."

Chu-ch'ôl listened in silence. He smoked cigarette after cigarette, struggling to control himself. It was his duty as a father to put up with this disgrace and scorn in order to save his son. He was torturing himself for having imagined his son a bloodied corpse.

"I've made a careful study of the so-called opposition forces, and you know what? If this country went communist, those people would be the first ones purged. More than eighty percent of them are from the bourgeoisie or petit-bourgeoisie. They're just a bunch of romantics being jerked around by a few hardcore communists. No, you know what they really are? They're actors who strut around on stage trying to boost their own popularity."

That was an insult. Chang was stomping all over him. Chu-ch'ôl felt like grabbing him by the ankle and knocking him to the ground. He wished he could dump Yun-gil and all the problems he was causing, but that was impossible. He had to be a father.

Perhaps Chang was right. Chu-ch'ôl wasn't confident in his poems. He wasn't sure about the masses either. In a way, he really was a bourgeois socialist. He firmly believed that violent struggle wasn't the answer. Wealth had to be redistributed through a reconciliation between the capitalist and working classes. To achieve that, capitalist absolutism had to be avoided, and the power of the working class increased. The labor movement couldn't destroy the capitalist class or eliminate private property. It simply had to empower itself so it could check the capitalists' power. Violence must never be used. The capitalists needed a sense of ethics, and the state would have to help them find it. Nevertheless Chu-ch'ôl didn't tell Chang what he thought. He knew that his revisionist ideas wouldn't sit well with a government prosecutor. Who knows? he thought, maybe my thoughts, my poetry and my predicament all exist in isolation from one another. They must. How else could I meet this contemptible man? Chu-ch'ôl reeled from the contradictions, the alienation, and the confusion.

"This is a capitalist society. You'd have to demolish it before you could make it socialist or communist. Blood would have to flow. But there can be no blood. I want to make that perfectly clear. The communist nations were created by the propertyless majority by spilling a sea of blood, but they've all failed economically. Now they're trying to convert to capitalism. We've accumulated this much wealth under a capitalist system, and we've got to solve our distribution problem gradually, building on our strengths as a capitalist society. We've nothing to gain from importing Marx or Engels, or Lenin or Kim Il Sung's self-reliance ideologies. Korean intellectuals and members of the middle class have to open their eyes. They have to stop the radical conspiracy to destroy the capitalist system in the name of this apparition they call 'the people.' The sad thing is there isn't a single intellectual willing to defend the capitalist system. They're all afraid. The professors, the reporters, the opposition politicians.... They're all afraid of a few reckless students. That's the greatest tragedy facing our society today."

Chang Ki-ho went on and on. He had been watching the people in the democracy movement, he said, and there was really only a handful of hardcore communists and socialists. Be careful, he warned. It's only a matter of time before they're crushed like flies in a single stroke of the fly swatter....

"You've never sent me a book of your poetry but I've read every poem you've published. I've got them all. I don't know what other people think but in my view you're a revisionist, an opportunist, a middle-of-the-roader. You won't be welcomed on either side. You'll be criticized for not taking an active stand against the capitalist system. At first they might praise you for your activist poems but you'll be criticized sooner or later. The communists use the bourgeoisie and the petit bourgeoisie until they've established the basis for their struggle.

"Everyone has their own contradictions but from what I can see, you have more than your share. You've got to break free of them as soon as possible. We're not from the basic class so they'll never accept us, no matter how hard we try. It's just like the Chosôn Kingdom. You couldn't sit for the state examinations unless you were a *yangban*. They'll always criticize you for your bourgeois roots. And criticism means punishment and destruction. It could even mean purge and death. You saw what happened in Kampuchea. The left wing adventurists wiped out everyone they didn't like, everyone they thought was tainted."

Chang was barking from the drink now.

"I'll see what I can do, but don't get your hopes up. Those bastards don't tell us who they've got until they've finished the investigation. I can't ask. That would be showing my weak side. I'll try to get them to let him go when they turn him over to me. People think we're like cats ordering mice around, but mice have pride, too. You have to remember that." These final words drove Chu-ch'ôl to anger and despair.

They left the restaurant, and as Chang's black sedan pulled up to the front door, he turned to shake Chu-ch'ôl's hand. "If he's lucky, my boys have got him. Otherwise, well..."

Chu-ch'ôl groaned and pulled open the bathroom door. He bit the end of his tongue as he stood over the toilet. The telephone in the living room rang. His wife hadn't answered the phone since her son's arrest. Chu-ch'ôl rushed out and picked up the receiver. "Hello, hello," came a harsh, nasal voice. It must be Chu-ôn, he thought. His flesh crawled at the thought of his cousin. Wasn't he satisfied with arresting Yun-gil? What more did he want? Chu-ch'ôl's blood rushed to his head.

He wanted to scream into the receiver, to spit out all the fury that had built up inside him, like a doctor draining rancid blood from a bruise. But he didn't. The whole family would wake up. He lowered the receiver for an instant, then brought it to his ear again. Perhaps Chu-ôn had some good news.

"Who is this?" he asked.

"You're awake!" Chu-ôn exclaimed happily. "I was afraid you wouldn't answer. I'm so glad you did. I know it's late, but I've got to spend the night at your house. I have something to discuss with you. About Yun-gil." Then he hung up.

Chu-ch'ôl stood motionlessly at the center of the living room, his eyes closed. A cockroach was flying toward him, out of a dim and distant hell. It wiggled its long ugly feelers into his consciousness. Still, Chu-ôn was bringing news of Yun-gil. Chu-ch'ôl tried to control his disgust.

As he returned to the bedroom, Chu-ch'ôl cleared his throat and frowned. The devil inside him was waiting for something horrible to happen to Yun-gil. Something awful, something irreversible. He wanted Chu-ôn to bring the news. That Yun-gil had suffocated during water torture, that he had gone insane from the electric probes. Chu-ch'ôl bit his tongue until it hurt, as if he were torturing himself for harboring that devil within.

It was bad karma, evil destiny. There was no reason why things had to turn out this way. It must be bad karma between Yun-gil and me. Maybe Yun-gil wants something terrible to happen to me too. Maybe that's why he insisted on doing everything I despise. Was it all fate?

As he looked down at his sleeping wife, an overwhelming sense of alienation and despair spread over him like a poisonous fog. The Patricide Society, he thought. I've been ostracized by my family for years. It all began around the time Yun-gil entered high school. Hye-suk began handling the children's affairs on her own, discussing their problems with them, never bothering to include him. No doubt she did it because she didn't want to inconvenience him, but gradually he began to feel left out, like a drop of oil floating on water.

One of Chu-ch'ôl's friends, a self-made man whose father had died when he was quite small, had once said he felt children would be better off if their fathers died when the children reached a certain age. "I know it sounds cruel, but kids have to learn to be independent, to blaze their own path and make their presence felt in the world. A powerful father is a windbreak. He makes his children weak, like seedlings grown in a green house. A strong father can handicap a child. It can be a great misfortune."

Chu-ch'ôl stood looking at the shadows of the tree on the window pane. He felt like a sea gull circling an uninhabited island, a tiny rowboat on a vast sea. Should I die for Yun-gil's sake? he thought. But when? Have I waited too long? Is now the time? Should I wait until our youngest son enters university, or until he graduates? Sorrow squeezed his heart.

Chu-ch'ôl's wings were tired. He traveled back and forth between his office and that boarding house of a home like a pendulum. His monthly salary of one-million won disappeared before the month was gone. The poems he published in literary journals barely covered the price of a couple of drinks.

He had to do whatever his boss, an old friend, asked him to do. He had to proofread when they were short of editors. He had to go to the printer's to check the film and give the final go-ahead. I have to keep going for ten more years, he thought. No, for longer than that. Until the day I die. Yun-ho's only in the seventh grade. Damn it! I wanted to quit this job when Yun-gil graduated and started bringing in some money. I don't want to spend the rest of my life wrestling with those words that squirm around like thousands of tiny ants. But it was all just a fantasy.

That bastard, that little bastard! How could he do it? Why did he have to join the leftist movement? Why did he feel he had to act on his beliefs? Couldn't he leave the action to others? And if he had to act, why couldn't he do it peacefully? Why did he have to make molotov cocktails? What made him go all the way to the far left and throw those firebombs?

I know. It was my father. My father's ghost drove him to this. It's karma. Is there any way to melt through it?

2

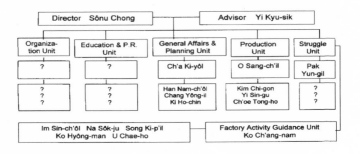

The Anti-American & People's Liberation Struggle Committee

A single sheet of typing paper lay on the desk. It was an organization chart for the Anti-American & People's Liberation Struggle Committee. A squat, muscular man looked down at the paper and began the interrogation. The man had heavy eyelids and dark purple lips. He wore a brown shirt and a flashy tie with vertical red stripes. The blue jacket he had been wearing when he entered the room was draped over the back of his chair.

Yun-gil was seated across from the man. He had studied the chart several times. The man asked him questions, referring to the chart from time to time. It was like a university entrance interview. The man acted like a good-natured professor who wanted to give the applicant ample time to prepare his answers.

Yun-gil was naked, his body cold. The man hadn't allowed him to get dressed after they dunked him in the icy water. Yun-gil was exhausted. He had writhed in the cold water, and now his body ached. It felt heavy, as if iron balls were hanging from his shoulders, chest, head and back. And when he relaxed, he shook as if by a gust of wind. He felt he might crumble like a dilapidated house in a flood.

He clenched his teeth, but he still trembled. He couldn't stop shaking. I have to be brave, he thought. I have to beat this.

The desk sat in the middle of a whitewashed room. A surgical cot stood across from the door, a bathtub at its head. Yun-gil faced the man, his back to the cot. The wall by the tub was spattered with drops of dried blood. Bloody fingerprints streaked the wall, as if someone had reached out in a struggle. Was it really blood that they'd left there on purpose, or had they simply splattered paint on the wall to scare him?

The room was in the basement. There was only one door. The room was lit by the transparent light of a florescent bulb hanging from the ceiling. The sound of a distant radio drifted through the door, together with the clicking of checkers and men's voices. The people next door must be playing *go* to relieve the boredom, and the radio was supposed to drown out the sounds of this workroom. Yun-gil had noticed it when he entered the room.

"Why don't you cooperate, all right? I don't want to see any more blood," the man said in a tired tone. "Sonu Chong, Yi Kyu-sik, Ch'a Ki-yol, O Sang-ch'il.... We've got these assholes in the other room. They've all talked. You're the only one who hasn't spilled his guts. Keep this up and you'll wish you were dead. Now tell me: Who headed up the Organization Unit and the Education & P.R. Unit? If you don't want to tell me, just give me the names of the people in your unit. Let's take it nice and easy. No yelling and screaming, all right?"

The man used a pleading tone. How many times had he asked the same questions? He had tried every trick in the book: he had coaxed and pleaded; he had called in the three men playing *go* and asked them to dunk Yun-gil in the tub.

The men were powerfully built. Two of them took Yun-gil by the shoulders and held him against the tub so he couldn't kick or struggle; the third grabbed the scruff of his neck and shoved his head under water.

"This is nothing," the stocky man explained when they had finished. "If you don't tell the truth, we'll take you next door for an electric massage. I don't want that to happen. A lot of people go nuts after being in that room. Frankly, I'd like to save that brain of yours. You're a smart boy. I have a brother your age. Let's be humane about this, all right? But you have to cooperate."

Yun-gil had nothing to tell them. He was determined to remain silent, even if it meant biting off his own tongue. The man was asking the most incredible things.

Their group was nothing more than an ordinary school club. Sonu Chong was the director. He had been expelled from school. Yi Kyu-sik was a graduate student who advised them on occasion. Of course, some of them were committed to the labor movement. Others were enthusiastic supporters of the anti-American movement, and still others demonstrated for the overthrow of the military dictatorship. The group didn't do anything but offer support to consciousness-raising activities in the field. They met once or twice a month and reported on what they had done. Then they discussed their individual activities, studied, and debated what directions to take in the future. Their "study" was achieved through discussion. There was no organization unit or education and P.R. unit, nor was there a struggle unit or general affairs and planning unit.

There was only this. Each week they read and discussed one book in order to be ideologically well-armed. They agreed not to tell anyone about the group, no matter what happened, and to never allow themselves to be caught. And if they were caught, they were subject to group criticism for their negligence and betrayal. Anyone who divulged a comrade's name to save himself was to be expelled from the group.

"Look, you little bastard! Are you going to cooperate or not?" The man was glaring at Yun-gil. His eyelids seemed slightly swollen. The reptilian eyes, as narrow as the slit of a knife, emitted a murky light.

"You seem to think someone's going to come to your rescue," he snarled, his nose crinkling with sarcasm, "but let me tell you something. That's all an illusion, nothing but a fantasy. You're in hell now, and no one can reach you here. Not even the King of the Underworld. I run things down here." The man spoke in a whisper. He seemed fatigued, as if he had been doing something strenuous before he came in.

They say that surgeons—people who make a living cutting people open, mopping up blood, sewing up twitching flesh and mending broken bones—tend to be heavy drinkers, and they often enjoy the company of women when they are drunk. Perhaps detectives who specialize in torture are partial to saunas and Turkish baths for the same reason. Some Turkish baths employ women who scrub men's backs and sleep with them for a little extra. Maybe this detective had visited one earlier. He was grimacing, as if the very act of whispering were a strain.

"It seems you know Prosecutor Chang Ki-ho quite well. Do you realize what a cruel person he can be? He wouldn't think twice about having his own wife dragged down here for a dunk and electric massage if necessary. He's the one who told me to do this to you. I think he's a real bastard. You know why? Because he doesn't have an ounce of humanity in him."

The man paused and leaned his head back against his chair. He closed his eyes, took a deep breath and ran his right index finger down the middle of his forehead to the tip of his nose. He didn't seem to want to look Yun-gil in the eye. It was as if he were waiting for Yun-gil to fall apart. Yun-gil hated the man for toying with him. He felt like a drenched rat, but he bit down on the rage boiling inside him and struggled not to shake.

"Come on. Let's get this over with so I can go take a nap. How about a little cooperation, eh?"

The man glanced leisurely at the chart, then pushed it across to Yun-gil. Trembling, Yun-gil looked at it. The names in the rectangular boxes seemed like part of some brutal criminal organization. He found his own name. The three characters seemed to shimmer with a strange blue light. Separate, alienated from him, they huddled like vicious outlaws, making him shiver even more.

"So are you going to cooperate or not?"

"There is no Struggle Unit. Really. You can ask me a hundred times, a thousand times and my answer will be the same. It's the truth. You've got it all wrong. I don't know anyone named Chang Ki-ho."

Yun-gil stumbled over the words. He spoke in a husky voice, his eyes trained on the desk in front of him, his jaw loose. He was ashamed to let the man see him trembling, but what could he do? He had caught a cold. He was falling apart. He had to hold on. There must be something that I'm willing to stand for till the very end.

"Do you want another taste of that water? Is that it? You're driving me crazy." The man glowered at Yun-gil with those snake-slit eyes and pressed a button at the edge of the desk. A bell went off outside, somewhere in the direction of the radio and clicking *go* checkers.

That was the fifth time he had called in his three assistants. They're going to drag me over to the tub, like furniture movers, and dunk me in the water. Yun-gil shuddered at the thought. He wanted to tell them the truth. A dizzying despair wrenched his heart. This man didn't want his truth. He wanted Yun-gil to fill the empty boxes with the names of people he knew. The names of high school classmates who went on to other universities, the names of friends in his department, the names of people who had graduated before him, those who had come behind him.

But how could he? If he filled in the names, their owners would be dragged in and tortured. They would be transformed into criminals, and the world would buzz with the startling news. Yun-gil closed his eyes, trying to look as relaxed and composed as the man across from him.

He thought of his father. He must have met Chang Ki-ho. Yun-gil had secretly hoped he would. Then he would be released and could despise his father for asking favors of a reactionary puppet. The investigator's words worried him, though. "Do you realize what a vicious person he can be? He wouldn't think twice about having his own wife dragged down here for a dunk and electric massage."

Yun-gil hated himself for counting on his father and Chang. I still haven't freed myself from my familial dependencies, he thought. That's how I got caught. Maybe I inherited that from my father. Yun-gil sneered at the thought of his father playing up to his buddy Chang, groveling to get his son released.

The door opened and footsteps entered the room. The sound of the clicking *go* checkers had stopped; only the radio played.

"This little bastard's stubborn!"

"We should have given him a nice electric massage first thing..."

"Let's take turns. You hold him down this time."

"Are you kidding me? That's the rookie's job!"

The men bantered back and forth as they approached Yun-gil.

"Do it right this time," the stocky man said in a feeble tone. Yun-gil had hypnotized himself. He left his body to take his spirit elsewhere.

Two men took him by the arms and dragged him toward the tub.

Eyes closed and teeth clenched, Yun-gil tried to push his spirit into the past. They stopped in front of the tub. Yun-gil kept his eyes closed, a prisoner waiting for the noose to be slipped around his neck. He struggled to keep from shaking.

"Hold it," said the stocky man. The other men paused. "Are you going to talk or do you want some more water?" he asked in an irritated tone.

Yun-gil imagined a lonely mountain path in winter. He was walking with his father. As they headed north from his father's hometown, the snow thinned. By the time they reached Changhung Township, the snow was little more than a scattering of cherry blossoms over the hills and fields, and after Yuch'i, there was none at all. Yun-gil concentrated, trying to hold the memory in his mind.

"See that mountain over there? Is it young or old?" Chu-ch'ôl asked, indicating a taro-colored mountain with a toss of his chin. Yun-gil thought the mountain must be old because it was covered with exposed rocks. A young mountain would be covered with soft soil and dense forest like a healthy head of hair, while an old mountain would be bald from centuries of floods. He didn't answer immediately, though. Why had his father asked such a question?

"So what do you think? Is it young or old?" Chu-ch'ôl repeated.

"It's old."

His father walked on, head bent in silence. They crossed a brook by a small steppingstone bridge, and Chu-ch'ôl paused to light a cigarette.

"This is probably a silly question, but which comes first, communism or capitalism?"

A stabbing pain shot through the sole of Yun-gil's foot when he heard the question. He had hurt it fleeing barefoot through the snowy forest that night. He hadn't let it bother him before, so why did it hurt now? Yun-gil pretended not to hear his father and limped on. Chu-ch'ôl continued.

"Marx and Engels believed that capitalism was the final stage of history, to be followed by socialism or communism. I can see their point, considering the age in which they were living. But these days socialist and communist countries are trying to embrace capitalism. The problem is: Do we want human liberation or a welfare paradise? Can a communist society realize human liberation if it doesn't recognize private property? And can a capitalist society create a welfare paradise?

"So what about that mountain over there? Actually, it's relatively young. It will take thousands of years before it has the soil and trees that older mountains have. You have to change the way you think. Capitalism isn't the last step on the road to socialism and communism. When it's done right, capitalism can bloom into a flower more beautiful than anything the other political systems have to offer."

They jammed Yun-gil's head into the water. His lungs screamed for air. He sucked water into his nose and mouth. He tried to breathe, swallowing again and again, but he couldn't find a single bubble of air. His lungs filled with water, and he lost consciousness. It was a distant yet comfortable state. He pictured his father's hand.

Yun-gil nursed at his mother's breast until he was four. He slept in her arms until the age of six. His mother miscarried three times when he was small. Each time, her breasts filled with milk, and Yun-gil would drift off to sleep sucking the sweet liquid, his nose buried in the plump mounds, drunk on her acrid scent. It was disgusting nursing a child with a full set of teeth, she complained, but she held him tight, her breathing quickening as he sucked.

One morning Yun-gil jerked awake to a feeling of abandonment. He reached out, but his mother's breasts were gone. Feeling deprived and empty, he crawled across the room to his father's quilt near the window where his parents lay sleeping. He buried his nose in her shoulder and reached for her breast, but the soft, round mounds were covered with a hand, as large and hard as a wooden bowl. Yun-gil's eyes sparked with a blue fire. He jerked back his hand as if he had touched a hot stove and curled in a lonely ball, the hand clutched to his chest.

Mother didn't belong to him. She had been Father's all along. Still, he felt frustrated and saddened at losing her. He had graduated from middle school, high school, then college, but he still hadn't rid himself of the despair and disappointment he had felt that morning he found his father's hand on her breast.

His mother was strikingly beautiful, different from the other mothers. People said that when she was in school, love-sick boys gathered around her gate like dogs after a bitch in heat.

Her skin was as white as rice cakes, her face a perfect oval, her features strong and clear, especially her large eyes. She was so tall and shapely people were dazzled by the sight of her.

As Yun-gil grew older, however, he began to think his mother ugly and coarse. His parents' room always smelled of a pungent odor, like chestnut blossoms or fetid bodily secretions. His mother seemed to carry a strange breeze in her long, seamless skirts, and when she sat down at the table or plopped on the floor, it wafted out in all directions. It too had a sour odor, like mother's milk or armpits, a dark, secret female scent that attracted men as a flower attracts bees. That was why her father was always after her. They weren't in their twenties or thirties. They had a son old enough to marry and they were still trying to attract the opposite sex! Gradually he came to hate the smell of his mother's make-up. He hated the sight of her broad behind when she wore pants in winter. The bright pink underwear peeking through her broken zipper made her seem so slovenly and coarse. In his eyes, she not only ignored her appearance, she was debauched without the slightest sense of womanly virtues.

And his father! How could a poet live with such an unkempt woman? A clean poet, a man who wrapped his life in rainbows and white clouds, should love a clean woman, a woman who didn't shed a single particle of skin, a single drop of body fluid, no matter how he licked her. But his father was just as lazy and ugly. He rarely bathed, and he was always forgetting to close his fly. Hye-suk was forever nagging him to wash his hair at least twice a week, but he never did. It was always messy and littered with specks of dandruff. He was known for writing clean poems but his body was the opposite. When he came home from work, his wife had to push him to the bathroom to get him to wash. She had to nag him to change his underwear. It was laziness, incompetence, though Chu-ch'ôl called it freedom. "Stop trying to fence me in. Please, of all people, you should let me be free. I'm so sick of it all..."

Yun-gil popped open his eyes, as if waking from a deep sleep. He could hear the radio in the next room; the florescent light stung his eyes. Someone was slapping his cheek. He focused on the face. It was the stocky man. He didn't see the others.

"Wake up!" the man said in a clear, crisp voice. He spoke rapidly; there wasn't a hint of fatigue in his face. He looked different. His skin glowed as if he had just had a shot of morphine; his eyes sparkled like black jewels. That look of total exhaustion had all been an act. Yun-gil closed his eyes again. The man's glowing skin and shining eyes roused the fear and despair in him once more. Yun-gil shivered. He was all wet. The room was cold. He was cold. His teeth began to clatter. What is this? he wondered. It's not important. I'll tell them everything they want to know.

The man sat Yun-gil down in front of the desk and spread a sheet of paper out before him. It wasn't the organization chart for the Anti-American & People's Liberation Struggle Committee. It was a list of names, including all his high school classmates who had gone on to the same university. The names of his close friends from middle school and high school were underlined.

"You know what'll happen if you don't tell us? We'll drag in every last one of these guys and beat them. When they find out you're the one who ratted on them, your name won't be worth shit. We have to fill in these blanks. That's your homework. Do you know who gave me this? I hear Prosecutor Chang Ki-ho and your dad are buddies."

The man crinkled his nose. The florescent light refracted off his forehead.

"I'll fill in these blanks. It's too bad. It's not my fault for not interrogating you well, and it's not your fault for not telling the truth. We're all to blame."

He looked down at the list.

"An Yông-ho, Hong Min-shik, O Ch'un-gu, Ko Ch'ang-jin, Kim Il-sun, Yi O-sông.... How about putting these guys in? Then we'll pick them up and torture them. Is there anyone you'd feel sorry for? Better tell me now. I can take their names off the list if you want."

He was like the king of the underworld. With a jot of his pen, his underlings would roar out like a black wind and arrest the person. Yun-gil felt as if he were tumbling from a cliff. He shook his head weakly.

"I haven't even gone out for coffee with those fellows since we entered university," he whimpered. In fact, the names all belonged to members of his group. What if they think I ratted on them? he wondered. What'll happen to me after I get out of prison?

"You know, I'm exhausted. I don't want to hurt you anymore.... After all, you've got a bright future. Don't you realize how I feel? If I take you into the other room for an electric massage, that'll be the end of you. You've got to realize: I'm letting you off easy. I want to get this over with too. I want to be free of all this!"

He was filling in the blanks with a ball-point pen. Yun-gil didn't have the strength to tell him to stop. He felt as if he were in a dream. He was dizzy. He closed his eyes and thought of the path to Unju Temple. They had walked all the way from Porim Temple in Yuch'i to Unju Temple in Hwasun. Yun-gil strode ahead, hoping to lose his father, but Chu-ch'ôl had kept pace with him. They plodded across the snowy mountains and fields, as if they had bet to see who would give up first. Dark clouds, laden with snow, whispered overhead. Ravens circled, stirring the air. The evening sunlight floated over the eulalia fields like tufts of angora. Yun-gil thought back to all the names of plants and trees his father had taught him on their walks to the spring behind their house in Ui-dong. This is an azalea, this is a hazel nut, this is bush clover...

"All right, now there's one more thing, and it's a real headache. Hey, wake up!" The man pulled a paper from the bottom of the stack and stared at it. "I can't give an inch on this, I'm afraid. Looks like we'll have to see some blood."

The light on the ceiling burned into Yun-gil's optical nerves. An ominous flash shot down his spine. The man scowled and continued.

"About those tunnels. What's the story with them, huh? Where did you hear about them? I hope we can settle this nice and quiet."

3

The clock struck two. A black wind hurdled over the wall and swept up the dead leaves in the garden. Chu-ch'ôl lit the oil stove and boiled some water for coffee. The glass beads hanging from the lamp on the living room ceiling sent shafts of yellow light around the room. He stood with his back to the stove, warming his hands behind him. The glass door to the foyer stared at him like a dark television screen.

He was waiting for Chu-ôn. He must be in the taxi now. No, he's probably flying through the darkness like a cockroach. What did Chu-ôn want? Where were they keeping Yun-gil?

He still couldn't believe that Yun-gil had been arrested. He felt as if he must be hiding somewhere in the darkness. The image of Yun-gil wandering among the pagodas and stone Buddhas in the valley by Unju Temple passed before his eyes.

His son was a riddle to him. He had walked with Yun-gil that night because he wanted to solve the riddle. And that night at Unju Temple, he had finally grasped what Yun-gil was all about. No, that wasn't exactly true. Perhaps what he had "grasped" was not the truth at all.

"Father, do you consider yourself a member of the middle class?"

Chu-ch'ôl did not answer right away. He was trying to figure out what his son was thinking about. Yun-gil didn't wait for an answer.

"What's the difference between a prostitute and an editor who writes poems like you? Who's better in your opinion?"

It was an insulting and difficult question. How was he supposed to approach it? How was he to judge greatness? Chu-ch'ôl was confused. He was no match for Yun-gil when it came to sensitivity or quickness. Yun-gil didn't wait for his father's answer.

"According to Marx, every laborer is the head of his own factory. That factory produces a commodity called the 'self.' A prostitute works to improve her commodity. She goes to the bathhouse everyday and makes a regular visit to the beauty parlor to have her hair done and get a facial massage. She's careful with her make-up. And of course she buys lots of pretty clothes. She learns how to better serve her customers from her madam or more experienced prostitutes, she studies how-to books and reads pornography, and she practices everything she learns. I once heard a gynecologist say most people think prostitutes don't take care of their bodies, while housewives and young unmarried women do, but it's the other way around. Prostitutes take special care of their bodies. They have to if they want to stay in the good graces of their madams and customers."

Yun-gil paused in front of a statue of Maitreya, the Future Buddha.

"And what about you, the editor-poet? What's so different about you? You try to produce better books than your competitors so you can sell more. You use your Japanese language skills to gather information about Japanese publishing. You make friends with language professors to get good books in English, French and Russian. You wine and dine them once or twice a month, and that's not all. You and your boss play cards with reporters who cover culture and publishing, and lose to them on purpose. You slip them a few hundred thousand won to play up your books so you don't have to pay for advertising.

"What do you sell? A good eye for literary trends and the ability to make an appealing book. You work hard to enhance your value as a commodity. You struggle not to be abandoned by your friend, the capitalist-publisher, and your readers. In that sense you're no different from the prostitute. In a capitalist society like this, there is no true human liberation."

Yun-gil stared down at the stone Buddha's worn nose. Unlike most Maitreyas, the statue's eyes were wide open. It stared back at him. Chu-ch'ôl felt as if Yun-gil and the Maitreya were both thinking of a distant paradise, several thousand years in the future. What was the difference between Marx's belief in human liberation through communism and the Buddha's belief in the need to lead the masses through a philosophy of nonexistence? What was the difference between an ideal world that could never be realized on this earth and a paradise 10,000 years hence?

"The president of your publishing company is your friend. You once told me that he lived on instant noodles and slept in his office when you two first got together. One tiny room served as the editorial room, business office and warehouse. But now he's a big capitalist, a publishing tycoon, and you're still a lowly laborer. Your friend's millions have been accumulated at the cost of the surplus value of your labor over the decades. You've become his slave. If a prostitute is a slave to her madam, then what about you? I'm sorry to have to tell you this, but who's to say which one is more of a slave?"

There was a certain logic to what Yun-gil said, but Chu-ch'ôl couldn't help but laugh as he looked at the Maitreya's worn nose and wide eyes. A prostitute and a poet may be alike in that they both work for a living, but the results of their labor were as different as night and day. If his son's logic doesn't account for that, it was nothing more than the half-baked ideology of a naive child.

"Things have to change. The capitalists' property and power have to be turned over to the people. Only then will this divided land be unified and a paradise on earth be built."

Yun-gil spoke with ease. Chu-ch'ôl was frustrated. Just think how many had died since liberation, hoping to convert this country to socialism or communism? Some may have escaped alive, but they had to live in the shadows for the rest of their lives. This boy is living in a dream, he thought.

"It won't be long now. The people are waking up. The problem is the power elite—the capitalists who exploit the masses and the bourgeoisie who think they're part of the middle class. They're all against unification and a redistribution of wealth. They are the enemy, but another greater force is protecting them. American imperialism. The Americans think of Korea as their colony. We have to wake up and realize they're not our friends. Do you think they've deployed nuclear weapons on Korean soil for *our* protection? Far from it. And who dug those tunnels? The North Koreans? What evidence is there? They're just making fools of us. The Americans need a bridgehead in Asia to sell their goods. That's what Korea is to them: a bridgehead. They'll do anything to secure their footing here. They're the ones who dug those tunnels."

Chu-ch'ôl was speechless. His son really was as foolhardy as the proverbial puppy facing down the tiger. The North Koreans dug those tunnels to invade the South. There was no question about that. They were just waiting for a chance to communize the South. Everyone knew that. It was dangerous to hint at such things, to suggest that the Americans dug the tunnels to justify their presence, or that the South Korean government had done it to convince the world that they were living under the threat of a communist invasion and to have an excuse to keep on oppressing their people and maintain their dictatorial regime. No one dared question such things. If you did, you'd be arrested, and no one would hear from you again. To question the government line was tantamount to aiding the enemy. Furthermore, it was an insult to Korea's closest friend. If Yun-gil had begun to doubt, there had to be something wrong with him.

"You stupid fool, do you realize what you're saying? How can you be so careless?" Chu-ch'ôl burst out in anger.

Yun-gil stared at his father. Their eyes collided in mid-air.

"What's wrong with you?" Chu-ch'ôl sighed, lifting his eyes to the sky.

"I'm just telling the truth," Yun-gil scowled, as if his father were the one who had spoken out of line. "It's no crime to tell the truth."

"How do you know that's the truth? You don't understand what the North Koreans are up to. You don't know what they're really like. And even if what you're saying is true, this is hardly the time to be talking about it. These are dangerous times." Chu-ch'ôl's face reddened as he spoke.

"There are times when we have to tell the truth, even at risk of death. Now is one of those times," Yun-gil retorted.

The doorbell rang. The sound darted through the living room like an angry cat. Chu-ch'ôl picked up the intercom. Chu-ôn's voice drifted from the receiver.

"Cousin, it's me."

Chu-ch'ôl pressed the button that opened the gate. He felt as if he were opening his home to a burglar who had already stolen him blind. What more does he want from me? he wondered. The gate clanked open, then shut. Chu-ch'ôl opened the foyer door to face his cousin.

Chu-ôn bowed deeply.

"How have you been?"

"How have I been?" What kind of question is that when you're the one who took Yun-gil from me? Chu-ch'ôl felt like shouting at the top of his lungs, but he suppressed the temptation. Chu-ôn sat on the sofa and warmed his palms over the stove. The cold air that Chu-ôn carried with him spread across the room, chilling Chu-ch'ôl's skin like a frightening conspiracy.

"Yun-gil's fine. I dropped by there this morning and asked the man in charge not to be too rough on him. There's no need to worry. That's what I came to tell you. Is your wife sleeping? She's angry with me, isn't she? She doesn't understand."

Chu-ôn rubbed his face with his warmed hands. "There's a bit of a problem, though. It's those tunnels."

The words punctured Chu-ch'ôl's temples like a drill. A shiver ran through him, as if someone had poured ice water down his spine. He remembered what Yun-gil had said at Unju Temple, and a dizzying sense of despair swept over him. He felt helpless.

"Now don't get excited. Things have taken a strange turn. They're starting to wonder if they shouldn't be looking into your thoughts as well," Chu-ôn said with a grimace.

Chu-ch'ôl looked across at his cousin in silence. He recalled what Chang Ki-ho had said. "You write poems 'for the masses,' but who are the masses anyway? They're simply an apparition, a figment of your imagination."

Chu-ôn pulled out a cigarette. "There's no need to worry. When they suggested you were a commie, I smacked them right in the chops, and I told the guys handling Yun-gil's case to take it easy on him. Yun-gil's lucky to have been taken there. It's like the measles. He had to go through it sooner or later. That's the only way he'll be free of all this. He's caught a bad case of the bug. In a way, you could say he's in intensive treatment. He'll be a new person after this."

"Would you like a cup of something?" Chu-ch'ôl asked in a deliberate tone. He didn't want Chu-ôn to see him worrying. He picked up the jar of Maxwell House and put two spoonfuls into a cup. Chu-ôn looked on as if he were observing a solemn ritual.

"I've a favor to ask," Chu-ôn said, wrapping his hands around the cup. "Of course that's not why I came in the middle of the night like this."

Chu-ch'ôl didn't ask what kind of favor. Chu-ôn sipped the coffee appreciatively. The tick of the clock and the whir of the electric heater in the bedroom circled the room.

"Let me have a grave site back home. It doesn't have to be the best spot. Any place will do, as long as it overlooks Black Island. I want to move my parents' graves. To bury them together. My father spent his life looking down on that island, you know. They're both buried on the sandy hill beside the beach. It floods when the big waves come. No one will object if you say yes. I realize it might look like I'm using Yun-gil, but I can't help it. I'm asking you to decide. Don't connect it to Yun-gil. Just consider my poor father."

Chu-ch'ôl's mind swam in confusion, and his hatred for Chu-ôn boiled in his chest. So that's why you were so intent on catching Yun-gil! You wanted to vindicate your own parents.

You wanted to get back at the people who beat you and your parents, the ones who ordered you around like their own private slaves. That's why you grabbed that rotten rope of power.

Chu-ch'ŏl cleared his throat. It would never happen. Chu-ôn's father was an outsider. And to make matters worse, he had spent his life doing the lowest of tasks: emptying other people's latrines, burying unclaimed corpses, carrying funeral biers and wedding palanquins for other families. Chu-ôn's mother was a crazy woman. She had simply wandered onto the island, met Chu-ôn's father and had a child.

"I can't do it. I can't decide something like that on my own. Go down and ask the family elders yourself. You know our uncles wouldn't let anyone decide on his own. The whole family has to discuss it." That was what he wanted to say. It was the truth. He wanted to take Chu-ôn down a peg, but he couldn't. He cleared his throat again. This was no time to make Chu-ôn angry.

"I'll talk it over with the others. As you've probably guessed, there'll be plenty of opposition to the idea, but let's try to figure something out. After all, it's good for everyone."

Chu-ch'ŏl despised himself for fawning to his cousin.

Chu-ôn nodded. "I knew you'd say that. Actually, I went home a while back and visited all our uncles. I asked them for a grave site, and you know what they said? 'Go ask Chu-ch'ŏl in Seoul.' They said your great-great grandfather bought that mountain and donated it to the clan, so it's up to you."

Chu-ch'ŏl felt as if an iron spike had been driven through his heart.

"My great-great grandfather may have bought it, but it belongs to everyone now. I can't decide on my own. They told you that because they didn't want to decide right there and then. Just wait. I'll see what I can do. Next time I have a chance to go down there, I'll bring it up with the uncles."

Chu-ch'ôl had already decided he would never give Chu-ôn a grave site. Even if he wanted to, he knew that most of their uncles would froth at the very idea. Chu-ôn seemed to sense this. He placed his cup on the coffee table.

"It's no use. I know they'll never let me bury my parents there, no matter who comes out in my favor. I was just asking. My folks are probably more comfortable where they are anyway. If they moved to the bottom of the Pak's grave site, the respectable men in the family would probably beat my father for looking at their wives the wrong way. They'll make him do the dirty work all over again. It's bad enough that he had to put up with it while he was alive. Why should I make him go through it again in the afterlife? It's all because of my own stupid greed. Forget I ever mentioned it."

Chu-ch'ôl's face flushed. Chu-ôn was toying with him. Chu-ôn stood. "I'll sleep in Yun-gil's room," he said in a quiet voice.

Chu-ch'ôl didn't answer immediately. There was something sacred in Yun-gil's room. They had only taken Yun-gil's body. His spirit was still in his room. Allowing Chu-ôn to sleep there would be tantamount to handing Yun-gil's spirit over to Chu-ôn. He'll search through Yun-gil's things, Chu-ch'ôl thought. He will ransack his drawers, open his books, read his journal, go through his letters and writings. He'll gather the fragments of Yun-gil's thoughts, his very consciousness, and report them to the investigators.

Chu-ch'ôl shook his head.

"I'm sorry, but you'll have to sleep out here in the living room. Or you can go to an inn. I have my reasons. You may not understand this, but there's a strange channel connecting that room to Yun-gil's mother's heart. It's as if blood and oxygen flowed through it. Don't even touch the doorknob."

"How can you say that? I feel pain too, you know. I have blood in my heart too. I won't lay a finger on Yun-gil's things.

Don't worry. This business with Yun-gil has made me realize that blood is thicker than water. Actually, I need to find a few things. Yun-gil hasn't been telling the truth. That's why I came. We don't want to hurt him, but we need to find out more about his activities. Like where he got that information about the tunnels. Was he listening to North Korean radio? Has he read some questionable books? He'll be in big trouble if they find anything like that. I've got to get rid of it ahead of time. If you don't trust me, you can come in with me."

Chu-ôn stepped toward Yun-gil's door without waiting for Chu-ch'ôl's permission. Chu-ch'ôl couldn't find the words to defend Yun-gil's room. He stood motionless, watching Chu-ôn open the door. Only when Chu-ôn fumbled for the light switch did Chu-ch'ôl rise from his chair and follow him inside. He felt he had to know what Chu-ôn was after. No, he wanted to watch as his cousin gathered the fragments of Yun-gil.

"I'll have to open this drawer. To tell the truth, there was something strange in there last time I was here. I think it might make things easier on Yun-gil. I need to go over it again."

Chu-ôn opened the bottom desk drawer. There were two notebooks. Between the pages were several bunches of manuscript paper, twenty or more pages each. There were also several smaller pieces of paper covered with tiny words, like ants crawling across the pages. Chu-ch'ôl had read them once after Yun-gil's arrest. It was the "Riddle Story."

Chu-ôn left the notebooks where they were. Instead he pulled out the drawer, placed it on the corner of the desk, then reached into the dark gaping space and removed a bundle of newspapers and a book.

"This is what I'm looking for," he said, indicating the newspapers and book. Chu-ch'ôl unfolded the newspapers. They were all about the tunnels. The book was entitled *The*

Tunnels I Dug. It was written by a North Korean soldier who had defected to the South.

"Actually, these aren't very important. This is the problem. The radio," Chu-ôn said, indicating the radio on the desk with his chin.

"Yun-gil used the radio and this book and clippings to write it."

"It? What are you talking about?"

Chu-ôn turned on the radio. He twisted a knob and a tinny voice came on, speaking in a thick northern accent.

"What are you talking about?" Chu-ch'ôl asked again.

"The wall posters," Chu-ôn replied. "The wall posters claiming the tunnels were the work of the U.S. and Korean governments, not the North Koreans. Someone was putting them up everyday."

"You mean, Yun-gil wrote them?"

"Of course!"

"You really want to get him killed, don't you?"

Chu-ch'ôl felt like he had dropped off a cliff. At the same time the devil in him began to laugh. He wanted to cry out loud because of the devil's laughter.

"How can you say that, Cousin?" Chu-ôn frowned, as if offended. Chu-ch'ôl looked down to avoid his gaze. Chu-ôn didn't pursue it.

"We can't leave these here," Chu-ôn said as he gathered the newspapers, book and radio together. Chu-ch'ôl couldn't help feeling they would be used to frame Yun-gil. I have to stop him, he thought, but he didn't do anything.

"Oh, I almost forgot. What's his name? Prosecutor Chang Ki-ho. Did you go see him? That was a mistake. You should have talked to me first. Do you realize what an insult that was to my colleagues? Yun-gil's the one to suffer if they're provoked. Prosecutor Chang could be of some help when Yun-gil's charged, but there's only so much he can do. The case we prepare is what matters. No one can do anything, not him, not anybody. If you try to get him out or get the charges reduced through other channels, it'll only make matters worse. We pretend to do what the prosecutors ask us, but actually we can do anything we want. Dunk them in water, give them an electric massage. Of course, things are different for Yun-gil because he's got me..."

Chu-ôn picked up the things and rose from the chair.

4

A bird landed in the flower bed beneath his window. It was covered with dark gray feathers, and its beak was almost black. There was a splattering of white and yellow feathers on its back and sides, and a few dark blue and purple feathers at the tips of its wings. A wild magpie—what was it doing here? If only he could catch it. He'd put it in a cage and give it to his girlfriend Sûng-hûi.

Sûng-hûi majored in Korean painting and often painted birds. The flower bed was only a few steps from the foyer where Yun-gil was standing. The magpie didn't seem to be afraid. He could tell it had been tamed. There were some steamed chestnuts in the kitchen. He took a handful outside, peeled one and tossed it to the magpie. The bird didn't fly away; it simply pecked at the chestnut. While the magpie was eating, Yun-gil tried to think of a way to catch it.

He returned to the house and got a bamboo basket. He propped the basket up with a pole and scattered a few peeled chestnuts inside. Then he tied a string to the pole and waited by the foyer door. Finally the bird fell for his trap. When it stepped under the basket, Yun-gil yanked the string. He was excited by his catch. He felt as if he had caught a deep blue secret from an endless river. He asked his mother for ten thousand won, went out and bought a cage, several times larger than the lotus lanterns people hung in temples on the Buddha's birthday.

He reached inside the basket, but jerked his hand out in surprise when the bird pecked him. He screamed in pain. "Wild magpie, wild magpie, where are you going? If you cry..." Yun-gil had thought the magpie docile and sweet-tempered, like the song by that singer with the husky voice, but now he remembered it could be fierce. He dabbed some mercurochrome on his wound, put on a leather glove and went after the bird. It pecked at his gloved hand. Blue eyes rolling, it shrieked and flapped. Yun-gil lost hold of it again and it flew at his face, trying to peck him.

Yun-gil opened his eyes at the sound of something pounding the desk. A man's eyes, tinged with the same blue as the magpie's, flew at him. He had been dreaming. The tip of the bird's beak was sharp and turned up like a fish hook. The bald man's glare was trying to gouge his eyes like the magpie's beak.

"You wrote this, didn't you?"

He spoke in a thin, gravelly voice. It was a different man. Yun-gil felt dizzy. He couldn't distinguish dreams from reality. The stocky man had just replaced the sharp-beaked bald man. He pushed a photocopy across the desk. He was asking the same question as the bald man, who must have asked it thirty times himself. How many times did he have to answer the same question? If only they would let him sleep.

"Yes, I wrote it."

"Read it, out loud," the man said in a low, cold voice. The bald man had made Yun-gil read it at least thirty times already. Yun-gil could recite it from memory now.

"Read it slowly. I want to catch the full meaning."

They were trying to keep Yun-gil awake. He picked up the paper and began to read. His eyes were still closed.

The tunnels, which the U.N. Forces Command and Korean government have proclaimed the work of North Korea, were in fact fabricated by the governments of Korea and the United States. The following proves this beyond the shadow of a doubt.

The first tunnel was discovered by U.N. Forces on November 14, 1974 and opened to reporters shortly thereafter. Mun Bin-do, columnist with the *Seoul Shinmun*, noted graffiti on the tunnel walls, including slogans such as "Speedy Victory in Battle," "Path to Unification," and "Poim Observatory, October 6." The U.N. Forces also showed reporters what they claimed was evidence left behind when the diggers heard the U.N. Forces' shots. Included were clocks, compasses, canteens, mess kits, telephones, levers, picks, mines, dynamite, and composition gunpowder for setting off bombs.

Mun noted: "You could tell from the half-empty rice bowls that the North Koreans had been working right up until the tunnel was found. It was no laughing matter. They clearly fled at the sound of the U.N. Forces' guns." However, the slogans written on the walls of the tunnel are not used by the North Koreans. Rather, they are used by South Korean forces. Why would the North Koreans write such things on the walls of a tunnel being dug for military use? And would a tunnel of that kind really be useful in modern warfare?

At the time this tunnel was discovered, the international press was saying that the Korean peninsula had stabilized enough to merit the withdrawal of U.N. Forces. The United States felt pressured by the media. They feared they might have to give up their bridgehead in Asia. They wanted to remain in Korea even if the forces from other countries were withdrawn. How could they leave after investing so much here? They had to invent a way to stay. The tunnel. By fabricating the tunnel and convincing the world that the North Koreans were warmongers, they strengthened the U.S.-Korea Defense Pact. It benefited both sides. The South Korean government was happy to have proof of how militant the North Koreans were. At this time, demonstrations calling for the overthrow of the Yushin dictatorship of Park Chung-hee were being held every day. The tunnel was the perfect excuse to put down the anti-establishment forces. And with the tacit understanding of both countries, more tunnels were dug. Technology improved with the second and third tunnels.

Oh citizens of Korea! Do not be deceived by the shallow lies of the U.S. imperialists and Korean government. We must realize that it is not North Korea but the American imperialists who are the true warmongers! Let us see the truth and fight!

The Anti-American & People's Liberation Struggle Committee

The stocky man listened with his eyes closed. Did I really write this? Yun-gil thought. He felt as if he had been living in a white night. He didn't feel like himself. He didn't know where he was. He felt as if he had been dragged off to another world, a completely different space and time. He wanted them to set him free. He wanted to give the stocky man everything he was demanding and go home. Everything he had tried to achieve seemed meaningless.

I've been awfully lucky, he thought. He had always bragged about how he didn't believe in fate, about history being a matter of overcoming contradictions and conflict, but he was often surprised by the good luck that surrounded him like a warm breeze. On several occasions when the students had occupied office buildings, they had drawn straws to see who would jump in protest. There were plenty of volunteers because they believed it was the best way to hold off the riot police, to prove their own intentions, and to expose the government's vicious tactics, and they had to draw straws to decide who would have the honor of jumping. Yun-gil always volunteered, and he always ended up with a short straw. A tremor passed through him each time he pulled the straw out. It was a shudder of joy: he had survived.

"What a bunch of nonsense!" the man said wearily. There was a tinge of irritation in his voice. "Read it again," he whispered, glowering from beneath his heavy eyelids.

Yun-gil picked up the piece of paper again and yawned. A wave of helplessness and drowsiness swept over him; he was sinking into a deep, dark hole. He yawned and let his body slip back into sleep. He was walking along a snowy mountain path. His father was walking beside him, silent as a shadow. His father slipped and tumbled to the bottom of the valley.

Kkkwang! Yun-gil jerked awake. How long had he been dozing? The man was slamming his hand on the desk, yelling in a tinny voice.

"Listen, you little asshole! I told you to read! How come you keep slipping off to never-never-land? Open your eyes and read!"

Yun-gil struggled to open his eyes. In the florescent light, the black letters looked like tiny ants swarming across the page. He read. A deep voice rose from his throat. It was a stranger's voice. He had never heard it before. His eyes followed the ants; his mouth spat out the words as if they had been written by someone else. The wriggling ants dizzied him. The sad song of two chickadees echoed in his ears.

He and his father were hiding behind a bush watching a pair of chickadees. Beeyo, peeyo, one cried as it plummeted toward the branch of a dead birch tree. A second chickadee followed. They looked as though they might collide with the tree, but at the last moment, they veered into the sky again, to repeat their flight over and over again.

It was late spring, his freshman year in university. Parents' Day. His father went to the mineral spring behind their house every weekend and holiday. Yun-gil didn't have the heart to refuse him. His father was trying to inspire a love of nature in him.

Father watched the birds, holding Yun-gil's hand in silence. A wild magpie sat in the outer branches of the birch tree. The chickadees were aiming for it.

Yun-gil thought of the magpie he had given Sûng-hûi. She hadn't kept it long. At the time, she was sharing a rented room with her mother. She kept the bird in the kitchen and took it in the room to sketch from time to time. The bird sang an eerie song night and day. The neighbors complained that the bird woke them. It ate constantly and defecated so much her old mother couldn't take care of it. Finally Sûng-hûi had to let it go.

The wild magpie wasn't afraid of the chickadees. Maybe it was the magpie that Sûng-hûi had released, he thought. It was so cocky. Every time the chickadees hurled down at it, the magpie yanked back its head and tried to peck them. Then it explored the tree until the next attack. It was looking for something to eat. From the glint in its eye and the chickadees' desperation, it was clear the magpie was looking for more than bugs. The chickadees' nest must have been nearby. The magpie hoped to find something to eat there, and the chickadees were trying to protect whatever it was. Was it eggs or chicks? Would a wild magpie eat the eggs or offspring of another bird?

The magpie finally found a hole hidden in the tree bark. It peered inside. The chickadees' cries grew louder, their attacks intensified. The magpie jerked its head more rapidly now. It pecked at its attackers, then turned, pulled something from the hole and swallowed it. It smacked its beak and jerked its body. A lump passed through its throat to its chest. The chickadees hurled themselves at the predator, but the magpie kept eating, glancing back to ward off their attacks, eyes sparkling.

"What's it eating? Eggs or chicks?" Yun-gil asked, extricating his hand from his father's grip. He picked up a stone, but his father caught his hand without a word. Yun-gil glanced from his father to the birds. His father just stood back and watched as the magpie stole from the chickadees. Yun-gil was incensed. His father was so callous.

When the magpie had finished, it flew into the sky and landed on the top of a towering oak. The chickadees continued to attack. Undistracted by its meal now, the magpie was free to repel them. The chickadees charged with all their might, braving the larger bird's pecking. The magpie finally flew away, disappearing around the mountain. Perhaps it felt guilty, or maybe it was full. The chickadees sat in the oak tree, weeping sadly. Yun-gil's father simply watched them. Perhaps he was waiting for them to fly back to their nest and cry even more sadly.

The tiny birds circled the dead birch tree but did not land to look inside their nest. They must have sensed the two men watching them. His father didn't wait any longer. He pushed his way through the branches, Yun-gil following behind him. The dead birch tree stood on a slope covered with elms and lacquer trees. With some difficulty, they made their way to it. There was a nest in a hole half-way up the rotting trunk. It was empty. What had the wild magpie eaten? His father peered into the nest and studied the fallen leaves decomposing around its trunk. There were no egg shells or chicks to be found, not a single bird dropping.

"I wonder what he ate," Yun-gil's father muttered.

What a stupid question! Yun-gil thought. He wished he had thrown the stone. He should have killed the magpie.

One summer day during his sophomore year, Yun-gil argued with his father about the magpie and the chickadees.

"That's what capitalist society is all about. The strong eat the flesh of the weak. If we are going to make this society livable, we must transform it from an animalistic society to a human one. In other words, we must transcend the food chain. In that sense, Marxism is the ultimate humanism."

Yun-gil stared at his father's fly as he spoke. It was unzipped. He was too embarrassed to tell him. His father had so many sloppy habits. He had made some incredible mistakes at work. Once he added an extra stroke to the title of a book so the Chinese ideograph for *The King and the Servant* became *The Jade and the Servant*. He sometimes forgot to put the publisher's telephone in newspaper advertisements. That was the most important thing! He often had a speck of red pepper powder stuck between his teeth after meals. His necktie was never straight, and the collar of his sportscoat was often turned under.

Yun-gil despised his slovenly father, and he hated his mother for treating him with the respect due a poet.

"I love the way nature is organized. I respect the natural order," his father said. "The food chain is governed by divine law. If man interferes with it, everything will fall apart. Capitalism is the closest thing to the natural order. It's not perfect, of course. The capitalists often exploit the workers, and when that exploitation causes the workers to rebel and prevents capitalists from reinvesting their surpluses, our international competitiveness deteriorates, and both the capitalists and workers suffer. Everyone has to stop being greedy. That's the most important thing. Capitalists have to set an example by returning their profits to society on their own. Only with that spirit of self-denial can the contradictions and conflicts between the two classes be mitigated. That's the only way we can strengthen our international competitiveness.

"And how do we get the capitalists to stop being so greedy? By instilling them with a sense of ethics. The traditional ethics of Buddhism or Confucianism, or the spirit of a Christian philanthropist perhaps. The Japanese say: 'The *Analects* in one hand and an abacus in the other.' The strength of the Japanese economy lies in the spirit of Confucius' *Analects*. That's why Japanese capitalists and laborers work together to enhance productivity and put their country at the top of the international economy. We should be teaching our children *A Handbook of Reminders* or the *Analects*. We should give them the opportunity to study Buddhist sutras and the Bible. As far as I'm concerned, the only way to keep our economy from collapsing is to create a Korean-style Confucian capitalism."

Yun-gil snorted in amusement. That's why this country is in such a mess, he thought. Because of middle class fools who think like my father.

"Where did you get this?" the stocky man asked in a sinister voice, his eyes glinting like the magpie's. "Who handled your ideological training?"

"Do you think someone had to teach us that? You can find that information in any daily newspaper. All you have to do is read. A three year-old child could figure it out!"

Yun-gil spoke with confidence for it was true. The man shook his head slowly, eyes half-closed. He moistened his lips with a flick of his bright pink tongue and spoke in a low, husky voice.

"You must have been under the orders of someone familiar with the North Korean regime. I know I'm right, and you'll have to admit it sooner or later. Here, write it all down. The name of the person who told you that the tunnels were fabricated, where you met him, and how you wrote the posters and printed and distributed the flyers. If I don't like what you write, I'll make you redo it a million times. We might even dunk you in that cold water again or take you next door for an electric massage. Let's settle this nice and quiet. If you've got a problem, you can bring it up in court. Why make the ghosts in this smelly old basement any angrier?"

The man's husky voice made Yun-gil feel dizzy and helpless.

"I have a brother your age. We ran a check on you: I know you're a smart kid. I'd hate to ruin that brain of yours, so just do as I say."

Yun-gil heard the faint sound of the radio. The florescent light on the ceiling floated down like silvery powder. Yun-gil shut his eyes. Why did I go back to Temple Hollow? I had gone there to persuade the villagers not to give in to the Buddha Light High School Foundation. I didn't want them to accept anything if the Foundation didn't hand over the land to the tenants.... But the plainclothesmen were waiting for me.

Bombs never fall in the same place twice. That's why a bomb crater is the safest place in a battlefield. Yun-gil had gone to Temple Hollow with that in mind.

No, he thought, shaking his head. He had gone there because of that woman, the one who was always grinning like a Hahoe mask. She was strange. While Yun-gil was there, she bathed every day in the early evening. She bathed in the stream that flowed past the dormitory until early autumn, and when the weather grew colder, she heated water in the kitchen and bathed there. After her bath, she always put on make-up. Then she dressed in clean clothes and came to Yun-gil's room. She polished his floor with a rag, cooked him ramen or boiled him potatoes or eggs, made spicy noodles, roasted chestnuts, brought persimmon punch, and peeled fruit. And while he ate, she talked. She told him about her encounter with a buck on the way to

Sunrise Peak. She and the buck climbed into the sky on a rainbow. She told him about one of her dreams. A spring had gurgled up from beneath the temple bell pavilion. The fields and alleys turned into rose gardens, and a garter snake chased her through the flowers. She said she thought she might be a fairy. Her husband had hidden her wings but she found them and flew back into the sky, carrying one child on her back and the other in her arms. Sadly, she had awakened too soon. She told him of another dream too. She was crawling through the dark alleys of Kyerim-dong in Kwangju, trying to escape the bullets, when she floated into the air as if she were riding a cloud. The woman laughed as she talked about flying over the mountains, across the sea, over unfamiliar villages.

Her laughter reminded him of the giggling of a small child being tickled. Her face flushed as she talked.

Listening to her, he felt as if he were living in a fairy tale. As if he were dreaming. Life's troubles seemed so trivial.

"Are you going to write it or what?" the man snapped.

"What shall I write? Who should I say told me to do it? Tell me. I'll write whatever you want," Yun-gil replied with a grimace. He had no choice. He couldn't bear the thought of being dunked again. He wanted the man to give him a script to follow.

"You bastard! You're just jerking me around!" the man snarled. His eyes flashed like an ax blade. He glowered at Yun-gil for a moment, then lowered his eyes and spoke in a tired voice.

"Everyone has an emergency store of energy. Never let a drowning man get hold of your arm or leg. He'll never let go, even if you break his arm. Where does a dying man get such strength? It's emergency energy. That's what keeps a marathoner going after 25 miles."

What is he talking about? Yun-gil thought. The face of the woman floated before him. He could hear her talking and laughing like a baby being tickled.

"Shall I tell you a really funny dream?" she giggled. "I have this dream a couple times a week. I'm getting married, and I'm wearing the bride's crown, and you know what?.... Ha, ha, ha...you're the groom! Ha, ha, ha!"

The stocky man swallowed and continued.

"When a person is pushed to the very edge, his emergency store of mental energy comes into action. Imagination that you never expected, superhuman strength, wit, the power to unearth memories buried in the subconscious, the logical forces to create fictional memories that seem real.... In other words, people create the power to overcome the crisis at hand. Of course, it doesn't just happen. We have to help you create that energy. I hope you don't get me wrong. We have to push you to the edge. For your own sake."

The man pushed the button on the corner of the desk. The faint chirp of a bell rang through the sound of the radio. The three men would come in soon, yawning and cursing. Yun-gil closed his eyes and cried silently as he tumbled into that black despair. "Mother," he cried, but he knew he shouldn't be calling her. "Avalokitesvara, Bodhisattva of Compassion! Bodhisattva of a thousand hands and faces! God, all knowing, all powerful! Please save me!"

5

Hye-suk was wrapping a thickly padded *hanbok* and several pairs of underwear in a large scarf. They were for Yun-gil to wear in jail. Her cheeks were puffed in anger. She loathed her husband. He was so cold.

Sunlight streamed through the window to the south. Chu-ch'ôl was sitting with his back to the sun, waiting for his green tea to brew. He was always so calm, so solemn when he brewed tea, as if he were meditating or praying. First he poured the water from the mineral spring into an electric tea kettle. He warmed the stoneware teapot and cups with hot water, then poured hot water into a bowl to let it cool to the precise temperature: just warm to the lips. He put tea leaves in the teapot, poured in the cooled water, and waited for the tea to brew.

As he waited, his mind was empty. His consciousness faded white, like a blank piece of paper, untouched by a single stroke of the pencil. At that moment, he was completely alone in his own universe. The moment stretched on as he slowly sipped the first batch of tea, poured in more water and waited for the second and third, drinking each with the same studied appreciation. If Hye-suk spoke to him, he simply grunted in reply.

Hye-suk had always felt her husband was like a man possessed. This morning she hated that quality in him. He seemed so cold and distant.

"Aren't you going to call Prosecutor Chang?" she asked. She wanted him to ask his friend to make it easier for her to visit her son. She had been pestering him about it since the night before. Chu-ch'ŏl frowned and smacked his lips in irritation. He hadn't been able to focus on his tea that morning. It didn't taste right if the water was too hot or too cool. He felt distracted when the tea wasn't right. Then he got irritated. It irritated him to see his wife wrapping the clothes for Yun-gil. He was disgusted by the thought of calling Chang Ki-ho, but he also hated the idea of his wife staying out all day. Her every move seemed to break the rhythm of his tea ritual.

He didn't go to office that day. He had cut a week-long business trip short and returned home four days earlier. For the next four days he planned to stay home and write two poems and a column he had been putting off. He had always treasured the time with his wife when the children were at school.

When the two of them were alone, he acted like a child. He slid his hand inside her blouse and fondled her breasts. He allowed her to draw a tub of hot water and bathe him. When his bath was finished, she cut his finger and toe nails. He laid his head in her lap and she plucked out his white hairs. With his face against her belly, he couldn't help breathing in her scent, the ripe citrus smell that wafted from her breasts, armpits and skirts. There was a hint of chestnut blossoms there, of silk tree flowers and sour body odors. That was how his mother had smelled. As he lay there, surrounded by that scent, he dozed off peacefully.

It was always comfortable to stay home with his wife. She created a cozy atmosphere. But now she had found some reason to go out and leave him behind. He lost his appetite for tea.

They had seen him once since the case was sent to the prosecutor's office, a month and a half after his arrest. During that visit, Hye-suk was speechless. She simply cried. Chu-ch'ôl was confused. He couldn't tell whether he was sad and resentful or happy and thankful about his son's imprisonment. It was as if there were a devil inside him, ordering him around. He tried to play the supportive father, saddened and angered by his son's arrest, yet persevering with quiet dignity, but he felt like a hypocrite and ended up scowling in silence. Yun-gil must have thought that his father was too stunned to speak. He tried to comfort his parents.

"Don't worry. It's not so bad," he said, looking up after a long silence. "You don't need to visit me. Why don't you meet the other parents and discuss what you can do as a group?"

Yun-gil then rose from his chair, although visiting hours were not yet over.

Chu-ch'ôl tried to make up for his silence in a letter. He had mountains of advice for his son, both as a father and as a member of the older generation. Their spiritual communication as father and son had been cut off for too long.

Chu-ch'ôl read a great deal in preparation for his letter to Yun-gil. He leafed through Adam Smith's *Wealth of Nations*. He read Marx's *Das Capital* and reconsidered the problems of labor, exploitation and alienation. He read Bruce Cumings' *Origins of the Korean War* and looked through the *History of the Korean Communist Movement*. He read about opportunism on the right and left and studied the Pak Hon-yong line. He read the *Modern History of Korea* compiled and published by the North Korean Social Science Research Institute.

Chang Ki-ho made it possible for him to write to his son. Of course, they let Yun-gil write to his father too, and made sure every letter reached him.

They wanted to use Chu-ch'ôl's letters. They figured a poet's letters would be most persuasive. A good letter might turn Yun-gil around, and failing that, at least it might make him realize that radicalism was not the right path.

Chu-ch'ôl had put off writing a second time. His son's response to his first letter had upset him. Yun-gil was heavily armed with Marxism and Leninism, with a relentless criticism and the will to overcome his father's generation. Yun-gil had once told him about their Patricide Society. It was made up of the children of rich parents and high government officials, from various universities. Of course, they weren't demanding that anyone kill their father, he explained. "We just have to take a critical attitude toward our parents' thoughts and actions. We have to overcome them."

Annoyed by his tiff with Hye-suk, Chu-ch'ôl called Chang Ki-ho. The man's arrogant voice, so quiet and sinister, repelled and, at the same time, overwhelmed him. He was angry at himself for being intimidated and snapped at Hye-suk as he told her of the special channel Chang had arranged.

Chu-ch'ŏl cursed his son as he watched Hye-suk leave the house with the bundle of clothes. If it weren't for him, I'd never have to fawn to these miserable worms! He drew a long breath and his face crumbled in despair.

Images of his son collapsing from the torture rose in his brain. Yun-gil taking his last breath, Yun-gil being placed in a coffin. The images were etched before his eyes. His devil wanted it to happen. Chu-ch'ŏl bit down hard on his tongue, then called after his wife. "Tell him to eat what they give him and exercise as much as he can. What use are freedom, nation and unification if his health is ruined?" She had already stepped out of the gate, though. He slammed the foyer door and looked at Yun-gil's room. It was empty, of course, but it didn't feel like it. Chu-ch'ŏl felt as if Yun-gil had hidden his spirit there when he left home. The spirit was just like Yun-gil: It spent all its time in the room, then dashed out in the middle of the night or early morning, without a word to Chu-ch'ŏl or Hye-suk. Where was it now?

Chu-ch'ŏl crossed the living room. A drawer was open at the bottom of the bookcase. Who had opened it? Amidst the drills, wrenches and hammers, the adze looked strangely large. At the sight of its white blade, he was suddenly reminded of the legend of the deer.

Deep in the mountains, a deer scurried into a small hut to hide from a hunter. A middle-aged couple was sitting in the hut; the man was carving wooden shoes, the woman cleaning vegetables for kimchi. The deer collapsed in front of them. It was a doe, ready to foal. She was wounded in the leg and bleeding profusely. The woman hid the animal under her skirts. The hunter dashed breathlessly into the hut and asked if they had seen a deer. No, they said, and he left, puzzled. After the hunter was gone, the man and the woman began to have second thoughts. It was a long time since they had tasted meat, so the man whacked the doe on the head with his adze. When he split open the animal, he found two fawns in her belly. The man and woman feasted on deer meat for a month. They made deer soup and preserved some of the meat in salt and soy sauce, and they drank stock from the bones for six months. It was not long before the middle-aged couple regained their youth and the woman became pregnant. The husband was thrilled and stroked his wife's belly happily. They had never been able to afford memorial rites for their ancestors, nor did they have any children to perform rites to them after they had died. But now the woman gave birth to triplets, first a daughter, then two sons. The children seemed to bring good luck, for the wooden shoes were soon selling like hotcakes. The couple tore down the old hut and built a four-room house. Their lives were filled with laughter and happiness. Then one day the father died. He had gotten drunk and fallen asleep as he was working on a pair of wooden shoes. The children had a fight, and the eldest son threw his father's adze at his sister. It landed on their father's head instead. After watching their father die, the three children fell ill and died one by one. In a single month their mother buried four corpses and went crazy. She camped beside the graves on the hill behind their house, beating the ground, throwing her arms around the mounds of earth, crying herself to sleep. Then one day she heard her children's voices from inside the graves. Was it a dream? "Mama, we should have killed the old woman, too," her youngest son said. "No, that old hag will shrivel up and die on her own, just like a worm in a fire," her daughter answered. It was only then that the woman realized her three children had been the reincarnation of the mother doe and her two fawns. The woman ran from the graves and tumbled off the edge of a cliff.

Perhaps Yun-gil and I share the same kind of bad karma, Chu-ch'ŏl thought. He then shook his head firmly, chiding himself for the thought.

Chu-ch'ŏl went into his room and took out Yun-gil's letters. His son was a talented writer. They had received one or two letters a week. His handwriting was small and neat, like sesame seeds arranged in neat rows. The tiny letters filled all three sides of the pre-stamped envelopes. They would probably fill 20 sheets of manuscript paper, Chu-ch'ŏl thought. I could make a bestseller out of these letters. Maybe I should set up my own publishing company and print it. Then I'd be president of the company. He scorned himself for the thought. That's the way everyone in the publishing business thinks. You dirty bastard! Did you send your son to jail so you could own your publishing company?

The first letter Chu-ch'ŏl opened was Yun-gil's response to his own letter.

Father, you said, "You're right, but that doesn't mean you can live according to the way you think. The world doesn't work that way. They say a man of virtue is above the ways of the world..." That's what the older generation always says. You share the consciousness of a generation trained as slaves of imperialism and flunkyism....

In your letter you said there are two ways to dedicate oneself to one's country and people: "First, demanding rapid reforms before you're fully ready, like you, and second, suppressing your anger and studying hard until you can achieve something truly great, even if it means being ostracized as a coward or traitor by other members of your movement. What do you think is the best way to serve your country and people?" My professors have told me the same thing a thousand times. That position typifies the mystification and fraudulent logic of a generation that has lived under imperialism and flunkyism for too long.

Our movement is struggling to help people live as human beings. In my view, man can only become truly human when he lives within the context of social relationships. By renewing and recreating our relationships, we can make the most of our humanity. This process of change and creation is what we call the "movement." You must rid yourself of your old thoughts and let Mother join the committee organized by the families of political prisoners. If you want to visit me, visit as a group. If you want to bring me spending money, bring it together, for all of us...

Chu-ch'ôl felt something hot rising within himself as he read the letter. He was angry and embarrassed. Yun-gil might be right, though he couldn't admit it.

"To criticize means to punish and destroy for the communists," Chang Ki-ho had said.

Chu-ch'ôl picked up Yun-gil's third letter. In it, Yun-gil wrote of his girlfriend, of his views on women, and explained, in detail, how his father should improve things at home. Chu-ch'ôl began rereading it in hopes of finding gaps in his son's logic. The writing was so small he had to put on his reading glasses.

Suddenly the telephone shattered the silence.

"Hello? Is this Yun-gil's house?" A middle-aged woman asked in a quiet voice. When Chu-ch'ôl confirmed it was, the woman asked for Yun-gil's mother. "She's out," replied Chu-ch'ôl. The woman asked if Chu-ch'ôl was Yun-gil's father, then introduced herself as the head of the Support Committee founded by the families of the students arrested in the Anti-American & People's Liberation Struggle Committee case. She began by sympathizing with him, saying how angry and bitter he must be.

"I'm Ko Ch'ang-nam's mother. Yun-gil and my son have been very close since high school. Now they're stuck in the same boat."

The woman started to get agitated. "I've called several times but it's either busy or no answer. All the other mothers have gotten together. Please listen to what I have to say and tell Yun-gil's mother."

She spoke rapidly, like a starling. She said the authorities were torturing the students in unimaginable ways, doing everything they could to fabricate a case against them. That's why the mothers had to come forward, at risk of death, to make the world see their children's innocence and the injustice of their arrests.

"We're having a meeting right now. Please tell Yun-gil's mother to call me at home when she gets back."

He jotted down the number.

"I won't be home until after nine this evening," she added with an air of importance.

Chu-ch'ôl put down the receiver and stared blankly in front of him. All he had said was "Yes, yes." He began to feel a certain resentment toward Ko Ch'ang-nam's mother and her group. Her voice rang in his ears, like the wailing of Yun-gil's spirit drifting from his room. Chu-ch'ôl chuckled bitterly. He would never let his wife attend those meetings. And she wouldn't go against his wishes. She always obeyed him.

It wasn't simply because Chu-ôn had told him not to allow her to go. And it wasn't because he believed Chang Ki-ho would find a way to get Yun-gil out sooner if they avoided the group. He simply wanted to sit back and watch things develop without attracting any attention.

...First of all, you must abandon the notion that Mother, a woman, is the property of you, a man. How can one human own another? Are women really nothing more than slaves to men? That's a misconception of a people living under imperialism. True human liberation begins with the liberation of women....

Chu-ch'ôl jotted some notes on a piece of paper: The biological structure of men and women...how to realize true happiness for men and women.... He was searching for ammunition to use against his son.

The door bell rang. Who could it be? "May we have a word with you? We've brought the Lord's good news." What if it was one of those exasperating women? he thought, and let the ringing continue. The ringing stopped for a moment, then resumed. Whoever it was, they were determined to outlast him. He went into the foyer and lifted the intercom.

"Hello? It's me, Sûng-hûi," a childish voice rang out.

"Who?"

"Sûng-hûi, Yun-gil's friend. I've been here several times."

Chu-ch'ôl hesitated for a moment. It was that girl, the one Hye-suk said was no bigger than a sparrow. She had studied Korean painting at some third-rate art school, and now she was working in the labor movement. Sûng-hûi had visited several times on Yun-gil's errands, once for his escape money and another time for his clothes.

He thought of Yun-gil's spirit once more. It was as if his son's spirit had returned in the form of this girl.

"I have something to tell you, Father."

How dare she call me Father, he thought, as he pushed the button opening the front gate.

The girl got down on her knees and bowed to Chu-ch'ôl as soon as she stepped into the living room. He stood awkwardly, refusing to sit to receive her greetings.

"Has Mother gone out?" she asked, pausing at the hall leading to the kitchen. She looked no more than half Yun-gil's height, Chu-ch'ôl thought, recalling his wife's description. Chu-ch'ôl switched on the oil heater. Most short girls made up for their height with large faces and distinct features, but not Sûng-hûi. Her features were small and crowded, her body was skinny as a rail, and her face was covered with freckles.

"Yes, she went out," Chu-ch'ôl answered as he put a cigarette between his lips. He lit it and plugged in the electric tea kettle. He didn't ask her to sit down. He wasn't going to make a space for her in his home, he thought. He would have liked to drain the air so she couldn't breathe. Maybe she would leave Yun-gil alone when she realized that his family had rejected her.

Sûng-hûi was an audacious girl, though. Or was she just thick-skinned? After all, she was a painter; she must have sensed how they felt, but she behaved as if she hadn't noticed anything out of the ordinary.

"Coffee?" he asked gruffly.

"Yes, please," she answered with a sweet smile.

Chu-ch'ôl smiled to himself. He treated his honored guests to green tea. For his closest friends and important callers he brewed the Korean leaf tea he kept under lock and key in the refrigerator. A monk at Ssanggye Temple had sent it to him, saying it came from the first crop of the new year. He also stored the green tea his former student had brought from Beijing in the refrigerator.

...The tendency to stress a woman's beauty and physical appearance over her spiritual nobility is feudalistic and capitalistic. Cattle ranchers want hefty females and large males to produce plump calves with high-quality meat. The desire for beauty and a good body from a woman is a bourgeois sickness of men who care for nothing but their own pursuit of possessions. The love between a man and a woman must be considered within the context of the movement. It must be judged in accordance with the principle of human liberation....

Chu-ch'ôl recalled Yun-gil's letter as he spooned the instant coffee into a cup. Yun-gil was trying to rationalize his relationship with Sûng-hûi. He was trying to reorganize Chu-ch'ôl's household.

...Why does Mother have to work alone in the kitchen all the time? Why is she stuck with all the washing and cleaning? Why can't the family take turns with the cooking and laundry so she can be freed from that prison of a kitchen? We have to open a road for her involvement in society.

Chu-ch'ôl scoffed at his son's naiveté. Lips pursed firmly, he stirred the coffee and handed it to the girl. He waited for her to explain why she had come. Head bent, she wrapped her hands around the cup.

"From the way they're controlling the news, it looks like they're going to make a bigger deal out of this than we expected," she said after taking a sip. "You've probably guessed as much yourself."

Chu-ch'ôl drew on his cigarette. A woman has to look like a woman, he thought with a frown. Something must be wrong with Yun-gil. Her skin is rough, she's skinny as a rail, and she doesn't have a curve on her. How could she ever produce a child? What could she do in bed?

"The families have to come forward before the conspiracy goes any further. I'm handling general affairs for the family committee. The head of the committee called earlier, didn't she? Actually, I've thought of marrying Yun-gil while he's still in prison and joining the committee as his wife, but I figured it might seem too presumptuous and you and Mother might disapprove, so I decided to wait. I came to tell you that Mother must come to the meetings. The mothers have to stick together. They have to go to the political party offices and social organizations, and to the press. They have to tell them that the case is a fabrication. It's been blown out of proportion. All the other mothers came. Mother was the only one who didn't show up. I was so embarrassed."

Chu-ch'ŏl took out another cigarette. He was waiting for a chance to reject her idea. He picked up his lighter. She placed her empty cup on the table. The dwarfish girl looked like she wouldn't budge until he agreed to send Hye-suk to the committee meetings.

Chu-ch'ŏl avoided her sparkling eyes. He stared at the table and nodded. A bitter nicotine taste spread through his mouth as he exhaled. He closed his eyes for a moment, then opened them and stared at the empty cup.

"I can't make her do anything," he began. "I'll tell her what you said, but it's up to her whether she goes or not.... She generally doesn't like going places like that.... You put in a good word for her if she doesn't go, all right?"

6

I was eating the meal they had shoved through the slot in the door when I heard the magpie. I was thankful to the jailers for letting the sound in. When I heard the magpie I thought of the sky. I started to grow wings and turned into a bird. You may laugh at my sentimentality, but lately I live for that...the joy of becoming a bird and flapping my wings. I turn into a bird and travel, traversing the clouds, flying through the sky. I wander through the woods, the mountains and valleys, over the fields and rivers and sea. I pass over virgin forests that no one's ever seen and fly over the raging sea. They cannot take this freedom from me.

Chu-ch'ôl thought of his son's letter as he climbed. The hill was steep. He gasped for breath. A thin fog hung over the trees—pines, oaks, alders, hazelnuts—and a thick milky sea of fog spread around the foot of the mountain. He felt as if he were on an island in the middle of nowhere. The sounds of the city shook the island-mountain like roaring waves.

After coming here I've learned what walls are. Everywhere I look I see a wall. There is even a wall between the friends I came here with. You and I have exchanged many letters but the wall between us is as high as before. There's even a wall in my dreams. I'm imprisoned in my own universe. I've learned how to escape, though. I sprout wings. But I haven't told anyone about them. My friends would say it's just sentimentality and fantasy. Sentimentality and fantasy do us more harm than good.

The months had passed like a whirlwind. The case of the Anti-American & People's Liberation Struggle Committee burst into the press. The reports said they had listened to North Korean radio broadcasts and devoured every communist book they could get their hands on. They had been stained by Kim Il Sung's self-reliance theories. They were accused of setting up a vast student organization under the direction of the North Korean government. It was front page news, the lead story on the television news, replacing the usual coverage of the president's daily activities. The trial was closed to all but the immediate families. The prosecutor asked for a seven and a half year sentence for Yun-gil. He was sentenced to five. How could he survive five years in prison? His best years... Chu-ch'ŏl's heart was as dark and desolate as a winter landscape. It stung. He groaned in agony.

His household was destroyed. It didn't seem like home anymore. Hye-suk was never there. She made breakfast for their college-age daughter and middle school son and left the house with them in the morning. She made the rounds to the party offices, social organizations and churches with the other parents. They joined forces with families involved in other cases, visiting the courts, disrupting trials, writing petitions, and staging demonstrations.

Today was Sunday, but she had gone out without telling him where she was going.

It didn't take much for her to lose her temper. When the children came home with food in their lunch boxes, she nagged them: "How can you waste food like that? Some people live on rice and salt. They're imprisoned inside cement walls. Are you trying to show off your good fortune?" Or when the children poked at each other and giggled in a teasing mood, she shrieked, "How can you be so heartless? You never even ask about your brother!" Soon the children were self-conscious around their mother.

There was a heap of laundry—socks, underwear, dirty pants, blouses and shirts—in front of the washing machine in the bathroom. The water in the bathtub had a layer of dirty scum at the bottom, and there was a grimy ring around the sink. The wastepaper basket next to the toilet overflowed with soiled toilet paper. A thick layer of dust covered the bedding, Chu-ch'ŏl's desk and bookshelves. He couldn't remember the last time he had taken a bath. And Hye-suk didn't cut his fingernails anymore. She didn't pluck out his white hairs either. He was being pushed from her life.

He felt lonely and sad, an orphan. When he got home from work around eight or nine, she wasn't there. The house was filled with cold wind. He sat on the sofa smoking a cigarette. He didn't even take off his jacket. He was like a guest in his own house. I should have gone out drinking with a friend, he thought with displeasure.

Women were his weak point. When he was living in town by himself during middle school, he cried himself to sleep at night, pining for his mother. On Saturdays, he dashed three miles home from town, without even dropping his school bag off at the lodging house. Once home, he spent the night fondling his mother's breasts, breathing in her scent, then whimpered the whole way back to town the next day.

Chu-ch'ŏl married Hye-suk when he was twenty-five. Come to think of it, he had simply replaced one woman with another. It wasn't long before he had settled down to a comfortable life in the warm atmosphere his wife created at home.

Chu-ch'ŏl often used the image of an island and the sea as a metaphor for the relationship between men and women. He had once written about it in a column for a women's magazine.

Man and woman are like an island and the sea in their physiological structure. Man's structure is lonely; woman's is made to embrace that loneliness and thus fill up her own emptiness. Men have no choice but to act like children around women, and women are born to be generous, like a mother. This is why men rule the world, but women rule men. There is a woman behind every man that stands tall in history and society. In the traditional Korean household, the relationship between a man and wife is like the relationship between the outer fabric of a traditional overcoat and its lining. The outer fabric is made of thin hemp, the lining of silk. Why is the expensive and beautiful fabric put inside? Because it prevents the outer fabric from wrinkling. What if they did it the other way around? The silk might look nice on the outside, but it would simply invite trouble.

It would attract dirt, the clothes would balloon in the wind, and the garment wouldn't hang right.

Several young female readers called to complain. What a hackneyed point of view! they cried. Do you really think the greatest womanly virtue is to support men from behind the scenes? How can you take such a negative approach to women's rights and social advancement? He felt embarrassed and ill at ease.

"I didn't mean it that way," he explained. "I simply wanted to say that women are the foundation of a healthy society. I'm not taking a negative approach to women's social advancement. I'm just expressing my concern that when women get overly involved in society, they forfeit what is truly valuable and great about their sex."

What was his wife doing out all day? She had gone beyond working for Yun-gil's release or protesting the injustice of his situation. She was trying to overcome the corruption in their society. "How can we sit in this nice warm room stuffing ourselves like pigs when bright kids are being dragged off to be beaten, even killed?" she finally blurted out. When he suggested they wait and see what happened, her voice broke. "I can't wait. My anger's all I've got left."

He understood, but at the same time he felt lost and restless without her. He tried to convince himself that he had to accept it, but he wasn't that generous. Yun-gil had his life and they had theirs. What was the point of running around making such a fuss? It was the devil inside him. Why should I take care of that boy when he's jabbering about a Patricide Society?

The fog gradually invaded the valley like an army of occupation. The sky was filled with thick clouds. Chu-ch'ŏl walked through the eulalia grass. The rhododendrons had exploded into bloom on the surrounding hillside. He gazed over the forest: the azalea blossoms had fallen already; the oaks, birch and bush clover were covered with young leaves. He recalled the days he pointed them out, teaching Yun-gil their names one by one.

"In the mid-1860s an American envoy to Russia, a man named Clay, made a recommendation to his government. He said, 'We must establish a base for our army and navy in northeast Asia if we are to dominate the region politically and economically. We should occupy Komun Island off the southern coast of Korea for it can serve as an Asian Gibraltar.' Don't you see what this means? The older generation has to wake up and realize that the United States is not our ally. It never has been! Ever since the *General Sherman* invaded in July 1866, the Americans have been storming our country. In the end, they actually occupied part of Korea. They are our enemy! They didn't drive out the Japanese to liberate us. They did it so they could take over our land!"

This was how Yun-gil's final statement began. He looked haggard in his white padded *hanbok*. His pallor was set off by his unkempt thatch of hair and stubbled chin. His cheekbones stuck out, his eyes seemed larger. His neck was thin; the Adam's apple stuck out like a head of garlic. His voice, usually so clear and strong, was raspy, perhaps because he was weak. He spoke in a high, even tone.

"Hey, he's really smart."

"He's Pak Chu-ch'ôl's son. You know, the poet."

"Pak Chu-ch'ôl's a little ambiguous at times, but his son is completely different."

The hushed whispers of two men seated somewhere behind him flew to Chu-ch'ôl's ears. His face burned. The months in prison had made Yun-gil even more resolute in his beliefs. He hadn't gotten any smarter, but he was truculent. His *t'aekwondo* training in the army, the water torture on the Seven

Star board, the electric torture—it had all made him more belligerent. He wasn't talking in a normal voice; he was screaming, shrieking. The words were filled with hatred and revenge. There was no good will there, no desire for peace. No, he wasn't any smarter: His speech was a sign of mental illness.

Hye-suk sat at Chu-ch'ŏl's side, clasping his shoulder. She didn't breathe for a moment, then let out a string of trembling sighs. Sûng-hûi was sitting beside her, and Chu-ôn stood behind Chu-ch'ôl.

"The older generation says the Republic of Korea is a democratic nation..."

Later, in a letter, Yun-gil described the despair he felt as he spoke.

I felt dizzy. I'm not sure why. It was as if all the words I had prepared simply slipped away like the tide. My brain was empty, a black mudflat. I fumbled through my brain, grasping for the tails of those fleeting words, but they whirled through the air like a wildcat. Perspiration ran down my back and forehead. "Fuck this, fuck this," I kept whispering to myself. I had to present some kind of image to my parents, to Sûng-hûi, to the other defendants, to my friends who couldn't get tickets to the trial, to the lawyers who were defending us without pay, to the prosecutor, to the judge, and to the plainclothesmen in the Communist Investigation Unit, to Uncle Chu-ôn, to the United States, to the Korean people....

It was my duty to our society, to history. But that duty felt like a mountain. The summit was so far away, out of reach. My legs and arms were too weak, too skinny to make it to the top. I was dwarfed, a tiny insect. I felt so helpless. I wanted to step back. I wanted to make some kind of excuse, to step out of line, to give up my turn.

FATHER AND SON

What you had said about dedicating myself to something bigger, about not letting myself fall like an unripened flower, about a virtuous man flowing with the times.... I was tempted by your words. I had been discouraged so many times after they got me down in that basement. It was the same despair I'd felt in army *t'aekwondo* class. In fact, I've felt it since I was a child. Every morning you made me do chin-ups and push-ups. You pressured me to increase the number each day. It took all my strength to do a single chin-up or a dozen push-ups, but you wanted more. "Just grit your teeth and do it," you said. "You have to make yourself do one more." You stood right behind me. I could feel your breath on the back of my neck. Hanging from the bar or lying on the floor, I was filled with that despair. "How come you never make the top five of your class? You make the top ten, without even trying. With a little effort, you could be in the top five. Just screw up your confidence and try. It's easy. When you get home from school, just go over what you studied that day."

You were always so interested in my grades. "You've got a good head. You're just not trying. You could be first in your class if you tried. All my friends' kids are good students. I guess you've got to be smart to write poetry or novels." Sometimes I wondered if you were trying to use your children' grades to prove your own intelligence. You actually lied when people came over. "We don't have to tell our kids to study. They're good students on their own." Every time I had a test, I'd get dizzy. I never did well on exams because of that despair. That's probably why I failed the university entrance examination the first time around. I was paralyzed. It took me five minutes to solve a question that should have taken thirty seconds.

"You can't confine me in your box. I want freedom and liberation for my people. This can only happen when we are free from the United States and have unified our nation. When all private property is shared, when our people are free from servitude..." When I said this, an even heavier feeling of helplessness swept over my body. I clenched my teeth, cursing myself for my weakness. I took a deep breath and looked for an escape. I thought of you, Father, sitting next to Mother in the bench behind me. And the feeling of helplessness miraculously disappeared. No, it wasn't really miraculous. I pictured you fawning over that prosecutor Chang Ki-ho in some secret room. My hatred for you boiled up, I clenched my fists and was able to continue, in a strong, clear voice. "When private property is shared by all and the Korean people are independent, there will be true freedom and human liberation."

I was finished. I felt like a giant. The people in the courtroom seemed like insignificant creatures. But I felt lonely and empty, as if I were the only one left in the world. I was plunged into loneliness.

Chu-ch'ôl was imprisoned by the fog now. It was sweeping toward the top of the mountain. He thought back to Yun-gil's statement in court. Chu-ch'ôl had shut his eyes and clenched his teeth in anger. "Ha, he just had to say it, didn't he?" he sighed to himself. Hye-suk was still clutching his shoulder, trembling all over.

"All right, you little bastard, that's the end of you. It's your ideology. It's yours, to live or die by."

Chu-ch'ôl paused, overlooking a valley and the mountain beyond. He felt as if his son were standing somewhere on the mountain. As if he and his friends had gathered there to plan some new conspiracy. He recalled what Yun-gil had said about the Patricide Society.

Ha, he snorted. Did they really think they could overcome their fathers' legacy? Try, just try! I'm not that old and feeble. I'll keep going for another twenty years, at least until I'm seventy. Twenty years is a long time. The mountains and rivers change in a decade—that's what the proverb says. Just imagine what can happen in two decades. But what am I going to do? What do I need to do while Yun-gil sits staring at a blank wall in prison for the next five years?

The fog swirled before him, carrying the song of the chickadees.

Modern Fiction from Korea

Father and Son: A Novel by Han Sung-won
Translated by Yu Young-nan & Julie Pickering
ISBN: 1-931907-04-8, Paperback, $17.95

An age-old struggle between the generations of modern industrialization and the battle for democratic freedoms in Korea. The author explores the role of the intellectual in modern Korean society and the changing face of the Korean family.

Reflections on a Mask: Two Novellas by Ch'oe In-hun
Translated by Stephen Moore & Shi C. P. Moore
ISBN: 1-931907-05-6, Paperback, $16.95

Reflections on a Mask explores the disillusionment and search for identity of a young man in the post-Korean War era. *Christmas Carol* uses the themes of hope and salvation to examine relationships within a patriarchal Korean family.

Unspoken Voices: Selected Short Stories by Korean Women Writers
Compiled and Translated by Jin-Young Choi, Ph.D.
ISBN: 1-931907-06-4, Paperback, $16.95

Stories by twelve Korean women writers whose writings penetrate into the lives of Korean women from the early part of the 20th century to the present. Writers included are: Choi Junghee, Han Musook, Kang Shinjae, Park Kyongni, Lee Sukbong, Lee Jungho, Song Wonhee, Park Wansuh, Yoon Jungsun, Un Heekyong, Kong Jeeyoung and Han Kang.

The General's Beard: Two Novellas by Lee Oyoung
Translated by Brother Anthony
ISBN: 1-931907-07-2, Paperback, $14.95

In *The General's Beard*, a journalist tries to solve the mystery of a young photographer's death. In *Phantom Legs*, a young girl studying French literature meets a student wounded during demonstrations and begins an ambiguous relationship with him.

Farmers: A Novel by Lee Mu-young
Translated by Yu Young-nan
ISBN: 1-931907-08-0, Paperback, $15.95

The novel is about Korea's Tonghak Uprising the 1894. A farmer-turned Tonghak leader who left the village several years ago in the wake of a severe flogging returns to his village to take revenge of his exploiters.

More titles from Homa & Sekey Books

Flower Terror: Suffocating Stories of China by Pu Ning
ISBN 0-9665421-0-X, Fiction, Paperback, $13.95

"The stories in this work are well written." – Library Journal

Acclaimed Chinese writer eloquently describes the oppression of intellectuals in his country between 1950s and 1970s in these twelve autobiographical novellas and short stories. Many of the stories are so shocking and heart-wrenching that one cannot but feel suffocated.

The Peony Pavilion: A Novel by Xiaoping Yen, Ph.D.
ISBN 0-9665421-2-6, Fiction, Paperback, $16.95

"A window into the Chinese literary imagination." – Publishers Weekly

A sixteen-year-old girl visits a forbidden garden and falls in love with a young man she meets in a dream. She has an affair with her dream-lover and dies longing for him. After her death, her unflagging spirit continues to wait for her dream-lover. Does her lover really exist? Can a youthful love born of a garden dream ever blossom? The novel is based on a sixteenth-century Chinese opera written by Tang Xianzu, "the Shakespeare of China."

Butterfly Lovers: A Tale of the Chinese Romeo and Juliet
by Fan Dai, Ph.D., ISBN 0-9665421-4-2, Fiction, Paperback, $16.95

"An engaging, compelling, deeply moving, highly recommended and rewarding novel." – Midwest Books Review

A beautiful girl disguises herself as a man and lives under one roof with a young male scholar for three years without revealing her true identity. They become sworn brothers, soul mates and lovers. In a world in which marriage is determined by social status and arranged by parents, what is their inescapable fate?

The Dream of the Red Chamber: An Allegory of Love
By Jeannie Jinsheng Yi, Ph.D., ISBN: 0-9665421-7-7, Hardcover
Asian Studies/Literary Criticism, $49.95

Although dreams have been studied in great depth about this most influential classic Chinese fiction, the study of all the dreams as a sequence and in relation to their structural functions in the allegory is undertaken here for the first time.

More titles from Homa & Sekey Books

Always Bright: Paintings by American Chinese Artists 1970-1999
Edited by Xue Jian Xin et al.
ISBN 0-9665421-3-4, Art, Hardcover, $49.95

"An important, groundbreaking, seminal work." – Midwest Book Review

A selection of paintings by eighty acclaimed American Chinese artists in the late 20th century, *Always Bright* is the first of its kind in English publication. The album falls into three categories: oil painting, Chinese painting and other media painting. It also offers profiles of the artists and information on their professional accomplishment.

Always Bright, Vol. II: Paintings by Chinese American Artists
Edited by Eugene Wang, Ph.D., et al.
ISBN: 0-9665421-6-9, Art, Hardcover, $50.00

A sequel to the above, the book includes artworks of ninety-two artists in oil painting, Chinese painting, watercolor painting, and other media such as mixed media, acrylic, pastel, pen and pencil, etc. The book also provides information on the artists and their professional accomplishment. Artists included come from different backgrounds, use different media and belong to different schools. Some of them enjoy international fame while others are enterprising young men and women who are more impressionable to novelty and singularity.

Dai Yunhui's Sketches by Dai Yunhui
ISBN: 1-931907-00-5, Art, Paperback, $14.95

Over 50 sketches from an artist of attainment who is especially good at sketching stage and dynamic figures. His drawings not only accurately capture the dynamic movements of the performers, but also acutely catch the spirit of the stage artists.

Musical Qigong: Ancient Chinese Healing Art from a Modern Master
By Shen Wu, ISBN: 0-9665421-5-0, Health, Paperback, $14.95

Musical Qigong is a special healing energy therapy that combines two ancient Chinese traditions-healing music and Qigong. This guide contains two complete sets of exercises with photo illustrations and discusses how musical Qigong is related to the five elements in the ancient Chinese concept of the universe - metal, wood, water, fire, and earth.

More titles from Homa & Sekey Books

Ink Paintings by Gao Xingjian, Nobel Prize Winner
ISBN: 0-931907-03-X, Hardcover, Art, $34.95

An extraordinary art book by the Nobel Prize Winner for Literature in 2000, this volume brings together over sixty ink paintings by Gao Xingjian that are characteristic of his philosophy and painting style. Gao believes that the world cannot be explained, and the images in his paintings reveal the black-and-white inner world that underlies the complexity of human existence. People admire his meditative images and evocative atmosphere by which Gao intends his viewers to visualize the human conditions in extremity.

Splendor of Tibet: The Potala Palace, Jewel of the Himalayas
By Phuntsok Namgyal
ISBN: 1-931907-02-1, Hardcover, Art/Architecture, $39.95

A magnificent and spectacular photographic book about the Potala Palace, the palace of the Dalai Lamas and the world's highest and largest castle palace. Over 150 rare and extraordinary color photographs of the Potala Palace are showcased in the book, including murals, thang-ka paintings, stupa-tombs of the Dalai Lamas, Buddhist statues and scriptures, porcelain vessels, enamel work, jade ware, brocade, Dalai Lamas' seals, and palace exteriors.

The Haier Way: The Making of a Chinese Business Leader and a Global Brand by Jeannie J. Yi, Ph.D., & Shawn X. Ye, MBA
ISBN: 1-931907-01-3, Hardcover, Business, $24.95

Haier is the largest consumer appliance maker in China. The book traces the appliance giant's path to success, from its early bleak years to its glamorous achievement when Haier was placed the 6th on Forbes Global's worldwide household appliance manufacturer list in 2001. The book explains how Haier excelled in quality, service, technology innovation, a global vision and a management style that is a blend of Jack Welch of "GE" and Confucius of ancient China.

www.homabooks.com

Order Information: U.S.: $4.00 for the first item, $1.50 for each additional item. **Outside U.S.**: $10.00 for the first item, $5.00 for each additional item. Please send a check or money order in U.S. fund (payable to Homa & Sekey Books) to: Orders Department, Homa & Sekey Books, P.O. Box 103, Dumont, NJ 07628 U.S.A. Tel: 201-384-6692; Fax: 201-384-6055; Email: info@homabooks.com